One Man: No Plan
K'Barthan Trilogy: Part 3

Here are some things readers have said about M T McGuire's books.

The Wrong Stuff, K'Barthan Trilogy: Part 2

"This one is even better than book one and if there is any justice it will be a best seller.... " – Susan (Gingerlilly) Watson.

"The story is tight and unpredictable and the pacing excellent. The characterisation is superb and the humour delightful." – Tahlia Newland, Awesome Indies.

"The K'Barthan trilogy is the kind of writing that gets me excited about reading and inspires me to write!" – Kate Policani, Compulsively Writing Reviews

Few Are Chosen, K'Barthan Trilogy: Part 1

"I found I was turning pages as fast as I could... there wasn't a single character that didn't engage me in some way" – http://gracekrispy.blogspot.com

"Once I got used to the tone and style of the dialogue, I really began to appreciate The Pan's self-depreciating humour and sharp wit, and how his cowardly nature allows him to look at events with a more detached view, enabling him to make rational, intelligent observations.

"Filled with a host of brilliant characters from various wonderfully weird races, none of the different personalities introduced fail to fascinate." – http://www.thebookbag.co.uk

One Man: No Plan

K'Barthan Trilogy: Part 3

M T McGuire

HAMGEE
UNIVERSITY PRESS

First published in 2014 by
Hamgee University Press,
www.Hamgee.co.uk
Version 1 June, 2014

ISBN 978-1-907809-20-0

This book is written in British English, with a bit of light swearing
UK film rating of this book: PG (parental guidance)

Written by M T McGuire
Designed and set by M T McGuire
Published by Hamgee University Press
Edited by Mike Rose-Steel
Cover design by A Trouble Halved
This copy printed by Lightning Source UK Ltd, Milton Keynes

For
Gordon McGuire and all the clan.

M T McGuire is 46 years old but still checks inside
unfamiliar wardrobes for a gateway to Narnia.

Thank you for buying this book.
If you enjoyed it you can keep up with
news of the author online by
visiting www.hamgee.co.uk

You can also sign up for the
M T McGuire mailing list by
e-mailing list@hamgee.co.uk
or buy Few Are Chosen merchandise at
www.zazzle.co.uk/drawnbyhand*

Thank you to:-
The Editor – Mike Rose-Steel for help, advice and support over and above the call
of duty.
Press Officer and Ninja Sister In-Law – Emily Bell; ditto
The Beta Readers – Emily Bell, Kel Crist, Geoff Hughes, Hayley Humphrey, Claire
McGahan, Kath (Ignite) Middleton, Kate Policani, David Staniforth and Dr R J
Westwell.
Gerard, at ATH for understanding exactly what I wanted for the cover... as usual.

And thanks to my husband and family, for their support and understanding.

Chapter 1

The Pan woke with a start as the door of the room he was in hit the wall with a loud bang. His spirits descended to basement level, which was exactly where he was, he realised. What little light shone from the hall was almost completely blocked out by Captain Snow.

"On your feet, trash!"

Stiffly, and painfully, The Pan sat up. He was temporarily disorientated, and tried to recall what had happened to him.

****

He remembered the raid on the Underground's HQ in Ruth's version of reality. After they were captured, he'd been chained to Big Merv but when they arrived back in K'Barth at the Security Headquarters there was a delay. It turned out there had been a nationwide purge that morning; a series of dawn raids across the length and breadth of K'Barth. As a result there was a crowd of over a hundred of the nation's most wanted individuals waiting for processing. Captain Snow had grumbled about the delay with increasing volume, but spectacularly little effect. Eventually he had confronted the Major overseeing the intake of prisoners.

"I've got better things to do than spend my whole smecking day here. When'll you be ready to admit these?" He swung an arm in the direction of The Pan and his friends.

The Major shrugged.

"We won't be clear until sixteen hundred hours at the earliest."

"Then I'll stick them in a holding cell, if I may, sir and I'll come back then."

The sarcasm with which the Captain used the word 'sir' clearly annoyed the Major.

"Watch your mouth Captain. You may be Lord Vernon's special pet but you're not in charge round here. I am."

"That's right. I'm not in charge, but Lord Vernon is and these are his toys I've got here. I don't think he'd take kindly to hearing that you'd messed me

1

about. So if I ask to stick them in a holding cell, Major, sir, I'm sure you're not going to refuse. Are you?"

"I can't allow it while they're conscious. I don't have the staff to put a trooper on the door."

"Fine. I can fix that." Captain Snow took out his crowd control stick, primed it with one swift movement and blitzed Sir Robin. For a brief second, the old man's back arched and his lips drew back from his clenched teeth as the charge ran through him. Then his eyes rolled up into his head and he flopped to the ground. The Pan heard Ruth gasp and met her gaze. Bound, helpless, he tried to reassure her without words. Captain Snow blitzed Trev.

"I'll be back when they wake up."

Captain Snow turned the control stick on Gladys and Ada.

"Hey—" The Pan croaked, his voice hoarse from having been half strangled by Lord Vernon. He stepped forward, trying to intervene.

"Get out of my way," sneered Captain Snow and one of his guards pulled The Pan roughly back. "Just for that piece of cheek, you can watch."

They held him still while they applied control, as they liked to call it, to the rest of his friends. Blitzing them unconscious as he fought, pointlessly, to free himself and stop them. Finally, the Captain turned to face him, adjusting the setting of the control stick to maximum.

"Guess what? It's your turn now, you pathetic nothing." The metal had felt cold against The Pan's skin as the Captain pressed it between the eyes, and then... nothing...

****

"Come on, underling, I haven't got all day." Captain Snow's sneering tones brought The Pan abruptly back to the present. "I said, 'on your feet' you scab."

Slowly, The Pan stood up. He grimaced and rubbed his forehead with the heels of his hands.

No wonder he had a headache, and General Moteurs had warned him about the sore throat. He wondered if Lord Vernon would have actually strangled him had General Moteurs not intervened. There was no sign of his other friends, or Ruth. He moved towards the door, cursing himself for agreeing to take part in Sir Robin's ridiculous plan. Now that they'd let the Grongles capture them, The Pan was even less confident of its success. Lord Vernon would never drop his guard and if the Candidate had any sense, it wouldn't flush him out of hiding.

2

"Arnold's hair," he half muttered half croaked, "I should never have let them agree to this."

"What's that, freak?"

"Nothing," mumbled The Pan. He was hoarse and his voice had the timbre of a barking sea lion, but he could still speak. Just. It could have been worse, he supposed.

"Good, 'coz it's time to go."

"Where are you taking me?" No, no, no, don't ask questions.

"To your luxurious penthouse suite, right boys?"

There was a general snickering from the hall behind Captain Snow; clearly, he had the usual goons with him.

"That's good to know, I paid a supplement for room with a view."

"What are you doing? Don't annoy them or they'll hit you," said a voice in his head. A voice that was so realistic it almost sounded as if it was coming from the outside.

"Belt up." Captain Snow swung his arm, hitting The Pan across the face with the back of his hand.

"See?"

For a moment, The Pan wondered if Captain Snow was throwing his voice. No. It was the same one he'd heard before, back at the Underground HQ in Ruth's version of reality.

"Cluck?"

The Pan scrunched up his eyes, trying to dispel the last vestiges of post control stick muzziness as Captain Snow moved forward, grabbed him by the arm and pulled him out into the light of the corridor. Ahead of The Pan was a wall, and to his left the corridor ran a few feet to a door. Captain Snow and the goons were standing on his right so presumably he was meant to go left. They moved back a little. Yes. He looked at the door and immediately, by instinct he found himself judging the distance, the speed he could reach it, the odds of escaping.

"Wait, you agreed to be captured."

Who or what was that?

The Pan sized up the door. It had a flat plate on it; no handle, and across the top of the plate was the word, 'push' in Grongolian. It was an open invitation to run and before he could stop himself, The Pan did. Ignoring the shouting of the voice in his head, with no thought of the consequences, he fled. With lightning speed, and a precision of movement he'd not have expected of himself

3

after being controlled, he was through the door and half way up the next corridor before Captain Snow had even started to react.

"Smeck! The little runt's got away! Stop him!" The Pan accelerated. "You wait till I catch you, you rancid little turd!"

Captain Snow's shouts continued as The Pan turned the corner at the end of this corridor.

"Don't bother. I'll get you sooner or later. There's nowhere to go!"

The Pan was approaching a flight of stairs. He heard startled shouts as he passed the open guard room door, and hurtled up them. The security wasn't as tight here, it was only the holding cells. The guards spilled out into the hall in time to tangle with Captain Snow and his goons, who were only a few seconds behind. That had delayed them but not for long. At the top of the stairs The Pan dodged past another Grongle, rolled through the legs of three more and darted up the next flight. He knew that to stand any chance he must get to ground level. That meant going up.

A couple of laser rounds pinged off the wall but The Pan knew they couldn't get a clear shot, not on the stairs. Another floor, but still no windows. He must go higher! Three more floors, his chest was burning and his breath coming in gasps, but the footsteps were further behind him now. At the top of this flight was a landing with French doors opening outwards. The stairs continued up, so did The Pan. As he bounded up the next flight he almost collided with a party of Grongles on their way down. He turned back, leaping down the steps up which he had just come and running across the landing. He dived through the bottom pane of one of the French doors, arms up over his head, elbows taking the force of the impact. Outside, he rolled head over heels across the balcony in a shower of glass.

Somehow, he knew that there were hand holds on the balcony, that he could climb down the columns supporting it and hide under the portico below. He flipped himself over the balustrade and clambered swiftly down the face of the building, jumping the last ten feet or so, rolling when he hit the ground and running under cover where he couldn't be seen from above.

He stopped, put his hands on his knees and took stock. He was in one of the quadrangles, the upper one, he thought. It was lined on all four sides with columned cloisters. He straightened up, his breathing returning to normal now, and surveyed his surroundings.

The quad was an open space with a statue in the middle. Cobbled paths leading to and around the statute in a cross shape bisected perfectly manicured

4

lawns, peppered with white signs sternly warning all users to keep off the grass, black on white, in Grongolian. It sounded as if he'd lost his pursuers. Even so he didn't fancy crossing the quadrangle. Instead he stayed under the cover of the cloisters. He jogged the length of one side, wondering what to do and where to go now. When he reached the corner pillar, he stopped.

Now what?

He'd escaped. But he hadn't thought beyond that. Indeed, he hadn't thought at all. He'd just run. He was at large in the Old Palace. But Captain Snow was right, there was no way out. And even if he found a way to leave, his friends were still in custody.

"Cluck," said someone.

"Am I hearing things, or was that really a chicken?"

"Cluck."

Somehow, although it had only clucked, The Pan had the distinct impression the chicken was expressing concern about his colleagues. He tried not to listen. He'd got out of the holding cells. It was simple enough. He would get back in and get them out; except he couldn't; and it wasn't simple.

"Arnold's trousers!" He put both hands to his head and cast an exasperated glance skywards. "What in The Prophet's name am I doing?"

Surrendering to instinct he supposed, when what he actually should have been doing was... well... surrendering. The Pan might not like Sir Robin's plan, but he'd agreed to it, which meant he must keep his word and stick to it. Even if he were to find a way to get out of the Palace, he could never leave without the others. He thought a moment. No. The very idea of leaving Ruth here, alone, made his heart ache. There was nothing for it.

"Cluck."

"Yeh, I'm going to have to give myself up."

He heard the sound of footsteps thundering closer and he stepped out into the centre of the cloister, waiting.

A door in the wall a few yards away burst open and Captain Snow, his goons and all the other Grongles who'd joined the chase spilled out in front of him, a few feet away. Laser pistols drawn, they stopped. Dead. The Pan stood facing them. He held his hands out at about shoulder height, palms facing out and downwards, fingertips spread to show he had no concealed weaponry. Not that his short flight had been exactly rich in opportunities to arm himself, even if he'd wanted to. Concentrating on trying to stop his hands from shaking he looked his pursuers in the eye, one by one.

For a moment they almost looked frightened of him.

No. Not likely.

Captain Snow was breathing heavily. There clearly wasn't much running in him. Something to note for future reference perhaps. Not that it mattered now. The Pan doubted he had a future and he'd probably earned himself a spell in solitary for most of it. At least now he'd had one last look at the sky. He glanced sideways and upwards. Two.

Still with his arms raised, he took a cautious pace forward. As one, The Grongles at the other end of the corridor primed their laser pistols and took aim.

Sweaty and still breathless, Captain Snow nodded at a couple of them and jerked his head sideways, indicating that they should move outwards, into the quad, presumably to outflank The Pan should he decide to run again.

"Sorry, Captain. Force of habit. I'll come quietly."

"That's right, you scab, you will," snarled the Captain, and he pulled the trigger.

The Pan saw the muzzle of the gun flash red, the world was filled with blinding light the colour of blood and then he heard rather than felt himself collapse onto the cobbles.

Chapter 2

Several floors above the Upper Quad, in a luxury suite of rooms overlooking the roof-tops of Ning Dang Po, Deirdre Arbuthnot stirred. The first thing that forced its way into her consciousness was the pain. The second thing was an ardent longing to be asleep still. She supposed there were some parts of her that didn't ache. Yeh, her eyelids were OK. And her nose. That didn't hurt. Or her left ear. Anywhere else pain free? No, it would seem not.

Ugh.

These reflections were then disturbed by Deirdre's usual first thought upon waking in the morning, which was that she could quite do with a wee. So she was going to have to get out of bed. But please, not yet. She wasn't quite ready for that. Any movement was going to smart. The need to wee wasn't that urgent. It could wait.

In the meantime she would take this slowly, try to relax away as much of the pain as possible before she moved but, eventually, she would have to sit up. She closed her eyes and concentrated on the pain management techniques she'd learned in her training. This was a lot of pain. It was only to be expected of course; she'd spent nearly two hours, maybe more, fighting at levels of intensity that few people would expect to maintain for more than ten or fifteen minutes – even in combat. It wasn't just that she had taken a beating, she was aching and stiff from such marathon levels of exertion. She briefly consoled herself with the fact that her opponent would also be nursing a few bruises this morning, but hand-to-hand combat with Lord Vernon was not an experience she wished to repeat. Not without reinforcements, anyway.

She added some relaxation techniques to the pain management routine and began to feel better. When she was convinced she'd managed about as much pain as she was going to, she steeled herself and sat up.

"Arnold's smecking, sweaty—"

"Hello Lieutenant," said a voice and there, next to the bed, perched casually on a chair, was a Blurpon.

"Snoofle!" She was delighted to see her friend from the laundry and laughed, which hurt. "Ouch."

"I was going to bring you some breakfast, but you were still asleep so I thought it'd wait until you woke up."

"I was worried. Captain Snow zapped you with a crowd control stick."

"Yes."

"It must have hurt."

"Only when I came round. I'm guessing you're the same in that respect."

"Yes. I'm sorry they got you. I shouldn't have let that happen." Deirdre wasn't very used to apologising and she seemed to be doing a lot of it these days.

"I can't see what you'd have done to stop it."

"I should have anticipated. I've never lost one of my people."

"You didn't lose me. Anyway I'm not actually under your command you know, you're strike operations and I'm espionage."

"It's all Resistance..." She shrugged (with a grimace) and let the matter drop. "How did you get here?"

"General Moteurs. He tells me you turned up here, suffering from exhaustion and half delirious and you..." he tailed off.

Deirdre buried her head in her hands.

"I told him about you? Is that what he said?" Would she really have been that much of an idiot?

"He said you were mumbling, 'No not Snoofle'. That piqued his interest so he looked me up in the staff records." Why did Snoofle's version of General Moteurs sound so much more benign than hers, Deirdre wondered. Snoofle was still talking. "There was no need to worry, Captain Snow's goons dumped me in the dormitory. Head Launderer Sid saw them leave and came to find me with a couple of the others. They were still with me when General Moteurs arrived."

"He went to the dormitory?"

"Yes."

"Himself?"

"Yes."

"But he's a General!"

"Imperial Guard, you have heard about them?"

"I know they exist but I've never encountered them; my targets have always been members of the regular army and the security forces."

"That might make sense. Rumour has it that the Imperial Guard are better behaved then their Armed Forces colleagues."

"Yes, D'reen – Mrs Pargeter – in the Laundry told me that," said Deirdre.

"The ones in the grey are almost decent," quoted Snoofle, in a very passable impression of Mrs Pargeter's voice.

Deirdre smiled.

"Just so," she said. "All the same, if he or any of those goons touched you—"

"Quite the reverse. He got a Medical Orderly to check me over. There was talk of a stay in the infirmary but I persuaded them to let me come here and keep you company."

"How?"

"It didn't take much. He thought the presence of someone familiar would be... helpful to you when you woke up."

"Then thank you."

Snoofle shrugged.

"It's nothing. I've been enjoying the scenery. This place is like a museum exhibit. He has some seriously quality stuff here, and the art works... There's a Maracaggio out there in his sitting room, you've heard of Maracaggio right?"

"No."

"Really? He was a hot contender to be the most bad tempered dude who ever lived – he died in a duel eventually – but, Arnold's hair, he could paint."

"I can't say his name is familiar."

"Are you serious? He's one of the most famous painters in the world! And there's one of his paintings right there over the fire place – a portrait of Commander Thistwith-Mee. It's just amazing. There's hardly any of Maracaggio's stuff left. If his clients didn't get mad at him and destroy it, he ripped it up himself to stop the ones who hadn't paid from getting them after he'd died. To have one in your own apartment is like... Well, all I can say is, our General Moteurs must have a lot of cash and I'd say he knows a thing or two about art works."

"Or his decorators do," Deirdre stretched and winced, noting that she must stretch more carefully for a day or two. "It must be unusual for the Imperial Guard to be outside Grongolia."

Snoofle adjusted his whiskers.

"Not really, they guard individuals. In this case, Lord Vernon."

"But his own troops do that."

"Exactly, Captain Snow and his lot. I'd be interested to find out what the

Imperial Guard here *really* do."

So would Deirdre.

She looked around her. She was in a bedroom. Sunlight streamed in through floor-to-ceiling windows along one side. Through them was a balcony and beyond it lay the city of Ning Dang Po in all its glory. As living quarters went, these were pretty ritzy. So was the room: understated, for sure, but elegant; expensive, antique elegant, as Snoofle had said. Except for the double bed which was clearly new and fitted with crisp white sheets. They were clean on for her use, Deirdre realised. Then there was her shirt, someone else's expensive shirt. It was a pale cream, unbleached, soft and comfortable. Raw silk? Yes, by the feel of it. She rolled up the sleeves, which were a bit long and noticed the bruises round her wrists where Lord Vernon had held her down and... she turned her head abruptly away from Snoofle. She had to put that from her mind. So easy to say, so hard to do. She closed her eyes and clenched her teeth. She. Was. Not. Going. To. Cry. Without thinking, she drew her knees up and hugged her arms round them. The sudden pain very nearly succeeded where her recollections of Lord Vernon had failed.

Snoofle's beady black-brown eyes followed every movement.

"Lieutenant, Ma'am?" he said gently. "I am a great believer in the restorative properties of coffee."

She could have hugged him but that would probably have hurt, too so instead she took the cup he was offering her and drank it gratefully. It was still warm but only just.

"Thank you," she smiled wanly.

"Forgive me if I am speaking out of turn but I am aware of what you must have been through. Everyone knows what Lord Vernon does to the female staff – that's why Room A is a Blurpon only pick up. After Captain Snow blitzed me with the control stick, I kind of put two and two together. My apologies if it has come to something other than four."

"No Snoofle, you're correct, as usual." Deirdre heaved a sigh. "We have to get out of here."

"I don't think we can at the moment, Lieutenant."

"Snoofle, don't call me that. You're not under my command. Deirdre, if you please."

Snoofle smiled.

"Deirdre. More coffee?"

She held out her cup.

"If you need it, the bathroom's just down the hall," he told her as he poured.

"But… I gave General Moteurs my word that you wouldn't escape. Or go anywhere near his desk. Until we can find a way to neutralise his hold on us, I believe we should obey him."

"He's not going to know," said Deirdre.

"I fear he is. He's put three armed guards at the end of the corridor – if we try, they'll tell him."

"When they come round…"

Snoofle smiled.

"You are in no state to do any more fighting," he said.

He was right. Bummer. Gingerly she got out of bed and stood up. It wasn't as bad as it could have been but she still felt distinctly wobbly.

Noting the three guards the other end, Deirdre made her way slowly down the hall to the bathroom, with Snoofle following. Somewhere along the way he acquired a big fluffy towel and some clean clothes, which he handed her.

"Will you be alright in there?"

"Yes, Snoofle. I think I can cope with a few bruises."

"I didn't mean the bruises. I was thinking more of—"

"Snoofle," Deirdre cut in. The expression of concern on his face betrayed his thoughts.

"Sorry."

"Understand this; I may be feeling emotional but I'm not going to go in there and cut my wrists—"

"Well, no, of course you're not because any sharp objects in there have been—"

"No. Not because of that, because I'm a trained assassin, a member of the Most Holy Order of Ninja Nimmists and I don't do self-harm. I do revenge. If someone knocks me down, I get up and get even."

"But—"

"Snoofle. I'm not going to kill myself, OK?"

"Ma'am."

Deirdre took the towel and the clothes from him

"However, your concern is noted." She did appreciate it, even if it was a bit irritating. "Thank you."

"Sorry… you would like some breakfast when you finish, yes?"

"Yes."

"I know you prefer muesli but maybe today you should have something more substantial. Kedgeree?"

"You're the boss, Snoofle. Cooking is not usually my concern."

"With orange juice?"

"Yes... please." She added the 'please' as an afterthought.

"It will be ready and waiting when you're done."

"Thank you," she said again and shut the bathroom door.

Chapter 3

The sun rose: dawn painting the sky pink. In the square at the bottom of Turnadot Street, the clock chimed six. On the street itself, the air was filled with the roar of diesel and the thunderous rumbling of caterpillar tracks on asphalt. Many of the residents came to their windows, unamused by this auditory invasion.

"Lorks," said Betsy Coed as she looked out through the heavy net curtains in the front window of the 'lodging house' she ran. "They've come to do us over." She cast a quick glance at the door, to check that the chain was on and the bolts shot home and then ran to the bottom of the stairs clapping her hands loudly. "Chop chop! Ladies, females, gentlemen and males," she shouted. "We're about to get raided. It's time for clean sheets. This is Laundry Day."

Doors opened in the hall above and a group of scantily clad females gathered on the landing.

"Third time this week," grumbled one of them.

"That it is," said Betsy. "Ours is not to reason why. Come along, spit spot. Get your things together. Angie and Persephone, would you explain to your clients and send them down? They'll have to go out the back."

Muffled OKs drifted down from above as Betsy ran to the side of the reception room and started lifting one corner of the rug. A young woman wearing nothing but a silk bathrobe, high heeled furry mules and an expression of alarm hurried down the stairs to help her.

"Bless you, Merlinda, quickly now."

Pub Quiz Alan, who helped out with the odd DIY task, appeared in the kitchen doorway. His face was framed by even wilder blonde curls than usual. Either he'd overdone the perm since Betsy last saw him, or he'd forgotten to brush his hair. Otherwise he was dressed in the standard Alan ensemble: stonewashed denim jeans, penny loafers, stripy polo shirt and black blouson leather jacket. Today's penny loafers were grey, Betsy noticed.

"I heard the carrier go by. I had to go garden hopping from Frontock Street. Not a lot of people know this but those personnel carriers can run silently when they don't want to be heard. They're only making that racket to shake us up, get on our wicks. You know the Grongles scrap them after two years, as well. Even if there's nothing wrong with them, even if they've only done a couple of miles. I thought I'd—"

"Alan," Betsy cut him off – after all speed was of the essence. "You must get back in the kitchen and get a fry up going. There's a chef's hat on the peg on the back of the door."

If Betsy's unlicensed bordello was to be taken for a respectable lodging house it had to look the part. Pub Quiz Alan went off and Merlinda took the other end of the rug. Three more scantily clad females appeared and moved the furniture out of the way as Betsy and Merlinda rolled the rug back to reveal a trap door in the floor. Betsy pulled it open.

"Quickly girls!"

The only two punters who had stayed the night, a young Grongle officer and a fat middle-aged sales rep, arrived in the hall, hurriedly dressing as they went.

"You're respectable lodgers staying at Ms Coed's lodging house," Merlinda coached them as the rest of the girls ran up and down the stairs ferrying whips, masks, hand cuffs, kinky underwear, and some other alarming objects whose uses are best left to the imagination. Betsy Coed checked the items off on a list as the girls flung them into the hole in the floor. Once all of it was in she slammed the lid and with the middle-aged businessman's help rolled the rug back. The furniture was replaced and Alan came out of the kitchen with a tray of crockery and a white linen table cloth.

"Now girls, up you go, and it's twinsets and pearls when you return, please. And NO red lipstick or nails. It's a dead giveaway."

Betsy checked her watch; one minute, near as dammit, and the bordello had turned into a boarding house. 'Laundry' was complete.

The girls ran back to their rooms and Betsy went to the window. The Grongles were out of the carrier but round the other side of it where she couldn't see them.

"You gentlemen can stay and pretend to be guests, or go over the scullery wall into the scrap yard and take your chances with Wayne Jenner's dog."

The Grongle officer joined her for a moment, standing well back so he was obscured by the nets. The two of them watched, in silence, as a sleek, dark green staff snurd pulled up, further obscuring their view. An officer got out and by the way they were fussing round him Betsy guessed he was in command. He was short, for a Grongle and wearing a different uniform; grey.

"They're Imperial Guard. They'll throw the book at me," groaned her Grongle 'guest'. He was one of her most faithful, regular customers. Presumably because he didn't realise that, being a Grongle, Betsy charged him twice what everyone else paid. "I'll take my chances with the dog." He drew his laser pistol and strode purposefully towards the kitchen, where the back door was.

"It's a vicious thing, that dog, but please don't—"

"Rest easy Betsy. I've set this to stun," he said, holding up the pistol. "It'll wake up a few minutes after I'm gone."

He was alright, for a Grongle. He'd been a customer for over a year now, although she'd never asked him his name: it wasn't the form. He seemed quite smitten with Persephone. He even brought presents for her from time to time and he would see no-one else.

"Thank you," she told his departing back.

"Is the excitement extra?" asked the businessman as Betsy heard Alan's voice in the kitchen and the back door banging closed.

"No but if you want to eat the breakfast it's $5 Grongolian," she said quickly.

"That's a bit steep."

"Times are hard. I took $2 off because you helped with the rug."

There was a moment of silence as she and the businessman continued to watch events across the street.

"Alright," said the man.

The Grongle across the road was still out there, speaking to another officer, presumably the one in charge of the personnel carrier. Both of them turned and looked straight at her front door. Betsy held her breath and then... they swung round and headed towards the door of the Parrot and Screwdriver.

"Arnold be praised," she said as the front entrance of the pub was opened, from the inside, by another Grongle. The officer who had arrived in the snurd went inside with his subordinate. Through the opened door, Betsy could see movement. They were searching the place. Thank goodness the owners, her friends Gladys and Ada had taken Their Trev and gone away on holiday. She was distracted by the sound of ferocious barking from next door and a pinging sound. There was a yelp and then the barking stopped. It sounded as if her Grongolian customer had got away.

The first of the girls arrived, devoid of makeup and demurely attired. She sat at the table.

"Are they going to raid us?" she asked.

Betsy moved away from the window and ushered the middle-aged businessman to a seat in the carver chair at the head.

"It's difficult to tell. I think we'd best keep the clean sheets on today but, no. I'd say it's someone else's turn."

Chapter 4

King Denarghi, XVII of the Blurpon Nation – and Supreme Leader of the Resistance – was in a towering rage. Then again, as a Blurpon, he was a member of a species famed for its towering rages so nobody was very surprised. Things hadn't been going very well for the Resistance in recent days, what with Big Merv and his driver escaping.

Professor N'Aversion tried to make himself look as unnoticeable as possible. Becoming incognito is a challenge for a Swamp Thing since they are green, clammy-looking, over six foot tall and have antennae. But the Professor had a good go anyway

Denarghi stood on his throne-room desk, to gain height. The ends of his eye whiskers almost brushed the low ceiling as he bounced irately up and down on his single leg. His pointy cat-like ears were lying flat back against his head. Yes, the Professor reflected, Denarghi was fully lit, his red fur bristling with angry static, like a puffed-up pooch. He looked unbelievably cute like this but would probably take the head off the first person who mentioned it. The Professor zoned out the noise and let his mind wander; not that it could drag itself far with so much on it. He started as a particularly loud shout from Denarghi brought him back from his reverie.

"You are supposed to be the cream of this organisation!" Yeh right. Most of Denarghi's commanders were there because they were yes men or relations. Professor N'Aversion had better things to do than listen to a bunch of idiots being told their job. He wondered how soon he could leave without being rude. Denarghi continued, "You are here because you are supposed to be able to get results. I want Big Merv, I also want that little Hamgeean smecker and I want them alive. One way or another, they're going to give me what they stole. And when they have, they will pay for what they did."

Professor N'Aversion weighed up the facts. Big Merv and his getaway man, The Pan of Hamgee, had disappeared into thin air, in front of Denarghi and two members of his personal guard. He doubted anyone was going to catch them any time soon. There'd been a big shake up about it all. Had been? What was he thinking? It was still going on.

Lieutenant Arbuthnot, who had brought them back to base, carried the blame, unfairly, in the Professor's view.

Belatedly, the Professor realised that Denarghi had finished shouting. Silence reigned. He concentrated on the background noises that had accompanied his train of thought, replaying them in his head to make sense of them. Did Denarghi ask him a question at the end of all of that? No he didn't think so. He kept his antennae very still so as not to betray his boredom, or his thoughts, and practised the Ninja Nimmist blending-in technique he was working on. As Head of Tech Ops, it was unavoidable that Denarghi would ask him what the prisoners had used to get away, and The Professor wanted to put the moment off for as long as possible. Mainly because he didn't really know. Or at least, the few shreds of an idea he had did not add up to a hypothesis that would please his Master.

"You!" Denarghi pointed to Smeen, recently reorganised into the position of Colonel Smeen, in charge of Military Ops, and with it, Denarghi's personal guard – although in light of the kinds of jobs they usually did, his department was unofficially titled 'henching'.

"We're doin' all we can, Sir."

"It's not enough."

Professor N'Aversion's stomach rumbled. Arnold's socks! There went incognito. Sure enough, Denarghi swung round and extended the pointy finger of accusation his way.

"What did you say, Professor?"

"I- I'm sorry." He patted his stomach. "I haven't had breakfast." The Professor had been rudely woken and summoned to the meeting before he'd so much as had time for a coffee and he was feeling it keenly.

"Are you being insubordinate? I am not in the mood for insubordination."

"No, sir."

"Good." Denarghi cracked his knuckles. "Since you are in the spotlight, Professor," Oh here we go, "I wonder if you have any theories as to how they escaped?"

The Professor heaved a sigh.

"Not at this time."

"Why not?"

The Professor suspected that *I haven't a blind clue how they did it'* was probably not the answer Denarghi was looking for but, *I think they used some kind of quantum device but I have no evidence to prove it'* wouldn't go down well either; and he'd have to explain quantum; and it was so early in the morning.

"I can only conclude that the rumours of matter transportation among upper echelon Nimmist Elders are truer than we think," he said, opting for noncommittal.

"Professor, the fact they are mentioned in the writings of the priests does not make them true."

"There are many kinds of truth, Denarghi."

"Don't quote The Prophet at me."

"My apologies," said the Professor, and left it at that.

The irritating thing was that in many respects he shared Denarghi's view of the religious commentaries, especially the ancient ones. Even reading them in their original languages, he appreciated that they were skewed by the conventions of their times. But there were aspects that he recognised as echoes of modern science. The Professor had always wondered if the miracles were merely some advanced level of quantum mechanics kept secret. Denarghi would never understand that, though. He liked his world black and white. In some ways the Professor envied him his simplistic approach. It must make everything so wonderfully straightforward.

"If these stories are true I assume you will be replicating the technique. When can we see a demonstration?"

"I don't know. I don't even know if we can. The writings tell us the effect but seldom the cause. If they say the Architraves hold a sphere that allows them to listen to every conversation taking place on the planet at once, all I know is that the equipment used is spherical. If I want to build it, its shape is redundant information. What I need to know is what's inside."

"No-one told me about this sphere."

"It isn't real, Denarghi, I made it up as an example. Once we find The Pan of Hamgee I can talk to him—"

"When we find him, you will not be engaging him in casual conversation, Professor. This is not a social engagement, he is not joining us for tea. He is an enemy of Free K'Barth and we are bringing him here to stand trial."

"Quite, quite. I understand that but—"

19

"There will be no further discussion on this topic. Next on our agenda:" Professor N'Aversion relaxed a little. At least Denarghi was about to grill someone else. "The decimation of our Revenue Acquisition arm." Or maybe not. "Why are our crews disappearing, Professor?"

"Because they cannot outrun the Interceptor, sir."

"Then they will have to learn, or you, Professor, will have to invent something that will give them the edge."

"I am working on that, sir."

"Then perhaps you should try harder."

"We are, sir, but our equipment is old and obsolete."

"Times are hard for all of us, Professor. But you are straying from the subject. How many Interceptors are there and what are their weaknesses? No wait, don't tell me, you're working on that."

Professor N'Aversion took a moment to control his rising irritation.

"Yes, sir. We now have confirmed sightings and the times suggest one vehicle. We also have photographs, which we have enhanced and—"

"Enhanced!" Denarghi spat, "had them bodged by geeks with over active imaginations and too much time on their hands."

"I assure you, sir, none of my 'geeks' has too much time on their hands."

"No? Well whatever they're doing with it, perhaps they should stop and spend it doing something that gets results."

"I have results, here, if you will listen. And I can get you more, if you let me talk to The Pan of Hamgee. If I can broker a deal—"

"No, Professor, you will not be brokering anything with The Pan of Hamgee. We do not negotiate with scum."

"Then with respect, sir, how do you expect me to—"

"Silence. You will return to the subject under discussion."

"I believe I—"

"Your Majesty, if I may..." Colonel Ischzue interrupted the Professor smoothly. The Professor thanked The Prophet that the Colonel had sided with him. As well as being head of Revenue Acquisition, Ischzue was a Blurpon, like Denarghi, which meant there was an outside chance the jumped-up little hamster would listen to him. "The Professor has been working hard to alleviate our difficulties. He has given us valuable advice which has allowed us to minimise the damage."

"Really?"

"Sir. We lost two teams out of eight last night; one escaping a heist in Ning Dang Po and another returning from Tith."

"And that is good?" asked Denarghi incredulously.

"On recent reckoning, yes. No-one escapes this thing. No-one. The week before, we lost seven out of eight." There was a moment of silence as everyone took that in. Ischzue continued. "If the Interceptor travels at the speeds the Professor estimates then we can assume the team returning from Tith were engaged in combat by the same vehicle which downed the team in Ning Dang Po. The journey times correspond exactly with the figures he gave us. Usually the attacks are so quick and lethal that our teams just disappear. However, the second crew managed to get us a text away before they were destroyed. It cited a black snurd, with lasers. There are no survivors from either group but the evidence, here, clearly points to it being one vehicle and to that vehicle being the Interceptor. The other six teams were successful and I believe we have the Professor to thank for that."

"Bravo, Professor," said Denarghi acidly. "Can they build a second Interceptor?"

"Indubitably, but it is becoming increasingly clear that despite the advanced technical specifications, it is the skill of the driver which makes this one lethal. It will take them some time to find another fellow that good."

"So you say."

"So I know and potentially, we have a better one at our disposal."

"The Pan of Hamgee has betrayed us, Professor. We are not going to recruit him."

Lieutenant Wright, Colonel Ischzue's number two at R.A. spoke up.

"We wouldn't need to," she said, "not if we can find out how he does his disappearing trick. We won't need getaway drivers or vehicles."

"Oh, I'm not so certain of that," said the Professor. "If he could use it to get into a bank vault, he would have done so with the Mervinettes."

"He may not have known how before," said Colonel Ischzue.

"Then we must ask him."

"No. Any questions you have will be addressed through the proper channels. Nobody will be accessing the Hamgean but Colonel Melior, and his team in Information Retrieval." Colonel Melior the yes-man, or at least, yes-Blurpon, now heading up the Resistance's once efficient Information

Retrieval section looked up suddenly.

"Yes," he said.

"But—" began Professor N'Aversion.

"The matter is closed," growled Denarghi.

"Sir," said the Professor, irritably. He noticed that Colonel Smeen, sitting a few feet to Denarghi's right, appeared to have nodded off, and envied him.

"Plumby," Denarghi's attention turned to the other yes-Blurpon; the one heading up Espionage. "Do you know how long it will be before they build a second Interceptor?"

"No, sir."

"What about our contacts at the Palace? Have they found anything?"

"Not yet, sir."

"And has Lieutenant Arbuthnot succeeded in assassinating Lord Vernon?"

"No word yet, sir. She disappeared yesterday evening. We believe she was sent to him shortly after you spoke with her. She and Snoofle were supposed to be locking up the Laundry but something happened. Snoofle was found unconscious in the dormitory, Head Launderer Sid reckoned he'd been zapped with a crowd control stick, and the Lieutenant was gone. The next thing they knew, this Grongle General arrived, with a medic, and took him away for treatment. Neither he nor the Lieutenant have been seen since."

"A General? That is unusual."

"Yes, sir."

"Is Snoofle double?"

"If Snoofle was a double agent, I doubt we'd still be here," said Professor N'Aversion. "He's very, very good."

"Like you would know," muttered Plumby.

"True enough, he has an exceptional gift," said Denarghi. "Both he and Lieutenant Arbuthnot have served the cause well. Colonel Plumby, you can confirm they are in custody?"

"No, sir."

"They will be rewarded greatly for their dedication in the afterlife," said Melior.

"They're not dead, yet," said Professor N'Aversion.

"No, not yet. But are they dead to us? If they come out of custody alive will they be compromised? If they are they cannot be spared," said Denarghi.

"Wait!" said Professor N'Aversion. "You're not liquidating them, are you?"

"He has no choice," said Colonel Melior.

"Exactly. The Grongles will turn them," said Plumby.

"If Snoofle were to turn double we should use him because, I assure you, his loyalties would be with us. As it is, he may be on to something. What if this General was a rescue team, a disguised—"

"Silence, Professor. You are making a fool of yourself," snapped Denarghi.

Across the table, Professor N'Aversion noticed Colonel Ischzue, in charge of Revenue Acquisition write something on the papers in front of him and show it to Lieutenant Wright.

"I believe there is a clear danger that they will betray the cause," said Plumby.

"As do I," said Melior.

"Poppycock!" said, Professor N'Aversion. "Snoofle and Deirdre are two of our best operatives in their fields. That sort of thing would never affect them. If they're incommunicado, it's because they're deep under cover. All they need is time. They have not turned. I'd stake my life on it."

"I wouldn't do that, Professor," said Denarghi ominously. "I may have no option but to take it."

"You go ahead. And good luck when I'm gone. I'm sure you'll crack the secrets of teleportation in no time at all." Not only was the Professor loved by his staff – something he never ceased to be amazed and thankful for – but, as one of the leading brains of his generation, he was completely indispensable. "Snoofle and Lieutenant Arbuthnot are both highly professional, I can't see either of them betraying us! Plumby's very suggestion insults them."

"Stick to science, Professor, you know nothing about managing beings," sneered Denarghi. "I have heard enough. I am the leader of this organisation and it is *I* who will make this decision. I will give them 24 hours. However, if we have had no contact by then, I will be forced to declare them turned and order their liquidation.

"Now, back to the matter in hand. The recapture of Big Merv and The Pan of Hamgee."

"The Grongles have him," said Plumby.

"You know this for a fact?"

"No, but he has dropped off the grid."

"He could be in hiding," said Colonel Melior stating the blindingly obvious.

"So where would a cowardly insect like this run to? I suggest somewhere he believes he would not be found; a little known backwater," said Denarghi.

"Agreed, but we have no confirmed sightings," said Colonel Plumby.

"There is nothing to report from our teams either," Colonel Ischzue volunteered. "Lieutenant Wright and I have ordered our agents everywhere to be on the lookout."

"Someone talking sense at last," muttered the Professor.

"You have something to contribute?" Denarghi asked him.

"Yes. I, too, believe all units should keep their eyes open. If I was a frightened young man trying to disappear, I would not head to the sticks where my arrival would be a notable event, but to the cities where I might be lost in a sea of new faces. Furthermore, he's young and Ning Dang Po is the capital. He'll head for the bright lights."

"Professor you are a middle-aged academic. What would you know?" said Denarghi.

"I remember my youth well enough."

"I believe the Professor speaks wisely," said Colonel Ischzue, "I have given Lieutenant Wright orders that her teams, too, should be vigilant. It is easier for them than Bank Division. My operatives in the remoter areas are in hiding, themselves."

"When you two – and Lieutenant Wright, who isn't a Colonel by the way, and therefore shouldn't even be here – have finished telling me my job," snapped Colonel Plumby. "I know what to do."

"Of course," Professor N'Aversion agreed politely. "That goes without saying, but we would like to help. What is your plan of action? How may we assist?"

"My plan of action is not your concern and your greatest assistance would be to stay out of it."

Naturally. Plumby couldn't manage his way out of a paper bag. He wouldn't want his working methods scrutinised by anyone who could. It was doubtful that there was much to be gained by appealing to Plumby's good sense – he had none – but the Professor tried anyway.

"Colonel Plumby, this is important. The boy has access to something that would change the balance of power from the Grongles to us. We need to find him and to do that, we should try to work together."

"Thank you for those pearls of wisdom, Professor," Denarghi cut in, "but the balance of power does not lie with the Grongles. We have the real power here. We are ruthless, nimble and unafraid of death. We cannot be stopped."

"I think we can. But if we get hold of The Pan of Hamgee and persuade him to trust us, we could change that. By The Prophet, he can disappear into thin air! Think what that would mean for us."

"Professor. I have already told you this subject is closed. We do not trust criminals and we don't need him to explain his remarkable gift. That is what you are here for."

"But Your Majesty, he could advance my research by months. This is a completely new application of reality theory and time is crucial—"

"Then you'd better get started. I want answers, Professor, and I want them fast. You are excused."

The room was silent and still as the others waited to see how the Professor would react. Then, out of the corner of his eye, he noticed Colonel Ischzue and his number two exchange looks. All eyes were on the Professor, so the rest of the assembled company missed the way the Lieutenant's eyes rolled. The Professor decided he must sound out those two.

"I believe I dismissed you, Professor," snapped Denarghi.

"Yes, sir. Thank you." The Professor stood up, banging his head and crushing one of his antennae painfully against the ceiling, "Smeck!" He nodded to the others, Smeen, who had woken up, Wright, Ischzue, Melior and Plumby. "If you will excuse me."

Gah! How he loathed these meetings! Though now he was being summarily dismissed from one, he found he wanted to stay. Mainly because no matter what heights of delusion they had to scale, they'd find some way of pinning something on him in his absence. Like poor Lieutenant Arbuthnot. Blimey, they'd probably be blaming him for the shape of the planet by the time they'd finished, and the next week's weather. The Professor sighed and wondered how in The Prophet's name he got anything done. Once again he was going to have to pull a rabbit out of the hat to save the organisation's bacon. Perhaps Ischzue and Wright would help. He resented that it was always he who dragged the Resistance out of the poop and Denarghi who took the credit each time he succeeded.

"Management. The same the world over," he grumbled irritably as he shambled down the dreary corridor.

Chapter 5

Deirdre felt a great deal better after her bath. She dressed in the clothes; correct female underwear – not her own; new with the labels still on but exactly the right size – another shirt, like the one she'd woken up in, only tailored for a female figure the same shape as Deirdre's, a pair of grey britches, with a lighter stripe down the side, another exact fit and a pair of long black leather boots, ditto. She wondered if they'd measured her while she was unconscious. The idea made her feel vulnerable. If anyone had, they'd better have been female.

She folded the towel, draped it over the side of the bath and made her way back to the bedroom. There was a full length mirror on the inside of the wardrobe door and even for Deirdre, the vision it presented looked good. Pity they were Imperial Guard trousers, they really were flattering. The side zipper, she supposed. There were no braces on the female version. She tried a couple of high kicks – proving, painfully, that the trousers were practical, too; cut to allow plenty of freedom of movement. But Deirdre made a mental note not to move freely too suddenly until she felt less stiff and achy. Snoofle arrived with a tray and put it on a table at the far end of the room, opposite the bed. It was a beautiful day and she wondered about suggesting they move outside onto the balcony. However, when she glanced through the glass doors she realised a new guard had appeared out there. Standing facing the doors, rapid-repeat laser gun trained on them, primed and ready to fire was a female Grongle. She was, pretty much, the Grongolian equivalent of Deirdre; tall, good looking and long legged. Her hair was tied up in some kind of complicated plait and she wore a peaked cap. Deirdre had never seen a female Grongle soldier and couldn't help but stare. The night before, when she had stood shivering and exhausted in General Moteurs' rooms, he had said she didn't know her enemy. Much as she hated to admit it, she realised he might be right.

She sat at the table and Snoofle served breakfast. The usual protocol, for an officer of Deirdre's seniority, would be to dismiss Snoofle and eat alone but she didn't want to send him away. She didn't relish the idea of solitude. And whatever the military protocol might say, it was very bad manners to make him sit and watch her. So, instead, she invited him to join her. She was glad of her decision when he confessed that he hadn't eaten since the early hours.

"What d'you make of him?" she asked Snoofle.

"The General?" She nodded and immediately wished she hadn't, the movement sent a wave of pain through her aching shoulders. "He's either our guardian angel or our nemesis," said Snoofle. "At the moment I don't know which."

"I do. When Captain Snow tried to take me back to the cells, he said," she aped General Moteurs' clipped officer class accent, "'Captain, are you looking for this?' As if I was a piece of trash."

Snoofle made a face.

"Ouch, I wouldn't have liked to have been in his shoes after he did that. I bet you tore him off a strip."

"No. He had a laser pistol trained on me at the time."

"Ah. You two didn't hit it off then?"

"No."

"I suppose he is a bit pleased with himself."

"Just a bit. You have a different view?"

"I'm not sure yet. He is a General and he came to the dormitory to find me. As you said, that's notable. Then he got a Medical Orderly to examine me. He isn't like the others and I am a little intrigued."

"I'm not," said Deirdre. No. That wasn't what she'd meant to say. "Correction, I am. I need to know my enemy but I don't like him and I don't like this." Deirdre stopped. "I prefer strike operations. Espionage is complicated and I am not."

"No. Denarghi should never have sent you here—"

"Agreed."

"Deirdre, we are not playing to your strengths but we are playing to mine. We must be patient, wait and see what the General wants, we may yet prevail." The conversation lapsed while she and Snoofle ate their breakfast, each locked in their own thoughts.

Deirdre's turned, again, to General Moteurs. Which was annoying enough in itself. She didn't want to give him the mental air time. He'd called her 'this'. The stuck up, snot-coloured get. It was exactly the kind of thing she'd expect from a member of a species she'd sworn an oath, in a zealous moment, to cleanse from the planet. Except that having behaved absolutely true to form in the minutia of conversation, she had to admit that when she looked at the bigger picture, his overall behaviour was impeccable. He'd saved her from Captain Snow and Lord Vernon, lent her his bed and sent Snoofle to keep her company. All very decent. For a supercilious prig.

Deirdre's recollections were hazy after the moment she'd sat on his sofa, huddled in his jacket and started eating his supper or at least, most of it. He'd gone to run her a bath but after that she had nothing but vague half-conscious impressions of events. Only a few things had stuck in her mind. Someone had picked her up and carried her, presumably to this bedroom. She had no visual memory of him, which merely made the fragments she recalled all the more tantalising. She wondered if it had been General Moteurs, himself, but she doubted it. He was such a clean, green Grongle, Deirdre couldn't see him sullying his own hands with a non-being. He'd have human servants for that. Whoever this person was, he had lifted her in his arms and carried her gently, tenderly, as if she mattered. She remembered a scent – one that she liked, despite her state of semi-comatose exhaustion; traces of a very pleasant cologne mixed with his own. She felt again the soft sensation of his shirt against her skin and the contours of his body underneath. He was fit, a fellow martial artist, perhaps, and he had made her feel... safe, protected even.

Oh get a grip. No-one protected Deirdre. That was her job and she was more than equipped to do it. Better equipped than anyone else; especially some anonymous male, who was unlikely to resemble her fevered imaginings, anyway. So, what next?

There had been a brief period of nothing. She must have lost consciousness for a while, and then she had a sensation of lying flat and someone cutting the slip off. A female voice apologised that the scissors were cold and then they, she was pretty sure it was more than one person, carefully washed and dressed her wounds. Had General Moteurs been there when they undressed her? Arnold, please not. It was unlikely though. As she'd already decided, he'd have summoned his minions to deal with her the minute she'd fallen asleep on his couch.

"You alright?" asked Snoofle.

"Yes, I'm thinking."

"What about?"

"Last night. I don't remember what happened."

"I think I can tell you some of—" Snoofle began but he was interrupted by a quiet knock at the door. She glanced at him across the table.

"Yes?" said Deirdre.

"Good morning, Lieutenant, Group Leader." General Moteurs strolled into the room.

Despite her intention to stay pointedly seated, Deirdre found herself standing up, politely to greet him. It was as if this Grongle were able to affect her behaviour somehow, make her do uncharacteristic things. She didn't like the unpredictability he sparked in her and at once she was on her guard.

"I see you are awake at last."

How dare he say that to someone who had actually collapsed from exhaustion?

"Yes," she snapped.

"I trust you slept soundly," he said.

"Well enough." She rubbed her aching back. As well as disquiet, her politeness in standing up had caused her pain.

He looked at her with the practised eye of a commander inspecting troops.

"You wear that well."

"I'd rather not wear it at all."

"Of course; please accept my apologies. I appreciate that you will not be comfortable in an enemy uniform. I have ordered my troops to find something more suitable but I am afraid that even we cannot arrange that instantaneously."

"Noted," said Deirdre.

"I must also apologise for my own, somewhat dishevelled appearance," General Moteurs went on. "When I lent you my bed I was foolish enough to leave my clean clothes here with it." He looked immaculate. Deirdre knew how much effort went into keeping a uniform looking like that – especially suede boots – and she couldn't help but be impressed, despite who he was. If he thought his appearance was dishevelled, now, Arnold knew what he looked like when he wanted to make an impact. Then again, perhaps he did, maybe he was playing it down, trying to make an impression.

She watched him, standing there in all his finery. He was clean shaven but his short brown hair was a little unkempt and he had bags under his eyes. Wherever he'd slept, the couch perhaps, he clearly hadn't got much rest. The tiredness of his expression softened his features.

"Get on with it then," she said at exactly the same moment as Snoofle held out a casual arm and said.

"Go right ahead."

An almost imperceptible change around the corners of the General's eyes suggested a smirk. The smug get. He made a slight bow before walking over to the wardrobe and removing a clean shirt, identical to the one Deirdre had woken up in. That one had been his shirt then. He walked with a grace and economy of movement that would have appealed to her if he'd been someone else. And he'd been kind enough to lend her his bed. Unfortunately, there was a small technicality, Deirdre reminded herself; that he was a Grongle and the only good Grongle was a dead one.

"You require anything else?" he asked. She glanced over at Snoofle. The Blurpon's face was set in a noncommittal expression.

"I would like to return to my work in the Laundry."

"That will not be necessary for either of you, not today."

"No. It will. If I don't go back people will notice. I don't want to draw any more unwelcome attention to myself."

"Only natural. Although since you have already excelled yourself in that respect, I doubt you have much to fear."

"I don't do fear. I'll leave that to you." As she said this, she felt a strong sense emanating from Snoofle, that he wished he was elsewhere.

Their host ignored her taunt.

"Since neither of you is well enough to return to your duties, you must remain somewhere quiet where you may recover. However, I regret, I cannot allow you to stay here – these are my personal quarters and they are not suitable accommodations for guests such as yourselves."

Guests? Who was he kidding? Deirdre and Snoofle exchanged glances.

"I have arranged somewhere more secure," he continued smoothly. "Despite the strong deterrent in my favour, I'm afraid I do not trust you to stay put – mainly because I would not do so, were our situations reversed – so I believe it prudent to remove all temptation."

"Understood," snapped Deirdre. Snoofle started to groom his whiskers with an air of studied casualness.

"I apologise that your new quarters will be more severe than these, but I hope you will find them comfortable. My troops will escort you there shortly."

Smeck. By the sounds of things, it was the cells after all.

"Understood."

His eyes met Deirdre's: superior and utterly self-assured.

"When you are settled in, I will arrange for the Medical Officer to see you again."

Again? Of course, Deirdre remembered, someone had helped wash her and dress her wounds, but she'd been sure that someone was female. It must have been a nurse. Yes, thinking about it, that would be the Grongolian way, the M.O. would have a quick look and then he and the General would go and socialise, leaving the female nurses to do the work.

General Moteurs seemed to be waiting – presumably for another 'understood' – but Deirdre stayed silent. He read her reticence as consent.

"One more thing Lieutenant. Do not think I would underestimate you. I know you are a dangerous adversary, even winged as you are now. So be advised that I do not make idle threats. If you harm any of my troops or try to escape, I will withdraw my protection and return you directly to Captain Snow and Lord Vernon."

Deirdre threw another glance at Snoofle who shrugged.

"We have some honour, General," she said.

"Yes, Lieutenant, but your devotion to your cause outweighs your sense of honour, I think. We have a file on you. It makes for very interesting reading."

She glared at him. Could she outfight HIM, she wondered. He seemed to read her thoughts.

"I wouldn't try anything now," he said drily. Making a point, he turned his back on his 'guests' to search in the chest of drawers for some clean socks. Deirdre was angry. So angry. But it was better than the alternative, which was still to feel wretched. She waited, watching General Moteurs. She wondered if he could feel her hatred for him and his kind burning the back of his neck. Socks retrieved, he draped the rest of his clean clothes over one arm and turned to face her and Snoofle again.

"When you are settled in your new quarters and I am a little more presentable, I will come and see you."

"If you must."

He raised his eyebrows and made a half bow. She watched him turn to leave.

"Wait." He stopped. "Last night, they put me to bed."

Slowly, he turned round again until he was facing her.

"Yes." He gave her a look as if to say, 'do you want to make something of it?'

Deirdre took a deep breath. This wasn't going to be easy but she wanted him to know that K'Barthans were decent and honourable, unlike his kind.

"Whoever it was, I would like to thank them."

He seemed surprised.

"Thank them?"

"Yes. That's what we K'Barthans do when somebody shows us kindness."

"I am familiar with the concept; it's what most civilised beings do. You can thank one of them, yourself."

There was a long silence as the truth dawned on Deirdre.

"You?"

"Naturally. You passed out on my sofa so I picked you up and carried you to the bedroom."

Smecking Arnold!

"Then I summoned my M.O. to help treat your wounds. You were suffering from exhaustion and the M.O. advised me against moving you elsewhere so I lent you my bed. As a male, it would have been improper for me to remove your clothes and dress your wounds alone, without your consent. And since you were unconscious it was expedient that I summoned others." He stood there waiting for her response; tall, dignified, calm. There was no way out of it. This was going to be almost physically painful. And he knew it. His face was impassive but, again, she noticed that minute change to the corners of his eyes; a smile.

"Then thank you," she mumbled.

"My pleasure." He bowed.

"I'm sure it was."

He shook his head, as if she were nothing more than a temperamental child. Then, without a word, he walked out. His reaction cut her – more than she expected.

There was an awkward silence. When she turned to Snoofle, he wore a slightly panicked expression, as if he feared he would bear the brunt of Deirdre's rage. But, only a bad commander would vent her anger on her troops.

"I told you he was a smecker." She wanted to cry.

33

"Yes. That was not good. I can see now that the two of you do not get on." He was thoughtful. "Or perhaps your remark hit home. Maybe our General has a weak spot."

"Which is...?"

"You."

"No. Not him. There's absolutely nothing."

"Conspicuously nothing."

"No, Snoofle, nothing, nothing. I've felt more chemistry from Group Leader Phillimore and it is well known throughout HQ that he is... you know... happy; happier than a product tester in a laughing gas factory."

Snoofle chuckled.

"General Moteurs is in espionage and he's good at it. He's not going to give anything away but there's something there. He complimented you. He said you looked good in the uniform."

"It's his uniform. He said that to needle me. I may not know about espionage, Snoofle, but I know about males. I'm not on his radar."

"Hmm..."

"He's a Grongle. As you are aware, they struggle to class the rest of us as sentient."

Chapter 6

Professor N'Aversion sat at his desk staring into space. He was thinking. Hard.

Snoofle was not answering his phone. It looked very much as if he was in custody. But the Professor found it difficult to believe that the situation was as cut and dried as Denarghi had made out. Some General had come to the employee dormitories and Snoofle had gone with him, of his own accord: no guns, no coercion. Why?

Where are you, my friend?

He thought, with sadness, of Lieutenant Arbuthnot. She was as prickly as she was beautiful and she had been far too much in Denarghi's thrall, but there was an honesty to her that he liked. Was she dead? He glanced at his watch and tutted. In a few short hours, unless he could find a way to stop it, Denarghi was going to declare Snoofle and Lieutenant Arbuthnot as compromised. After that, even if they managed to survive whatever it was they were enduring, their fellow agents would kill them.

The Professor dialled Snoofle's number again.

Still not picking up.

Arnold's nostril hair.

He sent a half-hearted text over the secure system to his second in command, Simon, who was in Ning Dang Po negotiating the purchase of some contraband electrical components.

'How is it going?' he typed.

"Such a waste of resources, this reinventing the wheel," he grumbled as he pressed 'send'.

Yet another thing Denarghi disapproved of in his Head of Tech Ops was the way the department used their mobile phones. All messages were supposed to be sent in code. The Professor was of the opinion that sending random groups of numbers which were obviously code, or messages that said things like, *the mist is rising and soon the geese will fly* was a bit of a giveaway. What's more, in the Professor's view it was guaranteed to result in surveillance. If a mobile phone with those sorts of messages on it fell into Grongle hands, the first thing they'd do would be to start surveillance on every single other number the phone had dialled. The mobile phone system was secure in that, unlike the landline system, calls were not tapped as standard. However, call logs were automatically stored in the phone for a period of time and could easily be accessed by the network provider and the authorities if need be.

If the messages were the kind Denarghi preferred it would be hard to convince anyone that the handset was some honest, upstanding Grongle's lost phone. The Professor therefore considered it a risk to use the Resistance's somewhat enigmatic code system. The fact no phone had ever fallen into enemy hands didn't mean it wouldn't happen one day. He had told Denarghi as much.

He turned his attention back to the Database and The Pan of Hamgee's trick of disappearing into thin air. He glanced up. There wasn't much daylight coming through the light pipe. The Resistance HQ was lit using a sophisticated system of polished metal light tubes which funnelled natural light from the treetops of the woodland above. A system of mirrors mounted about the walls and ceilings maximised the light shining in, reflecting it across the corridors and spaces. However, unless they were regularly polished, the shine on the insides of the pipes soon faded. That was the trouble with building these things out of scrap metal; not all of it polished to a mirror shine and even if it did, there were no expensive lacquers to put on to keep it shiny. The Professor sighed and switched on the desk lamp. He knew the rumours well enough; the early Nimmists were supposed to have been capable of transporting themselves thousands of miles in an instant. Most of the lore was verbal but there was a sprinkling of mentions in scholarly religious writings. There were other rumours, too; stories of artefacts – items of great power which were known only to the Architraves and a few favoured advisors.

The rationalist treatises dismissed these tales as lies. The religious ones said it was faith, a Ninja-Nimmist technique. The Professor believed these early accounts were descriptions of advanced science and equipment by simple beings who didn't fully understand it.

Whatever the answer, ancient K'Barthans being as they were, the Professor was sure it would be written down somewhere, even if they were concealed in code. Accordingly, he had tasked his assistant, Nar, with developing a programme that would check for possible codes concealed in the books of Arnold and the accompanying early religious treatises.

If he uncovered any truths behind these rumours of the early Nimmists' super powers he was no longer certain what he would do. The Professor was as keen to send the Grongles home as any of his colleagues but he knew his views differed with Denarghi's on the subject of what to do afterwards. The Professor believed the Resistance should conduct the Looking and restore the old order. Back in the old days, when he'd joined, the Resistance had believed this too, not that he'd been aiming to join them. At the time he'd believed it was the Underground he was joining. A naive young Thing, by the time he'd discovered what he had done, it was too late. Nobody left or retired from the Resistance. Once you were in, you were in for life. Like Mrs Burgess in Catering, the only other moderate left in charge, the Professor was an anomaly, in that he was simply too good at what he did to remove. He was under no illusions, though, if they ever found a fundamentalist being who had the same level of scientific intelligence, he was dead. Then again, that looked unlikely. These days, things within the Resistance had changed. Denarghi made no secret of his view that a new order was required, centred around a secular supreme ruler.

"No guesses as to who that would be," muttered the Professor resignedly.

It was a few moments before he realised that the annoying beep he kept hearing was his phone alerting him to a return message from Simon.

'Gng gr8. Shld close deal this eve. Back 2mrw.'

The Professor didn't like text speak. He couldn't see what was wrong with vowels and proper words. Although, as Simon was a Spiffle, and had smaller hands and probably found it harder to type, the Professor could give him a little leeway. He composed a reply.

'Smashing, let me know how it goes,' he sent. Except the phone's predictive text programme made the unilateral decision to change 'smashing' to 'smorgasbord'. Well, with the kind of day he was having, that was par for the course. The Professor laid the phone aside and was about to turn his attention back to his studies, but his elderly tablet beeped. It was a new e-mail. He opened his e-mail interface, only to find it was a round robin about a black out in the lavatories in Sector 7. All the same, it reminded him.

He pulled up the photograph of The Pan of Hamgee which Denarghi had sent to all the Resistance Department Heads and forwarded it to

Simon's webmail, with the message, *'While you're in Ning Dang Po, could you have a look for this chap?'*

There, that should do it. Totally innocuous, simply helping Plumby, he thought as he clicked 'send'.

Now where was he? Ah yes. Back to work. He was complementing Nar's programme with some good, old fashioned cross referencing. To help, he and Nar had developed a comprehensive database and dictionary of the religious writings.

"Teleportation," he said under his breath as he typed.

Nope. Hardly a surprise, that.

"Matter transference."

Nope, still nothing.

"Reality theory," he mused as he typed it in. His search returned thousands of results, the vast majority, irrelevant – he'd come back to that later.

"Quantum?"

No results.

"Of course not, the religious elders of 2,000 years previously would never have heard of quantum or reality theory."

So, all he had to do was work out how somebody who'd never heard of reality theory would describe it in the language of a people new to science. He opened the Thesaurus programme on his tablet and looked it up. No. Nothing there. And then he realised his antennae had tied themselves into a knot.

"Arnold's toe jam!"

He concentrated, trying to untie them but they merely pulled themselves tight. How he wished they wouldn't do this. All Swamp Things can knot their antennae but the Professor was one of a small minority unable to undo them again without using their hands. He took out the mirror he kept for just these sorts of entanglements. Despite his care, the one he'd bruised against the ceiling in Denarghi's throne room was tender. Antennae sorted out, he closed the database, leaving his subconscious to work on a suitable description, and turned to his to-do list. Ah yes. He strode to the door of his office and opened it. Immediately his ears were filled with the banging of hammers and whining of electric motors – not to mention engineers – while the smell of solder assailed his nostrils.

"Nar!" he called.

A lanky creature with dog-like features, covered in mauve hair, looked up from the prototype laser gun she was trying to construct – from covert photographs of the original, the kind of scrap metal that the Grongles would consider too knackered to even bother melting down and, hopefully, the stolen electronics Simon was trying to buy.

"Professor?"

"Have you got a minute?"

"Of course."

"In my office."

The Professor went back to his desk, leaving the door open. Nar followed him in, closing it behind her.

The Professor had never married and Nar was the closest thing he had to family. If he'd had a daughter, he hoped she would have been like Nar. Nearly 30 years his junior, she was one of the two indigenous species of the mountainous region of Smirn; a Galorsh. The other was the Blaggysomp. Nar was about the same height as a Blaggysomp but far less humanoid. Indeed, in her home environment, her fur would be a great deal longer than it was here. She also had a long tail, with a fluffy black tuft at the end and a ring of black fur round her neck.

When they came down from the mountains, most Galorshes shaved their coats short over the summer to keep cool. Now that Autumn was coming in, the Professor could see that Nar was letting hers grow back. Apart from her long neck she was humanoid-ish, except for her drooping soft-haired ears, deep brown, expressive eyes and long snout. Conversing with Nar was rather like talking to a highly intelligent mauve spaniel, Professor N'Aversion found – although he tried not to, because it was species-ist to think things like that. Nar was wearing a threadbare lab coat, darned extensively with neat patches of white cotton, much like the Professor's own. Like his, it was also laden with pockets, all of which contained electrical equipment. Clipped over the top pocket was the ubiquitous collection of biros that marked her out as an engineer. The lab coat was strangely lumpy because she was wearing a jumper underneath it. The jumper itself was lumpy, too, knitted as it was from a motley collection of recycled wool unravelled from other worn out jerseys scavenged from the recycling bins on collection day.

"You chilly, Nar?" he asked.

"Yes, professor; usual thing, time of year, my blood pressure..."

"Of course, you poor lass." The mountains of Nar's homeland were high and the air was thinner. The average Galorsh's blood pressure was therefore lower than that of K'Barthan humans and lowland species. In Smirn, the Galorshes' blood pressure gave them the distinct advantage of never suffering from altitude sickness. However, in the lowlands it meant they could be sluggish and feel the cold in autumn and spring while their coats were re-growing or if they clipped them too early.

"What can I do for you, Professor?"

"How's work on the laser?"

"It's ready for the parts."

"Good stuff. I wonder if you could help me with a couple of things. What do you know about Big Merv and The Pan of Hamgee?"

"Not much."

"We need to find them."

"I've met Frank the Knife and Smasher Harry. They're petrified of their old boss. They didn't have a good word to say about The Pan other than that he was what we would call, in Galorsh, a 'smarveen'."

The Professor knew what a 'smarveen' was; the literal translation was, roughly, 'he who can only walk the precipitous ledge if he has brought spare underwear'.

Nar continued.

"They thought that's what made him so good, though." She quoted The Prophet. "A frightened being runs better and faster."

"Hmm... Could you start searching for any traces of him? They have to be somewhere and I think it's Ning Dang Po. I just hope that the Grongles haven't captured them. I need to talk to The Pan of Hamgee. I want to find out what he did and whether it's something we can use. We need to be the very picture of discretion, though, because only I.R. are to be allowed to speak to him. You know what they're like; if we want to get any sense out of him we need to find him and have a quiet chat before they do."

"Yes, Professor. Would you like me to check the Palace mainframe?"

"You can do that?" Why was he even asking? Nar's team of analysts could hack a hole in anything.

"Of course. It will take time."

"Thank you. While you're working on that, there are rumours that

Snoofle and Lieutenant Arbuthnot are in custody."

"I heard. I hope it isn't true."

"So do I. They're inside the Old Palace somewhere but they seem to have disappeared. This is rather a departure from protocol, I appreciate, but while you're looking for The Pan of Hamgee, could you just see if the records show..." he left the sentence hanging.

"Of course Professor."

"Thank you. Oh and Nar? Our Leader's stance on this is different from ours. I shouldn't really be asking this of you. So be careful; only your most trusted people are to work with you and the results are for my eyes only."

"Yes, Professor," she said.

"Oh and, one last thing. It's getting terribly gloomy in here, if you can spare someone to scrape the worst of the grime off the light pipes again..."

She nodded and left.

Professor N'Aversion sat looking at the closed door after Nar had gone. He could feel the tension tightening in his neck and shoulders. He must do some relaxation exercises or he'd give himself a headache. Nar would be alright. She was intelligent, and sensible, but the Professor hoped he had not put her in too much danger. Uh-oh. Now his antennae were waving towards one another again. Not another knot; he must distract himself from his thoughts. His eyes were drawn to the tablet computer, and the database. No. It was time for some practical work. He got up, slipped his phone into his pocket and went out into the workshop.

Chapter 7

With the ubiquitous fruit smoothie by his side, Lord Vernon sat at the desk in his apartments, working on a speech. He looked up briefly and, as he moved, a flash of light from the buildings opposite caught his eye. The sun was rising over Ning Dang Po. It turned the windows of the buildings across the square to fire and the stonework a delicate pink. It was all the more striking against the dark blue of the retreating night sky. He glanced at his watch. Dawn had come, on schedule, like any other day. But this was not a normal day. This was the beginning of a new era. The Underground in K'Barth was no more. Lord Vernon had switched on the radio and, as he sat and admired the view, he listened to the day's news roundup. Top story: the latest body-blow to those who opposed him.

Naturally the radio station was not using the name 'Underground' since, to the average K'Barthan, it was little more than a rumour. They had only heard of the Resistance.

Chapter 8

Acouple of hundred feet below Lord Vernon's apartments, in the darkest most stinky section of the High Security cells, Private Skule and Private Klub stood at the head of a dimly lit corridor. Private Klub was carrying a wooden box, some shackles and a set of keys. Private Skule was only carrying a slop bucket. It was Private Skule, therefore, who opened the glass fronted control box for the cell lights. He pressed one of the red switches and shut the control box door.

"Let's get this done," he said. "I should have been off duty hours ago. Why're we having a purge on a smecking Saturday, anyway?"

"I dunno, but with all these idiots I've processed today, it's taken me effin' hours to type it up," grumbled Private Klub.

"You'll have to learn to use more than two fingers then."

"Ah shut up Skule," said Klub as he moved ahead. "It's not my fault you're too thick to pull your weight. If you could even half spell I wouldn't be lumbered with it at all."

Private Skule stopped walking.

"Well at least I can count, that's the cell we want," he jerked his thumb at the door beside him. "You've gone past it."

Glowering at his colleague, Private Klub retraced his steps.

"It's your fault. All your smecking argy bargy put me off."

"Get on with it then. I hate coming down here. This place gives me the creeps."

"Yeh, me too," said Private Klub as he selected one of the keys. "But we've been assigned to this prisoner, so until he snuffs it we're stuck with him," he grumbled and he unlocked the door.

****

The Pan woke up, or perhaps, came to is a more apt description. After running off like that and getting himself shot, he was quite surprised to be regaining consciousness at all. When Captain Snow fired, he'd been sure it was death he was facing, but no, apparently it was a stun shot.

"Unless I'm dead. Am I dead?"

"Cluck."

"I guess not." Although it was so dark that it was hard to tell. He realised that, after inconveniencing Captain Snow to such an extent, he was unlikely to regain consciousness in five star accommodation, but this exceeded his worst expectations. He sat up. He could see nothing, not even his hand in front of his face. Not even the luminous dial of his watch. He ran his hand round his wrist to check.

Oh.

They'd taken it.

No surprise really.

"Smecking Arnold," he said. His throat was dry and his voice still croaky but it didn't ache as much as he expected. However, now he had a raging thirst.

"I spy with my little eye, something beginning with 'd'. Dark," he croaked.

Far away in the distance, he thought he heard laughter.

No.

Nobody laughed down here.

A few more seconds inched by and The Pan sat where he was, waiting for something to happen. All the while, in the background, he could hear an irritating whistling sound in his ears, tinnitus with knobs on. Or was it some special madness-inducing soundtrack that the Grongles were playing to him? He cocked his head on one side and listened. No. It might have sounded as if it was coming from outside but he was ready to bet it was inside his head. An aural hallucination, definitely. Mmm. Perhaps, after they'd shot him, they'd drugged him. He closed his eyes and concentrated. He felt woozy but his mental capacities weren't nearly muzzy enough for drugs. He couldn't discount it of course but he was as certain as he dared be that this was simply the aftermath of taking a stun shot after being blitzed with a crowd control stick.

The darkness wrapped itself around him, making him blind, and the cold clamminess of the air felt as if it was smothering him. The Pan wondered about his friends. Were they awake yet? Probably. He'd been zapped unconscious twice. He'd have been out longer than all of them.

For a moment, he concentrated on Ruth. It was a comfort to know he loved and was loved, but the fact that he had let her and the others agree to take part in Sir Robin's ludicrous plan still frightened him. Giving Lord Vernon everything wouldn't make him relax his guard, and even if he did, the Candidate could never defeat him. No-one could. The Pan considered it academic, anyway. He doubted the Candidate would bother to show at all – mainly because, faced with the same dilemma, he knew he would run. For someone so intelligent, so adept at manipulating others, Sir Robin was being naive, at best.

"Stupid," said The Pan dourly. His voice echoed through the surrounding darkness. Yes, it was definitely a bit gravelly but at least he could speak. He listened, half hoping one of the others might be nearby. "Anyone there?" He waited but there was no answer. He knew, with a terrible heaviness, that instead of using his head and running away with Ruth he had handed her to Lord Vernon, and with her, K'Barth. And now he was alone, and there was nothing he could do.

He felt as if he were trapped in a pit, unable to climb out, with no light and no hope, waiting for his doom.

"Yeh well, a bit melodramatic but that sounds about right," he muttered.

Suddenly, a glare filled the room. It's amazing how bright 40 watts can be to someone who's been in total darkness. The Pan screwed up his eyes and looked round. He was in an old fashioned dungeon. It had black slimy walls, a concrete floor rather than earth – but still filthy – and in the middle was a table, complete with leg and arm restraints. No water canteen or slop bucket, he noticed.

There was a pile of sawdust in the opposite corner and, just in case a demonstration of its purpose was required, they'd kindly left some under the table, stained the unmistakable reddy-brown colour of dried blood.

"Mmm. Homely." The Pan looked around him. "I think I preferred the dark."

The annoying ringing faded as his ears picked up on a new sound; footsteps.

The door crashed open and two guards walked in, or at least the first one walked. The second one carried a slop bucket, which somehow got caught up between his legs as he tried to pass the other one, sending him sprawling across the floor. He leapt up, swearing and muttering something about lice. They wore black and red uniforms, similar to Captain Snow's.

"Skule! You stupid tool," said the other one.

45

The Pan got slowly to his feet as Skule went and retrieved the bucket and dropped it on the ground at his feet.

"Ah, I see you've brought the en suite."

"Oh," said the other guard, "Looks like we've got a joker here."

"What's an en suite?" asked the one who'd fallen over.

The Pan had no idea what the time was, whether it was still morning, or afternoon or even the same day, but judging by the way he felt at the sight of the slop bucket, there'd been time enough for his bladder to fill up. He retrieved the bucket from the floor and in the absence of any other cover, retreated behind the table.

The two of them watched him and waited.

"Can you two...?"

"What?"

"Can you give a man a little privacy here?"

They stared at him.

"I don't mind if you go outside and shut the door."

"What?" asked the one that wasn't Skule.

"I'd like to... Oh suit yourselves." With a resigned sigh, The Pan turned his back on them and used the bucket.

"That's disgusting, that is," said Skule.

"What did you bring it for then?"

"To use after we've gone."

"How's he going to use it after we've gone you plank? We're supposed to put him in chains."

"Oh yeh, I hadn't thought of that."

The Pan retrieved the lid of the bucket from the floor and put it on.

"Thank you gentlemen," he said.

He held it out to them. Neither of them moved so he went and put it in the corner.

While he was doing so, one guard got a wooden box from outside in the corridor and placed it against the wall. There were two chains hanging from the wall above it and The Pan realised their intention at once. He made to dodge. He couldn't go anywhere, but if he could keep out of their reach for long enough, he might be able to argue. Unfortunately, despite being stupid, they were fast.

"Hold him, Klub!" shouted Skule as the other one grabbed him.

So now he knew their names, Klub and Skule. Klub held him tight and

Skule drew his laser pistol, moving a couple of paces back so The Pan didn't try to jump him. As if he would, as if there was any point. Klub let go, moved round and stood in front of him.

"Put your arms out in front of you," he said.

The Pan did as he was told.

If Skule was dumb, Klub wasn't much smarter. It took him several goes to figure out how the locking mechanism on a pair of iron manacles worked and lock them round The Pan's wrists. Each manacle had a hook. Klub dragged him over to the wall and made him stand on the box. He raised The Pan's arms in turn, clipping the metal bands onto the chain links so his wrists were held upwards, above his shoulders.

"Is that it?" asked The Pan.

"Yeh. Skule, take the bucket, it's an offensive weapon that is."

"Eh? How?"

"He might chuck it at us."

"How? I'm shackled to a wall," muttered The Pan.

"Shut up, you little turd," said Klub and he walked to the door.

"You forgot the bucket, Skule."

"No I didn't."

"Yes you did, I'm not taking it. I carried the box."

"Why do I have to take it?"

"Coz I'm smarter than you; that's why."

Grumbling and muttering Skule lumbered over to the corner, retrieved the bucket and carried it out into the hall.

"Sweet dreams non-being," said Klub and he slammed the door. The key turned with a metallic grating sound, then Klub and Skule's footsteps faded and the lights went out with a pop.

Chapter 9

It was still early. The Chosen One was asleep. But that was good. Surprise was part of Lord Vernon's plan. Quietly, he closed the door to the rooms he had allocated her a few yards down the cloistered corridor from his own. Soundlessly he moved across the carpeted floor to the bed where she lay. According to Captain Snow, she had become hysterical when she was brought to the Palace and, afraid that she would damage herself or one of the others, he had been forced to control her and then tranquillise her with a sedative. Lord Vernon suspected it had been the Captain's laziness rather than any hysterics on the Chosen One's part, and that angered him. But there would be time to deal with Captain Snow. They had not undressed her but left her sprawled on the bed in her own clothes with a blanket thrown half over her.

He breathed deeply, slowly. He had planned for this, expected it, capturing the Chosen One was merely another step along the path to world domination. Yet, the closer he came to achieving his goal, the more tense he became. He must ensure he took some time out to relax himself. He looked down at her. She was the Chosen One, destined to love the Candidate and Lord Vernon was the Candidate. Now, after a good night's sleep − albeit drug induced − she would be ready to meet her future husband.

Slowly, carefully, so as not to wake her, Lord Vernon peeled off the blanket. He took off his sunglasses, tucking them into a pouch on his belt and stood admiring her, lost in thought. Destiny apart, she would take some owning. There was a wilful spirit, an energy, a strength of character in her that would be a match even for him. Yes, this one was going to be interesting. She hated and feared him and yet he knew that in time, one way or another, she would give herself to him; willingly and yet so unwilling. He smiled to himself. It was time to rouse her. She needed to appreciate her situation. She needed to be frightened. Lord Vernon knew exactly how to frighten her most.

She was lying on her back with her arms up, either side of her head. He put one knee onto the bed and leaned over her, locking his hands round her wrists. They sank into the soft pillows either side of her head as his arms took his weight. She stirred. He leaned down and kissed her neck softly, gently. She almost purred.

"Defreville..." she mumbled sleepily.

"No, someone better," he whispered.

Her eyes snapped open, filled with horror.

****

Ruth's brain climbed muzzily towards the light of consciousness. She was lying on a soft bed but she was cold. The covers were off – and there was somebody there, leaning over her. She thought she felt a light kiss on her neck in the disorientation of that blissful, dreamy state between waking and sleep. The shock of hearing Lord Vernon's voice was almost physical, and when she opened her eyes and found herself looking into his face – so close – she felt a wave of fearful nausea. When it passed, the emotion left in its wake was rage. A burning anger so immense it made her shake.

Perhaps Lord Vernon mistook it for fear because he smiled. As usual there was no warmth in it.

"How dare you? Get off me," she snapped.

"This is a very brusque way to treat your future husband."

She glared straight into the cold grey eyes and said, "If you think I'll marry you, you're mad as well as vile."

"Oh but you will, Ruth. You *will* be my wife, I assure you."

His voice was soft, gentle almost, but that merely increased her fear. It was too much. Ruth moved suddenly upright, or at least, as upright as her pinned arms would allow, turned her head to the side and gagged. With lightning speed he let go of her and moved backwards, off the bed, out of range. Clearly he didn't want anything untoward spattered over that pristine uniform. Good. Even better, from Ruth's point of view, she wasn't actually sick, which would have been deeply humiliating.

"Clearly the idea of our betrothal appeals," he said drily.

"Like open heart surgery without an anaesthetic. I will never love you, Lord Vernon."

"You are the Chosen One and I am the Candidate. It is your destiny. You will no more be able to fight it than extinguish the stars," his air of

49

absolute confidence scared her. "Furthermore, I am a Grongle, an exalted, supreme being—"

She leapt up.

"There's nothing exalted about you!"

Unperturbed, he looked coolly down at her.

"And yet here I am with a whole nation at my feet and here are you, also at my mercy..." he flashed her a nasty smile and moved closer. "You know what they say, 'every woman loves a bastard,' and I can assure you, it's true."

"Not this one."

"But yes. Whether you like it or not, you belong to me. And if you're suitably..." he paused to pin down the right word, "accommodating, I will protect you." She pulled the zip on her top up; as far up as it would go. "But if you are unkind I may have to be a little more... authoritarian than you would appreciate. I am sure you wouldn't want that."

"I might prefer it to the alternative."

He laughed. Absolutely not the reaction she was looking for.

"So fiery. That is why I like you," he said. He took his mobile phone from his pocket, flipped open the case and consulted what Ruth guessed was his diary. "I believe your boyfriend should be ready to see me by now. I'd be a poor host if I kept him waiting."

"Leave him alone," she said, trying to keep the anxiety out of her voice. She failed.

"I couldn't possibly do that," he said lightly, "I am so looking forward to seeing him."

"No," said Ruth but it came out as more of a sob, ruining everything.

"I see you are not so fiery now." Lord Vernon was still supremely calm but with an added air of smugness which she hated. "I will leave you. I wouldn't want to be late. Captain Snow will bring you breakfast."

"I won't be eating it."

"I would if I were you. You will need the energy."

He turned to leave.

"Listen," he stopped. "If you hurt The Pan I will give you nothing, do you hear me? Nothing. You might as well kill me now."

He turned back to face her. When the grey eyes met hers, it felt as if he was sucking her very soul into the vortex of that cold, all-seeing, gaze. It wasn't real, she told herself, it was just a knack, a way of looking at people.

She mustn't let it faze her. So easy to say... She glared back at him with all the defiance she could muster and did not turn her head away.

"You will give me everything I want; and more. You will fulfil my every desire – of your own free will – and that is why it will be so exquisite." He made a mocking bow. "Now, if you will excuse me, I have much to attend to. Until tomorrow, my darling..." He strode from the room.

The door slammed shut and she was alone.

Chapter 10

Alone in the dark, chained to the wall, The Pan waited. The minutes crept by. He was amazed at how painful it was to stand with his arms raised. Soon, his chest ached, a dull pressure that increased as he breathed in leaving him short of breath. That wasn't good. It felt as if all the blood fighting against gravity to get up his raised arms was losing the battle and collecting in his body cavity. He stood on tiptoe which helped a little. There was some slack in the chains but not enough to allow him to drop his arms. He was able to grip them and take some of the weight with his hands though. That was better. The minutes crawled on. He tried not to be afraid. It was a big ask. Perhaps it would raise his spirits if he sang?

No, not least because of his sore throat and the aching weight round his lungs.

The annoying, whistling tinnitus returned. He closed his eyes and tried to think of other things but his thoughts seemed to be stuck in a loop.

I'm going to die.

No I'm not.

Yes, I am.

No, I'm not.

Shut up.

At last, the lights went on. The Pan squinted his eyes and listened, as he adjusted to the sudden glare. Footsteps again; getting louder. Even though they were outside in the corridor, The Pan could hear the arrogant swagger in that walk. The door was unlocked and this time, Lord Vernon himself walked into the room, cracking his black suede clad knuckles as he advanced. A yard from The Pan he stopped and removed his sunglasses. He folded them and wrapped them carefully in a soft cloth before putting them into a pouch on his belt. The rings he wore over his gloves reflected the dim light as he did so. He was flanked by the two guards from earlier.

"Good day to you, Hamgeean."

The Pan tried to reassure himself. Lord Vernon wanted to keep him alive. Otherwise, he'd already be dead. Unfortunately, his nerves weren't listening to that kind of logic. The Pan knew that the trick here was bravado. He must act like a man; calm, collected, not showing his fear. But that was a difficult part to play for a coward, especially one who wasn't a natural thespian.

"Wotcher. Thank you for turning the lights on." Unable to move his arms to point The Pan nodded at the table. "But I'd fire your decorator if I were you. Dried blood is so last year." No, no, no. That wasn't acting like a man. That was acting like an idiot. The Pan wondered how it was that, after all that time on the blacklist, he could still only gibber, or behave like a total arse, in any situation where he had to face danger standing (or in this case hanging) still.

Lord Vernon laughed humourlessly, "I see you appreciate that I cannot kill you... yet."

The Pan looked Lord Vernon in the eye, which took courage, but not as much as he'd expected, and said, "Yes."

"Interesting; for all your cocksureness, I assume you also know you are exactly where I want you."

"Apart from dead," said The Pan glibly.

"I can wait." Lord Vernon moved closer to The Pan. Because of the box, he was higher than usual and their faces were about level. Those inhuman, human eyes glared into The Pan's: cold, merciless, impassive. "I have already signed your death warrant." Lord Vernon held a piece of paper in front of The Pan's face. "And when you have served your purpose," he put his other hand to The Pan's throat, pushing him against the wall and squeezing hard enough to make the point, "I will have my wish." The Pan swallowed and tried to hide his fear but the rattling of the chains as he shuddered belied it. Lord Vernon responded with a slow, sinister smile, "Nothing to say?"

The Pan bit his tongue; he'd said quite enough already. Standing, chained to a wall, doesn't afford a man much dignity and he decided that the remaining shreds were best preserved with silence.

"How disappointing." Lord Vernon let go of his neck abruptly and turned to the guards. "Get him down."

The guards unhooked the shackles round The Pan's wrists. Immediately, his legs gave way and he fell off the box and onto the ground in a crumpled heap, right at Lord Vernon's feet. There went his dignity then. Lord Vernon stepped back and waited while The Pan rolled over slowly, clumsily and crawled over to the table. Holding onto it, he hauled himself shakily to his feet. Lord Vernon nodded to the guards.

"Leave us."

The Pan moved away from him, round the table, putting it between the two of them and leaning on it. His arms felt leaden and heavy and moving made him dizzy, but he knew he must try to get the blood distribution in his body back to normal as soon as possible. He leaned on the table and took deep breaths. As his legs recovered, he walked and then jogged on the spot. Lord Vernon let him get on with it. With the table between them The Pan felt safer, even though logic told him it made no difference. He windmilled each of his arms around in turn, to try and persuade the circulation back into his numb hands, while Lord Vernon watched and waited with a disdainful expression.

"You have led me a merry dance, Hamgeean. I must applaud you on your evasive skills. Perhaps you believe I will waste my time pursuing you round that table. I think not. You forget that I want you alive." He waved a dismissive suede-clad hand, "...temporarily. However, unfortunately for you, condition is an issue. You see, should I avail myself of your services to..." He paused to think of the word, "Influence the Chosen One, I will need her to understand that I mean..." He unhooked the laser pistol from his belt as he spoke, adjusted the power setting and aimed it at The Pan with cool precision, "Business."

He fired; two bolts in rapid succession.

The Pan threw himself sideways, avoiding the first shot, but the second caught him square in the left shoulder. The force of the impact lifted him and flung him against the wall. Slowly he slid down onto his knees and fell forward onto the floor. To say it hurt was probably the understatement of the millennium. His whole body burned and for one fearful moment he wondered if he was actually vaporising. Instead, gradually, the pain drained away from his limbs. But as it lessened in the rest of his body it increased in his shoulder where he'd been hit. Gasping and breathless, he rolled around on the floor, his good hand clutched to the wound, but nothing would contain the agony. He was almost mad with it. His breath came in sobs and, worse, tears ran from his eyes. He curled into a ball, head down, so Lord Vernon would not see them and after what seemed like an age, he finally managed to acclimatise himself to the pain enough to breathe normally.

He heard Lord Vernon walk slowly towards him. Hurriedly, he tried to get to his feet, wiping his face with the sleeve of his good arm at the same time, but his shaking legs would not hold his weight. He made it onto all fours but no further. Lord Vernon kicked him over onto his back. Even though he guessed what was about to happen next, and even though he braced himself, when Lord Vernon put his boot against the wound and leant on it, The Pan could not bear it. Pinned helplessly to the ground, crying out and writhing in agony, he clutched ineffectually at the suede-clad foot clamped against his injured shoulder. He tried to push it away and free himself. Lord Vernon reacted by increasing the pressure, holding him fast to the floor. After an eternity of embarrassing screaming The Pan managed to control himself enough to lie reasonably still. Faint and panting he looked up at his tormentor.

"I'm so sorry does that hurt?" asked Lord Vernon, glibly.

Though he tried, The Pan could not speak.

Lord Vernon leaned forward, putting a little more weight on his foot. The Pan's back arched, his fingers curled and a strangled cry squeezed its way out through his gritted teeth despite his attempts to keep a manly silence.

"I'll take that as a 'yes'. It is merely a broken collarbone, easily mended but excruciatingly painful. I must say, your brother took it better than you."

"Leave my brother out of this," gasped The Pan.

"Perhaps you would like to know how he died?"

Arnold no. He was in no state for that. He said nothing.

"Aren't you even a little curious?"

"No."

"I think I ought to tell you."

"No. Stop," croaked The Pan. Lord Vernon tutted.

"Manners, Hamgeean. I didn't hear you say please."

The Pan closed his eyes. "Stop... please."

Lord Vernon jerked his heel venomously against The Pan's shoulder. The Pan felt his eyes roll, it was almost beyond pain now. He was shaking and sweating. He began to feel sick and light-headed. With any luck he was about to faint. What a relief that would be.

"Oh no, Hamgeean, you don't get to pass out. Not with me," said Lord Vernon. He reduced the pressure just enough to keep his victim the right side of conscious.

"Get on with it," whispered The Pan. "Just do what you have to do and then go."

"Oh I have done what I came here to do." Lord Vernon put a tiny bit more pressure on his foot but The Pan managed to bite back the pain.

"I was going to tell you about your family; Mother, Father, Brother, Sister."

The Pan didn't trust himself to speak. Slowly, painfully, he shook his head.

"I'm going to tell you how they died..."

The Pan closed his eyes again, and tried not to hear, but there was something hypnotic and powerful about Lord Vernon's voice. He could not block it out, and as Lord Vernon continued, sparing no detail, The Pan began to cry, wracking sobs, which made the whole foot-on-the-shoulder aspect to his current position so much worse. Lord Vernon looked down at him, dispassionately, observing his reaction. The Pan turned his head away and closed his eyes. He put his good hand across his face but nothing would block out Lord Vernon's words, or stem the flow of tears, as six years of guilt and loneliness overwhelmed him. At last, snivelling and snotty-nosed, he half shouted, half sobbed.

"Stop this. You have said enough."

"You are in no position to give me orders." Lord Vernon ground his heel into the wound. The Pan didn't even try to curb his reaction. He was beyond caring. Lord Vernon kept up the pressure, and when The Pan's sobbing had quietened down enough he leaned forward. "Did I not tell you, Hamgeean, that I would break you?"

With a supreme effort The Pan managed to slow up his tears enough to speak, although it seemed that nothing in the world would make them stop.

"Just kill me and have done."

Lord Vernon raised his eyebrows.

"It's interesting, but that's exactly what your father said. Several times, if I recall. Alas, as you well know, I cannot oblige. I may regret my decision – your girlfriend seems very taken with me and I wonder if I will have need of you – but I value General Moteurs' counsel and I will not go against it." He smiled with the usual reptilian level of warmth. "Ah... Ruth... She is so spirited isn't she? Such a fighter." He glanced contemptuously down at The Pan. "Not like you." Again he hefted his foot against The Pan's shoulder and, again, as if the point needed demonstrating, The Pan treated him to a most unmanly exhibition of writhing and screaming. Lord Vernon looked down at him and said. "I will have her before long."

Cold horror gripped The Pan.

"No you won't," he gasped.

"Oh but I will. You underestimate the weight of tradition. I am the Candidate; handsome, powerful, intelligent and indomitable." Lord Vernon jerked his foot downwards against The Pan's shoulder with each adjective. "What's not to love?"

"Everything," croaked The Pan. Lord Vernon gave him one last, savage kick and stepped back. The sudden release of pressure merely provoked another mind numbing wave of pain. He rolled around on the filthy concrete, sobbing and nursing the wound. Lord Vernon walked across the room and banged on the door.

"Sir. You have finished?" The Pan heard one of the guards ask.

"I haven't even started," snarled Lord Vernon. "Put him on the table and tie him down."

The guards dragged The Pan to the table by his arms, the pain beyond agony, and flung him onto it like a piece of meat. He didn't struggle when they locked the straps round his wrists and ankles, there was no point. Anyway, the torture had exhausted him. Lost in his own private world of misery he lay, unmoving, waiting for the blessed oblivion that would come when he slipped into unconsciousness, which he would soon, surely. His hatred and anger burned strongly within him, but over and above the misery of hearing the truth about his family, it was the separation from Ruth – and the knowledge of what Lord Vernon planned for her – that overwhelmed him now.

Lord Vernon returned to the table with a syringe.

"I am going to begin the fascinating process of deconstructing your sanity. I must admit, I am a little disappointed to have broken you so soon. After the resourcefulness with which you fought for your freedom I expected something more... challenging. Perhaps I mistook your desperation for courage. No matter, we are going to have fun together, you and I..." He squatted down, his face level with The Pan's. Despite wanting to turn his head away, The Pan could not find the strength to do so. "I'm afraid it will be less fun for you but for me... oh the pleasure." Aside to one of the guards he said, "He is losing consciousness, wake him up."

The Pan felt something cold press against his neck. His body jolted as, with a burst of white hot pain, he absorbed a low level bolt from a crowd control stick. A smaller, hand-held version he realised when he had finished screaming.

"Excellent," said Lord Vernon. "I think I have your attention now." He waved one of the hypodermic syringes from the trolley in front of The Pan's glazed eyes. It was the one with the red liquid. "Here is a little something to help you focus." He grabbed a tuft of The Pan's hair and held his head still. "It goes in the usual place. Just. Below. The. Eye. But I think I will put it... here." He jabbed the syringe savagely into The Pan's neck and depressed the plunger. "You may be impervious to Truth Serum but I do not think you will resist this. It is a compound which will make your life most interesting for the next twenty four hours. You are tired and thirsty and doubtless you would like to sleep. This chemical will ensure that you do not, or that if you do, you will wish you hadn't."

The Pan looked blearily into the merciless grey eyes.

"Do I get to find out what's in it?" his voice was slurred, now, and it took a few breaths to get each word out. Arnold, this stuff worked fast.

"A hallucinogen, a stimulant – several times the prescribed safe dose, naturally... oh and colouring."

"Colouring?"

No-no, you idiot, don't make conversation. If The Pan had possessed the mental energy, he'd have kicked himself. As it was he lay there, semi-comatose, while his nemesis helpfully answered the question.

"Those who serve me at this level do not always understand the nuances of lengthy pharmacological names. All the chemicals used in information retrieval are colour-coded for ease of reference."

"Information retrieval? The K'Barthan word is torture," said The Pan; at least he hoped that was what he had said, but the red stuff was beginning to take hold. Following the conversation was starting to take applied concentration.

"Your name for this little... chat we are having, is immaterial."

"And drugging me is. Pointless—"

"But no more than you deserve," sneered Lord Vernon.

"You know anything I could tell you already."

"Who said I want to KNOW anything. I just want to watch you suffer."

Well, The Pan realised, he had asked.

58

"What will it do to me?" he whispered.

Lord Vernon held the empty syringe out sideways. One of the guards took it from his hand, exchanging it with a full one.

"I can't tell you that. It will ruin the surprise," said Lord Vernon as he jabbed the second syringe into The Pan's neck. "Wait and see." He handed the second empty syringe to the guard, stood up and strolled to the door. There, he turned and surveyed the scene for a few moments. The Pan, strapped to the table, tried to stare back but the red stuff – or was it the after effects of being shot – was making it difficult to focus. Lord Vernon cocked his head on one side and looked at him, thoughtfully. "Interesting," he said to one of the guards. "He is weaker than I thought. Make sure he does not die."

"Yes sir," said the guard nervously. Lord Vernon put on his sunglasses.

"If he does, I will hold you personally responsible."

"Yes sir," replied the guard, except it was more of a fearful squeak. Lord Vernon turned to the other guard who was looking more than a little relieved. "Both of you," he said. The door slammed and The Pan listened to the footsteps as they faded into the distance.

Chapter 11

Left alone, Ruth bit back the tears of rage and exasperation. Crying might, possibly, make her feel better but it wasn't going to help. She needed to be calm, incisive and devise a plan of action. She thought about Lucy, who would undoubtedly have come out with the favourite quote of one of her heroines; a member of the Suffragette movement called Emily Wilding Davison, the one who'd been trampled by the King's horse at Epsom races. How had it gone? Ruth tried to remember, yes, that was it, 'rebellion against tyrants is obedience to God'.

"Ha! Very apposite," Ruth muttered. And everyone thought Emily Wilding Davison committed suicide for her cause. Which was a complete misinterpretation of events.

"You and me both on that one, Emily."

Ruth knew that many K'Barthans would hate her for marrying Lord Vernon. They would see it as a betrayal and nobody would ever know the truth, just as few people realised how unlikely it was that Emily Wilding Davison had intended to die for her cause. As Lucy had forcefully explained, she was trying to stick a protest rosette on the horse as it sped past, not throw herself under it.

If Lucy managed to survive this, would she realise why Ruth had acted as she did?

Suddenly Ruth wanted nothing more than to be back home, sharing a glass of wine with Lucy, while her friend regaled her with funny stories about the myriad temporary jobs she'd done to pay for her studies. Lucy had worked as a waitress, spent several holidays gutting chickens, stacked supermarket shelves at night throughout her time at university, and also typed up the dissertations of other students for them, for a small fee. Her admiration for Emily Wilding Davison was closely linked to her passion for education. Her idol had fought poverty and bigotry to finally get a degree.

'Even if I was poor, she had it far worse than me, and she never gave up,' Ruth remembered her friend saying. 'And because she didn't, I couldn't.'

Somehow, Lucy's admiration for Emily made her seem more immediate and connected to Ruth. And the knowledge that one of the poor woman's last conscious actions may have been so completely misinterpreted gave Ruth a sense of solidarity, of comfort.

"Yeh. I can do this," she whispered.

Although maybe before she thought about rebellion against the tyrant, she should start with some orientation.

"Good plan," she told herself. She stood up and moved around the room. Once she'd had the promised visit from Captain Snow, and she could do so undisturbed, she would look for routes of escape. For now she contented herself with taking stock. The entry door was set in the wall to the left of her bed, up six steps. This wall only stretched half the width of the room ending at the pillar one side of a huge arch, which ran across, at an angle, and met a similar pillar at the end of the wall opposite her, just to the left of the desk. The arch was glassed in, with doors opening onto a balcony – or perhaps it was more of a terrace because it was a good 20 feet in length, possibly more. She could see a table and chairs and plants in pots, olive trees by the looks of it and beyond that a wide open space flanked with buildings. To the other side of the bed, against the other wall was a large wardrobe; the kind you see in country houses with a hanging space either side and drawers in the middle. Only the lower half had conventional drawers. The upper half had those open drawers, for socks and undies, which are usually spaced at just the right width for the unsuspecting person reaching for a cotton hankie to rap their knuckles.

There were a lot of expensive under-clothes in there and a lot of slips, mostly in ivory or black silk, there was even a pair of silk pyjamas. Day wear looked thin on the ground. Oh no, hang on... she opened the wardrobe on the other side. Yes, it was full of clothes. Wonderful clothes, and shoes. They were all new, all Ruth's approximate size and all had that kind of tasteful and understated elegance that only money, a lot of money, can buy. There was even an evening dress, a beautiful long number in scarlet velvet.

Bum. Ruth's dream clothes but chosen by Lord Vernon. As such, even if they were the epitome of everything she liked, she couldn't wear them. She cast a regretful eye over the things on the rail and turned her attention to a chest of drawers by the bed. It contained more clothes, jumpers mostly, with the odd pair of casual trousers and some socks. The trousers were canvas jeans, like her own and everything was new.

To the right of her bed there was another door to a small, uninspiring bathroom. All white tiles, a piece of polished metal for a mirror, a basin with no plug, a loo and a shower. It had no windows, just a strip light and annoying fan that droned on for several minutes after she had switched the light off.

She checked the desk between the fireplace and the window. It contained crayons and writing paper, nothing sharp like a biro, a pen with a nib or even a pencil, she noticed. She almost laughed at the idea of herself taking on Lord Vernon armed only with a Bic biro and a fountain pen. As if that really posed a danger to him; as if she did. The sound of a key in the lock made her jump. Captain Snow entered, without knocking, followed by a girl in a black dress and white apron who was carrying a tray. She looked as if she'd stepped out of an Edwardian tea room. Ruth smiled at her briefly and then glowered at Captain Snow.

"Can't you knock?" she snapped.

"Nah." He looked her up and down in a way that made her skin crawl. She hugged her arms around her.

"I brought your breakfast. Porridge." He slapped the girl with the tray on the rump. Ugh, he was vile. Ruth made a point of addressing the girl rather than the Captain.

"Thank you. Can you put it there, please," she gestured to a table at the end of the bed.

"Wait," Captain Snow commanded. The girl stopped. "Let me check that." He put one greasy finger into the porridge and sucked it. Ruth wondered where his hands had been. Nowhere he'd washed them afterwards, for sure. "That's a lovely breakfast, I reckon I deserve a thank you for that."

"Thank you, Captain," said Ruth coolly.

Captain Snow nodded at the girl and she put the tray on the table where Ruth had indicated.

"I've been up all night serving the course of justice and then, when I could have gone to rest my weary head, I've stayed up that little bit extra to come and see you," he leered at her. "Don't I get a kiss from the lady?"

"No."

He walked over to the table, with an arrogant, rolling gait, put his finger in the porridge again and sucked it provocatively.

"I reckon that needs some seasoning," he said, and to her disgust, he spat in it, stirred it, still with his finger, and tasted it again. "That's better," he walked over to her and stood close, closer than was pleasant or comfortable. Near to, he smelled of stale sweat and had the kind of halitosis that could wilt flowers and probably render babies and children unconscious. "One way or another, little girl," he pulled her against him and pinned her arms, "you'll get to like the taste of me."

"I thought I was Lord Vernon's toy," she said.

He flinched as if he'd been struck, and let go of her abruptly. Result!

"For now," he said.

"There we are then. Every cloud has a silver lining," said Ruth, smiling sweetly.

"Oh, you'll get yours, human witch. He'll have his fill of you in no time, and when he's done, I'll be waiting." Laughing to himself he left the room. With a furtive glance at Ruth, the servant girl followed him.

Chapter 12

Deirdre and Snoofle were moved out of General Moteurs' private quarters shortly after the visit he made to collect his clean laundry, which, in Deirdre's opinion, had merely been an excuse to come and gloat. He sent a small detachment of heavily armed imperial guards to escort them to new rooms a little further along a sparkling, freshly painted corridor bedecked with art works, looted from other parts of K'Barth no doubt.

Their escort was a team of five led by the female Grongle who had been standing on the balcony while they had breakfast. She told them her name was Corporal Jones and politely avoided giving any in-depth answers to Snoofle's questions about anything else, especially her commander. Even so, the mere mention of General Moteurs provoked the kind of marked reaction in her that suggested hero-worship. It annoyed Deirdre, who would have found it easier to put up with his arrogant attitude if there was less evidence to suggest he had reason to be smug.

The door of their new quarters was a wooden one, reinforced with metal plates and with bolts added to the outside. Inside they found a plain room containing two beds at one side. At the other was an eating area – a table, two chairs and a higher stool for Snoofle – while close by was a space containing two easy chairs, presumably for relaxation. Yeh, as if. Through a door in one corner Deirdre had glimpsed a separate bathroom and when she had gone to check it out discovered that it was extremely secure, everything sharp removed, too. There were bars across the window, as there were in the main room and even the inside of the chimney, as Deirdre had discovered when she checked more thoroughly – but the metal was shiny and new. It was clearly an office rapidly converted for the purpose of containing her and Snoofle. Why hadn't General Moteurs put them in the main cell block? Was it just because he didn't trust Captain Snow? Or did he want to keep their custody a secret? Perhaps, if she could find out why, Deirdre could use the information against him.

Deirdre ran her trained eye over the room for any means of escape, and for the umpteenth time, it was still a 'no'. Their quarters had been expertly escape-proofed. The Imperial Guard knew what they were doing.

Corporal Jones arrived with a bevy of guards and breakfast: muesli for

Deirdre and kedgeree for Snoofle, with coffee, tea and orange juice.

"General Moteurs will be along to see you shortly," said Corporal Jones. "He asked me to stress that you are under his protection and remind you that you gave him your word not to abuse his trust."

"Understood." Deirdre glanced at Snoofle, who raised his eyebrows.

"He also asked me to return these to you," said Corporal Jones.

Deirdre took the items she was offered in disbelief. Her throwing knives and holster along with a brown paper parcel, tied up with white string, "Please make yourselves comfortable until my Commander joins you." She saluted and then left with the guards. Deirdre and Snoofle listened to the sound of the key turning in the lock and the bolts being shot.

Deirdre unwrapped the parcel. It contained a set of military fatigues, similar to those she habitually wore at the Resistance hide out, along with Snoofle's belt and phone.

"Amazing," said Snoofle as she held them up.

"You want them now?"

"In a minute; they can wait until I've finished this." He took a large mouthful of kedgeree, "I have to hand it to the Imperial Guard," Snoofle gestured to his plate, "their food's good. That's the thing about espionage, though, even the staff meals here are better than the stuff back at HQ. You know what? I haven't had one portion of boiled cabbage since I got here," he waved his fork for emphasis. "Aren't you going to join me?"

"In a moment, Snoofle." She picked up the fatigues. "I will return shortly." She headed off to the bathroom to change.

In the end, Deirdre decided to keep the Grongle shirt on. It was anonymous enough and she might need a clean one so she folded the green one up and put it to one side. She did swap the trousers, though. She suspected the new ones were Grongle army, too. They were certainly cut with the same made-to-measure precision as the others, with the same side zipper but they were full length and a shade of khaki. She checked her reflection in the mirror. Yes. Another excellent fit. Tight enough to highlight all her curves but loose enough to flatter. The trousers had elasticated straps at the bottom which went under the foot, to stop them riding up when she put the boots back on, which she did, in the absence of any alternative foot wear. She strapped the leather knife holster around her waist and right thigh. The effect was impressive, a definite 10 on the don't-mess-with-me-o-meter and yet at the same time, even for Deirdre, all woman. She smiled. Wary of any more high kicks she tried some slow stretches and discovered that yes, the khaki trousers allowed the same freedom of movement as the Imperial Guard britches. She returned to Snoofle who was sitting on the bed, his attention absorbed in his mobile phone.

"You have heard from HQ?" she asked him.

"Unfortunately yes," he said as he tapped away at the screen. "I hate this code and after all that sweat, all it says is, 'please report status'. I've said..." he tapped some more, "'not certain, will advise' or something along those lines. I wonder what General Moteurs will make of that. It'll be monitored, for certain."

"Should you use it?"

"No, but if I don't report back to HQ Plumby is quite stupid enough to think they've turned us. It would be smecking annoying to get out of here only for my brain dead commander to have us killed." The phone was still absorbing his attention. "I have a text from my good friend Professor N'Aversion warning me as much – and about 15 missed calls from him which were probably to say the same. I've told him we appear to be in protective custody and are being treated well. With any luck he'll pass that on. Not much signal around here." He held it up in the air for a minute. "There. All sent." He pressed the lock button, tossed it aside and for the first time since she'd changed, looked up at her.

"Wow, Deirdre."

"Good wow?"

"Very good. You're a big baldy so I can't be certain but yes, I'd say you look hot!" He hesitated. "For someone who isn't interested our General Moteurs is certainly making a fine clothes horse out of you."

"It's probably Corporal Jones. She seemed," Deirdre hesitated, "sympathetic." She smiled ruefully and sat down. "I am beginning to see many things differently. Close up with the enemy nothing is simple. The tradition in my family is to work in the civil service. For generations, we have maintained our position of influence by toadying to those in power. I have always disliked it; I still do. But now I am closer to understanding how it happens. Although I still- my family..." she stopped."

"What are you trying to tell me, Deirdre?" Snoofle clearly didn't want to use the c word. Not surprising, 'collaborator' was a pretty explosive adjective.

"My father is the mayor of Prang. He is famously cooperative with the authorities in a manner that has made him very rich." And Deirdre, not to mention many of the townspeople, loathed him accordingly. Snoofle seemed almost dumbfounded.

"You're THAT Arbuthnot?"

"Yes. I am."

"You certainly break the family mould."

"I would hope so."

"I take it your folks don't know what you do."

"No. I have told them I am a lumberjack."

Snoofle guffawed.

"Why ever did you tell them that?" he said and started giggling again.

"As you well know, I do not have an aptitude for subterfuge or the ability to sustain a lie. Timber camps are temporary, their locations are difficult to check and the work forces in them come and go. As a cover it seemed to allow for the most inconsistencies in my story."

"That's eminently sensible. Maybe you're not as bad at subterfuge as you think, Deirdre."

"No. I merely understand my shortcomings."

He laughed.

"Come on, come and eat your muesli. If it's as good as the kedgeree they've made me, you won't want to miss out."

She sat at the table at right angles to him and started her breakfast. She had to admit, it was possibly the best she'd tasted. Snoofle sat with her in companionable silence while she ate.

"Deirdre, I have to ask. How d'you explain the knife throwing?" he asked as she finished.

"I have been careful to avoid knife throwing in my parents' vicinity."

"You don't go home often, then?" he said, starting to chuckle again.

"No. I cannot trust my parents. If my father knew what I really do there is a chance he may inform the authorities. He will certainly cut me off and disown me. I would not be so concerned but my personal wealth has allowed me to give more than my loyalty to the cause. My troops need equipment, they rely on me to provide it for them." Snoofle stopped chuckling abruptly. Deirdre shrugged. "I have striven to achieve success on my own merits but since coming here and meeting you I have begun to doubt. I wonder what Denarghi sees when he looks at me. I thought he judged me by my actions; fifteen successful missions back to back. No-one else has equalled that, and two of them were death missions. He swore we wouldn't return; I myself did not expect to. But I proved him wrong. I still did my duty and I got my troops home in one piece. I thought he was impressed by that. I thought he believed in me. Now..." she tailed off the tears pricking behind her eyes.

"Now you are wondering if he just saw the colour of your money," said Snoofle gently.

"Do I have to wonder? It would appear I have done my own excellent job of upholding the family tradition. I am no more worthy to be a Lieutenant than Plumby."

Snoofle put his hand on her arm.

"That's not true, Deirdre. You are."

"I doubt you would have said that 24 hours ago."

"I hope I would have kept an open mind. You might have been Denarghi's flavour of the month but I had heard enough good things about you and your troops not to let that sway me. What about that time you got jumped in Smirn. Who was that?"

"The Interior Minister and his escort, the one who was advocating cleansing."

"That's it. Five people, with three throwing knives each, a couple of spare detonators and a commandeered lorry load of custard powder taking out a whole squad of 20 Grongles and a Class 1 target. That was genius, it's the stuff of legend."

"The explosive properties of custard powder are well known."

"To you maybe, I wouldn't have had a clue, and now you're here and I have seen you in action, watching, listening and learning, I'm ready to bet that every single tall story I heard about you is true."

"Maybe a couple are. But I've been a fool and blinded by my pride. If I'd possessed any foresight I could have avoided this. I should not be here."

"No you shouldn't, but you can't blame yourself. Denarghi was the stupid one, sending you. If it helps, now you are here I'm glad," he smiled. "And from what Mrs Pargeter in the drying room told me about your knife skills, you could always run away with the circus. I bet they would welcome you with open arms. That's if you wanted to of course," he paused. "You know, it's a bit like the logging business, itinerant, not much paperwork – a good way to disappear."

"It's not for me." Deirdre smiled weakly but she could no longer contain her emotions; a tear escaped and ran down her cheek. "Smeck," she said. She needed a distraction.

Snoofle put a tissue into her hand.

"Chin up soldier," he said. He glanced round the room. "Hey. What do you reckon? If we could get out of here, I quite fancy the circus. We can reverse tradition; pretend you're my stunning assistant and then surprise the life out of them when you start hurling the knives. Nothing appeals like a novelty! I think we could clean up." He grinned at her and she began to laugh.

"Thank you," she said.

"What for?"

"Snoofle. I know what you're doing."

"Me?" He looked up at her with an expression of wide-eyed furry innocence and then his focus changed to something behind her. "Oh I say... what a marvellous ceiling. It's Angel Michelo! I'm sure of it."

For all his dedication to the business of espionage, Deirdre noticed, you couldn't keep the art historian in Snoofle down for long, she began to chuckle.

"Then tell me all about it," she said, laughing properly now.

Chapter 13

After a very short time strapped to the table, alone, The Pan heard the sound of approaching footsteps again; running. The door was flung open and the two guards burst into the cell.

"Wotcher..." said The Pan, except that, because of the drugs what came out was more along the lines of "glrraub."

"Smeck!" said one of them, Klub, The Pan thought. "He's going to croak."

"Nah," said Skule. "He might throw up though."

"Yeh, he looks sick as a dog."

"Yeh."

"Same difference then. Can't have him doing that, he'll drown," said Klub, who was clearly the smarter of the two – not that there was much in it.

"Smeck," said Skule.

"Let's put him in the recovery position. At least if he snuffs it Lord Vernon will see we've made the effort."

"That isn't going to save us if he croaks."

"Yeh. I'm not stupid numb-knuts."

'That's a matter of opinion,' thought The Pan. He watched them as Klub, the smart one, approached the table.

"It's not fair—"

"He's the Lord Protector, he doesn't have to be fair. Now shut up and help me undo these."

The Pan lay in silence as they unlocked the straps holding the arm on his injured side, and his corresponding leg, to the table. They rolled him over and bent the free leg at the knee to keep him in position, but because of the tightness of the remaining two straps he was very near the edge of the table. In fact his knee hung well off it. The Pan liked the change of position. It was quite comfortable, although it was all relative. A bed of nails would probably have felt comfortable after Lord Vernon breaking his collar bone and then standing on it for 10 minutes. He wondered what the street value of the red stuff was; contrary to what he'd expected it didn't seem to be bringing him down so much as taking him up. He was beginning to feel better. Not physically, he was still in pain, but mentally. It was like being drunk – but fantasy drunk, as if he'd got plastered to forget about his sorrows and it was actually working. The guards stood back to admire their handiwork.

"Hmm," said Klub sucking the air through his teeth.

"Yeh," said Skule.

"Looks a bit risky that."

"Yeh."

"Health and safety wouldn't like it."

"No."

"He might roll off."

"Yeh, and take the table over with him. We don't want to break it."

"Should be alright. It's bolted down."

"You reckon?"

"I dunno."

The Pan's view of the guards was blurry around the edges and they shimmered and danced as if he was looking at them through a heat haze. The stuff Lord Vernon had injected him with was powerful. But even in his addled state, he suspected his mind was sharper than either of theirs. He felt a different sensation in his knee, as if it was moving forward or downwards and he realised, at about the same time as the two guards did, that he was, indeed, falling off the table. He tried to stop himself but his body felt as if it was made of rubber and his limbs responded to the messages from his brain at the speed of a tortoise with mobility problems. Anyway, he could only use his leg, because his serviceable arm was the one still strapped down, and it was the weight of his leg that was causing the problem. He gave into gravity, rolled over, fell a few inches and stopped suddenly, hanging in mid-air by one arm and leg. Oh. But at least he wasn't hanging by his bad arm. Even so, the sudden jolt resulted in a bout of pain that was truly unspeakable. He gritted his teeth and tried to put his foot down to take his weight but the floor was moving too much and he couldn't get a purchase. He was aware that the guards were watching him but they seemed unsure as to what to do next.

"He's off his tits," laughed Klub.

"Yessh I am," slurred The Pan.

"Shut up, Vermin," said both of them in unison.

"Sharming," said The Pan.

"If you want another dose of control stick you carry on talking," said Skule.

"Be my guesht," said The Pan. Result. With any luck it would kill him.

There was a long silence, while, presumably, the guards realised the same thing.

"Looks like we'll have to put him on the floor," said Klub.

"Well..." said his dim colleague, "it's not as if he can go anywhere."

"Nah," Klub agreed.

They unlocked the straps round The Pan's remaining arm and leg. Immediately he crawled under the table, pulling his jacket around him, and curled up into a ball, on his side, in the bloodstained sawdust.

"Is that the recovery position then?" asked Skule.

"It's close enough," said Klub. "He should be alright if we check him regularly. Go get some of the boys and we'll set up a watch party in the corridor. You play poker?" The Pan heard him ask as the two of them reached the door.

"Yeh."

"Good. Get a table and chairs while you're there then... Oh and a heater."

"Why can't you get it?"

"Because I'm the brains of this outfit so I have to stay here."

"OK but if he coughs it while I'm gone it's your fault."

"Smeck. We'll both go." They turned for one last look at The Pan.

"Listen up, you piece of dreck. If you die while we're not here, we'll kill you," said Skule.

"If I die, you'll die, too. Although, I'm guessing the Grongolian gene pool will thank me," said The Pan, except that what came out sounded like, "Ishy-glaarb," repeated several times. It was lucky, because whatever Lord Vernon had threatened, the guards probably would have given him a good kicking if they'd deciphered (or understood) what he'd said. Instead, there was another long pause while they stood looking at him thoughtfully, presumably trying, and failing, to work it out. Then with a shrug, smart guard turned and left, thick guard following in his wake. The door closed and the light went out with a pop. The Pan closed his eyes and lay in the darkness waiting to see what would happen.

Chapter 14

Professor N'Aversion sat engrossed in the database, a cup of Blimpet's clandestine coffee going cold at his side. He was roused from his studies by a knock on the door.

"Come!" he shouted.

"Professor?"

"Nar, I need cheering up, have you found anything?"

"Scraps. The Grongolian mainframe is a pig to crack, they change the codes every hour, but I have an intake list for Saturday; names and cell numbers. I looked for Group Leader Snoofle and Lieutenant Arbuthnot, too. I know Snoofle contacted you but I thought you would want to know where he and the Lieutenant were."

"Did you find out?"

"No. They're not accounted for on the main system. Wherever they are, it's very secret."

"Oh dear, how secret?"

"I'd guess black ops if the boys and I can't get to it."

"Arnold's armpits that's a worry. And yet, you know, he sent me text to say he and the Lieutenant are fine and being treated well. I can't reply, of course, it contained a trigger word so he obviously thinks the Grongles have planted a bug in his phone. But he sounded pretty chipper. Apparently Plumby is all hot under the collar because the text he got had a joke in it. I can't see the problem, myself."

Nar smiled.

"I heard that too. Whatever he and the Lieutenant are doing, they're in very deep."

"Yes. At the moment they seem to be alright but—"

"Do you want me to keep looking?"

"No, Nar. I've put you out enough. Let's see what you have on the others."

"I found something very interesting, Professor."

She put a piece of paper in front of him.

"There must a hundred names here, Nar."

"Don't worry, Professor, they're not all new intake. You see the columns to the right; the one saying 'held' means they're in custody, there's 'taken' which means they were arrested that day, 'status' that's just an 'a' for awake and a 'u' for unconscious, 'processed' that's executed and 'released' is obvious. I've highlighted the ones you want, at the bottom. They came in controlled, which is why it says 'u'."

The professor read the list; Big Merv, four women, and a man he'd never heard of; Ada Maddox, Gladys Parker and a Trev Parker who was noted as being her son, then Lucy Hargraves, Ruth Cochrane, The Pan of Hamgee and... The Professor looked up at Nar.

"Sir Robin Get?"

"Yes, Professor."

"Could that be a mistake?"

"I suppose it could be," said Nar slowly, "but it would be very unusual."

Professor N'Aversion read the names again.

"He died years ago, though. Are we certain it's him?"

"Pretty much, Professor."

"Could they have held him elsewhere?"

"Maybe, but he's survived a very long time..."

"Yes, much longer than anyone could expect."

"Are you sure this is genuine?" he asked.

"Mistakes are very rare."

"The famous Grongolian efficiency?"

"Yes, Professor, and we double-checked," she hesitated. "After the accident his body was never found, Sir Robin's, I mean. He could have faked his death."

"Yes and he certainly had the intelligence to make a convincing job. D'you know I met him once, a long time ago when I was young. Incredible intellect, so incisive, and a memory like my tablet here." He waved a hand at the computer on his desk. "By The Prophet I wish I had a brain like that. Alright then, Nar. Are you still friends with that lad Forrest in Information Retrieval?"

Nar looked down shyly and the Professor surmised that she and Forrest were a little more than 'friends'.

"Yes, Professor."

"Marvellous, perhaps if he could find a way to ensure his leader happens upon this? I don't think Colonel Melior would like it if the credit went to us; you know, poaching on his territory and all that."

"OK, Professor."

"And I don't like to batten on you but could he do so at the earliest available opportunity, if you please."

"Of course, Professor."

"Excellent work, really excellent, Nar."

"Thanks, Professor. If there's anything else I can do...?"

"Very kind of you but that'll be all for now."

Nar went out closing the door gently behind her.

The Professor sighed.

How typical.

Sir Robin, the man who could have answered any question about the secrets of Nimmism, arrested a matter of hours before the Professor realised he needed to ask them. Then again, if he'd been at large, undetected, all that time it was doubtful The Professor could have tracked him down. He wondered if it was worth getting in touch with Head Launderer Sid to see if anyone on the inside could get to Sir Robin. Then again, it was unlikely; he'd be under heavy guard and his presence might be classified information. It might be worth looking into but not at this stage. He chalked up 'finding Sir Robin Get' under the heading, 'Plan B'.

Now what?

"Have a pop at coming up with a Plan A," he muttered.

The Professor drained his coffee, grimaced and stood up. He needed a walk.

Chapter 15

"Find anything?" asked Snoofle.

Deirdre was making yet another tour of the room checking for any weaknesses in the security arrangements. They had been there several hours now, and she felt the beginnings of cabin fever.

"No. There is no obvious way out of here. You have heard from HQ?"

"Sort of..."

"Professor N'Aversion?"

"No. I used our trigger word, he'll know we're under surveillance. Command received my last message but they haven't picked up on their trigger word. Instead, it seems they think I'm trying to be funny. They've sent a rather terse one back about making jokes on a secure line."

Deirdre rolled her eyes.

"That Plumby is such a humourless robot. I can't believe it's a secure line any more, either. Still, I can see the General has him off pat. He probably only gave my phone back so I could keep sending status updates."

"You think so?"

Snoofle laughed. He was so relaxed, lying on the sofa gazing at the painted ceiling. How did he stay so calm?

"No, not really, or he wouldn't have given you your knives."

"Perhaps he wants me to kill him."

"I think he wants us to trust him. We gave him our word and this is his way of showing he trusts us."

"Or of taunting and belittling us."

"That doesn't strike me as his style."

"He's a Grongle, Snoofle, it's their national style. Why should he be different? Anyway, he wouldn't trust a K'Barthan."

"If he does, he will know he has to prove it."

"Maybe we should use Corporal Jones as a hostage."

"No. Not a good idea."

"Why not?"

"Because it's exactly what he'll be expecting us to do. We have to show him that we're better than that."

"Or less desperate," said Deirdre.

Snoofle laughed.

"You know something, Deirdre, this ceiling is a marvel..." Lying there on the sofa on his back, gazing up in rapt admiration, he seemed to be treating their captivity like some kind of glorified art tour. He'd already spent the morning examining the furniture, although he hadn't given her the low down on that, yet. Deirdre envied him and wished a few minutes staring at an Angel Michelo ceiling could ease her tension the same way.

"It is beautiful. But Snoofle, doesn't it make you angry? We scrape a breadline existence back at HQ and the Grongles are using a room painted by one of the world's most famous artist as a prison! I mean, no wonder we make no headway."

Before Snoofle could answer, their conversation was interrupted by the usual sounds of rattling and clanking that announced the unlocking of the door. Eventually it was opened but it was not General Moteurs that walked into the room. This Grongle was female.

"Thank you, Corporal," she said with a casual salute towards the rapidly closing door. She was wearing an Imperial Guard uniform. It appeared that they used the same insignia of rank as the Grongle army; she was a colonel, Deirdre noticed. She removed her peaked cap, immediately releasing a thick thatch of brunette curls, which fell in unruly waves about her shoulders. She threw the cap onto the nearest of the easy chairs. She was middle aged, probably in her early 40s, with twinkly eyes and a ready smile. She was also tall, or at least, average height for a female Grongle, which made her taller than General Moteurs; about six foot three or thereabouts.

The new visitor carried a black rucksack but otherwise she was conspicuously unarmed. Who, in the name of The Prophet was this? And a Colonel. Fine, so Deirdre had met Corporal Jones and understood that women were allowed into the Imperial Guard, but to find one at the rank of Colonel? That was so... un-Grongle.

"Lieutenant, Group Leader, I've come to see how you are," the Grongle explained.

"Good morning, Colonel," said Snoofle while Deirdre hung back, keeping her hand close to the knife holster on her leg, just in case.

"Colonel?" The Grongle's brows furrowed in puzzlement for a moment. "Oh, I'm sorry, what am I doing? Lieutenant, we've met but you were unconscious at the time and Group Leader, I had to send one of my colleagues to look at you."

'Colleagues' Deirdre noticed, not subordinates. Their visitor continued.

"I'm Dr Dot, the Imperial Guard's M.O.," she hefted the rucksack off her shoulder, put it on the floor and held out her hand. "How do you do?"

"You're the Doctor?" asked Deirdre incredulously as she shook hands.

"Yes..." said Dr Dot as she shook hands with Snoofle. "Is that a problem for either of you?"

"No... but this is... weird," said Deirdre. This was a female Grongle Doctor. In K'Barth male and female were considered equal under the old system. Though sexism raised its head from time to time, the attitude had stuck. There were no female Grongles of influence or power in K'Barth or Grongolia. Until she met Corporal Jones, Deirdre had encountered none in their military. Grongolian females were a silent enigma to most K'Barthans, and the widely held assumption that their culture did not class females as equal to males. It was one of the many reasons Deirdre had despised them. She wondered what this Doctor must have been through to get trained. How much determination would she have needed? Or were there others? Was it a simple case of women being kept out of the front line. Did they still see K'Barth as a war zone? Dr Dot laughed. With, not at.

"I promise I don't bite," her red eyes twinkled and then her smile faded, replaced by a look of concern. "If you're feeling really awkward, I can summon one of my colleagues to treat you. Would you prefer that?"

"No," Deirdre collected herself rapidly, Arnold no, "that will not be necessary. Thank you."

"Glad to hear it. Come on then, let's get started," Dr Dot picked up her rucksack and put it on the table. She didn't seem to have noticed that Deirdre was armed; or if she had, she was totally unperturbed. "Who'd like to go first?" she asked as she rummaged round in the bottom of the bag.

Neither Snoofle nor Deirdre said anything.

"OK, then, Snoofle, since your injuries are more straightforward, let's start with you. You were," she hesitated awkwardly, "controlled unconscious weren't you?"

"Yes."

"I'm sorry, some of my colleagues in the army are pigs. Nothing else?"

"Not as far as I know."

"Good. I know this is a bit cheeky but would you mind hopping onto the table for me?"

He did as he was told.

"Ah, it's a fabulous piece, this."

"I'm sorry?" Dr Dot's frowned in puzzlement.

"The table."

"I assume you mean it's old and shonky," said Deirdre.

She didn't think it looked much, it was old; dark wood with bulbous legs. Its surface was scrubbed clean but still bore the marks of many years' use, and it undulated in a way that made anything placed on it wobble. One of its legs was worn shorter than the others, too, giving it an additional dimension of shugglyness. It was intensely annoying to eat off. Intensely annoying, full stop.

"Shonky? How can you say that? And it's more than old," said Snoofle excitedly. "See the barley twist legs, the lovely patina, look at the way the bars along the bottom there are worn smooth, bit by bit, from thousands of beings putting their feet on them. You simply can't replicate that. It's at least 400 years old, I'd say, possibly more. It might even come from the studio of Gloombin of Tith, himself."

"Gloombin of Tith? Didn't he make that statue of Commander Thistwith-Mee that you use to navigate by."

"Spot on. Yes, but at the time, his art was considered very avant garde. He carved out of love and earned his living making pieces like this; things they did want, and need. It was his ability to make things like this so well that brought people round to liking his sculpture."

"I wish you could show me round Ning Dang Po Museum sometime, Snoofle," said Dr Dot.

"Most of it's in Grongolia," said Deirdre.

Shamefaced, The Doctor cast her eyes down at the table, running her fingers along the worn surface for a moment.

"Deirdre's right in a sense, but actually, a lot of it's here, in the Palace with many other pieces of note. I can show you the highlights of those."

"If General Moteurs ever lets us out of here," said Deirdre.

"I'll have to see if I can arrange it," said Dr Dot and she became a little more business-like. "Right, Snoofle," she said, "If you're ready, I'm just going to look in your ears first." She took out a torch and screwed a plastic end piece onto it.

"Any headaches?" she asked as she examined him.

"No."

"Visual disturbance?"

"No."

"Aches and pains?"

"A few... I feel quite tired," Snoofle admitted.

"Quite tired or I'd-like-to-sleep-for-a-thousand-years tired?"

Now it was Snoofle's turn to laugh and he was clearly surprised at himself. "Somewhere between the two, I'd-like-to-sleep-for-a-hundred-years tired."

"I see. I suspect you are playing this down. Even the voltage Captain Snow admits to was too much for a species your size. Heaven knows how much you really took. I'll sign you off for the day and inform Sid that you're staying here."

No 'Head Launderer' just 'Sid' Deirdre noted, as if her pretend boss in the Laundry and this Grongle were friends.

"You may feel tingly from time to time," Doctor Dot continued, "and you'll feel as if you're seizing up a bit. I can show you some stretches that'll help with that although I hear you're pretty hot at Hoo-Flung-Yoo. If you do your usual warm up stretches, GENTLY, that'll be as good as anything I can prescribe."

This was unreal, Dr Dot seemed not to have noticed the non-Grongle nature of her patients and her good humour was infectious. In fact, Grongle or not, Deirdre liked her.

"Thank you," said Snoofle.

"Just doing my job."

"I would like to return to my duties as soon as I can," said Snoofle.

"Let's finish this examination and then we'll see," said Dr Dot before going on to listen to Snoofle's heart and test his reflexes. "You're in very good shape, young fellow. I'd like to keep you here another day but you probably can go back to the Laundry after that, for light duties though. I'll pop back tomorrow, to have another look at you and we can decide then."

"Thanks, Doc."

"My pleasure. Right then, off you hop. Lieutenant," she turned to Deirdre. "Why don't you sit here?" She gestured to the stool Snoofle usually used. Deirdre did as she was told. "You're doing extremely well young lady, either that or you were born without pain receptors. I can't quite believe you are standing up. I would be in bed making a very big fuss if I were in your position."

Deirdre wanted to say that it was only natural since, as a K'Barthan, she had more courage than a mere Grongle. But somehow she couldn't quite do it, especially when Snoofle laughed again. So instead she just smiled.

"I don't think you need another scan, I've seen all I—"

"I've had a scan?"

"Yes, just an ultrasound, while you were unconscious." Dr Dot hesitated, "I'm sorry, it's not invasive, I just put some jelly on your tummy and then I run a hand-held scanner over it. I would have asked you but I couldn't risk waiting. If anything had been amiss it wouldn't have been the kind of injury I could leave. There was a high risk of internal bleeding. In fact, after the pummelling you've taken, I'm surprised your spleen's in one piece."

"Then, thank you."

"As I told you both a minute ago, I'm just doing my job, I am a Doctor, after all. OK, so you've suffered severe trauma young lady, you took a proper beating—"

"I gave one, too."

"I'm jolly glad to hear it."

Did she know what she was saying? No she couldn't possibly.

"I'm just going to test your breadth and range of movement. Let me know if it hurts and I'll stop at once."

"Understood," said Deirdre. The Doctor was gentle and seemed to know, instinctively, the exact point at which her ministrations became painful, which was well before Deirdre would admit it.

"OK, I'm signing you off for at least another four days, young lady," the Doctor eventually told her. "You're martial arts too, aren't you?"

Deirdre nodded.

"Ka-Pa-Te I believe. That's my discipline, and the General's, but I doubt either of us is as good at it as you." Deirdre looked away. "I think you should do the same as Snoofle to ease the soreness, use your warm up stretches. Let's see... downwards dog, backwards whistle, underwater elephant and when you start to feel a bit more supple, pooing yak. But be gentle; don't drive yourself too hard, your body needs time to heal."

There was something about Dr Dot, perhaps it was the obvious compassion underneath all that business-like efficiency; perhaps it was the kindly sense of humour, whatever it was, it made Deirdre feel a little emotional.

"Understood," she said.

"Remember that you are very bruised, and setting aside what you've been through, there's nothing like exhaustion to put you at a low ebb. I'll have another look at the pair of you tomorrow. OK?"

"Yes," said Deirdre.

"Oh and I almost forgot, you can take some exercise if you like but again, don't push yourselves." She looked from one to another of them. "Is that clear?"

"Yep," said Snoofle.

"Right then, I'm mostly done here but is there anything you want to ask me?"

Neither of them spoke.

"I'll give you a minute to think about it while I pack up."

She put everything into her bag and then opened a pouch at the front from which she removed two disposable hypodermic syringes and a bottle of liquid. She seemed slightly vulnerable now, unsure of herself.

"What's that?" demanded Deirdre. Snoofle began to groom his whiskers.

"This is usually part of the cure." Dr Dot perched on the edge of the table and heaved a sigh, "I don't blame either of you for being suspicious. OK, in different circumstances, this is what I'd do: over and above gentle stretches and exercise, I would prescribe you both some analgesics to be taken up to four times a day, as and when you need them. Unfortunately an overdose is lethal so, I'm sure you understand that General Moteurs has forbidden me to leave you the bottle. However, I will leave it, and the instructions, with Corporal Jones and her troops. If the pain gets too much, ask her for them."

"Thank you," said Deirdre, and Snoofle seemed to relax a little.

"Finally, I'd give you a good shot of this," she picked up the bottle. "It's my own personal cocktail to aid recovery in the post-combat body."

"What's in it?" asked Snoofle.

"Vitamins, minerals and a natural muscle relaxant to ease the soreness. It would benefit you both but you especially, Lieutenant. However," her face darkened in a blush, "General Moteurs warned me that trust might be an issue."

"Correct," said Deirdre.

"That's OK. My orders, at this point, are that I should give you no option. My Commander can be very forceful when he thinks he's helping. Except that I have to balance your physical health against your psychological well being. If I were in your position, I would be wary of having any kind of injection from an enemy being, such as myself. So if you'd rather not, that's fine by me." She smiled and winked, "I'm not going to say anything."

"Thanks, that's very thoughtful," said Snoofle.

"Not really," she glanced down at her hands and blinked a couple of times, it took Deirdre a few moments to realise that the Doctor was ashamed. "I can also offer you counselling, if you would like it; once again, Lieutenant, you especially, could benefit." She looked up again and her eyes met Deirdre's. They were full of sadness and something far worse, sympathy. It made Deirdre feel like a victim for the first time.

"I don't need it, or your condescending pity," she snapped, lashing out before she could stop herself. Dr Dot didn't actually wince but she came close.

"I quite understand and I'm sorry if I seemed condescending, I didn't intend to."

"I- understood," said Deirdre, hiding behind military formality. Arnold, her emotions were all over the place and she was afraid she would cry.

For a moment the three of them were silent and Deirdre got the impression Snoofle was slightly irritated with her for making the Doctor feel awkward.

"I will try some of your post-combat cocktail, if I may," he said. Yes, he was. Definitely.

"Good," said the Doctor, all cheerful efficiency again. "Lieutenant?"

Snoofle answered swiftly for her.

"She'll watch what happens to me and if I die she'll know not to try it."

"OK, so you're the poison taster are you?"

Even Deirdre managed a wan smile at that. Snoofle held out his arm and Dr Dot filled up one of the syringes and injected the contents into him.

"Right, I'd better get on. I'll see you both again soon," she said and cleared the rest of her things into the rucksack. Almost as an afterthought, she pulled out a leaflet.

"I'm sorry this is in Grongolian. After the last batch of purges I've none left in your own language, but it might help." She held it out to Deirdre. "And I mean it about the counselling, Lieutenant."

"Thank you," said Deirdre, as she took it and put it on the table beside her.

"Don't mention it," she said and was gone.

Chapter 16

"What just happened there?" asked Deirdre, incredulously, as the door was locked behind the Doctor.

"You were a little on the brusque side with a very well meaning being."

"I know, I'm..." she blinked back the tears, Arnold's trousers, where were they coming from?

Snoofle jumped back onto the table and picked up the leaflet.

"Deirdre, you're not made of iron." He put his hand on her arm. "You've taken some serious abuse and you're going to feel it. Sooner or later, it's going to hit you. It's nothing to be ashamed of," he said gently. "It'll hurt but it hasn't taken away your dignity or changed who you are in here." He pointed to her chest. "The pain will pass."

"She saw me as a victim."

"No she didn't, anything but. She pitied you for having to endure one specific event which is probably every female's worst nightmare. That's not the same as condescension. I'd say she was impressed at the way you've taken it," he squeezed her arm, "I'd say I am."

"Oh Snoofle," said Deirdre and a tear dripped onto the table at his feet, "I know she meant well but... this is so confusing. You said that it wasn't simple, but I never thought—"

"No-one ever does." He took a handkerchief from a pocket on his belt and held it out to her.

"Thank you." Deirdre wiped her eyes and blew her nose.

"Would you like me to hug you?"

She shook her head.

"I'll be fine." If Snoofle hugged her, she feared she might lose it completely. She changed the subject. "So, poison taster, how are you?"

"Grk." He put his hand to his throat, feigning theatrical death throes.

"Snoofle!"

"Joking aside, I think Dr Dot might have been telling us the truth; this stuff is wonderful. I can almost feel myself relaxing. You should have had some."

"Maybe tomorrow, if you're still alive."

He picked up the leaflet.

"You should read this."

She took it and went and sat in one of the comfy chairs. Snoofle jumped off the table and settled himself in the other one. She started to read and he took out his mobile phone. She couldn't apply herself. After she'd read the first paragraph for the third time, she gave up.

"Snoofle? What is going on? Who is he?"

He looked up from his phone.

"General Moteurs?"

"Yeh."

"I'm not very certain." Snoofle swiped the screen to lock it and put the phone back in its holder on his belt. "He arrived a few months ago. The official story is that he's a typical, old school hard-liner: impeccable honour, unimpeachable record and incorruptible: loves the State like no other. Lord Vernon certainly trusts him. That caused a ruckus when he first turned up here. The Imperial Guard were not welcome and Lord Vernon had them excavating the grounds of the High Temple. This place was strictly army: Captain Snow and his lot. Rumour has it General Moteurs found something at the High Temple, something Lord Vernon wanted. He was Colonel Moteurs then, so to get himself promoted four ranks in one go it must have been pretty big. Next thing, his feet are firmly under the table here, along with the Imperial Guard, and he's Lord Vernon's most trusted advisor."

"Intriguing."

"Yeh. He's good, too. Nothing gets past him. There's not a mouse farts in this place and General Moteurs doesn't know about it. He's made our ops here a great deal more difficult, I can tell you. Just ask Sid." He stopped.

"So...?"

"Something doesn't add up. Oh he's ruthless alright, he's shown us that. I wonder though... there is some history there and now that I have met him, I think my initial interpretation may be wrong."

"Why?"

"His behaviour is increasingly at variance with his image – and his back story."

"Which is?"

"That when it comes to being a pitiless, domineering smecker he is every bit his Master's equal, possibly worse."

"What's to wonder?"

"He sent us Dr Dot."

"He wants us fit for purpose, whatever that is."

"Maybe. The more I think about it, though, the more I'm beginning to doubt," he smoothed his whiskers hesitantly, "It's difficult to explain."

"Please, continue."

"He has a bit of a past, our General. It's not common knowledge but some of the Grongles like the way their nation has gone even less than we do. We tried to make contact with them once, before your time, but it was a set up. We lost a bunch of our best agents over that fiasco and afterwards, Denarghi decreed it should be struck from the record books and never mentioned again."

"An over-reaction," said Deirdre.

"Maybe, but I could see his point; we made a dangerous gaff that was best not repeated. I think he took it personally, too. That was when his view of Grongles really polarised, when he started all that the-only-good-Grongle-is-a-dead-one stuff. Anyway I'm drifting from the point. General Moteurs had a daughter and unbeknown to him, she was a full member of the Grongle Resistance movement. One day, she got caught. They tried her and found her guilty and..." He took a breath, "He executed her."

"His own daughter?"

"Not pleasant is it?"

"No. I believe even my father would stop at that, but I'd describe your initial summary as highly accurate, especially on the strength of the behaviour I've seen."

"Would you? I don't know. There's more to it than meets the eye. There has to be. Nothing could be that cut and dried. Why would he rescue us? He has treated us well: with respect, I'd say, and it looks genuine to me. In the flesh he is patently not the kind of being who would kill his only child in cold blood. Not even if they hated each other."

"How can you tell? You said, yourself, he is talented at espionage."

"He is. But so am I and there are some things that can't be hidden. He's different from Lord Vernon and the reason it's so convincing isn't because he's pretending, it's because he IS. And you can see that his troops love him. I'd give a lot to have my bunch adore me like that and it's not just Corporal Jones. You can see it in Dr Dot—"

"Maybe she has a crush on him," said Deirdre.

"They probably all do. Listen to this: one of the girls shrank his shirts once."

"What, the General's?"

"Yes. Sid had to sort it out, there was a good reason; the fire alarm went off – false alarm, something burned in the canteen and the smoke got into the hall.

But we didn't know that, so like good little employees, we all trooped outside, and Mandy, you know, the short dark haired human female who stirs the vats," Deirdre nodded, "she left a load of shirts soaking – not just the General's either, half the officers' stuff was in there. It was nearly an hour before we got back in again. The whole lot shrank. General Moteurs was not a happy bunny. You could see he was itching to tear someone off a strip. Even so, when Sid said 'I can explain' the General let him. When Sid had finished, General Moteurs accepted that it wasn't Mandy's fault. The other officers weren't being nearly so reasonable. General Moteurs found out about it and pulled rank on them. We didn't get any more flack. That's what doesn't fit. If I was profiling them and had to guess, I'd say it was Captain Snow who snuffed his daughter, every time, but General Moteurs?"

"So what do we do?"

"Sit tight. He will tell us what he wants eventually, and we're safe here, so until that time we may as well relax and enjoy the food." He grinned. "No boiled cabbage; it hasn't even appeared on the menu for a whole week. That would be a record back at HQ. We could even do a bit of gentle sparring – Hoo-Flung-Yoo is not so different from Ka-Pa-Te. At the least, we should start those stretches."

Deirdre arched her back painfully.

"In a while," she said.

Chapter 17

Ruth was not in the best of spirits. For starters, she was ravenously hungry, but she wasn't going to touch the porridge, and she didn't trust the orange juice either. Who knew what Captain Snow had done to it before bringing it to her. She shuddered. After he had gone she had thoroughly checked out her surroundings. The balcony was a long sunny eerie about ten feet wide and about 30 feet long; more of a terrace, then. It was set high up, and the drop to the moat below was long and sheer. No way could she escape by that route. There was a screen at the furthest end and when she peered round it, to see what was being hidden, she saw a similar screen and the balustrade of another, even larger balcony a few feet away. She looked at the long sheer drop between the two and wondered if she could get to it. Unlikely, anyway since she'd been told Lord Vernon's rooms were just down the hall, it was likely that other balcony was his – so absolutely not the place she wanted to escape to.

Back in her room, she stepped into the huge medieval fireplace and looked up the chimney. It was fitted with a metal panel with a trap door, presumably a sensible move to exclude draughts, since it could be opened if the occupant of the room wanted to light the fire and closed the rest of the time. It was padlocked shut. Ruth pulled at it. It moved a little, not much, just enough to open a small gap, about half an inch wide, at the opposite side to the padlock. Through the gap, Ruth could see the hinges. They were old and worn, the heads of the pins sticking out a little at each end. She wondered if she could get the pins out. She balanced precariously on one end of the fire basket so she could examine them more closely. Yes, they might have locked her in her room, but she hadn't promised to stay there. She smiled to herself.

"And I'm not going to," she said. It would be sensible to wait a day or so, establish how often her gaolers checked on her or brought her meals and when. But she knew her limitations. She lacked the self discipline to wait that long. However, she must be sensible about this, so she should go at night. It would be useful to know if there were guards stationed outside her room, too. If there were, she wouldn't want to make too much noise.

She tiptoed carefully up the steps and listened. She heard footsteps in the corridor and a loud crack as two sets of heels clicked to attention – which answered that question. She realised that the troops outside might be saluting somebody who was coming to visit her. She scurried back to the bed and sat down.

Captain Snow was back with two guards.

"Take her to interrogation room five," he told them, without even acknowledging her.

She stood up thinking they would escort her, but instead, they grabbed her by the arms and dragged her towards the door.

"Stop it! Get off me! I can walk myself," she shouted as they hauled her up the stairs. She kicked and struggled.

"Wait," Captain Snow told the guards.

"I am perfectly capable of walking," snapped Ruth.

"Yeh, I bet you are, but you can run, too, so you're going in the Chair," said Captain Snow.

"No." Ruth struggled even harder. One of the guards pulled her arms behind her back, wrenching them painfully upwards. The other went to the door briefly and returned with two of his colleagues. One had a metal chair. It had wheels on the back legs and handles, like a sack barrow. He clattered and banged it noisily down the steps and held it steady. Weakened by the pain from her pinned arms, Ruth could no longer fight as her gaolers dragged her back to the metal chair and forced her into it. Two of them held her while the others wound a rope tightly round and round her, knotting, or looping it onto the chair behind her back with each pass. She flailed and kicked angrily but they were too strong for her, forcing her legs against the chair's. She felt metal restraints close around her ankles with a click.

"That's better," said Captain Snow.

"You complete and utter—" began Ruth.

"We'll have to do something about that mouth of yours, darling. We can't have you disturbing the whole Palace," said Captain Snow. She realised he was holding a roll of gaffer tape. He tore off a strip.

"No—" began Ruth.

"This'll keep you quiet." He grabbed a handful of her hair, yanking it downwards so she was forced to look up, and stuck the tape across her mouth.

"Mmm!" she said angrily.

"Aw shame, I didn't get that. I can't hear what you're saying." Captain Snow smiled. "You're going to see Lord Vernon now, pretty girl. Won't that be exciting?"

"Mo!" She wanted to shake her head but he was still holding her by the hair.

"I can't wait till he's done with you. We're going to have so much fun." He leaned down and licked her face. Ruth was afraid she'd throw up – a worrying prospect with her mouth taped closed.

"Get off me, toad breath!" she shouted except that because of the tape, all she could say was a muffled, "gekof eee oadeth," which lacked the same impact.

All they did was laugh. Bugger.

"Gastards!"

Yes, definitely best not to try and talk.

She glared at Captain Snow with unbridled hatred but he just laughed the more.

"Come on boys. Let's get it down to the interrogation rooms. We don't want to keep the Lord Protector waiting."

Ruth burned with anger at being called 'it' but stayed silent.

The guards picked up the chair, carried it to the top of the steps and dumped it down at the top, like a sack of potatoes. Then they tipped it and wheeled her out of the room, along the length of the corridor and into a lift. She felt her stomach lurch as it sank downwards, into the depths of the building, and then stopped. A recorded female voice informed anyone who was listening that the doors were opening. Ruth was wheeled along a concrete corridor lit by a row of fluorescent lights down the middle of the ceiling. Finally they stopped, unlocked a door and wheeled her into a room. They parked the chair on the far side, close to the wall, facing outwards. There was some kind of docking station for it in the floor. She heard the fasteners engage round the wheels and legs with a clunk.

"I'll see you later," said Captain Snow, and with that, he and the guards left her alone.

Chapter 18

The Pan lay in the sawdust, nursing his wound, and let the red stuff Lord Vernon had given him do its work. He would have liked to sleep but at least the drug seemed to be deadening the dull, strength-sapping ache in his shoulder. He let his mind wander, watching the minuscule spots that made up the darkness on the back of his closed eyes. Gradually, as he lay, he became aware of the annoying noise in his ears again: the tinnitus with knobs on. It was a strange sound, a high pitched whistling, like a half-tuned-in radio, complete with the occasional hint of far off voices in the static. Well, he had been hearing, if not voices, then, a chicken for the last 24 hours. And one voice which had spoken about his resistance to Truth Serum back at the Underground HQ and warned him not to make jokes in front of Captain Snow. One voice and a chicken, then. Hardly a headlong slide into insanity but, nonetheless, a bit of a worry.

"Never mind, I'll be dead before it gets any worse," he thought.

"Cluck?" said the chicken, only he had the impression it was actually saying, "D'you think so?"

He sighed.

"Yeh. Thank The Prophet for small mercies." He said this out loud.

"Cluck," said the chicken hopefully.

The whistling continued. He listened. Yes. There were definitely voices in it, whispering, at the limits of his hearing.

"Arnold's ear wax, what is this stuff? I'm completely out of my box."

As well as the aural hallucinations, the chemical Lord Vernon had injected him with was increasing his thirst. He'd been held for – how long had it been? They'd given him nothing to eat or drink, so judging by his hunger, about three weeks. But on the strength of his continued existence without water, it couldn't be more than overnight. Yeh and going on his courage it was probably about three hours.

His mind dwelt on escape: and Ruth, not forgetting Ruth. He realised that, for all the short time since they'd met, she'd become his reason to live. A reason the Candidate had denied him by failing to appear. He would die now, and presumably so would she.

Arnold's pants! Where was the Candidate? If only he had come forward, maybe- Yeh what? Something, he thought lamely, something would have happened and the Grongles would have gone home.

"Well Mister Candidate, IF you exist, you're late; you snivelling, weasel-hearted smeck." His voice sounded slurred but his words were intelligible now. He immediately felt guilty about the 'weasel-hearted'. It was hardly fair. "Pot, kettle, black," he told the darkness. If the Candidate was safely hidden, why would he ever make himself known? Why would he stand up to Lord Vernon? Where would it get him? The Pan knew what he would do if he were the Candidate—

"Yes, we all do. Run away," said a peevish voice.

"Arnold's snot! Isn't the chicken enough?"

"Obviously not."

Yikes! That had sounded very real. The Pan tried to get comfortable. How he wished he could go to sleep and skip this bit. However, Lord Vernon had mentioned insomnia as a side effect of the drug. Yeh, and he hadn't been joking. Alright then, best not to think about sleep. Unwillingly, The Pan was drawn, again, to the sounds of distant voices. He concentrated, listening. He could hear snippets of conversation now: whiney argumentative ones. Oh, they would be; no chance of anything that would bring comfort or even make for pleasant listening. He wondered if he could persuade them to sing, that might sound better. Then again, no. They were probably all tone deaf. He switched his thoughts back to the Candidate's non-appearance. It hardly mattered. No-one could win against Lord Vernon, and, anyway, if he had shown up, The Pan would have been dumped. As It Was Written, apparently.

"Everywhere," he said morosely.

"Cluck?" said the chicken: an, 'are you certain?' kind of cluck.

"Yes."

Arse. Double jeopardy. Why couldn't The Pan have just stepped into Ruth's world and disappeared?

"Because the Grongles were after you there, too, if you remember," said the voice. It was rather sarcastic for The Pan's taste.

"Yes. I remember," he said. What was he doing talking to it? Then again, he'd been talking to the chicken.

"Exactly. So how would it have helped?"

"Arnold," muttered The Pan. This sounded like his virtual parents.

Sometimes, when The Pan had to make a decision or, usually, when he felt the need to give himself a mental upbraiding, he would put on mumsy and dadsy voices and say the kinds of things he thought his parents would have said. But he hadn't done it for ages. The day-to-day business of staying alive had taken too much concentration. And then he had met the Chosen One. He let his mind linger on that topic for a moment. "Oh Ruth," he whispered, "you are so—"

"Put it back in your trousers for Arnold's sake!"

Hang on, his virtual parents weren't this stroppy and they were him doing the voices. This was different.

"Of course we're not your stupid virtual parenting!"

"Cluck?" said the chicken, only this time, The Pan wasn't sure it was talking to him, instead, it seemed to be telling the other voice to belt up.

"Thanks hen," he said. The Pan liked the chicken; he felt its occasional clucks were meant with kindness.

"Arnold. I'm drugged; it's sending me schitzo and one of my alternative personalities is a chicken! What does that say?" he started to laugh.

"That he's the only one who can get through your thick, boneheaded, skull, you blithering idiot!" said the voice, which definitely was coming from outside... and wasn't him. He wasn't even sure he knew what 'blithering' meant.

"Look, whoever you are, this is not a good moment."

"It never is," said the voice at the precise second the chicken chose to say, "Cluck?"

"One at a time, please," said The Pan, wearily.

"Listen, young man, there is no good time for this conversation AND, I'll thank you to remember, we've all had to go through it before you."

The Pan laughed.

"If Truth Serum fails, give him – whatever that was and mess with his mind. It's working. Smecking Arnold it's working."

"Nobody's messing with your mind you buffoon, on account of the fact that I fail to see how anybody could make it any messier or more undisciplined than it already is! And I'm stuck in it, I should know."

"Ooo someone's got out of bed the wrong side. Now go away or I'm going to get angry." Not that anger would make any difference to anything, but the voice wasn't to know that and the bits of his subconscious that were controlling all of this might shut up.

"Arnold! The young people of today. Have you no respect for your elders?" This one was different, a female.

"Not until they've earned it," said The Pan acidly.

"Well really!"

"Cluck," said the chicken with a tone that clearly meant 'shut up' this time – although whether it was addressing him or the other voice, The Pan was unsure.

"Time out for ONE moment please, BOTH of you," he said. Silence. Good. "Thank you. Now, would you all form an orderly queue or elect one of you to speak to me on behalf of the others. Although, I guess not the chicken because," how to put this? "I don't speak his language."

"Cluck?"

"Well... not fluently – sorry chicken. And Lord Vernon may need me alive for the moment, but he's signed my death warrant, so it doesn't mean I'll be around long. If you have something to say I'd recommend you step on it."

"'Chicken' is no way to refer to the eighth Architrave," said a voice. It was the peevish, sarky male.

"The one with the thing about...?"

"Well, obviously."

"I see. So, I've an Architrave in my head have I?" In spite of his thirst and the pain in his shoulder this conversation was beginning to interest him.

"Yes."

"Arnold. Still, I'll run with it if it keeps my mind occupied." The Pan remembered Lord Vernon's comment about 'deconstructing' his sanity. "At least my imagination is undamaged. And flying, clearly."

"We're not imaginary. We've been here all along; you just refused to listen."

"Yeh right. You expect me to believe that?"

"Of course."

The Pan rolled his eyes.

"What kind of idiot do you take me for...?"

"One that talks, aloud, so that people can hear, when he could keep his mouth shut and speak with his mind. Tell me, can you read a book without moving your lips?" In spite of his situation, something about the pomposity of the voice struck The Pan as funny, *"Stop giggling! I see nothing amusing about this, you disrespectful little toad! Believe me, it's no picnic being stuck in your mind. I've never encountered*

94

anyone so downright contrary! And you're totally uneducated. There's nothing to read!
You spend your entire time mooning about some girl."

The Pan shuffled out from under the table and sat up.

"How could you not enjoy that?" There was a pause as if somebody was taking a deep breath ready to start shouting loudly. "Alright," said The Pan quickly, "don't lose your rag. I know you've been there a while or at least the chick— fine, I'll humour you, His Lofty Exaltedness Architrave Number Eight – where do I get this stuff? – has, but you have to understand that voices in the head are usually a bad sign. You get voices in your head, they tell you to do stuff and the next thing you know, you're chopping up your umpteenth victim and burying them in the woods for people walking their dogs to find."

"Perhaps you do not realise who I am," said the voice frostily.

"I'm afraid not, so if you've forgotten, you're in trouble." Far away in the distance, The Pan heard something which sounded like laughter. Although the voice in his head, or at least, the one he was talking to, had clearly failed to see the funny side.

"I'll have you know I am the Architrave."

"Which one?"

"The latest; the seventy-seventh. In these circumstances it is always the latest who speaks for the others."

"If you're the last Architrave, they beheaded you. How come you can talk?"

"I-" the voice began. *"Actually, that's a very interesting point. I don't know."*

"Don't you? Well, here's my theory. It's because you're not the seventy seventh Architrave."

"How can you doubt me?"

"Quite easily, as it happens. I'm dosed up with mind-expanding drugs."

"How dare you! You brick-headed fool. I know who I am."

"I'm sure you do; my point is, I don't."

"I am the seventy-seventh Architrave!" bellowed the voice, with more than a hint of petulance.

"Mmm, and I'm The Prophet, himself, come to save his people."

"You don't realise how close to the truth that is."

"Really."

"Yes. And I AM who I say I am."

"Shouting it louder doesn't make it true. If you really were an Architrave, I can't help thinking you'd know how to have a reasoned argument."

"Cluck," said the chicken, except The Pan was pretty sure it was actually saying, "not after you've wound him up." Whatever the chicken was, it had been benign so far, so he took the hint.

"Alright, I'm sorry, keep your head on—" he stopped, that wasn't the most tactful thing to say. "Look, just supposing this is true. Why would a couple of dead Architraves come and lurk round me?"

"I'm not at liberty to tell you, you're supposed to think it out for yourself, but I can say there are more than two of us."

In many respects, The Pan thought it unwise to get sucked into this conversation, but Arnold knew, he had nothing else to do.

"How many is 'more than two'?" An awkward pause. "All of you. It's all of you, isn't it?"

"Indeed," said the voice just as the chicken said, "cluck."

"But not The Prophet because I can hear you arguing and I think you'd get on better together if he was there."

Another pause.

"Hmph. Perhaps you are more intelligent than you seem."

"A lot of people say that. I wish it were true. It's a pity about Arnold." The Pan ran his good hand through his hair. "I could do with somebody to talk to." Several blissfully silent minutes went by. At the edge of his consciousness he imagined he could hear another argument.

"You could try talking to us," said the voice eventually. It sounded unwilling, as if somebody was poking it in the back with a stick.

"You and the chicken."

"Must you call us that?"

"Until you've proved otherwise, yes. Anyway, I don't think the chicken minds."

"Cluck."

"There you go."

"Here is your proof. Lord Vernon will remove your name from the blacklist. You will be given property, your own business, a full pardon and amnesty for the next year of your life while you adjust."

"How come?"

The voice made no answer, which didn't surprise The Pan, but neither did the chicken; which did.

"By The Prophet! What am I doing?" he muttered. He moved position against the table leg, trying to get comfortable and closed his eyes. He shouldn't allow himself to get drawn into this. It wasn't real. It was Lord Vernon's drug-induced 'sanity deconstruction'. "Smeck. The street value of that red stuff must be something." He shook his head to try and clear his thoughts, which brought on an attack of dizziness and made his shoulder hurt, "I've got to remember not to move my head."

"You can mock," said the previous Architrave, *"but we'll catch up in a little while shall we?"*

"Yeh," said The Pan, "let's do that." He hoped his cell wasn't bugged. He'd succumbed to the drugs so easily. He was annoyed to have given Lord Vernon the gratification.

A few more minutes passed, during which The Pan tried to collect his thoughts, and then he heard footsteps. The light came on and there was the sound of keys in the lock. Captain Snow stood in the doorway, flanked by the usual guards: four of them.

"Bring him," he ordered them.

"I told you," said the voice as the guards handcuffed The Pan, hauled him to his feet and half-pushed, half-dragged him towards the door.

"We could be going anywhere," said The Pan.

"But we're not, Vermin, we're going to see Lord Vernon," Captain Snow answered him.

"I wasn't talking to you," said The Pan.

"Course not. I expect you're talking to the voices in your head."

They all laughed and The Pan said nothing, Captain Snow having got him bang to rights.

"Ah, it's great when they start to go mental, right boys?" said the Captain and they all laughed again.

"I haven't. Not yet."

"You will. You won't know what smecking species you are by the time he's done."

The Pan swallowed. He didn't trust himself to speak and he didn't want to show his fear. Captain Snow took hold of his functioning arm and dragged him into the corridor, kicking the backs of his legs to get him moving.

Chapter 19

Ruth was out of breath. Not good. On the up side, at least she was angry. She decided that anger is good when the alternative is fear. It was horrible not being able to breathe through her mouth. She felt as if she needed more air than her nose could deliver. It wasn't true; it was only panic, but it didn't make her any more comfortable. It could have been worse: at least she'd had the presence of mind to button her lips together when Captain Snow taped up her mouth, so, she hoped it would mean marginally less pain when they finally removed the tape. Always assuming they bothered, instead of killing her with it in position.

Despite the melee when they had strapped her into the chair, she was still wearing her spectacles. She took in her surroundings. A grey room. Grey floor, grey ceiling, three grey walls, a grey metal bin in the corner – odd that – and along the fourth wall, a shiny glass mirror. Presumably there was somebody behind that, watching her. Oh marvellous. Three guesses as to who.

Two of the guards returned and stood either side of the door as Lord Vernon walked in. He wasn't wearing his sunglasses and now she wished her glasses had fallen off. That way, unless he got very close, she wouldn't be able to see him. An indeterminate green blob would be far less scary – and easier to face – than the high definition original.

With a glance at her he dismissed the guards. Ruth's anger was quickly turning to fear. She didn't want to be afraid. She took a deep breath and tried to get a grip.

"Ruth Cochrane," said Lord Vernon in the kind of suave tone of voice she'd expect him to use introducing himself at a cocktail party.

"Mmmpf." She glared at him angrily.

"Ah yes." Oh here we go. He reached down and she felt the corner of the tape lift as he took it between his thumb and forefinger. "This may be," a pause and an unpleasant smile, "painful." He ripped the tape off in one swift movement.

Blimey! He hadn't been wrong there. She winced and her eyes watered.

"Remind me to come to you if I ever want my face waxed," she said acidly.

"Perhaps I should put it back."

"It's hardly necessary in the first place, is it?" It wasn't as if anyone would hear her scream, she thought morbidly.

"Captain Snow is very diligent; it is why I value him so highly."

He drew a large knife and, putting one hand on the back of the chair, leaned in towards her. Without breaking eye contact he sliced through the bottom rope, one handed. Yes, that was one sharp blade. He sliced the next rope, and the next, working slowly up to the one at the top, which was almost round her neck. She felt the cold metal against her chin as he applied the slightest pressure, just enough to make her look up at him properly. "I do not intend to harm you," he said. The implication, in Ruth's view, being exactly the reverse.

"No, of course you don't."

"I'm glad we understand each other." Lord Vernon was impervious to sarcasm, it would seem. "I have a proposition for you," he continued, "which I do not expect you to refuse." His face was horribly close to hers and his expression – what was that? Something she couldn't place but whatever it was, she didn't like it. She glared at him to show she wasn't frightened and the slate grey eyes met hers with an expression of cold detachment, and was that...? Yes. Amusement. Arse. The show-no-fear approach wasn't working.

"Whatever it is. No," she said firmly.

"You are not going to listen first?" Mocking. "I can make you."

She wished he'd stop leaning over her but presumably disrespect for her personal space was part of his tactics. And why did it have to work so well?

"Do what you like. I'm not scared," she lied.

"Are you certain of that?"

Ruth shuddered.

"I know you are frightened. Yet I appreciate that you have courage. It has been a problem for me."

"Well, I'm delighted to have been able to inconvenience you."

"Ah Ruth, Ruth, so feisty." He picked up the ropes which had bound her, rolled them into a ball and threw them past her, into the bin in the corner. Once again, he made sure to do so in a way that involved maximum closeness, without actually touching. "That is what I admire in you."

Admire. Oh no. The metal restraints were tight round her ankles, forcing her to stay seated as he walked slowly round her chair, running one finger along the back of it until he reappeared in front of her again.

"My proposition is simple. I am the Candidate. I will be Architrave and you, my own one, are The Chosen."

My own one? Ugh.

"Not by you."

"Perhaps not but we go together, you and I. It makes perfect sense. When I am Architrave I will require a consort and that consort is going to be you."

"Never. I would die first."

"That will not be necessary. I am sure we will rub along."

"Not in your wildest dreams." She was angry now. Good. As usual, it was better than being frightened.

"You do not think I am attractive?" he asked lightly.

Yes, Ruth had to admit, he was but since she didn't like cruel, sneering faces, not in a way that was remotely alluring. How to put it?

"With a different personality, you might be." Yeh. That felt good.

He looked down at her, calm and unperturbed.

"If you are prepared to admit it now then I am sure later—"

"Oh you flatter yourself, or you underestimate me. You disgust me. If your face reflected the man inside then you'd be so ugly no-one would be able to stand within twenty feet of you, and what's more, the stench you'd give off would make it impossible."

He smiled without warmth.

"Clearly I am blessed." A pause. He leaned forward for some more personal space invasion. "Ruth, you would be wise to remember that I am a Grongle, not a mere human." For the first time, a hint of menace. That had touched a nerve.

"A mere human? I'm so sorry. If the rest of your species are like you then I wouldn't flatter you with a comparison. You are way beneath humanity. I will not be your consort, or at least, not while I am conscious and in possession of my faculties."

"That is what I suspected." A long, long pause. "But I believe I can persuade you to rethink your decision." He leaned forward and put his hand on the back of the chair again. She could feel the metal move and her ankles were released with a click. "Stand up."

She did as he had ordered.

He led her across the room and stood her in front of the shiny mirror glass.

"There is something I would like to show you." He clicked his fingers and somewhere, unseen accomplices turned the lights out. The glass was suddenly illuminated. Through it, another grey room which contained another prisoner.

Her heart fluttered the way it always did when she saw The Pan of Hamgee and then, immediately, she began to cry; fearful, silent tears. They'd hurt him. The shoulder of his velvet jacket was singed and soaked with blood; it was dark but it was reddish, not his usual – or was that unusual – blue, and he was in pain, cradling that arm with the other one. He stood, alone, in the middle of the room and swayed backwards and forwards, as if a little drunk. Was he concussed? Probably. Or drugged. As she watched, he looked at the glass wall quizzically. Yeh, whatever they'd done to him, he was smart enough to know about one way glass. The silent tears ran faster.

Lord Vernon gestured to the mirror.

"You recognise this renegade?" As the shock deepened, she was afraid she would fall apart. She wiped her eyes and nose with her sleeve, trying to stop crying.

"What have you done to him?"

"Nothing permanent. I shot him in the shoulder."

She was angry; the tears stopped abruptly.

"You've broken his arm."

"Actually, his collarbone. I am sure he will recover, if he is given the opportunity. But you have not addressed my original query, do you recognise this man?"

"Of course I do, and for your information, he's not a man, he's Hamgeean."

Two could get antsy about species.

"I stand corrected. However, his exact species is a technicality, since he will be executed in one hour."

"No," the authority in her voice surprised her. "You can't! He hasn't done anything."

Lord Vernon raised his eyebrows.

"I beg to differ. There's a small matter of treason, robbery, unauthorised portal use and naturally, as a Government Blacklisted Individual, his mere existence is already a capital offence."

"That's your fault – not his. You blacklisted him, on a whim as far as I can tell, or was it because of his father?"

Nice try but no reaction.

"I did, and since his existence is punishable by death I have already signed the warrant," he took a folded paper from his pocket, unfolded it and held it up so she could see. "Of course, I have the power to release him."

"Of course," she aped the way he said it. "And if you had the smallest, tiniest particle of decency in you, you would."

"Perhaps, I could be persuaded." He looked at her meaningfully and moved closer, "for a price."

"Which is?" As if she didn't know. The rest of my life, she thought. Was The Pan worth that? Oh yes. No hesitation. She would do pretty much anything to save his life, even sacrificing her own, or worse – she tried to mask her revulsion as the reality of the idea hit her – marrying Lord Vernon.

"Let me rephrase my previous request." Lord Vernon looked her up and down, with more than a hint of the sexual predator in his expression, and raised his eyebrows again. "The pair of you can die together like the renegades you are or you, Ruth, can become my consort, and, as a thank you for your kind endorsement, I will allow you to save another life that is precious to you."

"His?"

"I would assume; or one of the others, the choice is yours."

"Let me get this straight. You're saying you would free The Pan of Hamgee in return for—"

"You, my dear. Yes." Ruth doubted she had heard the phrase "my dear" used with such heavy irony.

"I may be foreign but I'm not a complete moron. We both know you would never do that. You've had it in for him all his life. There's too much baggage."

"Ah, but for you, I would."

No. Never. There had to be a catch.

"Would you free him properly though? Grant him an amnesty, take him off the blacklist. You're asking a high price. If you want me to pay it then his future has to be worth buying."

A pause, evidently the idea of removing the Pan from the blacklist rankled.

"I shall. He will be completely re-assimilated. Although, I am afraid I will be compelled to make an additional condition for that, something small, a mere trifle, my darling."

OK. My dear was bad, 'darling' was a bridge too far.

"Don't call me darling."

His lips curled into a malicious smile.

"Perhaps you should acclimatise yourself to it if you are to spend the rest of your days with me... darling."

"Perhaps you should tell me the catch before you make any assumptions that I shall," she snapped.

"I think we both appreciate you are now mine, Ruth. You care for him too much to refuse. I wish to be Architrave of this nation and to do that, I require the ultimate endorsement; the unwavering loyalty of the Chosen One. I am aware that you are unwilling but if you humour me, I will keep my word. I will free the Pan of Hamgee and remove his name from the blacklist."

"And your small condition? What's that?" There was bound to be a catch, this was Lord Vernon, after all – and it wasn't going to be small.

"That he believes you have willingly given yourself to me, that you have grown to love me, over him."

"He's not stupid. He'll never fall for that – always assuming I can act well enough to carry it off."

"There will be very little acting required. He is humble, in awe of you." He gestured to the glass. "And almost broken."

"He's not in awe of me; he won't break no matter what you do to him, and he is my friend. He'll know."

"Then you will have to find a way to ensure he does not know. I am confident you will do whatever is required to save his life."

"Why are you doing this?" Her voice wobbled. No. That meant he was winning. The tears began again. Why did her eyes have to let her down like that? She knew exactly why he was doing this; she'd been an idiot to ask, and now, Lord Vernon was going to tell her.

"Because without you, he will wish for death, because, since he lacks the courage to take his own life, he will have to live out the rest of his days, knowing and being reminded, every day, that you are with me. It will cause him more suffering than any torture I could inflict: why Ruth? You didn't suspect me of altruism, did you?"

No.

"You've already destroyed his life and taken his family. This condition isn't small or necessary."

"No? I am about to give him his prospects back, such as they are. Whether he takes advantage of my magnanimous gesture is up to him. Nothing is free in this world, Ruth. If I am to give so much I must have something in return."

"If I agree to be your consort, you will have me. Isn't that enough?"

"No. As you succinctly put it, there is too much," a wave of the hand, "baggage. These are my terms. You can take them," he glanced at the bedraggled figure through the one-way glass, "or leave them."

"I hate you. You realise that, don't you? And I always will."

"Ah but Ruth." He grabbed her arm, pulled her close to him and whispered in her ear. "Hate is so close to love."

She shuddered as his lips brushed against her skin.

"Not with you."

"Your answer?"

"I need time to think."

"You have thirty minutes. I am the Candidate. I will be the Architrave. As the Chosen One, one day, no matter what you currently believe, you will love me." He turned on his heel and walked out of the room. When he had gone, through the one way glass, she watched The Pan in the other cell until the lights brightened and the glass became a mirror once more. Then she flung herself down onto the concrete floor and sobbed in earnest.

She would have to throw in her lot with Lord Vernon. Sure, she could refuse and if it was only about her, she would. Far better to die than face a future of hopeless misery. But no matter how horrible the prospect of a lifetime with Lord Vernon, she could not choose a course of action which would cause The Pan's death – not without asking him. And asking him was impossible. So, no option.

No choice for The Chosen.

Again.

Was it supposed to be like this? How come she didn't get to do any of the goddamn picking? And while she was on the subject, was she even The Chosen, anyway? She was meant to fall in love with The Candidate at first sight and stay besotted with him forever. Well how was that going to work? She was already in love, utterly so – albeit at second or third sight – with The Pan of Hamgee.

She sighed.

"It's too late," she said aloud. No doubt about it. Any Candidate turning up now would have to be, well, sex on a stick: an angel with the body of a god and the shiniest, smashing-est personality to match. She stopped crying and sat up.

Yep. It would take a lot to edge The Pan out of the frame. Too good to be true didn't go half way; the Candidate would have to be too good to exist. Ruth wasn't about to fall for anyone without some time, years – or possibly the rest of her days – to get over the man she was already in love with. Which meant... Oh no. Why hadn't she thought about this before? There were only two possible explanations.

Either she hadn't met the Candidate yet and wouldn't do so for a long time, or she already had, in which case – if the love at first sight malarkey was even close to true – she was in love with him already. And that would make The Candidate – oh no, please no – The Pan of Hamgee.

The moment she thought it, she realised it was the only thing that made any sense – and he had opened the box. Not the one Sir Robin had shown her how to open but the other one that nobody else could. Which was probably the whole point.

Did he know? Did Sir Robin? Did anyone? Or was she the only person who had realised? She crawled over to the corner, sat with her back against the wall and closed her eyes.

She was as sure as she could be that The Pan would rather die than live to see her marry his nemesis.

"Well, that makes two of us," she said and in spite of her sadness, she laughed. But if she refused Lord Vernon's offer she would be executed and whether or not he knew who he was, The Pan, the only hope for the K'Barthan people, would die with her. She could not let that happen. It was a grim prospect. She had no choice. And she couldn't explain. Ever.

She was going to marry Lord Vernon.

That wasn't so funny.

And The Pan wouldn't break.

He would understand.

He would have to.

Chapter 20

Walking, for The Pan, was difficult and slow, especially when they kept pushing him. The dull pain in his shoulder tired him but at least it took his mind off his parched lips and dry throat. After walking what felt like one hundred miles, but was actually a couple of hundred feet of corridor, with a lift journey sandwiched in between, they arrived at a small, dimly lit, grey room. There were no outside windows but along one wall was a large mirror. The guards pushed him inside and closed the door.

He waited. Nothing. Standing was taking an effort but there wasn't a chair. He felt shaky but if he sat on the floor, he couldn't guarantee he'd be able to get up again. The Pan turned in a circle, taking in his surroundings. Grey, grey, grey.

"Perhaps they are going to bore me to death," he said drily.

"Cluck," said the imaginary chicken and The Pan smiled. The whistling in his ears had stopped and he could not hear the other voices. He thought he could feel them, though, at the edges of his consciousness, watching, listening.

A few more minutes passed and the room was flooded with light.

"Well, well. Things are getting exciting around here."

There was someone behind the one way glass, certainly, but no one replied. There had to be a point to this; something must be happening in there. He looked at the glass, quizzically. Yes.

He sighed. As usual, his thoughts returned to Ruth. Was she still alive? He wanted, wished he could see her again.

And then it was over, the lights dimmed to their original level. More time passed, ten minutes, twenty, The Pan wished he knew. He shuffled round the room, an interview room presumably, but nobody had come to talk to him. Strange, that.

As the minutes ticked on, his head began to clear. He wished he could have a drink but he tried to concentrate on something else – the thirst was probably part of the torture. He stopped shuffling and began to pace with more conviction. The lights flickered and went out again, plunging him into darkness. He stood still and waited, wondering what would happen next. Now it was dark, he could see through the mirror. Against his will, he was drawn to the glass as, in the cell beyond, he watched his darkest nightmare unfold.

Chapter 21

The thought of what she was about to do filled Ruth with dread but she tried to rein in her emotions. She needed to think calmly about this. Her future was going to be grim but at least she would have one, and while she did, perhaps there was hope. She would be a puppet: controlled, used, a prisoner, and she would never see her parents or her family again. That would put her in the same situation as The Pan, then, because buying his freedom wouldn't bring his family back either. She stood up, blew her nose, wiped her eyes with a handkerchief and checked her reflection in the one way glass. Lord Vernon was probably watching.

She waited, trying not to dwell on what she was about to do. Presently, she heard the sound of footsteps in the hall outside. A rattling of keys and the door was flung open as Lord Vernon, preceded by an aura of unbearable smugness, strode in.

"Well, Ruth?" He smiled his cold smile. "Your answer, if you please."

"I will marry you, Lord Vernon."

"As I knew you would."

"Don't be too smug about it, you gave me no choice and there is another condition."

"Oh you drive a hard bargain," he said, ironically. "Name it."

"OK. Before the actual marriage, you must show me proof that you have kept your word. That you have taken his name off the blacklist and given him a new life, and you must give me your word that after we're married you'll leave him alone. If you're not going to agree to that, the deal's off, go sharpen your sword."

"You would face death?"

"Rather than you at the breakfast table every morning? Yes, Lord Vernon, I would – and if this was about anyone's life but my own I would choose death every time. It may seem amazing to you but you are not my ideal mate."

"Oh so sarcastic, Ruth," sneering. "I didn't expect you to be such a poor loser."

"Don't bet on it Lord Vernon. You haven't won yet."

"Haven't I?" He walked over to her side.

"You are merely ahead on points."

"I hope you are not thinking of reneging." He moved closer.

"No." She stepped away from him. "Unlike you, Lord Vernon, I have some principles."

"Then I pity you such an encumbrance. Your lover already appreciates that you cannot remain true to him. As the Chosen One, he knows you are powerless to resist my charms." A pause to let the gravity of the message hit home. "Alas, so far, he seems to be... in denial."

"Yes, well I warned you, didn't I?"

At last. Her turn to be smug.

"That is so." A casual glance at one of his immaculate suede gloves. He curled his fingers, as if examining his nails and blew an imaginary speck of dust from his finger tips. "I am glad you are here to change his mind. He is," he sighed and cracked his knuckles, "irritatingly stubborn."

"You ARE still going to release him though, AREN'T you?" said Ruth.

"Possibly; it depends on you," said Lord Vernon moving closer to her again. "Doubtless you are pleased he does not believe me and yet it is," the usual pause while he sought the right word, "imperative, if you wish him to survive this day, that he does." His tone was ominous. "Remember, he must believe you love me. If I think there is the remotest chance he does not then I will be forced to put you both to death." He looked her up and down; a lingering, slow look. "And that will be a waste. Are you ready to say goodbye?"

"What do you think?"

"I think you have no choice."

"That's right."

"Good. Then you will have no objections in colluding with me to provide the Hamgeean with a... now, how would your friends put it, 'convincer'?"

He took her by the elbow, gripping her arm tightly so that his thumb dug into the joint and turned her to face him. She tried not to show how much it hurt, since she suspected that was the point.

"You can let go of my arm, Lord Vernon."

"Yes I can." He increased the pressure until the pain made her eyes water, "but I choose not to. As you know, that," he nodded towards the window, "is one way glass and since you have accepted my proposal, I suggest we re-enact it for the viewing pleasure of your ex. Are you ready?" Before she could speak, he answered his own question. "Oh, but I forgot," he said lightly, "you have no choice, do you?" He led her across the room and positioned her in front of the glass, finally releasing her from the vice-like grip. She rubbed her arm, watching as he took a box from one of the pouches on his belt and flipped it open. It contained a ring, the type of ring Ruth would have been overjoyed to receive from, yes, practically any other person who had ever existed. "I have come prepared. Stand with your back to the mirror, if you please, our friend may be able to lip-read."

"I can still refuse to do this."

"Yes, and if you do, I will kill him. If you are lucky, I may even let you watch."

Ruth felt sick.

He clicked his fingers and the dim lights illuminating the room brightened.

"Shall we begin, darling?" He dropped to one knee; holding the ring towards her. "Will you become my wife?"

"It seems I have to," said Ruth. Her hand was shaking as she reached out and took the ring.

"Try to show a little more enthusiasm, my dear, you are about to become engaged to Grongolia's most eligible bachelor."

"Grongolian bachelors can't have much going for them if you're at the top of the heap," said Ruth and against her will, very much against her will, she began to cry.

"Oh yes, tears. A masterstroke." He stood up and pulled her against him, brushing her hair away from her face. "You are, understandably, overcome with emotion."

"Yes I am," said Ruth, "but not in the way you'd like to think."

"Give it time." His face showed concern, even tenderness, but only for The Pan's benefit. His eyes showed nothing but cruel glee and his voice was quiet and malevolent. The two of them looked down at the ring; she couldn't stop her hand shaking enough to put it on. "Let me help you." He gripped her wrist, slipped the diamond over her finger and turned her sideways so she was visible, through the mirror, in profile. Then he leaned forward and buried his face in her hair. "Be careful what you say, Ruth," he whispered into her ear. "Now, I believe it is customary, in a situation such as this, for us to kiss." His breath was warm on her neck and, as she felt his arm tighten around her, a sob escaped before she could stop it. "Oh dear," he said, "I think it will take a more enthusiastic response than that. You know what will happen if he does not believe."

He kissed her cheek and as she looked up at him, he smiled; nothing to do with love; all to do with enjoyment at her distress. She glared into the impassive, grey eyes with all the hatred and anger she could muster.

"Remember, his life depends on this," he whispered as he leaned forward. Ruth closed her eyes, wrapped her arms round his neck and put everything she felt for The Pan of Hamgee, everything she wanted to tell him into a kiss for Lord Vernon. "Oh, my darling," he said, when, finally, he allowed her to stop. She felt as if she had given away her soul. Perhaps she had. With his arm around her waist, he swung her round and pushed her against the glass. He leaned in and as her head obscured his face from the room beyond said, "I want more than one of those, my princess; again, if you please."

However, Ruth had recovered her composure.

"I can only go so far, Lord Vernon. If I kiss you again, I'll be sick. Your call."

His mouth was inches from hers.

"No, my love, yours. You cannot refuse." She closed her eyes and took a deep breath. "That's better," he whispered, and his lips found hers. Ruth hadn't realised a kiss could be predatory. He took his time and when he clicked his fingers again, he waited a few unnecessary seconds after the lights dimmed to finish.

"You will never, EVER, get to do that again," said Ruth.

"Oh but I will."

"Not to me."

"Oh Ruth, such a tease," he let go of her and stepped back. "No matter, for the meantime, I believe our tryst has done its work."

As he stepped away from her, she turned to face the one way glass and stifled a scream. The Pan of Hamgee was standing right up close; he was leaning on one arm, which was raised, his clenched fist white against the surface, his forehead resting on his hand. He held his other arm lower, nursing his injury. She looked into his eyes, not that he would realise, of course. He was crying, no sobs, the same silent tears as she had cried. His good hand squeaked against the glass as he slid to the floor. He turned so he was sitting against the wall, rested his head on his bent knees and curled his good arm around his shins.

Lord Vernon tutted.

"He is so very upset. Such a pity."

The lighting adjusted between the cells and the one-way glass went black. Ruth rounded on Lord Vernon, pulling at the ring on her finger, desperately trying to remove it.

"I cannot wear this."

Lord Vernon eyed her coolly.

"You can and you will."

"No. I made you a promise, and I will keep it, but I will never wear this, or a wedding ring, or anything else that marks me out as anything to do with you. You only have me because I belong to him."

"Then perhaps I should fracture his other collarbone to focus your attention. We have an agreement. You have bought his life and in return I will stand by my word and set him free. However, if I am to do that, you must stand by yours. You have promised me loyalty and that is what I expect. Now, you will go in there, and you will tell him that you love me and no other, you will finish what you have started, you will break him."

"How can I?"

"With very little difficulty, I should imagine, because if you refuse, I will kill him and then I will take you as my wife, willing or not, do you understand?"

"Oh yes I understand."

"So you will marry me and you will wear my ring." Not really a question but she answered it as if it was.

"Yes, but because I have to; never willingly. An agreement is all it is."

"A matter of semantics, but have it your own way." He bowed. "We have an agreement. You will do what you must do." He took a clean handkerchief from his pocket and gave it to her. "I will allow you some time to compose yourself first."

Chapter 22

Ruth didn't expect The Pan to be pleased to see her but she wasn't prepared for the expression on his face when she walked into the grey room. In spite of everything, she believed he would grasp the reasons behind her actions. Perhaps her need for Lord Vernon to be wrong was clouding her judgement, but she instinctively turned to The Pan for friendship, support, comfort and he to her. Surely, he would realise that she would never dump him for Lord Vernon without a good reason. She was shaking and miserable and the only way she could retain her composure was to repeat, again, and again in her head, that whatever happened after this she would know that she had done one good thing in her life; or possibly two, if saving some other poor female from being married to Lord Vernon also counted. The Pan, on the other hand, seemed much sharper, now she was actually in his presence, than he had appeared through the one way glass; not drugged at all or at least not apparently affected by it. He stood very still, his manner calm and polar frosty.

"Well, well, well, hello Ruth," he said quietly.

"I've come to say—" she began.

"Goodbye. Yes. I know." Ruth had hoped that, maybe, without actually telling him the truth, she could make him understand her actions. She'd half-formed a plan to hug him so she could make a whispered explanation in his ear, but as soon as she looked into his eyes she knew it would be impossible. They glittered with bitter anger.

"I need to explain—"

"Oh spare me. I think the floor show was eloquent enough." She felt her face redden. "Yeh, I saw that but then, I was meant to, wasn't I?"

"You were but—" she glanced meaningfully at the glass wall. He didn't notice.

"But what, Ruth? But you didn't think I'd mind watching you hoovering Lord Vernon's face off? That's a nice big rock he's given you, better than the broken shoulder I have, I bet you're pleased with it."

She was going to cry. No. She couldn't do that. She took a deep breath.

"Actually, I would have preferred a diamond, and it's not your shoulder it's your collarbone." What was she doing? He stared at her.

"That's deep," he said acidly.

"Defreville; I'm sorry. I thought, I thought I could help who I am but I can't. I'm the brainless pawn prophesied, I am in love with the Candidate and that means," her voice cracked. No, she must not cry. "That means I have to do what my heart tells me."

"Your heart. Really?" Cold, sarcastic. "You mean to say you have one? Let's check the facts. I have been beaten, starved," he glanced down at his shoulder, "shot – yes, collarbone, shoulder-schmolder, whatever it is, he broke it by shooting me with a laser pistol. I've been injected with some mind-expanding red liquid – that's been interesting, by the way – I spent a fair old time hanging up by my arms, slowly suffocating, I'm sure you're concerned to hear that." He mimicked her, "'Oh no, Defreville who could have done this to you?' Guess? That's right. Your fiancé. Forgive me if I'm a trifle peeved, poor sop that I am, I thought you loved me, if not much, then enough for it to take you more than a couple of days to forget about me and shack up with my mortal enemy."

"If you think about this you'll realise I do love you—" She stopped short with an apprehensive glance at the one way glass, bad call, she'd been too obvious and Lord Vernon would certainly be watching. "Did," she corrected herself quickly.

The Pan glared at her with an expression of complete disdain and raised a sarcastic eyebrow.

"Did... yes, that's how it would appear." He hadn't picked up on her anxiety about the mirror, or at least, not the way she'd hoped. Hardly surprising, he was too angry; Lord Vernon knew what he was doing. 'The floor show', as The Pan had called it, was a masterstroke. How could someone who was in love with her think rationally after that? She sighed.

"Look, Ruth, I don't know what you think you're doing but you do realise, don't you, that Lord Vernon is not the Candidate and he will never be the real Architrave either; he's a fake." So much conviction but he hadn't picked up what she wanted to tell him. She tried again, she had to make him understand but she was afraid he was too angry.

"Defreville; all I know is that I am in love with the Candidate, just like your stupid books say and he has chosen me, too." Even now, it galled her to be so goddamn predictable.

"So you have to marry him. Yes, Ruth, I understand that you have to marry the Candidate."

"Yes, one day, I hope to."

Had he got there?

"My point is that the Candidate is not, I repeat, NOT – which bit of this are you failing to understand? – Lord Vernon."

No.

She moved closer to him and looked into his eyes, trying to make him realise what she couldn't tell him directly.

"Defreville, listen to what I'm saying. Properly." She rolled her eyes sideways at the one way glass. His eyes narrowed and the disgust, the anger in them intensified.

"Oh I'm listening," he was almost sneering. What would it take to get through to him?

"No, you're not."

"Well, I doubt it matters. You can go ahead and do what you like because I won't be around to care, they're going to behead me in a few minutes, anyway."

Blimey this was frustrating. How could he be so thick?

'Stop thinking about yourself and listen to me can't you?' thought Ruth.

"Actually, they're going to take you off the blacklist and set you free, and they're going to give you a year's total amnesty while you adjust to legal existence," she said.

"That's not the first time I've heard that today. I'll believe it when it happens."

"It will, I can guarantee you it will," she said meaningfully. Too meaningfully? She glanced at the window; surely The Pan would realise she was trying to tell him something! She couldn't go any further or Lord Vernon certainly would. "It's one of the things I am here to tell you."

"As well as goodbye."

For heaven's sake, could he not just think about what she was saying?

"Yes and that I'm sorry it has to be like this," she said.

"Yeh. Funny that. So am I." Was there hope? Was he softening?

"You're not making this any easier."

"I don't intend to," he said. No. His eyes were still full of anger and contempt.

"I can't blame you for feeling the way you do, but I promise, one day, when you're not angry any more, you will understand," Ruth said.

'And I'm hoping, if you would just stop concentrating on your anger for a moment and think about the real meaning of my words that you will understand now,' she thought.

"Yes, Ruth, I'm sure I will. I'm a very magnanimous bloke."

Nooo! What did she have to do to get this round his thick head? And did he have to be quite so sarcastic? She ploughed on.

"And I'm sorry I hurt you," she said. *'And it wouldn't be so painful if you'd engage your brain for one minute and think about this the way I am asking you.'*

"I'm sure you are, and at the risk of repeating myself..." he shrugged. The conversation ground to a halt. "Is that it?" asked the Pan. "Are we done? Only, if you've finished, I suggest you go." He stood waiting for her to leave and she felt the tears stinging her eyes. "Run along to hubby-to-be! Don't forget to send him my love and have a joyful, happy life together."

No. It would be anything but. She was in the process of alienating the only constant in a new and frightening world and if only he was a bit less goddamn STUPID he'd realise she was doing it to save his life. She couldn't hold back the tears any more.

"Oh bravo! Arnold! That's pretty despicable," he ran his good hand through his hair, "and shall I tell you what the worst thing about this is? It's that even now, seeing you cry like that I can't stay angry. By the Prophet! I've watched you happily playing tonsil hocky with the bastard who's taken everything from me, and even after that, I'm still in love with you."

Ruth's tears were blinding her and the strength of her emotions such that she was afraid she might collapse. She ached to run to him, to fling her arms around him, tell him she would love him forever and explain, for him to hug her back and tell her he understood. But with Lord Vernon looking on, she didn't dare, and he made no move to go to her. Instead, he stood and watched her sobbing. His voice was bitter when he spoke again.

"Maybe you haven't forgotten completely," he said with an air of cold indifference. "Even with your new boyfriend in there." He glanced towards the glass. "Oh yes, I know he's watching, to keep you happy."

"I wanted," she began, "I thought..." she took a deep breath, dammit, she had failed. "Goodbye shouldn't be like this. Not for us."

"No," he said sadly. "It shouldn't, should it? But it seems it is. Ruth, if you ever felt anything for me then do me a favour will you?"

"What?" Her voice was trembling.

"Leave me alone."

"Defreville," he looked straight at her. This was her only chance. She put her hand up to push her hair back, obscuring her face from the mirror for a few seconds as she did so and mouthed the words, "I have no choice." Had he even seen? She wasn't sure, a flicker of curiosity in the eyes and then the anger returned. Had it been enough? Had he understood?

"I think I'm done with this, just go." He turned his back on her. "Go away now." He put his hand out, backwards, towards her. "Oh and congratulations on your engagement, I know you'll make a charming couple."

She didn't remember much else. Captain Snow arrived but neither he nor the guards touched her. Instead, she followed him, crying, along dimly lit passages and corridors, upwards, always upwards, to her apartment on the top floor of the building. The guards opened the door.

"Inside," said Captain Snow, shoving her through it. She heard the door slam as she stumbled down the steps. She ignored the roof terrace, the fine furnishings and the view of the city. Instead, she threw herself on the bed and, burying her face in the pillow, she sobbed until she was too exhausted to cry any more. Then she sank into a dark, dream-free sleep.

Chapter 23

Lord Vernon leaned casually on his balcony reading an ancient tome, one of the many banned books in his collection. His plan was unfolding exactly as anticipated. His score on the Confibrulator already stood at nine, high enough, but he wanted perfection, he wanted ten and he was beginning to believe he could achieve it. The Chosen One was his, and the rest...

He took out his phone and flipped it open to consult his diary. General Moteurs would be arriving soon. Excellent. Lord Vernon's rage at being denied the blonde from the laundry, albeit for a logical reason, had abated. Now, he could only admire the skill with which his second in command had read the Chosen One. He smiled as he recalled his interview with Ruth. It was so easy to manipulate her; yet she'd resisted so bravely; a perfect combination. Forcing her to his will had been intensely enjoyable. She had agreed to marry him; he wondered what else she would agree to. The possibilities were limitless. Reluctantly, he put thoughts of Ruth to the back of his mind. He hoped the General would be as useful in solving his latest conundrum.

He closed the book and strolled back into his rooms, tossing it casually onto his desk as he went. Then he returned to the balcony doors, closed them and sat in one of the easy chairs in front of the long row of newly fitted windows. There was no trace of the torpedo damage the Hamgeean's snurd had inflicted. Lord Vernon's rooms had been fixed in record time.

There was a knock at the door. One of the guards outside let in a servant carrying two smoothies, and at the same time, announced the arrival of General Moteurs.

"Good day to you, General. Please, sit."

"Your—"

Lord Vernon eyed him meaningfully.

"Sir." General Moteurs sat down.

"Perhaps I was hasty in upbraiding you," said Lord Vernon and watched with pleasure as his number two failed to hide his shock. "For, once again, you have given me wise counsel. You were accurate in your summation of the Chosen One."

"Sir."

"If you had the time, I would assign her to your custody. As it is, Captain Snow can deal with her."

"I am at your command, sir. If you wish it, I will make time."

"No."

"Sir." General Moteurs would have said more, Lord Vernon surmised, but remained silent, so he continued.

"It seems that if I wish for her co-operation, I must pay with the Hamgeean. Once again, I am in your debt. I thank you for persuading me to spare him."

"Sir."

Lord Vernon noted, with interest, that praising the General had not relaxed him, more the opposite. He must make a point of praising him more often.

"I want her, so I have been forced to pardon him and remove his name from the blacklist."

"Sir."

"But I want him dead."

"Sir."

"I am wondering, if I must be denied the pleasure of ending him myself, how I may yet achieve the bloodiest and most painful demise for this upstart, without showing my hand in it." Lord Vernon regretted the emotion in his voice. He hadn't intended to betray so much of his anger.

"Sir," said General Moteurs. He had clearly detected the rage burning in his master's heart and was wary. Lord Vernon took a sip of his smoothie.

"Well, General?"

General Moteurs sat in silent thought and Lord Vernon watched and waited.

"We are merely one of many who sought him, sir," he eventually said, slowly. "It is a simple matter of ensuring one of the others finds him – the Resistance perhaps? I would wager they seek to kill him."

"Yes," said Lord Vernon slowly, although it was more of a hiss. "You can arrange it?"

"It will not be necessary, sir. Neither of us need sully our hands."

"Continue."

"He has, in his own way, given us everything."

"He has. But this is Sir Robin's deluded plan, is it not?"

"Yes, but we can give him some credit for his part in it." The inscrutable red eyes met Lord Vernon's grey ones and he understood.

"You are suggesting... a public acknowledgement?"

"Sir, when you announce your candidature, if you credit the Hamgeean's efforts for making such an announcement possible—"

"On GNN?" Lord Vernon almost laughed.

"Perhaps GNN Local, sir, or at a citation."

"You are suggesting a public ceremony to show my appreciation."

"Sir. If the ceremony is suitably emotive; something that touches a nerve with the populace—"

"There will be a riot."

"Sir."

"And we will do our utmost to protect him but... They will tear him apart."

"Sir."

"Excellent, General."

"Sir."

"I will leave the details to you and Captain Snow."

"As you wish, sir."

"Thank you. Before I dismiss you, the High Leader?"

"Sir."

"Will he be attending my installation?"

"Yes, sir."

"Have you arranged rooms for him?"

"Sir. Pending approval from you."

"Good, I want him to feel comfortable but the security must be... flexible."

"That is already in hand, sir."

Such efficiency.

"Good, keep me informed. When is he expected?"

"Thursday, sir, but my staff predicts Wednesday."

"Excellent work General, on both counts. I am so glad you have not let me down. When you demanded that Resistance wench, I feared you were losing your touch. Now I see your intellect is as sharp as ever. Perhaps I should upbraid you more often. I will concoct a suitably glowing eulogy for the Hamgeean and inform you when I am done." Lord Vernon retrieved the book he had been reading and flicked through the pages. "That is all," he said, without looking up. "You may go."

Chapter 24

The Pan waited in the grey room. Nothing mattered now; nothing but that monstrous betrayal. He felt numb, detached, robotic, as if the storm of emotions he was experiencing had overloaded his system and shut it down. He clung to this sensation of detachment like an emotional life-raft because it was the only thing holding him together; without it he would sink into despair. Alright, further into despair, he corrected himself. Never mind, they were going to execute him in a few minutes, and The Prophet knew, after what he'd just seen, death would be a relief.

For all his sense of calm detachment he realised the tears were waiting in the wings. It was only a matter of time before the storm broke. He wished he had his watch but the Grongles had nicked it. No surprise. It was a good one, a birthday present from his father, who had still been capable of generosity towards his wayward son, even if he could hardly speak to him or look him in the eye by that point. The Pan reckoned he had half an hour left to live. Surely he could keep it together until then. Coward or not he was too proud to die crying. Lord Vernon had won on all counts, easily. But The Pan would not give his nemesis that final victory. He would not die like the beaten pushover he was but like a Hamgeean... or at least, a man.

A part of him was relieved. No more running; no more struggling; no more pain... well... being beheaded was bound to smart but after that it would all be over. He was broken and he knew it. The detachment was temporary; underneath it was an emptiness so acute it was a physical ache. He closed his eyes but all he could see was the image of Ruth and Lord Vernon kissing.

How could she? How?

It made him so miserable he felt sick but he was also angry. That anger was his lifeline. He concentrated on Ruth's betrayal, replaying the image in his head; twisting the knife until it carried him past the pain, through fiery incandescence, to cold hard rage.

"I have no choice," he said, in a sing-song girly voice. "Did you

120

smeck? You treacherous bitch," he spat.

"Cluck."

"Arnold in the skies, I thought I'd got rid of you."

"Cluck." The Pan knew the chicken was trying to be comforting but he was too angry and unhappy to talk to anyone.

"Yes. I am bitter. And with good reason. Go away."

"Cluck?"

"No. I want to be alone and if I were you I'd really, really listen to me when I tell you that."

Sympathy, even from imaginary farmyard animals, would weaken him.

"No weakness. No tears," he said aloud. It was a tall order but he had to try and die with courage. He could blub all he wanted in the afterlife. There was a noise – keys in the door – and Captain Snow arrived flanked by two guards.

"You're early," snapped The Pan.

"And normally I'd give you a good kicking for that bit of rudeness."

"Go on then. As if I care."

"Nah. I'm not allowed to. It's your lucky day, you waste of space. You've been pardoned." One of the guards went out into the corridor and returned with The Pan's hat and cloak and a bag containing the contents of his pockets, which he handed to his commander. Captain Snow threw the Pan's hat and cloak on the floor at his feet. "Put on your things and let's get going." He kept hold of the bag containing the contents of The Pan's pockets. "Lord Vernon's given you a business to run and total amnesty for a year while you adjust."

"How kind," said The Pan sourly.

"Yeh, isn't it?"

This was just as Ruth had predicted. Slowly, without taking his eyes off Captain Snow – because it pays to be careful – The Pan bent down, picked up his hat and cloak and put them on. But he needn't have worried the Captain was busy rummaging about inside the bag.

"If I were Lord Vernon, I'd go with the first plan and cut your smecking head off."

"Lucky you're not then, isn't it?" said The Pan. Privately he almost wished Captain Snow would. He didn't want a business and total amnesty, not without Ruth and not in a K'Barth where Lord Vernon was Architrave. He preferred to die, even if a part of him knew he was being a massive drama queen to think it. Captain Snow took the keys to the SE2 out of the bag.

"I think I'll take these to make up for that piece of disrespect," he said holding them up.

"You won't get far, they only work with my finger print," said The Pan. He caught the bag containing the rest of this things as the Grongle threw it at him.

"I've got your fingerprint," Captain Snow sniggered, opened a pouch on his belt and pulled out what looked like the finger of a latex glove. "Had to get your fingerprint so General Moteurs and his lackeys could get the thimble out of the dashboard, didn't I boys?" The goons snickered as he put it on his finger. "I'd better set the alarm. I don't want anyone nicking it, do I?" He held up the keyring and pressed the button, it beeped.

"The snurd is mine," said The Pan.

"I don't think so. Nice wheels; very nice, and Lord Vernon's got what he wanted out of them, so I get to take what's left; spoils of war."

"It's still mine," said The Pan.

"Not any more. Boys, is this piece of trash arguing with me? How about we teach him some manners?" said the Captain. The two guards stepped forward priming their crowd control sticks as they went.

"Wait," said The Pan, and to his amazement all three Grongles obeyed him. "There's something I want to know first. Why have I been pardoned?"

"I can't say. Lord Vernon wants to tell you himself. He's ordered me not to spoil the surprise."

"Has he? How touching."

"That's right," said Captain Snow.

"Thank you. That's all I wanted to know." He looked Captain Snow straight in the eye. "Go right ahead."

"Do we control him, sir?" asked one of the guards.

"No. We're going to play nice."

"Very magnanimous. Then, I assume you'll be giving me my keys back."

"Not that nice. You have to come with us, and since I've got myself a shiny new snurd and I'm feeling generous, I'm going to give you a choice. Are you going to be a good little non-being and walk, or do we control you and drag you there in a sack?"

The Pan assessed his situation. On the one hand, it was grim. He had anticipated and feared this day. There was nothing left and no point in carrying on. Lord Vernon had taken everything from him, but the emotional numbness he felt made it far more bearable than he'd expected. Doubtless he'd pay the price later but right now, he didn't care what happened. It was a surprisingly liberating feeling.

"What's to be afraid of? What more can they do?" he thought.

"Cluck."

Yep, even the imaginary chicken seemed bullish.

The Pan glared at Captain Snow and felt a smug satisfaction when he won the game of stare-down and the Grongle blinked first.

"I'll walk, Captain," he said.

"Then let's move." Captain Snow stood back and gestured to the doorway, which was suddenly filled with the form of General Moteurs.

"A moment, Captain, if you please," said the General.

"Sir," said Captain Snow, the dislike in his voice audible. General Moteurs glanced at the Captain's goons who were still standing with their control sticks at the ready.

"I believe this prisoner has been pardoned," he said.

"Sir." Captain Snow shrugged and General Moteurs gave him the kind of gimlet glare that would have had The Pan quaking in his boots.

"That being the case, I would suggest control is not required." Except that this was most definitely an order rather than a suggestion. The two guards powered down their control sticks and snapped to attention.

"Sir," said Captain Snow.

"Thank you. I believe the usual procedure is to give the prisoner a medical examination before final release."

"Yes sir, I will see to it, sir."

"No need, Captain," said the General smoothly. "I know you are busy, so I have already made arrangements. My M.O. is waiting in the corridor. You may leave us. The prisoner will be ready for collection in ten minutes."

"Sir." Captain Snow and both his subordinates saluted smartly and left the room.

"What's going on?" asked The Pan.

"As the Captain has clearly told you, you are pardoned."

"Why?"

"I am not at liberty to say."

"Neither is Captain Snow."

"Correct." General Moteurs stepped out into the corridor briefly and returned carrying a fold-up chair. Two more Grongles followed him. The General plonked the chair down in front of The Pan and said. "Sit down, boy. We do not have much time."

"What in the name of The Prophet is going on?" The Pan asked him.

"As we ascertained earlier in this conversation, I cannot tell you." General Moteurs inclined his head towards the mirrored wall and raised his eyebrows. "I am under the strictest orders not to."

"Naturally," said The Pan acidly.

"Sit down, if you please." General Moteurs, pushed him firmly backwards so he half-sat, half-fell onto the chair, and thrust a canteen into his hand. "Drink."

The Pan took the canteen and drained the contents at speed. He felt a bit better.

"What day is it?" he asked.

"Sunday."

"Where are the others?"

"Alive."

"Are they—?"

"They have fared better than you. Enough talk, Hamgeean. This is Corporal Jones and my M.O. Dr Dot." The M.O. took off her hat. A cascade of brunette curls tumbled from underneath and for a moment The Pan was distracted from his misery by sheer curiosity.

"She's a—"

"Yes I am," said Dr Dot, "and so is Corporal Jones." The Pan glanced at Corporal Jones who was about six feet four and realised, with a shock, that she had legs that went on forever and the body and face of a goddess. Alright, so he was a bit preoccupied but how in The Prophet's name had he failed to notice her?

He managed not to actually say 'wow' but his mouth formed the word.

"Everyone says that," said Dr Dot cheerfully as she took off a small rucksack and put it on the floor in front of her. "I'm here to check your clavicle, your collarbone, and Corporal Jones is here to make it less painful." They both laughed and the Corporal slipped a rapid repeat laser gun from round her shoulder.

"And to ensure that you don't jump us all and escape."

"Yeh, right," said The Pan.

"Hi," she said.

"Hello," said The Pan.

124

She flashed him a brief smile before turning to the General and snapping smartly to attention.

"Sir, your orders?"

"Keep an eye out for Captain Snow, Corporal."

"Yes sir." Corporal Jones went and stood in the corridor but near enough to the door to take part in the conversation.

"I see you've been in the wars," said Dr Dot.

"No, just enjoying the usual Grongolian hospitality." When she flushed and looked down, he felt a pang of guilt, which was exacerbated by the way General Moteurs glared at him. "Sorry, don't mind me. I'm just bitter."

"What happened?" she asked.

"Lord Vernon shot me with his laser pistol." He tried to sound less bitter and more matter of fact. He failed.

"Take off your top, then," she said.

"What?" asked The Pan incredulously.

Dr Dot was older then Corporal Jones, in her forties with twinkly eyes and a kindly smile.

"I'll need to assess the damage," she said. "Judging by the mess it's made of your shirt and jacket, there are burns as well as a break."

"Ah right, yes. Sorry," said The Pan. He took off his cloak and tried to slip off his jacket. The wounded arm was too painful to use and it was difficult one-handed.

She watched him fumbling for a brief moment and then said, "Can I help you?"

"Thank you."

She eased off his jacket, undid the buttons on his shirt and took that off, too.

"Well. That's less of a mess than I expected," she said when the wound was revealed.

"Um... good," he said because it seemed to be the right sort of thing to say. It looked very messy to him — and bloody, to boot.

"Now, keep still, I have to assess the damage."

"Ah..." The Pan glanced up at General Moteurs who almost imperceptibly, nodded. "Right... thanks."

She moved backwards, looking at him, moving her head from side to side as if trying to ascertain whether he was quite symmetrical. Perhaps she was.

"You keep yourself pretty trim. What's your sport?" she asked. It threw him, no Grongle had ever talked to him like this.

"I do a lot of running and I climb sometimes," said The Pan weakly. He cast another glance at General Moteurs who looked away.

"Oh, my brother climbs," said Dr Dot as she moved round behind him. "He's coming over to visit Smirn, the high peaks round Driesch. I'm guessing you'll know them well if you climb, too." Who did she think he was?

"I'm afraid not. I do..." How to put this tactfully? "A different sort of climbing."

"Buildings," said General Moteurs dourly. "Fences, walls, trees—"

"Not free running?" Dr Dot broke in.

Desperate-not-to-get-caught running more like.

"Something like that," said The Pan. She picked up on his embarrassment.

"Are we, Corporal Jones and I, making you feel uncomfortable?"

"No. I don't have any hang-ups about women." He couldn't resist a dig. "I'm K'Barthan, not Grongolian. You are a bit of a rarity but you're also being remarkably civil, and that is novel."

"The boy is as ignorant as the rest of them," said General Moteurs and Dr Dot looked down to hide a smile.

"Don't mind my commander," she said. "It sounds as if you've been mixing with the wrong crowd."

"I've been blacklisted. It's difficult not to."

"Ah so when the General said you climb buildings he meant—"

"Up them, away from your less friendly colleagues. Yes."

"That's the army for you. Shoot first ask questions later," said Corporal Jones from the doorway. "They've no idea how to behave. That's why you haven't met any females, too. They don't let us into the army," she added dismissively. The Pan forbore to mention that on his one and only visit to Grongolia he hadn't seem many females there, either, and steered the conversation in a different direction.

"So, you're not army then?"

"No. We are Imperial Guard," said General Moteurs.

"Is there a difference?"

"Yes," said the General irritably. Oops.

"OK, that's enough chat. Mind on the matter in hand, young man; I'm sorry, but this is going to hurt. I'll be as quick as I can; tell me if it gets too much and I'll stop," said Dr Dot. The Pan watched with a sense of extreme unreality as she donned a pair of surgical gloves. She put her hands on his shoulder and felt gently along it. He bit back an 'ouch' or two when she pressed the burned areas but otherwise it wasn't too bad: nothing significant on top of the pain that was there already. When she was done, she looked up. "Sir?" she said, her gaze lit on The Pan's shoulder briefly before reverting to her Commander. General Moteurs inclined his head. When she spoke she addressed The Pan.

"Before I dress the burns I need to set the bone," she said.

"I wouldn't bother," he said.

With a heavy sigh, General Moteurs moved round and stood behind him. It made The Pan nervous.

"It will hurt less, if I set it," she said.

"What's the point?"

She smiled.

"I'm a doctor, I've sworn an oath to heal and you need healing. I'd be very grateful if you would indulge me." She wasn't taking it seriously at all.

"Will it hurt?" asked The Pan, who reckoned he'd endured enough pain for a lifetime over the last couple of days.

"A bit but it'll be worth it," she said, and before The Pan could reply General Moteurs grabbed his arms and put one knee against his back, high up behind the wound, while Dr Dot put one hand on his breast bone and one on his shoulder and pushed hard. There was a stab of unbelievable agony, a click and suddenly the pain level dropped substantially. They completed the whole process before he could even take a breath to scream.

"You smecking gets. You jumped me!" He didn't know whether to be grateful or angry. No, he did. "Thank you," he gasped.

Wordlessly, General Moteurs stepped back round in front of him, where The Pan could see him. He was a very light shade of green, and seeing where The Pan was looking, Dr Dot winked conspiratorially, and with a cautious glance at the one way glass, she leaned forward and whispered. "Our commander is not at home inflicting pain."

"I heard that, Doctor," growled General Moteurs.

The Pan glanced up at Dr Dot and she gave him a reassuring smile.

127

"Don't worry, he's just upset," she whispered as she cleaned the wound. When she had finished, she sprayed him with antiseptic and applied something that looked like a sheet of cellophane over the burns, "OK, leave this on. It's water and air proof. The burns will heal underneath it and it'll be absorbed naturally into your skin."

"Thank you for helping me," said The Pan.

"It's a pleasure. I'm a doctor. It's what I do," said Dr Dot as she rummaged about in her bag and finally produced a sling, a strange black padded harness, a syringe and a small bottle.

"This is a brace to keep your shoulder straight while it heals." She held up the black thing. "I'd wear the sling too, if I were you. It's only for comfort really, but it should help. You must move your arm as much as you can but gently, nothing sudden or harsh for three weeks."

"Three weeks," said The Pan. The mention of such a long period of time reminded him of the acres of emptiness ahead. She put the padded harness down and picked up the bottle and syringe.

"This is for the pain... if you want some."

"I'm sure it will make my last minutes more comfortable," said The Pan drily.

"You are pardoned, Hamgeean," General Moteurs reminded him.

"I'll believe that when I see it."

"OK, do you want the pain relief before or after I help you put on the brace and the sling?" asked Dr Dot.

"Before, please."

So the Grongolian Imperial Guard's M.O. injected The Pan, her supposed enemy, with a painkiller and helped him into the shoulder brace. Then she helped him put his shirt and jacket back on and tied the sling. It was all a bit surreal.

"You are done?" asked General Moteurs.

"Sir," said Dr Dot as she packed her things back into her rucksack and slung it over her shoulder. Then finally, to The Pan, she said, "I'm based here at Security HQ. If you have any trouble, come and see me."

"Er... thank you, I will," said The Pan.

"Goodbye, Hamgeean," said General Moteurs.

"Goodbye General, and thank you too; for this." The Pan gestured to the sling.

"Mere expedience." The Pan looked into the inscrutable red eyes. As usual, General Moteurs was giving nothing away.

"Maybe; but thank you, all the same."

The General clicked his heels and made a slight bow; a brusque, "Noted," was all he said. He stepped closer to The Pan and shook his hand. "Until we meet again," the red eyes flicked sideways, to the one way glass and then without moving his mouth, and very quietly, so that nobody else could hear, he added, "Trust me."

The Pan took a breath to speak but Corporal Jones beat him to it.

"Captain Snow is returning, sir," she said and she snapped to attention and saluted as the Captain arrived, flanked by the inevitable goons.

"Captain," said General Moteurs.

"Sir," said Captain Snow, saluting the General.

"I thank you for your patience. We are done here. I will leave you to carry out your orders."

"Sir," said Captain Snow again and he and his troops saluted General Moteurs, who left with Dr Dot and Corporal Jones. Captain Snow, his two troops and The Pan stood eying one another warily. Nobody said anything until the sound of footsteps had faded down the corridor.

"Let's go, Vermin," said Captain Snow and, flanked by the guards, The Pan followed.

Chapter 25

There is an old saying in K'Barth, 'nothing comes free without strings'. If Lord Vernon had pardoned him, The Pan knew it would not be out of the goodness of his heart. He completed the painful walk to his new business premises with trepidation. As the journey continued his misgivings increased, but as they turned the corner into Turnadot Street the tears welled up. He bit them back.

"Is this it?" asked The Pan, even though he knew where they were taking him now.

"Yeh. You're going to be a publican," said Captain Snow.

A publican. At home. In the Parrot and Screwdriver. Gladys and Ada's pub.

The Pan took in the scenery. Familiar, much loved but now alien; changed forever, a reminder of the people he had loved and lost. Presumably, that was the point.

As Captain Snow and the guards led him down the street, doors and windows opened. People began to come out of their houses to look; even the traffic had stopped. He straightened his back and tried to walk with some dignity. He'd lived on this street for over a year and he was on nodding terms with the ones who drank in the Parrot and Screwdriver. As he reached the outside of the Pub, The Pan understood their curiosity.

The Parrot and Screwdriver was set back from the road, with a patio area in front, which was usually full of outside tables. However, these had been cleared away. In their place were 20 or 30 Grongle troops, their black and red uniforms pristine, brass buttons and metal weaponry gleaming in the sunlight. They stood to attention, crowd control sticks at the ready, flanking a dais.

In front of the dais stood a microphone and on it stood Lord Vernon. He turned to look straight at The Pan, and even from several yards away, the malevolence emanating from that tall, immaculately dressed figure was almost tangible. Behind Lord Vernon, to the side of the terrace was the Interceptor, in broad daylight: black, shiny and as menacing as its Master. A weapon of immense power, a weapon which, until this moment had been little more than a rumour to most K'Barthans of a certain type, made real on Gladys' terrace. Further down the street, The Pan noticed a Grongolian National News van. What was going on? And then he saw the open door of the Parrot and glimpsed the overturned tables and chairs, the white stuffing spilling out of the slashed red cushions like blood in reverse. The Grongles had searched the place.

"Turnover before handover, I see."

"That's right. I expect it'll need a bit of straightening out, won't it boys?" said Captain Snow. The guards flanking The Pan laughed.

"What is this?"

"Your future," said Captain Snow.

"I have none."

"Looks like you do." He pushed The Pan forward up to the dais. Lord Vernon came to greet him, standing away from the microphone.

"Good afternoon, Hamgeean. Ruth sends her love." The Pan turned his head away; he didn't want Lord Vernon to see the hurt. "It seems I snapped your collarbone in vain. All women are attracted to power and yours – I'm so sorry, mine – is no different."

"She's not yours – she doesn't belong to anybody," said The Pan.

"How very politically correct of you; but in this instance you are wrong. I own her. I can do what I want with her," he smiled and licked his lips. "And I will." The Pan tried, but he could not hide his feelings. Lord Vernon radiated smugness as he continued. "I told you she wanted me. I am never wrong in these matters. So, for all your pathetic attempts to keep her for yourself, you have delivered her into my power, and the last of my enemies with her."

The Pan couldn't think of anything intelligent to say, but that didn't stop his motor mouth from going ahead without him.

"What do you want?" he said.

"For such a great service, I have put my personal inclinations aside and pardoned you, very magnanimously in my view, and I have arranged a little settling in ceremony for you. Welcome to your new life."

The Pan said nothing.

"The custom, in these situations, is for you to bow."

"I've never been one for custom." The Pan fought to keep his emotions in check. If he lost control he wasn't sure whether he'd thump Lord Vernon or cry like a baby. Neither option was viable.

"As you wish," said Lord Vernon. "Then let us proceed."

He moved back to the microphone and waited. Captain Snow gripped The Pan's arm and manoeuvred him forward onto the dais, towards Lord Vernon. A large crowd of locals had gathered now, and as The Pan looked out at them he could recognise some of the Parrot's regulars among them. Rather more worryingly, he could also see the TV camera that went with the news van. Captain Snow moved sideways and behind him, keeping out of shot but without reducing his escape-proof hold on The Pan's arm.

"Good afternoon, my faithful subjects," said Lord Vernon, suavely. Somebody jeered at the back – a dangerous thing to do; any gathered crowd of K'Barthans was not permitted to make a sound unless directed or allowed to by their Grongle masters. "Thank you," said Lord Vernon and there was a sharp crack as one of his guards controlled the heckler. Lord Vernon continued, "I have arranged this little event to show you that I am not ungrateful and that I reward those who serve me."

The Pan looked at the crowd, they were attentive, and they were looking back at him, mostly with expressions of mild interest.

"This is The Pan of Hamgee," said Lord Vernon. "At great personal risk, he has tricked some of the most wanted enemies of the State into my hands. Without his unwavering loyalty and assistance, I would not be at liberty to make the announcement I am today."

The faces in the front row were beginning to look at The Pan with different expressions; disappointment, shock, disgust and in some cases hatred.

The Pan glanced round him. The Grongles were going to fit him up as a traitor. Great, no need for Lord Vernon to kill him, his own neighbours would do it.

"Don't listen to him—" he began. Captain Snow pulled him backwards, out of range of the microphone.

"Hold your tongue, Hamgean, or I'm going to apply some control."

"You do that, moron. It'll show everyone what's going on."

Lord Vernon heard. He glanced round at the Captain with a look of enquiry that changed to one of understanding as their eyes met. With a nod, he turned back to the microphone.

The Pan started to struggle but without letting go of his arm, Captain Snow put his other hand on The Pan's injured shoulder and gripped it hard.

"There are lots of different ways to apply control," he said quietly.

The Pan stifled a cry as Captain Snow increased the pressure. The pain made him faint and dizzy; he started to sweat and his knees buckled. Suddenly, the Captain was holding him upright as well as still.

"Not so talkative now, are you? You piece of crap."

The Pan closed his eyes. Thank The Prophet for General Moteurs' M.O., but even with the analgesics, the pain was intense. He was shaking now, and he could feel the sweat running down the side of his face.

"That's right. It hurts doesn't it?" said Captain Snow.

The Pan nodded.

"So. If you give me any more trouble, I'm going to make it hurt a lot more." He waited but The Pan said nothing. "Are we reading, douche bag?"

"Yeh, I heard you."

"Good."

"Are we ready?" asked Lord Vernon, off mike.

"Yes, sir," said Captain Snow, at the same moment as The Pan said, "No."

Lord Vernon turned back to the microphone.

"My faithful Hamgeean servant, it is with great pleasure that I bestow upon you these gifts; your freedom – your name has been removed from the blacklist – amnesty for one year while you adjust to your new life and..." he held out the parchment to The Pan, "a future; the deeds to this pub."

"Take the parchment and bow to the Lord Protector," said Captain Snow.

The Pan shuffled forward and snatched the parchment from Lord Vernon's hand.

"I thank you," he said, adding a muttered, "for nothing, and I will not bow."

He saw the anger flash briefly across Lord Vernon's face before it was replaced by the usual expression of superior smugness.

"There is no need to thank me. I am sure you will make an excellent barman." The gathered crowd clapped half-heartedly and, too quietly for the microphone to pick it up, Lord Vernon added, "If this rabble spares you," before turning back to the crowd again. "My K'Barthan subjects, I give you, The Pan of Hamgee.

He turned to The Pan, and waited.

Captain Snow shoved a card into The Pan's hands.

"Step up to the microphone and read what it says."

The Pan saw what was written.

"No."

Lord Vernon smiled for the benefit of the crowd but his anger was tangible. He put one hand over the microphone and leaned towards The Pan with an expression of murderous intent.

"Read it, or I will kill her."

"You think I care?"

"I know you do."

"I don't think so. I have some dignity."

"Are you certain? Perhaps you forget. I only need her alive until Saturday. Read the card, Hamgeean."

"No."

"I'll ask you politely one last time; read it, or I will return to the Palace forthwith and despatch Ruth in such a way that she will envy your sister the mercy I showed. I told you what I did to your sister. You remember, don't you?"

The Pan took a deep breath to control his anger and misery, and did as he was told.

"My fellow K'Barthans, I thank my good friend and mentor, a great and benign being, Lord Vernon," he read woodenly.

"There, that wasn't so difficult was it?"

"That's right, there's a good little Vermin," said Captain Snow squeezing The Pan's shoulder until he was almost sick with the pain.

Lord Vernon held his hands out sideways in a here-I-am gesture and bowed. The crowd was silent for a few moments but began to applaud as members of the Grongle army passed among them, crowd control sticks at the ready. Their applause gathered momentum but not conviction. The phony show of appreciation went on until Lord Vernon signalled for silence and the guards allowed it to stop. He stepped up to the microphone again.

"Thank you, thank you."

"Bow to the Lord Protector," said Captain Snow.

As Lord Vernon turned towards him, The Pan raised his head, straightened his back and stood tall. He fixed his eyes on the smoke black blankness of the sunglasses his nemesis was wearing, and tried to put on a show of dignified calm. Without letting go of The Pan's shoulder, Captain Snow pulled him backwards, moving him off the dais and away, to the side.

"He's finished, let go of me, Captain."

"Oh no, he isn't done yet. Stay where you are and keep your mouth shut or I'm going to show you a whole new world of pain."

There was a kerfuffle among the crowd as the GNN crew changed cameras. Lord Vernon waited until they had finished, beckoning them closer. Captain Snow pulled The Pan further backwards out of shot.

"Don't get above yourself. They filmed you for GNN Local but you're not *real* news."

"My K'Barthan children, today I am able to share some wonderful tidings. I know you are lost; waiting, hoping, searching for a Candidate to be your new Architrave, a being to lead you and love you like an indulgent father. It has always worried me that no such person has been found. However, today, I can inform you that your search is over. You have your Candidate. I am he."

There was a stunned silence, and then somebody at the back shouted; the beginnings of a word; 'bol—' followed by the unmistakable crack of a crowd control stick discharging, and a thump. There were a few more jeers and shouts and similar cracks as their originators were also silenced. Lord Vernon continued.

"I will be installed as Architrave and take the Chosen One as my bride at midday, on Saturday."

His words hit The Pan like a punch in the gut, even though he had anticipated it and steeled himself. They were engaged weren't they? They were bound to get married. The Pan felt Lord Vernon's eyes on him as the troops among the crowd of K'Barthans compelled them into even greater heights of ersatz zeal. But The Pan clenched his jaw and stared straight ahead. He would not show his despair.

"That is all, my children, I have pressing affairs of State to attend to. I regret that I must leave you."

More fake cheering.

Lord Vernon switched off the microphone and stepped off the dais, stopping in front of The Pan.

"How unusual, Hamgeean. I see you are lost for words," he said. "I wish you luck. I think you are going to need it."

"Why didn't you just cut my head off?"

"Where's the fun in that?"

Lord Vernon turned to raise his hand to the crowd in salute – and farewell – and strode away, towards the Interceptor. The cordon of Grongles divided, the majority of them escorting Lord Vernon through the crowd, down a path already cleared by the others. The Pan caught a glimpse of him driving away and some of the troops leaving in an armoured personnel carrier. The GNN crew filmed the Interceptor climbing into the sky before running for their van. A small detachment of Grongles remained, and Captain Snow.

Lord Vernon, gone; the crowd started a slow, sarcastic hand clap. Unseen voices jeered and booed. Looking out at the angry faces of his erstwhile neighbours and fellow punters at the Parrot, The Pan wanted his new life even less. Some of the Grongles formed a cordon around him and he watched the crowd miserably.

"I should talk to them," he shouted over the escalating noise.

"I don't think so."

The locals started screaming obscenities at The Pan, clearly intent on... well, if not murdering him, then at least inflicting some grievous bodily harm. Someone threw a bottle.

"He's started a riot," The Pan yelled above the sound of Turnadot Street's inhabitants, baying for his blood.

"That's right," said Captain Snow as the Interceptor disappeared into over the roofs, "But don't worry. I'm here to protect you. Boys, control these smeckers."

The troops started laying about them with their crowd control sticks.

"No! Stop! These are good people," yelled The Pan above the shouting of the Grongle's victims, the electronic cracking and fizzing of control sticks discharging, and the thumps of unconscious K'Barthans hitting the pavement.

"Yeh. Sure they are." The cordon of troops moved with Captain Snow as he dragged The Pan towards the Parrot and Screwdriver.

"They are, it's not their fault after that sham. They don't understand what's going on," shouted The Pan above the din. "I can stop this. Let me talk to them."

"No."

"Captain, don't hurt anyone—"

"Or what? You aren't the one giving the orders round here, Vermin." Captain Snow dragged him onwards.

"I'm not vermin anymore."

The Captain grabbed The Pan by the scruff of the neck and pulled him close so their noses were always touching. "You'll always be vermin to me, *Vermin*."

The Pan glared at him. "I'll file a complaint," he said. Arnold! Pathetic. What was he saying?

"You do that, you pointless little cleggnut. Lord Vernon might have pardoned you but everyone knows what you are." Another bottle flew over the heads of the cordon and smashed on the pavement, peppering The Pan's trousers with broken glass.

"If you'll protect me while I talk to them, I can stop this."

"Why would I want to do that?" asked Captain Snow. "Boys!" he shouted to his troops, "this piece of garbage is cramping my style. Control him and lock him in the pub, then we can teach this rabble of scum a proper lesson."

"No—" began The Pan; there was a crack, a burst of pain and everything went black.

Chapter 26

Lord Vernon looked up from yet another sheaf of tiresome state papers as one of the guards from outside his door ushered General Moteurs into his presence.

"Your most—" the General began.

"General Moteurs." He stood up and strode round the desk to greet him. "Come, let us drink a toast."

"Sir." The General followed him nervously out onto the balcony. Lord Vernon was delighted to see that his friendly greeting had unseated his deputy profoundly and that he was already sweating.

"Sit." Lord Vernon gestured to a chair as he sat down.

"Thank you, sir," said General Moteurs and did as he was asked.

"The Chosen One is mine and the Hamgeean will soon be no more. I find my thoughts turning to the Resistance. How is progress with your female?"

"It is going well enough," General Moteurs shifted uncomfortably in his seat.

"A little too feisty for you, General?"

General Moteurs did not react to Lord Vernon's joke.

"She is certainly strong willed, sir. However, there has been another development."

"Which is?"

"New intelligence: the rift I mentioned goes deeper than Lieutenant Arbuthnot and Denarghi."

'Lieutenant Arbuthnot'. Interesting, General Moteurs had used her name, as if he thought she was worth something. Perhaps he did. He'd better not. No, General Moteurs was an old-school hard liner, most likely he found the idea of relations with other species repulsive. However, he was also old-school-courteous to females, regardless of genus, in deference to the Grongolian Code of Honour. That was a section of the Code which Lord Vernon and many like him, saw fit to overlook.

"I sense you want to use it."

"Yes sir,"

"Explain."

"There is a faction within the Resistance that is at odds with the direction Denarghi has chosen. There is a danger the entire organisation will collapse into anarchy."

"How convenient. You think you can make them implode?"

"With a suitable incentive, sir."

"Fear?"

"Sir, substantiated by facts."

"Which facts?"

"Sir, if we give them information about the portal we have reverse engineered, we can—"

"General, I almost thought I heard you suggest we share our advantage with the enemy. I hope, for your sake, I did not."

"Sir," the General hesitated, choosing his words carefully. Lord Vernon could almost hear his elevated heartbeat. "It will put them under pressure."

"How, exactly?"

"It will crystallise the two factions."

"And you believe they will crack?"

"Sir."

"What of our plan to let them assassinate the High Leader?"

"Lieutenant Arbuthnot and Group Leader Snoofle will still kill him. My ruse merely leaves us with—"

"Fewer loose ends."

"Sir."

"How much information about the portal do you propose we share?"

"A portion of the schematics, sir."

"Why can we not share something a little less..." Lord Vernon waved one hand as he tried to pluck the appropriate word from the air, "sensitive?"

"This is the most appropriate trigger, sir."

Lord Vernon took off his sunglasses and his cold grey eyes met General Moteurs' red ones.

"Because...?"

"As you know, sir, Denarghi is a hard-liner but he is in command of the only viable source of opposition to us. Many of his staff share the same broad aim—"

"To expel us from K'Barth."

"Sir, but not the same philosophy."

"Go on."

"Their Head of Technical Operations, Professor N'Aversion is a moderate. He has openly disagreed with Denarghi on many occasions. If he were to receive information from a Grongle—"

"Denarghi's distrust of the source will outweigh his faith in the Professor's expertise."

"Sir."

"And you think this Professor will defy his leader to use it."

"Yes sir."

Lord Vernon thought.

"Why something so precious to us? Why not have them build a bomb and trigger it when they are done?"

"For two reasons, sir. First, Professor N'Aversion is highly intelligent. He would recognise any bomb we can construct at once. Second, because an explosion is less precise."

"Agreed," said Lord Vernon. "A bomb would be... untidy." It would allow people to disappear without actually being dead, the way Sir Robin Get had done.

"Who will leak the documents?"

"I will, sir. Through Lieutenant Arbuthnot and Group Leader Snoofle."

"Would these technicians rise up against their leader?"

"I believe so, sir."

And while they were busy fighting among themselves, thought Lord Vernon, he would walk in and lay them waste. Just like the first time, when the Grongles liberated K'Barth. That would be exquisite.

"These fools never learn."

"No, sir."

"How long will it take?"

"Three days at the outside."

"You are taking a risk, General."

"A calculated risk, sir. They will have a wealth of information that tells them nothing. However, the concept, alone, will precipitate action."

"It is an interesting idea, General. I agree in principle but let us make it a little more... certain. If their Technical department believe your female

140

and her Blurpon friend have turned you, we will suggest, to Denarghi, that you have turned them."

"As you wish, sir. I will see to it."

"Oh no, General, I will."

The General's hand went to his face in that tell-tale gesture of insecurity.

"If that is your will, sir." He sounded was that...? Yes, hesitant. Lord Vernon congratulated himself on precipitating another first.

"It is," he smiled, racking the General's tension levels up a couple more notches. "I will keep you informed."

"Sir."

"Excellent work, General."

"Sir."

"I trust you will deal with the other details."

"Yes, sir."

"Good. When you are done, you will show me what you have sent and I will contact Denarghi."

"Yes, sir."

Lord Vernon stood up and General Moteurs, appreciating that this signalled the end of the interview, followed suit.

"Dismissed."

Chapter 27

Deirdre felt a great deal better. Her limbs were aching less – although she still felt stiff – and she and Snoofle had finished another excellent breakfast, courtesy of the Imperial Guard. For good digestion's sake they left a little time before a routine of gentle stretches. Once again, Deirdre passed up Snoofle's offer of a sparring session, deciding that even a light one was a bad idea when her joints still felt as if they were made of damp newspaper. Instead, the two of them prepared to move onto something less energetic – knife throwing practise – while debating the compatibility, for recreational sparring, of Deirdre's speciality; Ka-Pa-Te with Snoofle's; Hoo-Flung-Yoo. Their conversation was disturbed by the rattling of bolts and jangling of keys that heralded someone opening the door. It was Corporal Jones but she didn't come into the room. Instead she waited in the doorway.

"Thank you, Corporal," said a familiar voice.

"Sir."

When General Moteurs passed her, the young Grongle officer snapped eagerly to attention.

"As you were, Jones," said the General casually. He stood, with his hands behind his back, facing Deirdre and Snoofle. He waited while his troops outside locked him in; still, calm, confident and completely relaxed. Deirdre watched him, examining his face. He had a strong jaw line, a straight nose and a determined set to the mouth. He would be a fine male, were he not a complete get – and worse, a Grongle – therefore rendering the idea of fineness, in any respect, impossible.

Deirdre eyed him haughtily, trying to hide all of her emotions bar the hatred. His red eyes met hers, unperturbed.

"You're very trusting, General," she said and her fingers hovered above the knife holster strapped to her thigh. He flashed her a wry smile.

"I confess, not so trusting, Lieutenant." He took a laser pistol from behind his back. Deirdre's hand went to her first knife.

"I can put all three of these into you before you have a chance to use that."

"Very possibly, but if you do I will no longer be here to protect you, and you will be returned to Captain Snow." He holstered the gun, one-handed, in a single fluid movement. He had kept his other hand behind his back but now he brought it round to his side to show them a document folder made from buff-coloured card. He held his hands out either side of him, folder and all. "Go ahead. Kill me if you wish," he said. Deirdre's fingers twitched but she did nothing. Beside her, Snoofle shifted uneasily.

"I suggest we sit," said General Moteurs. He walked over to the table and waited. With a glance at Deirdre, Snoofle did as he was ordered, taking a seat on the stool. Unwillingly, Deirdre followed suit, settling herself in one of the chairs. General Moteurs tossed the folder he had been carrying casually onto the table between them as he sat. "Please," he gestured to it. She opened it and slid out the papers from inside.

"Your hit list, Lieutenant."

Deirdre recognised the sheets in front of her as actual Resistance profiles. How had he got hold of those? He answered her question before she asked it.

"Your organisation is somewhat compromised. Have you never wondered why you make no real progress? A step forward, a step back...?"

"I thought that was a different issue," said Snoofle.

"Your leader?"

"No," Snoofle bristled defensively. He had probably meant the inter-departmental in-fighting which was the bane of any Resistance officer's existence, but Deirdre knew Denarghi's leadership style would have been in his thoughts. After all, it had been in hers.

"There are many factors—" she began but General Moteurs spoke over her.

"Understandable; you both have the intelligence to see through Denarghi. However, his merits, or conspicuous lack of them, are irrelevant here." The General hesitated and fixed Deirdre with a penetrating look. She returned it with defiance. "Tell me, Lieutenant, what is your strategy when you choose a target?" he asked.

"I listen to our operatives in the field. When a particular official is tormenting the people – or perhaps I should say, tormenting them more than even your Government deems necessary – my team and I neutralise them."

"That is all?"

"Usually."

"I see..." He glanced down at the sheaf of papers on the table. "Then, I must commend you on some excellent choices. They are not strictly my countryMEN, of course, since they are Grongles."

"What does it matter? They're all evil."

"In the cases of these particular individuals, I can only concur."

"And you would be in a position to judge their morality would you?"

"Meaning...?"

"Meaning that you murdered your own daughter."

The General's expression did not change.

"I executed her. There is a significant difference."

"Not the way we see it."

General Moteurs' eyes narrowed, "Naturally."

Deirdre glared at him, fully intending to take him on in a bout of stare-down but Snoofle tapped her on the arm.

"Deirdre this will not help us..." he said quietly.

"Snoofle would make a better Lieutenant than you, I think," said the General.

"Agreed." It hurt to admit it but Deirdre was honest enough with herself to accept her failings. "I am especially unsuited to espionage."

"That is an interesting admission, coming from you."

"I am full of surprises, General," she said waspishly.

"So it would appear. Let me explain your presence here."

"I would rather you explained yours first."

"As you wish. The two are one and the same." He looked down at his hands and she noticed he was wearing a wedding ring. He put his right hand to it and moved it round his finger for a few moments, as if for reassurance, before he spoke. "It may surprise you to hear this but you and I are aligned in pursuit of the same goal."

Deirdre snorted.

"I find that difficult to believe."

"And I also. Nonetheless, it is true. I will explain—"

"Please do," she interrupted acidly. The General took a breath to speak but, pointedly, waited a few seconds – presumably in case either of his prisoners decide to interrupt again – before he continued.

"The code of my species, of my nation, is a proud one; it speaks of honour, good behaviour, clean living, strength of morals and consistency in all things. It also speaks of fairness, considered action and equality. Under the eyes of our state we are still classed as equal, male and female, Grongles and other species and yet in reality—"

"You have no other species in Grongolia," Deirdre cut in.

"That is true—"

"And those who haven't fled here, to K'Barth, have been cleansed."

General Moteurs sat still and straight and looked her in the eye.

"Yes," he said. "I regret that you are correct; long before my time."

"Which makes you no less complicit."

"Agreed. Cleansing is limited to my fellow Grongles now; those whose opinions are perceived to differ with the State's."

"And I'm sure you've played your part," said Deirdre, not giving him any quarter.

"Yes. I am a member of the Imperial Guard. We leave certain tasks to our less principled colleagues; those in the security forces and the army. Even so, indirectly, through my inaction, I have."

"That's quite an admission," said Snoofle.

"No, it is merely a statement of fact. For that deed, alone, I will burn for eternity. I was condemned a thousand times before I executed my daughter. I have shamed my family name, brought dishonour on my ancestors and if I do not make amends they will burn in hell with me. I cannot allow that."

His words moved Deirdre. They contained the power of a statement spoken from the heart. But they couldn't possibly be genuine. This was espionage, she reminded herself, and he was good at it. This had to be a ruse and it annoyed her that she was falling for it. She glanced at Snoofle. He showed no reaction but she suspected he was as affected by the General's words as she was.

"That's all this is? Family honour?" she asked.

"Deirdre…" Snoofle kicked her under the table. General Moteurs got up suddenly, standing straight, tall and imposing, very imposing. Deirdre fixed him with, what she hoped, was a look of fearless disdain.

"General?"

"Perhaps my sense of family honour woke the rest of my morals but no. This is about right and wrong, good and evil, who I am, who we are. What I have done, or not done, in the High Leader's name, sickens me." He was calm and still but the strength of his emotions was audible in his voice. "Our regime is a perversion of who and what we are, a travesty of our principles, our teachings... everything. It dishonours my species and my nation. By my complicity, I supported it, when my daughter, and then my wife, who were more courageous and principled than I, did not. I swore an oath to both of them that I would bring down the High Leader and I intend to keep my word. He will fall, and Lord Vernon with him, this Saturday."

Such an impossible dream but outlined with such conviction that it sounded almost achievable. Again, Deirdre reminded herself that General Moteurs was in espionage. He was playing her and Snoofle, he had to be.

"What you have just said, that's—" Snoofle began.

"Treason, I believe," said the General, suavely. He had collected himself remarkably quickly. "Yes. Perhaps now I have given you a hold over me, you will trust my intent."

"It doesn't change anything. If we betray you we will still be back in the custody of Captain Snow," said Deirdre.

"Unless Lord Vernon is grateful, in which case it is I who will be consigned to the Captain's care."

"He will not believe non-Grongles."

"On the contrary, he is no respecter of species when he is searching for the truth. It is one of his greatest strengths."

"You say that as if you admire him."

"In many respects, I do."

"That says a lot about you. We are not stupid, General, you are spinning us a line. Do you expect us to betray our brothers and sisters in the cause so easily?"

"No. I think it would be very hard for you. That is why I do not expect it and will not ask it. Furthermore, to prove my intent, I will give you a gesture of my goodwill. I have information which your organisation requires if it is to survive. I will give you this, to pass on to whomever you see fit."

"That's very generous of you," said Snoofle drily.

"I suggest your colleagues act swiftly since you are at our mercy. The location of your HQ is known to us and my Master would have ordered your destruction before now had I not counselled against it."

"If what you say is true, I thank you for staying his hand," said Deirdre coolly. "However, if there are traitors in our midst, the only thing that will save us is if you give me their names."

"I cannot give you names for there has been no tacit betrayal. I know this sounds impossible so I have arranged a demonstration to help you understand. You will stay seated, please."

General Moteurs went to the door and knocked. After a brief hiatus, unseen hands, presumably Corporal Jones', gave him a metal box, about the size of four house bricks stacked in pairs. It had wires hanging out of it. He carried it over to the table and put it down.

"This is a portal, engineered by my scientists from an original K'Barthan artefact. Currently it is fixed to a small number of our vehicles. However, my team are confident that in a few months it will be portable and issued to every officer in the Grongolian army. We will be able to transport troops and equipment anywhere, in seconds, in perfect safety. Every move will be instant; undetectable until the moment it occurs. Every attack will come as a surprise. You appreciate the gravity of this, I think."

"Understood."

Deirdre didn't dare look at Snoofle. She tried to compose her features into an expressionless mask but it was difficult confronted with an idea of such magnitude. The Grongles were close to indomitable already. This was invincibility: world domination, forever.

"This technology is based on K'Barthan science; old science. Our portal is only accurate to a distance of a few yards, which is perfectly adequate for moving troops in the field. However, for the purposes of an indoor demonstration I require something more sophisticated. Hence I have brought the K'Barthan version," he put his hand in his pocket and removed a gold thimble, which he held up in front of them. "This is a true portal. It functions on a quantum physical premise that is beyond my understanding, indeed it is different from anything my scientists have encountered before. It is powered by the thoughts of the user." He handed it to Deirdre. "Think about your leader, Lieutenant, and look into the open end."

Deirdre pictured Denarghi in her mind's eye and did as the General had ordered. Inside the thimble, she saw a tiny image of him. He was standing on his desk, and though there was no sound, she could tell he was shouting. This was real, alright. She could feel her composure slipping away and fought to keep her voice steady when she said, "Snoofle..." and handed it to her friend.

Snoofle put the thimble to his eye for a few moments and then slowly placed it on the table. His features were composed but even under the red fur, she could see he had gone white.

General Moteurs stood watching implacably. He had them in the palm of his hand, and though he was behaving more graciously than Deirdre would have expected, there was a confidence about him that showed he was aware of it.

"This is your surveillance?" she asked just to check.

"It is."

"How do we know it's real? You could be tricking us into this," said Deirdre with more hope than conviction.

"Yes, I could." He picked it up, "so let me prove conclusively that I am not." He held up the thimble so they could see what he was doing and curled his thumb over the edge. There was a loud sucking sound followed by a pop and he disappeared. He reappeared a few seconds later, slightly off balance, the other side of the room. "I have yet to master the art of moving from one place to another smoothly," he said.

"Smeck," whispered Snoofle as General Moteurs strolled casually back to the table.

"Agreed," muttered Deirdre.

"Now you understand why I can give you no names, since nobody in your Headquarters is spying for us. We have merely watched and listened using this – and others like it."

"There are others?"

"Five in all, counting this one."

"If they are K'Barthan, why do we not know of them?"

"You do. The 'secret' powers of the Nimmist elders? These portals are one of them. My superiors in the Underground gave me four and this, the last, was recovered, a few days ago, from The Pan of Hamgee."

"Big Merv's getaway driver?" asked Snoofle.

"The same. How else would he and his Master escape from your custody? He concealed it in his boot."

Oh no.

"Then it is my fault," whispered Deirdre, "I should have found it."

General Moteurs expression gave little away but his voice was surprisingly gentle when he spoke again.

"If I understand your operating procedures correctly, you are not solely to blame. What happened, Lieutenant?" asked General Moteurs.

"He was angry that neither I, nor my troops had searched them properly. I had just returned from a difficult mission, we succeeded but it was a trap, I nearly lost one of my team, there was a hard and bitter fight and we were exhausted. Denarghi met us as we arrived. I thought he was going to commend us on a difficult job well done. Instead, he berated me for being late and ordered us to bring the Mervinettes in. I refused to use my troops on the grounds that they had not slept for 36 hours and were spent. So, he let them go and sent me, alone, with a detachment of regulars. They were poorly trained imbeciles—"

"A punishment for your intransigence in attending to the needs of your unit before your Leader's," said the General. His voice was hard, he almost sounded angry.

"Maybe but I was the bigger fool, for I took out my bad humour on the troops I was given. I did not treat them well. There was... a misunderstanding between Denarghi and I as to whether he had signed for the prisoners when they made off. If he had, they were his responsibility. If he had not then, officially, though they were in his custody by then, they were mine. I am certain he signed, but he denies it and there is no paperwork."

"Paper is not so difficult to destroy," said General Moteurs.

"True," said Snoofle, "and his troops should have searched them again. If they didn't find anything either, the responsibility is shared. Those are the rules."

"I enquired. As I understand it, Denarghi's troops did not search the prisoners."

General Moteurs put his hands on his hips and his shoulders seemed to droop a fraction.

"I assume you voiced your concerns."

"Yes, and he sent me here."

"Naturally. He would not want anyone realising he was as culpable as you. Furthermore, if you challenged his authority you would have posed a very real threat. He would be forced to have you killed, and you are too useful to him for that. His answer was to give you time to forget, to send you here—"

"And let Lord Vernon kill her for him," said Snoofle bitterly.

"He would not have anticipated that," said General Moteurs.

"He didn't do much about it, though, did he?"

"No."

The three of them sat in silence for a moment.

"If he knows this information comes from me will he act upon it?" asked General Moteurs.

"What do you think?" said Deirdre.

"That he will not."

"In one," said Snoofle.

General Moteurs heaved a sigh. He ran his hand over his short spiky hair, down to the back of his neck, and massaged it for a moment.

"This presents a difficulty. Yet we must act. If my plan fails and Lord Vernon becomes Architrave, he will show the Resistance no mercy. If it is to survive, it must have this knowledge. But I confess, I now question whether I should entrust it to your leader." He looked down at the thimble in his hand for a moment and from one to the other of them. "The time for games is over. I am under orders, from my superiors in the Underground, to share the plans for our portal with your HQ, but I must know who to trust or I will be responsible for your organisation's destruction."

"I thought that's what you wanted," said Deirdre.

"Lord Vernon. Not me. You must tell me. Who can we trust?"

'We'.

"They're all in Denarghi's pocket," said Deirdre.

"Not all. One is definitely his own master," said Snoofle.

She was pretty sure who he meant but not quite sure enough.

"General, Snoofle and I must discuss this alone," she said.

"Understood. You have five minutes." She was surprised at how easily he had agreed. "Although," he added, "I regret that I must relieve Group Leader Snoofle of his phone for the duration. I will bring it back."

Wordlessly, Snoofle, held it out.

"Thank you." General Moteurs took the mobile from his hand. "Group Leader, Lieutenant, never fear. We can save your colleagues. We may even save the world. All you have to do is believe. I will not ask you to betray your brothers and sisters in the cause, merely to carry out the mission they have given you in a manner which suits us all."

"How very simple you make it sound," said Deirdre.

"Because it is, I think."

He walked to the door and knocked. With a rattling of chains, Corporal Jones unlocked and opened it for him.

"At ease Corporal," he saluted.

"Sir."

As he was about to leave, the General turned and looked back at Deirdre.

"Thank you," he said.

He was seriously good at espionage. The way he'd said that, she could almost believe it came from the heart.

"Lieutenant, Group Leader, I will return in five minutes."

Corporal Jones saluted at her prisoners, and then followed her commander, locking the door behind her.

"We may even save the world?" Snoofle laughed humourlessly. "He makes it sound so easy, doesn't he?"

"Agreed."

"And I'd really, really like to believe him, but something tells me I can't."

Chapter 28

"Blargh..." said The Pan and stirred.

"Get up!"

"What's he doing?"

"Lying on the floor, the great oaf."

"By The Prophet he really is useless."

"WAKE UP!"

The Pan was aware of something cool against his cheek; the flagged floor of the main bar at the Parrot and Screwdriver. For a few disorientated moments, he forgot why he was there; thought that he'd overdone Gladys' home-brewed beer and that the old lady herself would be down in a moment to tell him to get his lazy, good-for-nothing, drunkard's bottom off her nice clean flagstones. Then he remembered. He sat up and a wall of noise hit him. The tinnitus had turned into voices, the way it had when Lord Vernon had injected him with that red stuff. Despite being set and put in a brace, his shoulder was aching and the shouting in his head made it worse. He looked at his watch; it was morning. So this would be... what? Tuesday? No. Monday. Lord Vernon would be Architrave in five days.

"What sort of time do you call this young man?"

"What's he doing?"

"I don't know. Lying there."

"No, he's sitting up."

"Is he?"

"Yes."

"Get out of the way will you? I can't see."

"Don't push."

"Shut up," said The Pan.

"Cluck."

"Listen, chicken, can you tell your mates to keep it down a bit." He got wearily to his feet.

"Where's he going now?"

"I don't know do I? Watch and see what happens."

"But why isn't he going to find Lord Vernon and face him down?"

"Because I would prefer to..." The Pan began and stopped. He'd been going to say 'live' but he wasn't sure it was true any more.

Rubbing his aching head, he got unsteadily to his feet, and went and helped himself to a glass of water from the sink in the Holy of Holies, as Gladys and Ada called the kitchen area behind the bar. Then he made his way over to the front windows, in the main bar, and peeped through the closed curtains. The street outside was empty. Everyone was hiding indoors; a Grongle armoured personnel carrier rumbled past, alright almost everyone. The aftermath of a riot was obvious everywhere: broken bottles, overturned dustbins, smashed street furniture, a burned-out shop, bloodied clothing, a pile of charred wood, mostly comprising the remains of the Parrot's wooden outdoor tables and chairs. That would take a lot of clearing up – he let the curtain drop and turned his attention to the chaos inside – yeh, and so would this.

He walked back over to the bar. Four days until the end of everything in K'Barth, four days until Lord Vernon married Ruth. He was overwhelmed with the familiar sense of desolation. He put his good arm across the bar, rested his head on the polished wood and wept; great shuddering sobs, as if he was crying out his soul.

"Maybe I should just kill myself."

"In the name of The Prophet! You blithering idiot."

"Smecking Arnold. When's this stuff going to wear off?"

"It has you fool."

"I don't think so." Was he going to have to listen to the pretend Architraves rowing with each other for the rest of his days? "Please no," he said.

"I heard that," said someone.

"You were meant to. Help me, chicken," said The Pan. "Please, tell them, in the name of Arnold's snot to give it a rest."

"Must you blaspheme like that?"

"Yes," said The Pan belligerently. He stood up, walked out from behind the bar and stood in the centre of the room. If he did kill himself, how would he do it, he wondered. He lacked the courage to end his life directly. Mmm, but there must be a few indirect methods. He could bate some Grongles and be beaten to death or go to one of the dodgier parts of the city and get himself mugged to death. There were a thousand and one ways to end it all if he put his mind to it. Although he'd have to make sure they did it properly. If he was going to try and get himself murdered he didn't want to be maimed or put in hospital; he wanted to be put in a box. He supposed the best chance would be at night when everyone was drunk, but even then it wasn't very reliable. Or he could rob a bank and let it all go wrong. No. Knowing his luck he'd get away with it. Anyway, he'd had enough of robbing banks to last a life time. His thoughts scared him a little. He didn't really want to kill himself did he? No, he just longed for oblivion.

"Now, now, let's not get maudlin," said someone.

"For the last time, will you shut up!" said The Pan. He rubbed his eyes. What next? He glanced at his watch: one achingly boring, lonely, miserable day. He took in the chaos around him. "The state of this place." This was the nearest thing he had to a home and the way the Grongles had vandalised it made him angry. Gladys and Ada wouldn't have liked it either, which gave him an idea. Yes. He would tidy their pub. Leave it ship-shape the way they would have liked. Tidy up, sweep up, wash up and put everything away and then he would have some cheese on toast and... his thoughts reverted to getting himself killed. No. He would have enough time to think about the future when he'd tidied the pub. Good. That was settled, then. Suddenly, he felt better. He was a man with a purpose and with resolve. He had things to do.

"Yeh," he said, "time to make a start."

Chapter 29

General Moteurs was as good as his word. He returned five minutes later – to the second – and handed Snoofle his phone.

"You have conferred?" he asked as he placed a second buff coloured folder on the table.

"Yes," Deirdre said.

"And...?"

"We must send this to Tech Ops, direct."

"An excellent choice."

"Why?" Deirdre was on her guard at once.

"Professor N'Aversion is one of ours."

"What?" she felt shaky.

"He would never betray us," said Snoofle.

"I may be a Grongle but I am a Commander of the K'Barthan Underground. The Professor is 'ours', in that his ideals are aligned with the organisation I command, and he is honest, and true to them."

"What about you?"

"My actions will answer that," said General Moteurs. "I know this is hard for you and I thank you for your assistance. It pains me to be so heavy-handed but I have not the time to earn your trust and I cannot afford to give you a choice. Be assured I am grateful, all the same."

"Then, you won't mind showing your gratitude, will you?" she said. Arnold! That hadn't come out the way she had meant. General Moteurs seemed surprised at first and then she saw he was laughing at her, the get. Their eyes met. His: expectant, and amused. Hers: angry.

"And how would you like me to do that?" Without breaking eye contact, he walked slowly towards her. Deirdre stood her ground but as he approached, her skin prickled and her pulse quickened alarmingly. He stopped close in front of her: a tiny bit too close. She could feel his body heat and the tension crackling between them and she met those red eyes with a look of angry disdain; and then she caught a hint of his after shave. It triggered a sudden, unwanted flashback to the moment he had carried her; she felt the enveloping strength of his arms; the soft shirt, the warm skin, the sense of safety: relived it with an intensity that almost made her legs buckle. And she wanted— She gasped.

No.

She smecking well did not.

Arnold's snot. Where had that come from? If he sensed her emotional disarray, he made no sign. Instead he waited, his face a picture of polite enquiry.

"Well, Lieutenant?" he asked her. The red eyes looked calmly into hers, intelligent, unfazed and giving nothing away. She stared back, her soldierly *sang froid* unravelling under his penetrating gaze, desperately trying to remain aloof.

Snoofle cleared his throat and General Moteurs turned towards him, stepping backwards out of her personal space. Phew. Her friend was cleaning his whiskers nonchalantly and following his cue, but lacking any whiskers of her own, Deirdre flicked her long blonde hair, which she was wearing down, back over her shoulder. It was a gesture guaranteed to unman most males but General Moteurs gave it nothing more than a dismissive glance.

"What the Lieutenant might have been going to suggest, was that you share your plan of action with us," Snoofle said. "We are working blind and it's... difficult."

"That information would be useful," Deirdre agreed, "but my intended suggestion was that, if you are genuine, you will back up your words with action and give the Professor the K'Barthan portal," she gestured to the thimble.

"Group Leader, I cannot reveal my plans because they are dependent on the changing world of politics and on the whims of others. Accordingly, the details change from day to day, sometimes hour to hour. Lieutenant, all five thimbles are the personal property of Lord Vernon and he may want this one back at any time. If I lose it, he will have me executed."

"Does he realise what you're doing with it?" said Snoofle.

"I could not say, I would assume so, in light of my liaison with you," said General Moteurs as if it was the most natural thing in the world.

"He knows about us?" asked Deirdre, failing to mask her horror.

"Of course, you would not be here unless he believed you would serve him better working with me."

"But—"

"He is a being of great intelligence and power. I am no match. I am transparent to him. I must tell him the truth for if I do not, he will know it as surely as I breathe. However, he trusts my motives, believes that I am loyal to him and that, no matter what I say to others, I work to achieve his will. I update him on my progress in all my endeavours, including this one."

"What does he think you are trying to achieve?"

"Supreme power, for him, both here and in Grongolia. Certainly, if my plans go awry, that is what he will have."

"That is one hell of a gamble," said Snoofle.

"Agreed."

Deirdre could hardly speak.

"You are asking us to take a risk like this, blind?"

"You will not be blind, I am here to lead you. All you have to do is trust me."

Snoofle whistled.

"Deirdre has a point. It's a big ask."

"If I were a different species, perhaps it would be easier," said the General coldly.

To her embarrassment, Deirdre realised that yes, it would; for her part anyway. She glanced at Snoofle. He adjusted his whiskers again. Perhaps it was the same for him, too.

"As I thought," said General Moteurs. His voice was calm and level but Deirdre imagined she could detect some tension.

"It's difficult. Your species has shown us nothing but hostility—" she began with more heat than she'd intended.

"Naturally, and you K'Barthans? What have you shown us?" he asked. His manner was easy enough, but now, Deirdre was certain, underneath that smooth exterior, General Moteurs was riled.

"You invaded our nation, you are the ones subjugating us, you are the ones who want to cleanse the planet of everything non-Grongle."

"Not all of us: some. Of whom I am ashamed. Have some members of the Resistance not sworn an oath to cleanse the world of my species?"

Deirdre glowered at him. He meant her; she knew it.

"That's different," she said defensively. "You started it."

"You debate this like a child complaining to a teacher. What matters is that it must end, and to achieve that, one side must take the first step. I am here. Your move."

He won the game of stare-down. Deirdre turned her head away.

"We are sworn enemies, General—" Snoofle began.

"And I have much to prove?"

Snoofle hesitated, "Yes."

For a few seconds, General Moteurs was thoughtful.

"Understood," he said finally. "Perhaps one day you will learn to judge me by who I am instead of what I am."

"Perhaps if you were less of a smecker it would be easier," muttered Deirdre.

The General sighed wearily.

"Noted, Lieutenant. Though, were I The Prophet himself, you would paint me no different. Please accept my apologies for what I am." He bowed.

"I meant who *you* are, not your species," said Deirdre.

"I'm sure you did, Lieutenant." The irony was unmistakable this time. "I humbly suggest you reserve judgement until you do."

"I've seen enough to tell," snapped Deirdre.

"Then you will know that, if you have my word, you can trust me. If you are loyal to me, I will be loyal to you. I do not abandon those I have sent into danger. You will not hear me ask you to 'take one for the team'."

When Deirdre looked at Snoofle he was wearing a resigned expression.

"We have been tapping your phone, and Sid's, since the day they were purchased, Group Leader. We know mobiles fall into K'Barthan hands. Suspect accounts are flagged and monitored."

"But the mobile system is secure, that's—"

General Moteurs laughed derisively.

"So we would have the natives believe," Deirdre bridled at his use of the word 'natives' but Snoofle took it with equanimity, "I expected more from you, Group Leader. Every handset is equipped with an embedded surveillance application. Monitoring is a simple case of activating it. We can do that remotely. Your colleagues registered both phones in the name of a couple who had returned to Grongolia three days previously. Sloppy of them, I think, not to check the facts."

"Not necessarily," said Deirdre wading in, "to put the different pieces of information together, two of your government departments must talk to one another and join the dots. That would be a miracle."

"I concede it would, but they do not need to communicate, Lieutenant, they merely provide certain information to the Imperial Guard. We join the dots." General Moteurs paused for a moment to let the idea sink in before addressing Snoofle. "Group Leader, you have agreed that we will work together, yes?"

"Yes."

"And you have not changed your mind?"

"No."

He turned to Deirdre.

"And you?"

"I have no choice."

"She means yes," said Snoofle.

"Good. Then, I suggest you photograph these schematics." He placed the buff-coloured folder he was carrying on the table. "And then we will make a film for Professor N'Aversion."

Chapter 30

High up in the walls of the Old Palace, the draught played about the bars of a tiny window before being sucked helplessly into the room behind and down to the sub-aqueous gloom of the floor 15 feet below. As well as a selection of interesting smells, some more wholesome than others, it bore an almost bald parrot which, by some avionic wonder, was still able to fly. Screeching with delight, he flew down towards the old ladies below.

****

"Wipe my conkers!"

"Wossat!" Gladys woke with a start.

"Air biscuits!"

"Oh Humbert dear!" trilled Ada. "I've been so worried about you."

"Humph," said Gladys, but in truth after two days stuck in a dingy cell that was very much taller than it was wide or long, she was happy with anything that changed the scenery – even if it was Humbert in a confined space. It could be worse. These were the old cells, and while they were draughty and small there was, at least, a window. Rumour had it that the Grongles had dug down underground and built new ones, places of dark dread. Gladys was glad she and Ada hadn't ended up there. That was the great thing about being old, of course. Nobody can believe you're dangerous.

The two old ladies were sitting opposite one another on a pair of rough wooden palliasses which their Grongolian gaolers imaginatively referred to as beds. It was cold and boring and for the moment they'd had to suspend their discussion about escape plans. It was slopping out time and someone might be listening. Both old ladies sat dozing quietly. Soon the Grongle gaolers would be round to empty the slop bucket and serve the turgid fare they euphemistically called breakfast – although it tasted so vile that Gladys wondered, privately, if some of the former might get into the latter from time to time. After this, the Grongles would usually retire to a room at the end of the corridor and slam the door. They called this 'work' but both Gladys and Ada suspected that what they actually did was surf for internet porn on the computer in there and play cards. Certainly, there was no danger of anyone coming near the cells until the evening round of slop bucket emptying and food serving. It struck Gladys that the prisoners could probably go A.W.O.L. for the whole day without anyone noticing so long as they were in position for slopping out, each end of it.

Not long now and she and Ada could continue their discussion about escape plans.

Humbert, who was actually Escape Plan B, subsection 3i, settled on Ada's shoulder and dropped something into her lap.

"Polish my buttons!" he squawked.

"Bless me!" exclaimed Ada holding something up. Something large, metallic and covered in parrot slubber. Gladys leaned over to see.

"Is that what I thinks it is?"

"Not quite," said Ada. Holding up a large spoon.

Gladys frowned.

"It's a start."

"Yer."

"Bombs away!" shouted Humbert.

"Over there dear," said Ada pointing to the slop bucket. Gladys was impressed when Humbert obligingly did as he was told; flying over to the bucket and sitting on the edge of it. He sat the wrong way round, unfortunately, but Gladys reflected, you can't have everything and with a bit of effort, maybe Escape Plan B, subsection 3i might just work.

Humbert flew back to the old ladies and landed on Ada's bed.

"Tasty sprinkles!" he shouted, jumping up and down on the mattress and snapping up the bugs that leapt out.

Ada clapped her hands together, her eyes dancing with glee.

"Oh well done Humbert! Don't forget Aunty Gladys. She has sprinkles in her mattress too."

Gladys gave her friend, and Humbert, a nod of thanks. Fewer bites tonight would make things a bit less itchy tomorrow.

"'S, time fer slop and porridge I reckons," she said.

"I'd say they're due any minute now."

Bang on cue, there was a loud rattling and banging at the door, which startled Humbert, making him squawk loudly.

"Quick Humbert! Shoo!" said Ada but the noise had already frightened the parrot away. He took off with remarkable speed and as he left the way he had come, Ada quickly wiped the spoon on her dress and stuffed it into her cleavage. She hid most things under a certain size in her brassier, on the grounds that no gentleman would look there. A surly Grongle gaoler arrived with a thin grey fluid with lumps of gristle floating in it. It tasted vile but of course, it was supposed to. Gladys and Ada always ate it with gusto, sometimes asking for more, just to annoy their gaolers.

"Good morning young man," Ada trilled to the thug with the bowls. "And good morning to you too," she added to a second one who was holding the door open. He half-grunted, half-snarled in reply. Ada giggled. "Ooo you're such a charmer!" she said. That was another thing the old ladies enjoyed doing to their gaolers; being polite. The Grongles clearly didn't like it, which merely encouraged Gladys and Ada to even greater heights of courtesy.

"Less of your lip you old baggage or I'll show you the back of my hand," growled the Grongle in the doorway.

"Oh! Do you have a nice tattoo or something?" asked Ada, all innocence.

"Shaddup," said the one with the bowls. "He means he'll thump you, and if he don't I will." He wouldn't, of course, because he hadn't yet, and for that reason alone, Gladys and Ada suspected that he was under orders not to. "What are you old harridans up to?" he continued, "I heard noises."

"We were just doing our parrot impressions, dear. We used to be parrot impressionists, a music hall act, before you and your brethren closed them down."

"I wouldn't pay to listen to that."

"Of course not, you're not K'Barthan. But we have a rich history of bird impersonators," said Ada.

Gladys hoped Ada would remember all this cobblers she was telling them, and gave the guard her most guileless smile, the one which made people think she was slightly dotty, before changing the subject.

"Ooo you has brought us our lovely stew. You is too kind."

The gaoler dumped the stew on the floor and some of it slopped onto the stone flags.

"One of you old bats needs to empty the bucket," he said.

"Yer, I is sorry, I always forgets unless you reminds me," said Gladys mock-meekly. She went and picked up the bucket and did as she was ordered. She used her most doddery walk because it made the slop slop around in the bucket and she could sense how afraid he was that she'd spill some on his nice clean boots. Once she had finished the guard shoved her back into the room and slammed the door.

"Thank you kindly," Ada called after them.

The two old ladies listened to the grumblings of the guards, the squeaking of the trolley wheels and the slamming of doors as the slop and breakfast wagon receded down the corridor. After a minute or two Gladys gave a satisfied 'humph'.

"You reckons that parrot is going to remember?"

Many years ago, Humbert had been trained to fetch. Unfortunately, some time had passed and it was clear he didn't wholly recall *all* of his training.

"Of course," said Ada, as Humbert returned.

"Can't say as I shares your opti- opti- hopeful view."

"It'll be fine, dear," said Ada. "Now then Humbert dear, you need to get the key."

She drew it in the air with her finger.

"Pieces of eight."

"No dear. Key."

"Spoonful of honey," sang Humbert, sort of.

"No. Not a spoon, dear," said Ada. "A key."

"*The* key," added Gladys. "We needs to unlock that door."

She pointed.

"Spoon."

"Nearly, dear."

"Spoon," said Gladys.

"Key," said Humbert.

"Well done! Key," exclaimed Ada.

"Spoon," said Humbert.

"Humph," said Gladys. She suspected this was going to take a long time. Best let Ada get on with it, then. She sat back against the wall and rested her eyes.

163

Chapter 31

Professor N'Aversion had not slept well. Indeed, he had not slept at all. On Sunday evening, the news had broken that Lord Vernon was the Candidate. Debates as to whether this could possibly be true had ensued, followed by an emergency strategy meeting. Apparently, Lord Vernon had attended a ceremony to bestow a pub in Ning Dang Po on a 'close personal friend'. That had to be a set-up for starters, Professor N'Aversion couldn't imagine anyone getting close or personal with the Lord Protector, and in light of the Grongle line on alcohol, definitely not a publican. On this rare occasion, Denarghi, as well as the other department heads, agreed with him. Short of that single throw-away mention, neither the pub nor the 'close personal friend' had cropped up again. When there was nothing on Radio Free K'Barth it was dismissed as a human-interest detail; an imaginative piece of ornamentation to add flesh to the story.

As the night wore on, the Professor's spirits flagged. Denarghi returned to form: sifting the facts, picking the ones that would make up the most convenient party line and discarding the others as 'untruths'. The Professor could not make him see that half the facts would only give him half the picture. Once 'the truth' was decided, Denarghi went on to blamestorming. The Resistance's Candidate, Lieutenant Arbuthnot, was in the Palace with no known way out for three months and no matter how cogently the Professor argued the contrary, he believed she might be compromised, anyway. Obviously this had to be someone else's fault because clearly it couldn't be Denarghi's. The Professor tried to put a more positive spin on it by suggesting the old Palace wouldn't be so secure. It had been the seat of Government for over 2,000 years, he reasoned, and no self respecting leader, not even an Architrave, would want to run K'Barth trapped in a corner. Colonel Melior in Information Retrieval was to research any possible methods of entry and Colonel Plumby's people, both in and outside, were supposed to look for them. The Professor made a mental note that he must check the database and see if there was anything there that he could pass to Melior or Plumby.

He returned to his quarters, washed, changed and made himself presentable. Then after a brief word with Nar, who had been running his department like clockwork without any input from him, he went to the mess hall. He persuaded the fierce but kindly lady at the counter to open a can of the Resistance's precious supplies of spam and make him some spam fritters, fried with a couple of the Resistance's strained supply of eggs, and he sat at the table, enjoying them. Mrs Burgess, who ran the catering section, did her best but food was scarce. There is only so much you can do with a ready supply of baked beans and boiled cabbage, the Professor reflected. Everything else appeared in fits and starts and was eked out for as long as possible. Things were good now, there was a steady, if small, supply of milk and eggs. And Lieutenant Arbuthnot hadn't used *all* the custard powder when she'd blown up the Minister for the Interior. It had sat unused, in the twilight zone between food supplies and ordnance until the previous week, when two of the catering assistants had robbed a sugar lorry. Since then, the Professor had been almost enjoying some of the kitchen's imaginative creations. He'd been especially impressed by the crystallised cabbage pudding Mrs Burgess had dreamt up, with custard, the previous day. And he'd told her so. Perhaps the assistant at the counter knew. Maybe that was why she was ready to make him a fry up.

It was a deliberate decision. The Professor knew his mind required downtime but it was hard to switch off. The simple task of eating a meal, appreciating the food and trying to think of nothing else, would distract it for a while. Indeed he had relished the challenge of persuading the mess hall staff to make him a fry up after the hour when breakfast was officially served. Although it wasn't so much of a challenge. The Professor believed it did no harm to be decent to everyone, and once he'd been somewhere long enough this strategy tended to result in his getting the small things he wanted without having to ask. The supposedly 'difficult' mess hall staff were no exception this morning. It helped that they were mostly ladies of a certain age who enjoyed a little flirtatious banter with a Thing of advancing years. The Professor had been a bit of a Lothario as a youngster, and while his carousing days were mostly over, he could still turn on the charm.

He sighed with satisfaction as he mopped the final traces of egg yolk and fried tomato juice off his plate with the remaining mouthful of toast. It had only taken 20 minutes but this mental holiday had left him greatly refreshed. Yes, on a full stomach the Professor was ready for anything. Not that things could get much worse. Not only was Lord Vernon going to be installed Architrave on Saturday but one of the unknown women on the intake list Nar had procured, Ruth Cochrane, was the Chosen One, no less, and she and Lord Vernon were engaged.

"Well," muttered the Professor, "he is a good looking devil." But surely, even the most vacuous female could see beyond that, even if he was a very good actor. The Professor scratched his head and sighed.

His mood was broken abruptly by his phone. It vibrated across the Formica tabletop in front of him like a bumble bee with wind. As the sound reverberated through the hall, the only other occupants, a couple of Galorshes and a Blaggysomp who were sitting at the far end, nursing hot drinks, looked up suddenly.

"Sorry, it's a message," he explained.

They nodded their OKs but the Professor still flushed. He consulted the screen. He had a text on the secure system, number withheld, as protocol dictated.

"Open this alone."

Nothing else, just a video message.

Excellent. It would be from Simon. Maybe he'd got the parts and was on his way home. The Professor stood up, put on his lab coat, which he'd draped over the back of his chair and slipped the phone into his pocket. Remembering to hand his plate back into the hatch and thank the staff for their kindness, he headed back to his office. He thought to ring his second in command but decided against. It would be only polite to watch the video attachment first. Once back in his office, he sat at his desk and got comfortable, pen poised to make notes, and pulled up the text. It was only when he opened the video message that he realised it was not from Simon.

"Snoofle! How marvellous to hear from you!" he exclaimed in surprise before he remembered that this was a pre-recorded video.

"Professor, I hope this finds you well. Please put your headphones on." The Professor quickly jabbed the pause icon on the screen. Arnold! Where were the headphones? He scrabbled about in his drawers, the shelves, even behind the small sofa squeezed in between the wall and the workbench, which he sat on to read. No headphones were to be found. By The Prophet's socks. He ran out into the workshop. It was deserted. Everyone had gone for their statutory 15 minute break under the Resistance's employment rules – not that the Resistance employed them, exactly, they being freedom fighters or at least in this case, freedom technicians 'donating' their energies to the cause in return for free bed and board. He immediately found a pair on a nearby workbench and bustled back into his office only to find they didn't fit the headphone jack on his phone. Another trip to the Workshop, with the phone this time, and he found a set that fitted, left a post it note on the desk explaining where they were and retired to his office, locking the door.

Breathlessly, he sat down in his desk chair and pressed play. The tinny voice of Snoofle spoke into his ears.

"Are you sitting comfortably? Headphones on? Then, if you're ready for a few bombshells, I'll begin."

"Here's the first one; the Underground exists. I know you always thought it did," well yes, of course the Professor had. It was the Underground he'd wanted to join. It was only after they'd blindfolded him and brought him to meet Denarghi that he realised he'd been recruited by the wrong organisation. By that time, of course, he had no choice. He wondered if Snoofle had guessed as much, the video continued, "Bombshell number two, there are Grongles in it."

"Oh!" Professor N'Aversion hadn't known that.

"Bombshell number three; they plan to bring down Lord Vernon and the High Leader. Bombshell number four; we, Deirdre and I, have agreed to help." Involuntarily, the Professor suspected. "Bombshell number five; not surprising intel this, we may fail. Bombshell number six; the Grongles know everything about our organisation and..." Snoofle's voice cracked, "I'm going to show you how. Deirdre, I'll need to film this myself..."

The picture jumped and danced crazily before refocusing on Lieutenant Arbuthnot, for a delightful, and distracting, moment. To his disappointment, the image panned round again and the beautiful Deirdre was replaced by a Grongle.

"Arnold's sandals!"

"Good day to you, Professor. I apologise for disturbing you; after my Master's most recent announcement, doubtless you are busy. I am General Moteurs. Advisor to Lord Vernon on matters of security and Commander of the Imperial Guard here in K'Barth." the Professor had not heard of General Moteurs but he had heard of the Imperial Guard and knew their reputation. "I am also acting commander of the K'Barthan Underground and it is in that capacity that I contact you. I regret that I have some unpleasant news..."

The General projected an aura of intelligent self assurance that bordered on arrogance and set off all the Professor's warning klaxons.

"I hope you know what you're doing Snoofle," he muttered. "I think you may be out of your depth with this one. I think I might be." He watched and listened in increasing dismay as the video proceeded; the General gave a concise précis of the situation; the Resistance totally compromised, only himself standing between them and destruction, and then the denouement: teleportation, with a thimble, a very graphic demonstration. When it had finished Professor N'Aversion sat for some time, unmoving and fearful.

"This is trouble on every level," he muttered.

The Professor seldom met beings as smart as himself, and it galled him intensely to be pitched against one now, in a situation of such gravity. His tablet pc chimed with its usual annoying ding. New mail. He pulled it across the desk towards him in breathless anticipation. Sure enough, there was an e-mail from an unknown account containing a number of attachments; the schematics of the Grongolian portal, as General Moteurs had promised. He wondered if he should get Nar to run a check or two on the e-mail's header information when she got back. Yes. Although he was certain she wouldn't find anything.

The Professor opened the attachments and started to click through them. He had designed himself a special hat, a band with a sheet of card going across from the front to the back of his head, to separate his antennae and prevent knots. He put it on. The mere thought of what he was reading was enough to have them tying themselves into the kind of tangle it would take him the rest of his days to undo.

There was a report, with which he started. As the Professor read it his amazement grew. He would need time to examine the schematics properly but he understood the concept at once. So simple, so straightforward.

"So in all these years of scientific study, why haven't I thought...?" he asked himself. "Arnold's naval fluff."

He sat back in his chair staring into space for a moment.

"This is extraordinary."

More than extraordinary, it was life changing. He read on as the report outlined the theories behind the box's construction and how the Grongolian scientists had applied it.

"Fascinating..." he whispered as he read. It was filling gaps and answering questions almost as he thought of them. He spooled through the pages. He must ensure he understood them properly, and that he had the full knowledge at his fingertips before he acted, but even at this stage he could tell that the drawings on the screen were, almost certainly, genuine and complete.

He watched the video again. Yes. The rumours about matter transportation in early K'Barth were true. And the Grongles had captured the last five transportation devices and worked out how they operated. The Resistance was in trouble. Its enemies were omnipotent, they could watch anyone and go anywhere. Unless the Professor could build that box the Resistance was at the mercy of Lord Vernon, and the only thing standing between the HQ and wholesale destruction was a single Grongle... if he was telling the truth.

"And that's a big if," muttered the Professor. He heaved a sigh.

What to do? He trusted Snoofle and the Lieutenant, but he wasn't sure about the General. Or was that just that insufferable, Grongolian, officer-class arrogance that grated? No, he was a high powered being with little time for niceties, that was all. But there was an assured ruthlessness there. The General undoubtedly pursued his goals without compunction and the Professor felt more like his prey than a potential ally.

"I wonder. Are you watching me now?" Professor N'Aversion asked his empty office quietly. "Well if you are, I'll tell you something, General Moteurs. I am not one of your subordinates to bend to your will. I will act as I see fit. Not blindly, as you command."

Except that he had no choice. It was his duty to get the Resistance ahead and the only way he could do that was to accept the General's offer of salvation. Use the information as a starting point and come up with something better. But salvation always comes at a price and the Professor would be hard put to pay this one.

It could be a trick, it could be...

He opened the database and searched for the word 'portal'. It returned three results but even before he had read them he knew, in his heart, that General Moteurs told the truth; about the portals, anyway. The biggest question was, why?

He must discuss the situation with someone else: and the only ones he could trust with this, who were smart enough, were Simon and Nar.

He took off his headphones and stood up. Shoving the phone deep in his lab coat pocket and taking off his anti-knotting hat, he ran to the workshop. By the time he had returned the headphones, his antennae had already tied themselves into a veritable Gordian knot. Never mind. No time for that now. Thank The Prophet, his staff were drifting back from their break. He collared the first one to hand.

"Blimpet, I must find Nar, where is she?"

Blimpet gestured to the doorway where Nar was just arriving.

"Nar!" barked the Professor. The tension in his voice made him sound angry and everyone's heads snapped round to look at the object of his attention. "I must speak to you in my office, now."

The buzz of just-back-from-lunch chatter died as Nar walked across the workshop in silence.

"Forgive me, I don't wish to sound impertinent but it is most urgent that we speak." Professor N'Aversion ignored her staring colleagues, striding forward and grabbing Nar by the arm. "As you were, ladies and gents. Nothing to see here," he told the rest of the workshop before pulling her hastily inside. He slammed the door.

"I've found it," he told her.

"Found what?"

"The thing we are looking for but it comes with some grave drawbacks. Here," he held out his phone, "Arnold's bottom. Why did I put those ruddy headphones back—"

"It's alright, I have some of my own." Nar's voice was deliberately calm and soothing. The Professor hadn't realised he sounded that agitated. Her eyes travelled upwards to his painfully knotted antennae. "Can I help you wi—"

"No time for that now, Nar. The video message from Snoofle, please play it."

Chapter 32

The Pan would have preferred to begin the cleanup operation in the flat upstairs. Sure the Grongles had made less of a mess up there but it was his home and the sense of violation he felt at the state of it was stronger. However, he knew that Gladys and Ada would have begun in the pub. The Pan could almost hear them explaining how they could cope with living in a wrecked flat if having an un-wrecked bar meant they'd earn enough money to get it mended. That wasn't the only reason of course. He imagined Ada asking what the neighbours would think.

He started with the main bar. First he threw away the damaged cushions. Luckily there were plenty left undamaged, and he remembered that there were some spares in the settle by the door. Having primped the furnishings as best he could, he got the broom out. Sweeping up with one arm was difficult but not totally impossible and before long the room began to look less as if a tornado had been through it and more like a pub. Then The Pan spent a couple more hours rearranging the bottles and glasses behind the bar, throwing away the broken ones, polishing the survivors and checking the beer pumps were working and clean. He moved to the kitchen area behind it, where Gladys and Ada prepared the sandwiches and did the washing up.

"I is not leaving the Holy of Holies looking like we has exploded a beer keg in there," he said in a falsetto impression of Gladys.

"Quite so dear, it's absolutely shocking!" he said, switching to the role of Ada.

"Yer, I wants it ship shape, mind, no slacking."

"Oh come on," The Pan reverted to type, "I've only one arm."

He pretended to be Gladys and Ada's Trev and stuck up for himself.

"'S right Mum. 'E's armless."

"That was a shockingly bad joke... and this... talking to yourself is... not the way to go," he said.

Even so, he could imagine Gladys' nod of approval when it was done and that was a comfort. It was good to think he would spend the bleakest day of his life doing something more constructive than moping. This small kindness for the people he cared for was something they would have appreciated.

Finally the main bar, the hall, the stairs and the Holy of Holies were finished. Only the snug to do and that wasn't too bad. It was fitted out like a library, with all sorts of old books, mostly snaffled from skips and dustbins by Gladys, Ada and Their Trev. The Pan had tried to read one once, one of the more recent ones – some of them were truly ancient, by the looks of things. However, he had never finished it because the last chapters were missing. When he'd complained Ada had said, 'They're not for reading, dear, they're only there to look old and interesting...' and The Pan had said, 'I thought that was your job,' and she'd laughed. Despite his misery, memories of better days made him smile. He stuck his head round the door of the snug to check. Yeh, it wouldn't take long, merely a case of putting all the books back into the bookshelves.

He went back into the bar and glanced around him, proudly. Everything was as spic and span as a one-armed man who was already inept at cleaning could make it – what Gladys called 'Man Clean' when she was taking the Mickey out of Trev – but it looked cared for and that was the important thing. He went behind the bar and straightened the nut posters. The Parrot's bar nuts came in bags which were always attached to a cardboard poster. As the bags of nuts were sold, the picture beneath was revealed.

The posters on the cards varied, depending on where the nuts were sourced. One company sent their nuts on famous art works, the other, T&B Snacks, on a picture of a provocative looking female. The idea of the female was to kid the male punters into thinking that the bags of nuts were all she wore. The Pan could see the marketing sense behind this. Pub punters were mostly male and clearly, T&B hoped that, as such, they would buy the bags of bar nuts thick and fast to reveal what was underneath. He had never understood the logic behind the posters of art works provided by the other snack company, yet, it was their reproduction of a famous painting of Arnold, The Prophet, that was devoid of all its nuts bar one bag, over his hand. The T&B picture of a smouldering female Swamp Thing was only missing two.

Strange. The Pan supposed you never can tell. He straightened the two pictures carefully and moved back round the bar to admire his handiwork.

"Yeh. That'll do," said The Pan.

"Cluck."

"It's the thought that counts," said The Pan with a sigh.

"Cluck." The chicken sounded slightly sceptical but none of the other voices said anything. In fact, The Pan realised, the cleaning had absorbed him so much that, while he was concentrating on tidying up, he had almost blanked them out. Not completely, he could hear a general rumble of conversation, but; thank The Prophet, it sounded quieter, distant – as if it was in another room. However, absorbing or not, the cleaning hadn't distracted The Pan from the misery of losing Ruth. Her poisonous kiss with Lord Vernon seemed to be playing on an endless loop in his mind's eye. No. He mustn't think about that. He couldn't afford to stop and mope. Not if he was going to get the Parrot cleaned up. He was still toying with the idea of getting himself murdered that evening, and if he wanted to do that he must finish the cleaning first.

He stood in the middle of the bar looking around. The voices were returning, mostly to differ vociferously with the getting murdered bit of his plan. He glanced at his watch and smiled to himself; he was making good progress. Even so. He'd better get on. He hoped he would be dead before he slid completely into insanity. In the meantime, it was simply a case of being practical. Reality was all around him. He just had to hold onto it. Some more grounding manual labour would help. Yeh.

"Where next?" he wondered aloud. As if in answer, his stomach rumbled. "Good plan. The cellar." He could select a cheese to eat for his lunch at the same time. The Grongles were bound to have searched there, as well, so he should check the pumps were still properly connected and that everything was in order. There would be pickle down there, too, and homemade bread in the freezer. Yeh. There was lunch sorted. He ducked into the Holy of Holies and grabbed a sharp knife and a couple of plates. He would have to sort out the flat upstairs afterwards, ending up with the kitchen so he could reward himself with a last meal of cheese on toast.

"Mmm, and pickle. Let's not forget the pickle."

Your body is a temple. You shouldn't profane it with that gut rot. A lone voice slipped through his guard.

"Oh sod off." The Pan opened the trap door behind the bar and went down the stairs, into the cellar.

173

Chapter 33

Professor N'Aversion waited tensely until Nar finished watching the video on his phone. When she was done, she sat still and unmoving. He gave her time. She would need to process what she had seen.

"Has Simon seen this, Professor?" she asked eventually.

"No. I have only just watched it myself. I couldn't get through to Simon, so I left him a message and forwarded everything. I have suggested that the three of us have a conference call in an hour. If he hasn't come back to me; you and I must decide our course of action alone. I have another General Staff Meeting this afternoon. We must have made our decision by then so I can brief our Leader accordingly." He handed her a portable memory stick. "It's all on here; an excellent report. I think you'll have the basics in that time."

"Yes, professor."

"So, I asked Simon to think about these points. First, do we believe it's genuine? Second, if it is, he will undoubtedly need to procure some parts. To that end, what I must know from you, as accurately as you can in the time we have, is how many of the parts we have in stock, what – if any – extra we will need to procure and a time frame within which it can be built."

"Don't worry, Professor, I can do that."

"Ever efficient. Thank you, Nar. You won't need too much detail, bullet points will do at this stage."

"Yes, Professor, I'll start now."

"Good, good. Thank you, Nar," he said. His tone was upbeat, chipper even, but his heart was heavy.

Chapter 34

In the gloom of the cellar of The Parrot and Screwdriver, The Pan of Hamgee checked the freezer. There was bread, lots of it, and various things underneath, foil trays and containers all labelled with the names of Gladys' flag ship dishes. 'Squid for one' The Pan saw.

"Ooo, pity I haven't time to defrost that before supper."

He found another, 'Shepherd's pie for three,' the label said.

"Interesting."

There were the usual bags of frozen fruit, margarine tubs full of stock and, ah yes, bread.

He took out a loaf and put it on a plate, closing the lid and putting the plate on top to defrost. Then he set about tidying up. First he put the cheeses back on the shelves. There were a couple missing, he suspected, but it wasn't too bad. The pickle hadn't been touched – no surprise really – or the beer barrels by the looks of it. He'd half expected the Grongles to have destroyed them. They took a dim view of beer. Probably through pure pique that they couldn't drink it. Two drops of alcohol and the average Grongle would wake several hours later with a headache and no recollection of how he had acquired it. This wasn't common knowledge in K'Barth. Everyone assumed the Grongles disapproved of drink on moral grounds, but Gladys and Ada had graphically demonstrated the effect on some Grongles who'd come to The Parrot and Screwdriver searching for him once. He remembered how cross the old ladies had been when he'd accused them of using poison.

He moved further into the cellar, to the shelves at the back, where he found rank on rank of empty jars; all small, individual-portion-sized. They were clean but at the same time, clearly used. Each one was carefully labelled and they were arranged in pairs. He remembered what Sir Robin had told him about single use portals and the relocation scheme for the blacklisted.

"I wonder..." he said.

"Finally, some sign of intelligence."

"Absolutely! I was beginning to think this boy's brain was made of porridge."

"Smecking Arnold! Will you lot give it a rest?" said The Pan.

"D'you hear that? Put a sock in it he's trying to think," said someone else.

Arnold they were annoying.

"You took the words out of my mouth," said The Pan to the put-a-sock-in-it one. He supposed it might have been easier to deal with if they had liked him, even a little bit. He thought for a moment. No, the chicken did, and the sock-in-it one had stuck up for him.

He took one of the jars, removed the lid and held it up to his eye. In the bottom he saw nothing but grey fog... well, he was thinking about Ruth and she was... No. Don't think about where she was.

Start again.

He imagined the beach at Hamgee and there it was in all its glory, except that the weather wasn't as good in Hamgee as it was in Ning Dang Po. Instead of autumn sun, he saw the kind of grey skies and drizzle that perfectly suited his mood. He put a couple of the jam jars in his pocket and checked the connectors to the barrels as he'd seen Trev, Gladys and Ada do hundreds of times. All were fine except the end barrel, which was crooked. It was the one behind which he had kept his stash of loot in his bank robbing days.

Oh dear. The skew-whiff barrel would be his fault then. He remembered how a few nights previously, when he'd rescued Ruth, he'd returned home to warn Gladys and Ada that the Grongles were looking for them. He'd run down to the cellar and grabbed his bag of loot, thinking he might be able to sell some if he and Ruth ended up on the run. He realised he must have knocked the barrel out of position when he'd reached behind it. Except that he would remember knocking it, surely. He moved closer.

"What?" The bag was still there. He reached out and picked it up. "No. Impossible." He knew he'd taken it with him. A picture flashed into his mind's eye of a very similar red freezer bag, containing everything he owned, spiralling out of sight as he wrestled to control his snurd after it had fallen off the top of a building. He cringed at the thought. Yeh. He'd definitely taken it. And he'd lost it saving Ruth from Lord Vernon.

"And that was really worth doing wasn't it? Arnold! I gave up everything for her." He wanted to be angry, he wanted to hate her and call her a bitch but he couldn't. Worse, the idea of even thinking hurtful things about her just made him feel bitter as well as sad. "I know she loved me, I know it." No, no, no. If he wasn't careful he was going to cry again. The voices were silent but they were listening, The Pan could feel their awkwardness. Never mind, the fact there were voices at all was alarming. Maybe he should have a good sob, it was wise not to overload his system by trying to be stoic. Let it out. There was no-one around to see. No-one real anyway.

"Oh man up," he told himself. "You're Hamgeean for The Prophet's sake."

"Cluck?" said the chicken. It sounded sympathetic.

"I'll get over it, hen. It's just a broken heart," he said sadly. He blew his nose, forgetting that the thing in his hand was a red freezer bag and not a handkerchief.

Arnold's armpits.

"Yuck." He took the bag over to the lid of the freezer, emptied the contents onto the surface without really looking and scrumpled it up into a ball. Lucky he was cleaning the place. He had a rubbish bag with him. He stuffed the bogey-covered freezer bag inside it and then took a real handkerchief from his pocket and blew his nose again.

"By The Prophet's BO," he muttered as he put the hanky back in his pocket. Time for a snack.

"I ask you. The first time he stops thinking with his trousers his stomach steps in. Does he have an intellect?"

"Shut up," said The Pan at the exact same moment someone else, a woman, said, *"Be quiet!"*

"My dad always told me that eating regularly is essential, our brains need energy."

"Yours just needs using."

With a resigned sigh, The Pan cut into the cheese he'd selected – a large slice – and took a bite. Then he noticed what had been in the bag and stopped.

There were two things; the Importance Detector – the instrument which looked a little like a child's wind-up gyroscope, only not – and a box. The Box. The Pan put his slice of cheese down and accompanied by a deafening cacophony of shouting from what sounded like a hundred different people at once he took the box out of the bag and looked at it. Someone had left The Box. That Box. There. For him to find.

"Wow—" he began, but the voices drowned out everything.

He was shocked at how many there were, it was a wall of sound, almost deafening him; the unintelligible yelling of a crowd, each one bellowing the odds as loudly as they were able. The Pan's ears sang and his head buzzed. He flipped the box open and looked inside. There was the ring. He took it out and held it up to the electric light. The gold shone and the stone glowed a deep, bewitching dark red. He wanted to wear it. He so wanted to wear it. It was almost calling to him. And Sir Robin had told him to look after it. Where better to hide it than in plain sight where nobody would bother to look: on the hand of a humble publican? And who would be searching? Lord Vernon thought he already had it. The Pan tried to think as the voices screamed and his head reverberated with shouting. But he knew the box was real. And so was the ring. And some instinct told him that the ring would help with the ear splitting screaming he was enduring now. There could be something he didn't know. No, there *would* be something and putting the ring on might be dangerous. But he would take his chances with that. He held out his finger and slipped it on.

As the ring shrank to fit, there was a final deafening crescendo of noise, which brought The Pan to his knees. He almost lost consciousness and then he was kneeling on the ground, curled into a ball, his hands over his ears in silence: blissful, complete silence. The voices had gone.

"Hello?"

Nope. Nothing.

"Now that's what I call a result," he said. He pulled the ring a little way up his finger. He could hear distant shouting. The further up his finger he moved the ring, the louder the shouting became until, when he removed it totally, the deafening voices returned. He put the ring back on quickly and closed the box.

He remembered that, back at the Underground HQ, General Moteurs had taken the box from him and handed it to Sir Robin. The old boy had then demonstrated some ludicrous theory about thumb shape and Ruth had opened it. At the time, The Pan had been sure that the box Sir Robin used to demonstrate the thumb shape theory was a replica. When General Moteurs had given Lord Vernon both boxes, it had merely confirmed his suspicions. But, instead of betraying them, as The Pan believed at the time, the General must have persuaded Lord Vernon that the fake box was the real one. The Pan whistled softly and paused to re-evaluate his opinion of General Moteurs. 'Trust me,' he'd said. Yeh. The Pan shrugged. Maybe he should, carefully.

First things first though; before he got his knickers in a twist about anything, it would be a good idea to check whether or not it was the real box.

"Only one way to do that," he said. He wound up the Importance Detector, set it up on the lid of the freezer, next to the defrosting bread. He copied the hand movements he'd seen Sir Robin execute over the top of it. He wasn't sure if he'd got them right but an approximation would have to do. He pulled the tiny lever and the Importance Detector started spinning. As he moved the box closer, it was surrounded by an eerie – but not unattractive – green light. The Pan smiled.

"Well, well, well." How had Sir Robin put it? 'No glow, no show.' This box was definitely glowing green. It was the real McCoy alright. So now what?

The Pan realised he had the box which proved the identity of the Candidate. He also had the ring, worn by 40 generations of Architraves and a lot of single use portals. There was even an outside chance that, in the shape of General Moteurs, he had an ally. All Lord Vernon had was the Chosen One – even if that was a pretty big 'all', thought The Pan with a stab of bitterness. But the major worry was the Candidate because he had nothing.

So, if Lord Vernon had Ruth and the Candidate had nothing why did The Pan have all this stuff? Had the Candidate realised who he was but decided to stay hidden? Was The Pan supposed to find him? And what about Lord Vernon? As the fake Candidate, was he now real enough to pull it off? Was that why Ruth had suddenly fallen for him?

No. No way. Because as a fake, by definition, Lord Vernon would have to have every possible attribute to be convincing; the ring, the box AND Ruth. So what was going on? The Pan ran his good hand through his hair and tried to concentrate. Something big and obvious was eluding him.

"No change there then," he muttered bad-temperedly. If he could only put his aching heart to one side long enough to apply himself he might be able to work this out. But when he shut his eyes to focus his thoughts all he saw was Ruth and Lord Vernon locked together in an embrace, their arms wrapped around one another, their mouths—

"This has got to stop," he told himself through gritted teeth.

OK, forget about the thinking. His conscious mind was far too heartbroken to be diverted from tormenting the rest of him. He hadn't been strictly serious about the idea, but he definitely couldn't go and get himself murdered, now. Not until he'd found the Candidate or somebody else to look after the box and the ring. He looked down at his hand and drank in the silence of the cellar. Alright, no-one was having the ring but he must find someone to look after the Importance Detector and box, he could leave them the ring in his will.

"Yeh," he sighed. He would have to put off getting murdered until some other time.

"Cock-a-doodle-doo!"

"Aargh! Do you mind? You scared the life out of me."

"Cluck." It was a sort of apologetic cluck but it contained an unmistakable undercurrent of cheery smugness.

"You think topping myself was a bad idea?"

"Cluck." Yes. Very definitely.

"Then you've never been in love."

Suddenly The Pan saw an image in his head, it was a chicken but not the one who'd been Architrave.

"Alright so maybe you have... Is that her?"

"Cluck."

"I see. Did you two...?"

"Cluck."

"I'm sorry to hear that."

"Cluck," said the chicken but somehow, The Pan knew it was shrugging and saying 'kismet'.

"Can I ask you something?"

"Cluck."

"How come the ring blanks them out, but not you?"

"Buuuurck, cluck, cluck, cluck."

"Yeh. Doh. Because it's designed for K'Barthans and you're a chicken."

"Cluck."

"Hang on though. You are a K'Barthan chicken."

"Cluck."

"Ah, but not one of the K'Barthan life forms traditionally associated with the Architraveship, right? Pretty obvious I suppose."

"Cluck."

"So they are the Architraves?"

"Cluck."

"Ah. I've been quite rude to them."

The chicken clucked in a way that The Pan read as 'yes'.

"I suppose I should apologise to them."

"Cluck," said the chicken in an 'in-a-while' kind of way.

"You think I should let them sweat do you?"

"Cluck," said the chicken.

"Yeh, I guess it takes two to be rude. So you don't get on with them either?"

The Pan got the impression that, were it possible for a chicken, the eighth Architrave would be giving him a desultory shrug.

"I see."

A beat.

"Why are they there?"

"Cluck."

"What do you mean you can't tell me?"

The conversation lapsed.

"Well, if you're not going to talk to me, I'll listen to my rumbling stomach. I think I need some cheese on toast." The Pan took his cleaning things upstairs and left them in the snug, ready to start work. Then he returned to the cellar with a bag so he could carry the cheese, the bread and a jar of pickle back up to the bar in one go. He remembered Sir Robin explaining to him how, if he kept a portal with him at all times, the signal would block the view of anyone trying to observe him using another portal.

"Ah yes, good plan."

He filled the bag with pirate portals, too.

"I can't stop them coming here but with this lot but I can stop them listening," he said except that, obviously, it sounded like, 'gi gan't gortal goof ge gace give gis got gut gi gan gop ghem gistening,' because in order to have his good arm free to hold the handrail on the steep stairs up, he had to hold the bag in his teeth. Never mind, if the chicken really was the eighth Architrave, he probably understood.

The Pan didn't go to the kitchen in the flat. He didn't want to be distracted by tidying it up, so instead, he went into the Holy of Holies, behind the bar. He switched the grill on to heat up, boiled the kettle and made himself a cup of coffee.

He needed to think but to do that, he must feed his thinking apparatus with a plate of cheese on toast – if he could saw a slice off the loaf. He banged it on the draining board. Mmm, it hadn't defrosted at all. Never mind. He put the bread on a stool, knelt on it to keep it still and, bread knife in the hand of his functioning arm, he began sawing.

Chapter 35

It was more than an hour before Professor N'Aversion and Nar convened in his office to talk to Simon, but at least it meant he'd had time to draft a document for Denarghi and she had been able to prepare a rough outline inventory and read the report. Both were broad brush, citing the salient points. Denarghi seldom read much else, no matter how much detail he requested.

"Let's begin, shall we?" said the Professor, when he judged they were all settled. "First we need to decide if this is genuine or a ruse."

"The science is genuine, isn't it?" said Simon. "As I read it. Mind you, it's all quantum and reality theory, I'd say you're the only one of us who fully understands it, Professor."

"I am well acquainted with the theoretical concepts behind it but I have never seen them successfully applied. However, there's nothing there, as I see it, that suggests the portal will pose a danger to us. Nar, what's your view?"

"That is my reading too," said Nar, "like Simon, it is not my area of knowledge but I know it's yours, Professor, and I trust your judgement. It is a rare opportunity, and I am nervous as to why it has been offered to us but surely we have no choice."

"I agree, it's vital we do something to assure our survival if Lord Vernon really does become Architrave. There are already rumours that he's going to cleanse K'Barth," said Simon.

"Yes. That's what's worrying me. We should think long and hard before we decide to pass this up," said the Professor.

"I agree but it is a gamble, isn't it?" said Simon. "My reservations are not with the science so much as with this Grongle's motive in sending it to us."

"Indeed. Why is a General in the Imperial Guard giving us this information?"

"He can't really be Underground, can he?" asked Simon.

"I don't know. I suppose anything's possible."

Simon whistled.

"Right o," he said, "so, if we decide to go ahead, do you have an inventory for me?"

"Just two parts: contraband electronics. We can make the rest here."

"OK. I'm guessing I should stay put," said Simon.

"It might be wise," said the Professor. "Now then, just to be sure. Do we all agree we must build it?"

Nar and Simon both said, 'yes'.

"Then I will inform Denarghi."

"Professor. Should you do that straight away?" asked Simon. "I'm just playing Devil's Advocate here, but, will he allow it? There is a Grongle involved."

"Why would he not? We're not building this blind, Simon, I understand the schematics perfectly well. We have no option."

"That's certainly what General Moteurs wants us to think."

"Maybe but it's also what I think. We need to get ahead of them, and to start that process we must build this box. I am certain that even Denarghi will appreciate that."

"I hope so," said Simon, "but what's the plan if he doesn't?"

The Professor and Nar had anticipated and discussed this issue. He glanced at her, checking she still agreed, and she nodded.

"I would suggest we wait until we know his answer. I have another of his infernal councils of war this afternoon, what say we have another conference call at five? Is that alright with you two?"

"Yes, Professor," said Simon and Nar.

"Right then, I'll speak to you soon but I think it would be prudent, from now on, if we used a more private means of communication," said the Professor, "you know the one?"

"Yes," said Simon. One of the online forums, where the three of them were members, ran a private chat facility which could be accessed through the back-up PC in the Tech Ops store room. It connected to the outside world directly, rather than through the Resistance system, so it couldn't be easily monitored by Information Retrieval. If Simon used an internet café they could, in theory, send messages in complete privacy. The Professor hoped they wouldn't have to.

"Nar? Is that alright with you?"

She nodded.

"Good. We'll talk there, soon."

Nar sat quietly for a moment, worry lines puckering her brow.

"Surely you don't think Denarghi will say no?"

"He shouldn't. I'd have thought this is open and closed but you never can tell with him. Whatever happens, I have to do the honourable thing, I have to ask him. We must hope he says, 'Yes'."

Chapter 36

King Denarghi XVII, supreme ruler of the Blurpon nation, sat in his throne room alone with his thoughts. It was not a good place to be. He was angry. He was angry with everyone and everything. There had been a plan, until The smecking Pan of Hamgee came along. The Resistance was going to seize power. Lieutenant Arbuthnot, who worshipped the ground he hopped on, was going to establish herself as Candidate, there would be an uprising and the Grongles would be vanquished because no amount of weaponry can stand in the way of an angry mob; not if it's big enough and made up of K'Barthans who think they are being led by the Candidate. The mob would be everybody. The whole populous would have risen up. Sure, by Denarghi's tactical reckoning, less than half of them would have survived to sit down again but hey, you have to make sacrifices. Most of them would gladly lay down their lives doing Arnold's work, and he was sure he could persuade them it was Arnold's work they were embroiled in.

He would have been compelled to install Lieutenant Arbuthnot as Architrave, of course, but she'd be ruler in no more than name and she'd have done what Denarghi told her; hand the reins of power over to him. He'd even written some of the speech she'd give, *'I wish to pursue a life of greater spirituality and to do so, I must surrender the day to day running of this nation to my greatest friend and advisor, King Denarghi XVII ruler of the Blurpon and, as of today, the K'Barthan, nation.'*

So much for that now. Lieutenant Arbuthnot was... somewhere in the old Palace, the Grongles' Security HQ, being turned. Or not.

"No matter, I can use this," he muttered. It wasn't as if their pointless devotion to Arnold and Nimmism was getting the K'Barthans anywhere. If Lord Vernon carried on the way he was, Denarghi knew he might be able to stop them from hankering for the old theocratic regime and turn them to a new, better, government. A government that would reflect the wishes of the people, a government which would lead them as a collective, pooling their resources, working together, sharing everything equally. Although, as their leader, Denarghi would have a bigger share of the collective than everyone else, as befitted his status as their loving brother.

"Brother Denarghi," he said softly. That was to be his title and it sounded good. The country needed dragging into a more forceful, modern outlook and Denarghi knew he was the one for the job. He had plans for Lord Vernon. Strike Ops could not fail. One day, one of his teams would put a bullet through the Lord Protector's brain. After that, nobody was going to get in Denarghi's way. Then there were these ridiculous rumours, that there was an actual Candidate, who would come to save his people. Well Strike Ops had some pretty specific orders about him, too. Although Denarghi doubted he existed. In the midst of his irritation, his phone rang.

"What?" he barked.

"Good morning, Your Majesty," said a voice; it was electronically disguised, he could hear that, but he pressed the volume button in a specific sequence to activate the phone's call record application, anyway.

"Who is this?"

"Recording our conversation will not answer that question."

"Then you will."

The voice laughed.

"My identity does not concern you."

Denarghi bristled.

"Yes it smecking well does; this is a private number and a secure line."

"And you have nothing to fear from me," said the voice except that somehow, Denarghi felt exactly the opposite.

"I don't talk to anyone I cannot name."

"Then call me, The Candidate."

Oh how droll. Denarghi moved the phone away from his ear so he could read the caller ID. 'Number withheld,' it said.

"As you can see, I am not traceable, you can try, but I assure you, you will find nothing."

Again, the caller had anticipated his actions. In spite of his irritation, Denarghi was also intrigued. Was he under surveillance? He glanced round his Throne Room. It had been swept for enemy monitoring that morning, as it was each and every day, and declared clean.

"What do you want?"

"I have information for you."

"How much? You people always want money."

The voice laughed, and even disguised, it was chilling.

"No payment is required," said The Candidate and without giving

Denarghi an opportunity to reply, he, she, or very possibly 'it' continued. "Consider me a friend. Look in the top left-hand drawer of your desk."

Slowly Denarghi opened the drawer. It contained the usual detritus he kept there, stapler, Post-it notes, spare pens, staples, handgun, knuckle dusters, address book and wait a moment, there was something else. He pulled it further open. Yes, there was an envelope. Where had that come from?

No. No way. Except...

"How did you get in here?"

"I see you have found the Dossier."

The way he said it definitely gave it a capital 'd'. Denarghi regarded the envelope in his hand.

"Is that what you call it?"

'The Candidate' said nothing.

"I asked you a question. How did it get here?" demanded Denarghi.

"That question is one which I..." the caller paused as if trying to pin down the right word, "decline to answer. There is important information in the Dossier."

Denarghi opened the envelope, inside was an anonymous document folder of white card. It contained photos, the first of which was Group Leader Snoofle and Lieutenant Arbuthnot with a laundry trolley, the second a Grongle General crossing a street in Ning Dang Po. Totally unsuspecting, he was looking straight at the camera.

"Your agents have sent you information," said the voice as Denarghi examined the photo. That was interesting, because if his agents had sent anything, Denarghi hadn't seen it yet. Whoever had the intel, they'd better reveal it soon. There were no secrets kept in the Resistance. Not from Denarghi, at any rate. The Candidate continued. "This Grongle is their source. They think they have turned him. They have not."

"Where did you get this?"

"I warn you. The box will be your doom."

"What box? What are you talking about?" Denarghi demanded but he was talking to himself. The line was dead.

He looked down at the third photo in his hand. It showed the same Grongle with Group Leader Snoofle and Lieutenant Arbuthnot. They sat at a table and he stood next to it. There was a metal box between them. It was about the size of four house bricks stacked in pairs, with wires coming out of it. One of the Grongle General's hands was resting on the box, he seemed to be gesticulating urgently with the other. Group Leader Snoofle and Lieutenant Arbuthnot's, faces were upturned, listening. This last one was clearly taken from a hidden surveillance camera in the room. In addition to the three photographs was a single typewritten sheet. It was headed, in Grongolian, 'General Ford Moteurs, brief biography'. Denarghi read it and sat back in his chair. He took out his tablet PC, opened the internet browser and typed the General's name into the online encyclopaedia site, Pikiwedia. There was no mention of him; it was as if he didn't exist. On the other hand, the Strike Ops target database gave the same story, classing General Moteurs as a category 1 target, but concluding that he was not currently engaged in the types of activities that would warrant liquidation, and so closely guarded that the price of a strike would outweigh the benefits.

"We'll see about that," said Denarghi. He pressed the button on the intercom, "Get Melior and Plumby."

Chapter 37

Having made their video for Professor N'Aversion, neither Snoofle, nor Deirdre could concentrate on anything else. After 20 minutes, Snoofle's phone beeped.

"Anything?" asked Deirdre.

"No. Just a status request from Plumby."

"Smeck."

"Too right, Deirdre," Snoofle sighed and shook his head as he began to tap rapidly at the screen of his phone, "he really doesn't have a clue about field work."

"That's obvious."

"Cards?"

Deirdre shook her head.

"Sparring?"

"No, thank you."

"What about our knife throwing act? We should be prepared. If we upset Denarghi we might need to run away with the Circus."

"It is a coincidence that you should mention that. I told D'reen Pargeter, in the drying room, that my father was a knife thrower."

"No way!" Snoofle started to chuckle. "Why on earth did you tell her that?"

"I killed a rat. She appeared to find it remarkable."

"Yes, Deirdre, from 20 paces, with a knife, it is."

She pouted at him.

"It was 10 paces," she put her hand briefly on the holster strapped to her thigh.

"Blending in nicely then."

"I told you I was unsuited to espionage."

"I don't know. It was quick thinking... like that lumberjack line you've been feeding your parents."

"Stop laughing! Is this how you always cope? Making light of it?"

"It depends where I am, who with, what character I'm in... if my cover is some humourless automaton I can't. It's always harder then."

"The waiting?"

"Yeh. With any luck we'll be sent back to work. You know what The Prophet said, 'Time flies when you're having fun'."

Deirdre reflected on the mind-numbing boredom of the laundry.

"I would not term our work here as fun."

"No but you get my gist, it's absorbing."

Deirdre gave him a look.

"Seriously. Did you know that the great Blurpon forefather, Hieronymus Vringher, invented the trouser press over a thousand years ago? Within five years he had established our nation's reputation for its superb ironing skills. Then, because fabrics press better when they are damp, and consignments of ironing were drying out on route from the laundries, his assistant, Tallulah Twintaub invented the washing machine. In ten years the two of them made our nation synonymous with the highest skills of the laundering arts."

"Snoofle how do you know all this stuff?"

"It intrigues me, I suppose. I have an enquiring mind, and it's far more interesting than actually *doing* laundry."

"Most things are. Do you admire them, Vringher and Twintaub? "

"When I am not cursing them for dooming me to wash Grongolian socks forever and a day? Yes. Seriously though, boring or not, we need to get back there. If we're not careful Denarghi and Plumby are going to lose their nerve."

"If they have we're safer here."

"If they really bottle it we won't be safe anywhere."

"Agreed," said Deirdre, hiding her disquiet behind military formality as usual.

"We might be able to wangle a new I.D. from General Moteurs."

"I don't want his help."

"Don't let your pride get in the way."

"I'm not. I may have changed my view of Grongles, I can accept they are not all bad; Corporal Jones and Dr Dot are decent beings but General Moteurs..." she shrugged. "I don't know. Do you trust him, Snoofle?"

"I'm prepared to – with my eyes open of course. He's giving us an opportunity, and it's too good to miss."

"Perhaps that is why I doubt."

"You mean it seems too good to be true?"

"Like the delicious bait in the middle of a bear trap."

"I hear you. What's your gut instinct?"

"To trust him," she said slowly. "That is why I'm nervous. If I met him in other conditions, if he wasn't a Grongle, I would put my faith in him without question."

"Brain says no, heart says go?"

She blew the air out through her teeth.

"I wonder how Professor N'Aversion is using our intel."

"Very carefully, I hope."

Their conversation was disturbed as the door to their apartment was unlocked heralding the arrival of a visitor. It was Doctor Dot.

"Hello," she said, "I've come to take another look at you. Snoofle, did the tonic help?"

"Yes, thanks."

"Glad to hear it. OK, let's see how the pair of you are getting on. Who's going first?"

"I will," said Snoofle.

After a brief examination similar to that of the previous day, Dr Dot declared Snoofle fit for light duties if he wanted to go back to the Laundry.

Deirdre was not so lucky.

"Lieutenant, I'm sorry, but I simply can't authorise that for you today."

"Not even light duties?" asked Deirdre.

"I'm afraid not."

"But I only work in the drying room." The idea of staying there alone, fretting, even if only for another night, made her feel almost panicky. Smecking Arnold, would she look at herself? "Can I not go back to the dormitory then?" she asked helplessly.

Although thinking about that, perhaps not. A vivid aural memory of the incredible variety – and volume – of the snoring of the ladies in the dormitory sprang to mind.

The Doctor sighed. Deirdre could see she wasn't enjoying saying 'no' but she clearly wasn't budging either.

"The General did say you would find this difficult but it won't be for long and trust me, you need time to rest and heal. You're doing incredibly well, in fact, frankly, I'm amazed at your progress." She thought for a moment. "OK, what about this? I'll try to get you clearance to have

192

visitors, your colleagues are very anxious to find out how you are. Maybe Snoofle and Mrs Pargeter can come and see you before supper."

Deirdre perked up a bit.

"Thank you, yes."

"I can lend you some books as well, if you like. They're in Grongolian, I'm afraid but—"

"I would appreciate that," said Deirdre. Wow. How long had she been in this place? Three days, if that, and she hardly recognised herself. She cast a glance at Snoofle who winked.

"OK, I have to go now but I'll see what I can do," said Dr Dot and with that, she was gone.

"I'm sorry Deirdre, I really am. D'you want me to stay? I can always tell them I'd like to wait until I'm fit for heavy duties."

"No. You must go back. Today. If Plumby and Denarghi are losing faith in us, you need to be there, restoring it."

"That is a very good point," he said.

"Yes. I'll not have you dying on my account."

Chapter 38

Professor N'Aversion aimed to arrive at the afternoon's meeting first. He hoped a show of enthusiasm might atone for his getting himself chucked out of Saturday's.

However, needless to say, Colonels Melior and Plumby were already there; sucking up to their Master, the Professor reflected, with disdain. They were family and it was only to be expected, he supposed, but the way the three of them looked up at him as he walked in was worrying. They were clearly plotting something.

Once Colonel Ischzue had arrived with Lieutenant Wright, the Professor took the floor. He briefly outlined the principles of portal use, as he understood them and how they explained The Pan of Hamgee's escape. He went on to substantiate his theory with the quotes he had found in the holy writings. Nothing from The Prophet himself, but definite mentions from the fifth and eighth Architraves as well as the twentieth High Priest. As a coup de grace, he circulated the schematics General Moteurs had sent him. He kept the General's name out of it, instead stressing Snoofle and Deirdre's part in it. When Professor N'Aversion had finished his explanation, he opened the floor for questions.

"Well thank you, Professor. That was very interesting but you cannot expect me to let you build this thing," said Denarghi. He sounded irritated, as if he thought the idea was a waste of time. Plumby and Melior pompously puffed themselves up and nodded in agreement. Across the table from them, Colonel Ischzue and Lieutenant Wright exchanged looks but neither of them said anything. The Professor was disappointed. He felt he had put a pretty convincing argument.

"I- I was hoping so, yes."

"Out of the question. Perhaps you don't appreciate the source of this information. You didn't say where they obtained these plans. Do you know?"

"From the Grongles."

"How? Stolen? Leaked?"

"It's difficult to say."

"I do not doubt that!" Denarghi leaned forward, his voice acquiring a sinister edge. "But you're going to tell us, Professor, aren't you?"

The room was quiet and still, all attention focussed on his answer.

"Of course," said the Professor. What on earth was the jumped up little ferret getting so het up about?

"And...?"

"They got this information from a Grongle."

"I ask again, stolen? Leaked?"

"Leaked."

"Why?"

"He claims to be working against Lord Vernon."

"And how likely is that, Professor? Did you run any background checks on this Grongle?"

"There is very little information about him."

"Very little? And that did not alarm you, Professor?"

"Yes it did, I conducted exhaustive research."

"In your own amateur way, I am willing to believe you did. However," Denarghi nodded at Colonel Melior, "it appears you did not think to consult an expert."

"You mean Colonel Melior?" The Professor was careful to keep his tone neutral but really. Melior? The fellow wouldn't be able to find his own bottom in the dark with both hands.

"Colonel Melior, tell me, did the Professor ask you for help researching this General Moteurs?"

"No, Your Majesty."

"No. How fortunate that I received alternative intel from my own contacts within the Security HQ and briefed Colonel Melior in your stead. Circulate the information you discovered, Colonel."

Melior took a folder from under the table, removed a sheaf of papers and handed them to Colonel Plumby next to him. Out of the corner of his eye, Professor N'Aversion noticed Lieutenant Wright jotting something in the margin of her copy of the agenda. Colonel Ischzue took up his pen and put a line through it.

"Please take one and pass the rest on," Colonel Melior was saying.

"This is a summary of General Moteurs' service record," said Denarghi as the papers were passed round, "I will allow us all a few moments to familiarise ourselves with its contents. Then, I would be pleased to know, Professor, if you really believe Snoofle and Deirdre could turn this particular being."

The Professor read the document, which contained nothing above what his own department had discovered. Colonel Ischzue caught his eye, his brows raised in enquiry as if to ask 'what's going on'. The Professor shrugged apologetically.

"Well?" demanded Denarghi, in the face of the Professor's continued silence.

"I understand your misgivings," said the Professor. "Initially, I shared them. I appreciate that there is very little real information in the public domain about General Moteurs. Everything about him screams secret service, but I also see grounds for an open mind, if we proceed with caution." He glanced down at the paper in front of him. "For example, at the bottom here, it states he was in charge of the garrison guarding the Bank of Grongolia, which the Mervinettes robbed."

"He was posted here three months before the robbery, Professor."

"Perhaps, but the Mervinettes couldn't have pulled it off without an ally on the inside. General Moteurs is now based at the Old Palace, the Security HQ, where the intake records state that Sir Robin Get has recently been taken into custody. I agree that it might be a challenge for Group Leader Snoofle and Lieutenant Arbuthnot to turn a Grongle General, especially in the few days they have been there, but what if Sir Robin Get could? What if he already had? What if General Moteurs is telling the truth? What if he really is acting commander of the Underground?"

"The Underground doesn't exist," snapped Melior.

"Professor," said Denarghi. "Are you telling me you believe that Sir Robin Get faked his death, lived to found the Underground, recruited Grongles into it and that now they are trying to help us?"

"Yes."

"Your evidence for this is, at best, circumstantial and, at worst, hangs on nothing more than General Moteurs' word."

"He could easily have been the Mervinettes' inside contact at the Bank."

"Again, this is pure supposition."

"Not if he's telling the truth."

"He can have no concept of truth and he certainly won't be a member of the Underground. He's a Grongle."

"So?"

"Explain to him Melior."

"Look at this Grongle's record after he arrives here: a Colonel, doing nothing of import, clearly kept at arm's length by Lord Vernon and the powers that be—"

"Exactly, because he was distrusted by them—"

"Colonel Melior is not finished, Professor," growled Denarghi, his whiskers bristling with indignation.

"Thank you," said the Colonel with more than a hint of the playground gloater in his tone.

"As I was saying, General Moteurs was a Colonel when he arrived. He did something that got him promoted four ranks at once. By Lord Vernon."

Professor N'Aversion checked the faces round the room: Plumby, Melior and Denarghi exultant, they clearly believed they had delivered a debating ace; Ischzue and Wright guarded.

"What about Sir Robin Get?"

"What about him? He's been dead for years," said Colonel Plumby.

"No he—"

"Gentlemen, if I may," Colonel Ischzue stepped in.

"Well Colonel?" said Denarghi.

"We can argue about this all day, but putting aside our speculation about the source of our intel, let us look at the facts. We have a set of schematics and the Professor believes they will allow us to build a portal, an instrument of great power. Does it matter where the information comes from? Surely the key is that we have it and we must decide what we do with it."

"That is exactly what we are doing, Ischzue," snapped Denarghi.

"No, we are arguing about the source. The issue is whether we can trust the information we have been given. Personally, I would consider Professor N'Aversion to be a scientist of great enough intelligence to know what he is building."

"Thank you," said the Professor. "I'd like to think so, too."

"So would I," said Denarghi, "but I fear it is not true. Professor, you have been blinded by your desire for this box to work. I have other, reliable information that suggests it will not. I will not jeopardise the safety of this organisation just to give you a new toy."

Something in the professor snapped and he leapt to his feet.

"How DARE you trivialise this!" he shouted, banging his fist on the table. Everyone was silent. Arnold's bogies he shouldn't have lost his rag. Never mind it was too late now, "I apologise for raising my voice but this is not about 'toys' and with respect, Denarghi, it is preposterous of you to even think that. I believe that it is you who are jeopardising the safety of our entire HQ by refusing to let me build this machine. The plans are genuine. I don't know why we have them – I don't really care – all that matters to me is that we do and they are. Lord Vernon intends to become Architrave at the end of the week. If I can build this portal by then, and we can learn to use it, we might be able to use it to stop him. The Grongles have them already, they have the five original K'Barthan portals and this is our chance to level the field; if we act quickly enough. Say the word, Denarghi, sir, and I can build you a matter transference device by the end of the week. And before you answer think about what it means if they have one and we do not."

The tension was unbearable and the Professor realised, with irritation and pain, that his antennae had tied themselves into another knot.

"Professor, I assume you have proof the Grongles are using this device?"

The Professor said nothing.

"As I thought. If it works, why aren't they using it?" asked Denarghi.

"I believe they are."

"Why yes of course. That's why it's all over the press."

"It's black ops. General Moteurs is black ops."

"It's a fairy tale. A story made up by this General Moteurs and he is using it to get to you, and through you, to us."

"But he has no reason to do that."

"Oh but he does. He wants to destroy us."

"Denarghi. I can make it work."

"No you can't and you're not having the chance." He clicked his fingers. The door opened and Colonel Smeen, the Swamp Thing-sized human in charge of Denarghi's personal guard, walked in. He wasn't alone. He was flanked by five of his burliest guards and some of Melior's computer geeks.

"What is this? Are you arresting me?" asked The Professor.

"Smeen, you know what to do," said Denarghi before deigning to reply. "No, Professor, you are not under arrest. You will hand your phone, your tablet and any other electronic devices containing any form of memory to Smeen to be reformatted."

"You can't just—"

"I can and I will. Colonel Smeen's colleagues are at Tech Ops now, collecting these objects from your staff. I do not share your view that General Moteurs is our ally, neither do I share your view that this machine he wants you to make is benign."

"Denarghi listen I know it is, I understand the schematics, I KNOW—"

"Oh you think you know, Professor, but in this case, I fear your belief in your own superiority has clouded your judgement. This is beyond you."

"No it's not. It's quantum mechanics. It's challenging but I understand the principles and what the machine does."

To the Professor's rage Denarghi tutted.

"There you go, Professor, doing it again. I appreciate that you are loyal to this organisation – in your own undisciplined way – you would not knowingly put us in danger but if you build this device, you will. And I think the temptation to build it will be too much for you unless I take action. That is why any copies of these schematics," he held up the papers the Professor had prepared and ripped them in half, "have been deleted or destroyed. If you try to replace them, or build this device, I will see it as treason. This event never happened. It is struck from the records. You understand what that means, don't you, Professor?"

"Yes, I understand," said Professor N'Aversion. He was incensed and wished he could punch the little weasel-faced runt. But he must make a good account of himself; take it with dignity and grace. It was the only thing left to him now. He would rethink and regroup. Let Denarghi do his worst. Let him wipe every computer, every memory stick in HQ, let him wipe the main frame. The fact was, the Professor had read and understood the schematics. If required he could make a start on the portal from memory. The question, now, was whether he should.

As he was escorted from the room with Smeen he cast a final glance at his colleagues. Denarghi, imperious and intransigent, Colonel Melior and Colonel Plumby, smirking with ill disguised glee. Colonel Ischzue and Lieutenant Wright wore expressions of studied neutrality. So much for potential alliances. When he looked at them, both averted their eyes.

Chapter 39

The Pan sat in the newly tidied snug of the Parrot and Screwdriver finishing a second round of cheese on toast with pickle, lots of pickle but not too much or he'd be what Ada delicately referred to as 'not nice to know'. He had hoovered and put the books away, hoping, as he did so, that he would find an ancient tome containing something, anything that might shed light on his situation. The books were certainly antiquated, and Nimmist volumes, for sure. Indeed The Pan suspected it was a criminal act to own some of them under the current regime. However, despite such promise, the results of his searches had been an epic fail. Then again, it wasn't as if he had time to look at them properly and they all had substantial portions missing.

He glanced at his watch. Quarter to six. It was opening time at seven. Seeing as he wasn't going to be able to get himself killed until he'd sorted out stashing the box, he may as well open the pub. He picked up his empty plate, strolled through to the main bar and put it on one of the tables while he placed a good number of Gladys and Ada's pirate jam jar portals about the place. The signal from these portals would interfere with the five K'Barthan thimbles in Lord Vernon's possession, making it impossible for the Grongles to listen in on anything that was said in the pub. They looked a bit odd, dotted about the place. Mmm, maybe he could conceal them better.

He remembered that Gladys had some tea lights. Yes. Perhaps he should make the jars into a feature. After a rummage in one of the cupboards behind the bar, he found the tea lights. He put them in the jars and lit them.

"Very pretty," he said and smiled to himself. Then, not forgetting to pick up the plate, he went back into the kitchen area, the Holy of Holies, where he dumped it on the draining board. A sound from the bar caught his attention, a sucking sound, like the noise made by bathwater going out, and a pop. He froze. Somebody had just arrived by portal. He got down onto all fours, or at least all threes with one arm in a sling, and crawled silently, awkwardly, out of the Holy of Holies. Behind the bar, all was quiet.

The tea light in the pirate portal he'd left on the bar was burning brightly. He heard the same sucking sounds begin again and in front of his eyes, it disappeared.

"Smeck!" He leapt up, rushed back into the Holy of Holies and cast about for something heavy, nothing obvious jumped out at him but then he remembered... ah yes, there, on the high shelf in the knife block Gladys and Ada reserved for the really big knives which weren't used often; a meat cleaver. He grabbed it and ran back into the bar, smashing it down onto the empty portal, breaking it to pieces. Then cleaver in hand, he ran from table to table until he found the second empty jar and smashed that. Finally, with a great deal of swearing, and moderately burned fingers, he managed to remove all the tea lights from the remaining jars. Back to the Holy of Holies where he ran his fingers under the cold tap, washed the meat cleaver and put it on the draining board to dry. Then he got the dustpan and brush out from the cupboard under the sink.

Phew. That had been close.

What a moron. He was annoyed with himself. He was the only member of the Underground left. He had a very real and urgent reason to stay alive, now, and portal use was traceable. If he hadn't noticed so quickly and smashed the jars the Grongles could have picked that up, and it could have led them to the Parrot. At the best they would have taken all the pirate portals. The worst didn't bear thinking about. That signed death warrant was still floating about somewhere.

"Arnold's bogies!" Shaking and nervous he cleared up the two broken jars and put the others in less conspicuous positions, it would be a pity if somebody put something into one. He hoped he had got to the jars in time, but if the Grongles had detected portal use, The Pan was fairly sure they wouldn't have had time to find out where.

No wonder the voices thought he was an idiot. He felt the reassuring weight of the ring on his finger and was glad he hadn't had to listen to their reaction. The chicken was conspicuously silent, confirming that even he couldn't think of a way to be positive about this one. With a resigned sigh, The Pan put the dustpan and brush away under the sink.

As he turned to go back into the bar something on one of the high shelves caught his eye. When he'd pulled the meat cleaver out of the block, the baking trays wedged behind it had shifted. Tucked behind them, half hidden from view, was the corner of something; a book. He reached up and took it down. It was bound the old way; the paper torn to size, folded and stitched together at the spine a few sheets at a time. It made the edges of the pages rough. No straight sides like a modern book despite the recent dust jacket it was wearing. Interesting.

"The Beginner's Guide to Commercial Brewing," read The Pan, "oy-oy."

"Cluck." The chicken was back and he sounded excited.

"Mmm," said The Pan. He flipped the book open. "Hello what's this? The Prophetic Sayings of the Very Holy Arnold Elucidated," he read aloud. "Herein are collected the less appointed and understood sayings of The Very Holy Prophet, Arnold, given enlightenment by his Most Righteous Reverend, High Priest Bartle." The Pan raised an eyebrow. "Oh yeh?" The book was several hundred years old, possibly older. He wasn't too up on his history, what with his education coming to an abrupt halt when he was blacklisted, but The Pan had a suspicion that Bartle had been High Priest not long after the chicken had been Architrave.

"Cluck," the chicken confirmed, although how he was supposed to know, being dead by then, was anybody's guess. The Pan raised the other eyebrow.

"Mmm..."

He took the book through to the bar and stood reading. Carefully, he turned the pages. Many of them had notes in the margins in a variety of different hands. Searching through the text he discovered that, where Bartle had been right, there was usually an added note to say so. These confirming notes were seldom in the same handwriting. Clearly the book had been owned – or handed down – by a fair number of people. Not surprising given its age.

There were several referring to former architraves. Interestingly, it seemed that each one had a secret physical attribute which marked them out as unique and many were identified, in the prophecies, by these physical manifestations.

"I wonder if there's anything about the next guy in here. Then again, the future's not looking too rosy on that front."

"Cluck," said the chicken. It sounded hopeful.

"I wish I could share your optimism. If there is a Candidate, I should try to find him and give all this stuff back."

The chicken didn't say anything but he could almost hear its eyes roll.

"Don't get like that with me. I'm flying blind here," he said.

The chicken said nothing but The Pan's eyes were drawn to the ring on his finger.

"You reckon it's time to take this off and talk to them? Yeh, well, you may be right, IF they can stop shouting at me for a moment and listen." In his imagination the chicken was cocking its head on one side and giving him a bit of a look, "Yeh, I think so too but I need an hour or two first to get my head in order."

He riffled through the pages, reading a little here and there until he came to a page near the end. The text concerned one of the more abstruse sayings of The Prophet, which was helpfully underlined: *There will come an Architrave who will be given his nation in directions which oppose.'* it read. The Pan waded through the explanatory paragraph. Bartle declared, in the most flowery and turgid of academic language, that the phrase *'will be given'* was a mistranslation. In the original language, he said, the phrase meant something more like *'to be shown'* which, at the time The Prophet was writing also meant *'to see'*. He explained that he didn't understand why, but he was certain that this saying actually meant that the Architrave would be able to see his nation in opposite directions at the same time. Somebody had underlined that bit and written a note in the margin, *'How can the Candidate see backwards and forwards? Is he going to have eyes in the back of his head?'*

The Pan dropped the book in shock.

"Smeck," he squeaked. He clutched one of the beer pulls for support. "That really isn't funny."

"Cluck," said the chicken.

"No. It's not right." The Pan picked up the book, annoyed with himself for losing the place. He flicked through the pages trying to find the one he'd been reading but was distracted by a different chapter heading.

'General attributes' it said. The paragraphs below were surprisingly succinct and The Pan wondered if Bartle was quoting someone else.

"Hey, hen, this is interesting, listen to this: *'All architraves are endowed with an ability to bend space and time, to a greater or lesser extent.'* Whoa. *'This ability will not always be evident upon the Candidate's being chosen or even installed, but in many cases has manifested itself later on in life. Each and every instance has been reliably presaged by a singular alteration of the blood. The full capability to exercise this control will be extant within three weeks of the blood turning…'* What? Smeck, no. This doesn't compute."

"Cluck."

"Absolutely not."

"Cluck?" The chicken, no, the Eighth Architrave, The Pan reminded himself, sounded hopeful.

"I don't think so." Shaking, he put down the book. "It's alright, I'm just going mad that's all. You're not real, your mates aren't real and I've got a god complex."

He looked down at his hands and the ring. The ring worn by forty generations of Architraves. The ring that felt as if it was part of him, as if it wanted to belong to him. The ring which shrank to fit his finger but no-one else's; at least, it hadn't shrunk to fit Ruth. Then again maybe that was just the ring's way of warning him. After what happened with Lord Vernon… No. He mustn't think about Ruth. It would be his undoing. He picked up the book and re-read the page. Then, he managed to find the other bit and re-read that.

"Arnold's snot," he whispered.

His knees felt wobbly and the shock was making him dizzy. No he was just hyperventilating. Slow. Breathe. He concentrated on keeping his breathing normal and measured as he let the reality of the idea sink in. Well, on the up side, he'd found the Candidate. That was good. On the downside, look who it was.

"Arnold in the skies? What am I going to do?"

He was supposed to save his people. That was what everyone expected, that was what he had expected until the Candidate had refused to turn up; a powerful, charismatic leader who would stroll in with some giant army from – yes, nobody had really thought about where the army would come from – and defeat Lord Vernon, probably in one-to-one combat to the death. A man, or woman, who, by the sheer force of his personality would kick the Grongles out and unite all the warring resistance factions currently vying for control of K'Barth.

Unless it was a contest in cowardice, he didn't see how he could possibly defeat Lord Vernon. Why had he been so slow on the uptake? No, he knew why. And if he couldn't meet his own expectations, he was hardly going to live up to anyone else's.

"Arse. Now we're really in the doo-doo," said The Pan.

"Cluck," said the chicken casually, as if to say, 'Same-old, same-old.'

"It's alright for you. You're, already dead. How, in the name of The Prophet, am I going to fix this?"

Was he going to even try? Should he stay in hiding? And if he did, would he be safe? Did anyone else know? Stupid question. Sir Robin knew, and General Moteurs.

He stood a glass in the drip tray, under the pump that dispensed Humbert's Wall Smacker, the strongest beer. Gladys and Ada's first rule of running a pub was that no publican should ever pull themselves a pint. They confined themselves to brewing the beer and tasting it, in very small quantities, to ensure it lived up to their quality standards. But Gladys and Ada hadn't just found out they were the Candidate had they? The Pan glanced up at the bottles of shorts, lined up along the mirrored wall behind him. Maybe...?

No. That would definitely be going too far.

He gripped the beer pump and filled the glass to the brim. Where would all the re-assimilation cobblers the Grongles had promised him be now? He was straight back to being public enemy number one – this time, with brass knobs on – although maybe he could use his pardoned status as a blind. With a sigh, The Pan checked his watch, just over half an hour until opening time. He unlocked the door, went outside and checked for early customers.

None in the offing. Hardly surprising and even if they did turn up it would probably only be to lynch him. He took down the menu board and removed the chalk from Gladys and Ada's allotted place, a small hole between two bricks, behind where it hung, and wrote, *'Dear Patrons, On behalf of Gladys Parker and Ada Maddox, The Pan of Hamgee, caretaker manager, welcomes you to The Parrot and Screwdriver.'*

He underlined the phrase *'caretaker manager'*, replaced the chalk and the board and stepped back to view his handiwork. Hmm, it might work, if anyone could read his writing. With a heavy sigh, he went back inside. As he closed the door, something sharp dug itself into his good shoulder and The Pan screamed.

"Bite my winky!" shouted a voice.

"Arnold's toe jam, Humbert! You scared the life out of me."

When he had gone out, he hadn't noticed that he'd let Ada's pet parrot in.

"Wipe my conkers!" said Humbert, as if by way of apology.

"Alright Humbert. You know the drill, your place is over there." The Pan nodded at Humbert's usual perch by the bar and jiggled his shoulder to make him move. Humbert stayed put and all the jiggling did was tighten the pressure of sharp claws digging into The Pan's soft flesh. "Ouch. Don't you go knackering my other arm. Get off. Go on. I can't sort out the pub with you there." Still nothing doing. "Come on parrot. Please. Ada would want me to sort out the pub."

"Jiggle my tumpkin!" shouted Humbert, pretty much into The Pan's ear.

"Ouch, Humbert! Go on, over there."

Finally, reluctantly, Humbert took off but, avoiding his perch, he flew into the hall and The Pan heard the sounds of his gleeful squawking disappearing upstairs. Good.

He picked up his beer and downed it in one. He felt restless and he wanted to walk. He also needed to think, but after Lord Vernon's hand-over ceremony, he feared he might be set upon if he braved the streets. He put the keys in his pocket and went out via the back door of the pub to the alley where the bins were. He glanced at the drainpipe he usually used to climb up to the landing window. It went right on up to the roof, and when the need arose, so did The Pan. Much quicker than the fire escape.

However, tonight, he decided one-handed climbing would be a bridge too far, especially after a shock like he'd just had. So he went the conventional way, up the fire escape.

Chapter 40

Once he was on the roof of the Parrot and Screwdriver, the whole neighbourhood was spread out before The Pan. Some of it was on his level and a few notable buildings ranged above him, but most of it was below.

The houses on many of the City's streets were separated by narrow alleys – because of the risk of fire – but, for the same reason, most were linked with escape ladders and walkways at roof level. As an ex-GBI, The Pan knew many of these walkways as well as, if not better, than the streets below. At certain times of the day and night they were dangerous and best avoided but not now. It was early. That gap in people's evenings when they were bathing the kids, eating or getting dolled up to go out. If anyone had bothered to look up, they would have seen The Pan walking alone above the streets, silhouetted against the orange and red of the sunset sky.

He walked the length of Turnadot Street along the roofs and gullies, hopping the alleys, which were only narrow, as he went – it was easy enough terrain, little more than a stroll for The Pan, even with an injury. The air was cool and fresh on his face, and as he tramped through his home neighbourhood, the familiar sights and sounds – not to mention the odd smell – rose up from the streets below and soothed him. After a few minutes, he stopped to enjoy the view again.

He assessed his situation. His friends and family were gone. Once again, he was on his own – he glanced down at the ring – but somehow that didn't matter. He'd always been alone. He always would be alone. There was only ever one Candidate, one real one, anyway.

He was going to have to face Lord Vernon.

Alone.

Nobody could do this for him.

"Cluck."

"Yeh, that's right, hen. I'm in deep poop." But now, as he stood gazing out over the city he loved, his city, he knew what he was going to do. He couldn't defeat Lord Vernon in a million years but he could stop him from becoming Architrave. Ever. And maybe that was enough.

"Cluck?" said the Eighth Architrave.

"Yeh, it'll have to be."

He could and he would make things right. The thread would not be broken. There would be another Architrave, The Pan was sure of it. Lord Vernon would rule with an iron fist and thousands of K'Barthans would die but there would be someone else when The Pan had gone; a better man or woman, who could – who would – deliver them. He saw it clearly. His job was to die; his life for his people. No wonder Sir Robin had been so cagey, the old boy knew the score.

"Yeh and so do I now," said The Pan to himself.

He only had one chance to make things right and that made him nervous; far more nervous than the prospect of imminent death. Stuff up his part and everything would crumble; K'Barth would be gone forever. A way of life, a national outlook, a civilisation was depending on him.

"Smecking Arnold! No pressure then."

He took the box out of his pocket and flipped it open.

He would have to lay plans. Take measures to ensure his successor had the best possible chance, and then, in an action-packed Saturday, get killed.

He was no longer despairing and wanting to die. He felt the way he had in prison, when he'd heard he was going to be released. Nothing to lose; nothing to fear. Once again, he savoured the sense of liberation.

"Bring it on," he said and he began to make a mental checklist of what he must do.

"Number 1. Die. Hmm, there must be a better way of putting that."

In his mind's eye, he wrote in the other stuff. He had to sort out a support network, however lame, to look out for and guide his successor and he only had five days to do it in. Sure it seemed like an impossible dream but strangely, not so daunting. He couldn't fail any more comprehensively than this; the only possible direction was up. So, if he achieved anything he could count it a success.

"Arnold," he said. His head was buzzing with ideas, most of them decidedly dangerous. And while he was no longer frightened of death, he was nervous of dying at the wrong time, or in the wrong place. How he wished there was someone he could talk to.

The eighth Architrave didn't actually say anything but The Pan knew what it was thinking about; his predecessors. He wondered if they could help. It was probably time he spoke to them. He looked down at the ring on his finger and moved it upwards a little. Immediately he could hear the sound of voices, as if coming from far away. They were arguing.

"Marvellous. This is going to be fun," he muttered. Never mind, there were 75 Architraves in his head... and the chicken. Only Arnold was missing. They were properly educated, pointy-brained scholars and they were a powerful resource. If he could persuade them to stop bickering and help him.

"OK, Mr Chicken. I'm going to give you a few moments, to explain to the folks in here," he pointed to his temple, "that we need to have a chat. Do you think they would be able to help me?"

"Cluck." That sounded like a 'yes'.

"Help, in this case, does not comprise everyone shouting at me at once. OK?"

"Cluck?"

"Or I will immediately put the ring back on again, understood?"

"Cluck."

"And not take it off again."

"Cluck."

"Good, ditto if anyone so much as mentions the Chosen One, right?"

"Cluck."

"Right then. On you go."

"Cluck."

The Pan leaned against a nearby chimneystack and gazed out over the city. The sun was setting and the clouds in the sky tinged orange and pink. He glanced at his watch. He must open the pub in 45 minutes. There was just about time but he'd have to make this quick. Somehow, he realised the chicken and three of his predecessors were waiting to talk.

Alright. Here went nothing.

He took a deep breath and took off the ring.

The hubbub of voices that greeted what felt like his ears, fell silent.

"Right, ladies and gentlemen. I'm the Candidate, I'm your next-in-line and somehow, I am supposed to get my nation out of all this doo-doo. Any ideas?"

"You must raise an army."

The Pan put his hand up in a no-please-stop gesture.

"I have until Saturday. That's not enough time and actually, so far as there is an army, it's the Resistance and it belongs to," an image of

Denarghi appeared briefly in his head, "somebody who is unwilling to share it with me."

There was a long silence, which was unexpected. He had prepared himself for some more argy-bargy with his more old-school predecessors, or at least, the most recent one. When, eventually, one of them spoke, it was a lady.

"Good evening, I am the thirty-ninth Architrave, Rowena."

Well, that was easy to remember. When each Candidate was installed they would take an Architraval name. The K'Barthan Architraves were an unoriginal lot, most of the ladies chose the same name, Jennifer – there were 15 Jennifers – while the lion's share of the males plumped for Louis – there were 21 of those. Rowena was easy because it was different.

"Hi, Rowena," said The Pan.

"Please call me 39. We all answer to the number of our succession. It saves confusion."

Well, yes, with all those Jennifers and Louis The Pan could understand that.

"Alright. Hello 39," he said. "I guess that makes me 78." He couldn't help bowing, even though there was nobody there. "At your service."

"Not yet," said a male voice, which introduced itself as 43.

"Fair enough, then you'd better call me Defreville." He still felt slightly weird using his real name.

"What is your plan?" asked 43.

The Pan was thrown.

"What plan? I have no plan. You must know that, you live in my head," he said. He could almost hear 43 heaving a heavy sigh.

"What are your intentions?"

The same question, rephrased. What a numpty. The Pan shrugged.

"I'm not 100% sure yet. I thought I'd turn up at the installation and prove Lord Vernon is not the Candidate. As I understand it, to ensure the succession, that's all it will take."

"You are correct," said 39.

"Good, but that's not until Saturday. What I wanted to ask you about is what I do before then, how I can help the next—"

"How will you get into the High Temple?" asked 43.

The Pan hadn't really considered this but now he did.

"General Moteurs."

"Who is this General Moteurs? You said you had no army."

The Pan had assumed that, whether or not they were living in his head, the Architraves were privy to all his thoughts. Now it appeared they weren't aware of everything that went on in there. Interesting.

"A man on the inside," said The Pan.

"Unless the Grongles have changed a great deal in the last 5 years, they will not empower non-Grongles with the level of security clearance required to access tickets," said 77.

"Lucky it's a Grongle 'man' then, isn't it?"

"A Grongle?" spluttered 77.

"Yep."

"A General? And you trust him?" asked 43 incredulously.

"Yes. He's Underground and he saved my life."

"And that's all it took? How touchingly naive of you."

The Pan was beginning to develop a dislike for 43. He was used to being considered cynical and worldly. Being called 'naive' rankled.

"Perhaps, but I don't think so. He's a better man than I am."

There was a stunned silence.

"You're the Candidate, nobody's better than you are... except us because we're Architraves."

The Pan laughed.

"Don't be silly. Most people are better than I am."

"We're doomed," said 77 theatrically.

"Get a grip," said The Pan. "Alright, look, this isn't what I wanted to talk to you about, what I need your help with is—"

"Am I to understand that you have aligned yourself with Grongles?" demanded 39. She didn't sound very pleased either.

"Some of them."

"And alienated the Resistance?"

"No, just their leader, although, they take a pretty extremist stance right now and I don't know how many of their top people see things the way he does. I know they're compromised—"

"Your Grongle friends told you that did they?"

"No. Lord Vernon."

There was silence.

"Yeh. The guy who broke my collarbone."

"Who tortured you, yet you still prefer to work with Grongles than your own populous."

"No. I was recruited, or at least that's how it felt, by the last remnants of your government, 77; Sir Robin Get—"

"Who guided me to my execution." 77 cut in.

The Pan wasn't certain that's how it would have happened. If 77 was true to his public form his execution was likely to be in spite of, rather than because of, Sir Robin. Then again, he thought about where Sir Robin had guided him, in a roundabout way: to the grim task of proving that Lord Vernon was a fake and then getting killed, probably on world telly.

"Yeh, well, I give you that he's pretty ruthless."

"And clearly senile if he consorts with Grongles."

"Will you listen to yourselves? He runs the Underground. He *is* the Underground. Well... was. I suppose I am now. We have to be realistic about this. We don't have the power to get rid of the Grongles. Even if we overthrow them, here in K'Barth, their government will just declare war on us, inflict a crushing defeat and put them back. Look at me. Do you see a Warlord?" There was a long, long silence. "No. I didn't think so, and I'm all you have to work with and you have to accept that. As far as I can see, the only way to free K'Barth is to change the way Grongolia is governed, too. We can only do that with their help and by some incredible stroke of luck, I happen to have found a bunch of them who want to do just that. It's too good a chance to pass up."

"It's too great a coincidence to take up. What if this is a ruse, to trap any vestiges of meaningful resistance?"

"Even if it is, I should still get to ensure the succession. I know I have to die but if you want to, the place where you can make a difference is ensuring that it sticks; that the Candidate after me knows who he is and what he is for. I didn't until it was too late. Now, I have been given nearly a week, until Saturday, to find a way to fix that for him, to give him the knowledge he needs to succeed. You forget, you lot grew up knowing what you were for, you were educated to run a nation. It's hard to work it out on your own, the way things are going, he may not even be educated."

"Or he may realise, naturally. After all, there's a possibility he may be more intelligent than you," said 43.

"Yeh, or he may be less arrogant than you."

"What if 'he's' a she?" said 77.

"The same applies if they're an 'it'," said The Pan.

This wasn't going well. The Architraves seemed determined to question the things that he was sure about, and to stop him from asking the questions he wanted answered. He looked down at the ring in his hand and was tempted, very tempted, to put it on again.

"Do you seek unity with the Resistance?" asked number 39.

"It would be logical wouldn't it? Unity, full-stop would be great. The only problem is, Denarghi will probably kill me before I can get close enough to ask. I need to get to him, somehow, though, without him knowing it's me. It's only right that I should warn him. His whole organisation is in trouble and he hasn't a blind clue."

"So you said. But, if the Resistance are against you and helping them is so difficult why would you come to their aid? Let the Grongles remove them and your successor will have one less problem to face," said 43 calmly.

Arnold! What a ruthless smecker! Surely even Sir Robin wouldn't condone that. The Pan tried to hide his shock and made a mental note – hopefully not audible to the Architraves in his head – that he must find some history books and read up on 43.

"Tempting, but it's hardly the K'Barthan way. Anyway, if the Grongles have portals and we don't, it will impact on everyone in K'Barth, I'm sure you appreciate that."

"You clearly know nothing about the K'Barthan way," 43 snorted derisively.

"I'm sure that's true, but I know the difference between right and wrong. You seem to be having a bit of trouble with that."

"What is right is not always what is best. A little ruthlessness gets one ahead and a strong leader, with charisma, knows that," said 43.

"Yeh, that's what Lord Vernon says. I couldn't possibly comment."

"Do you impugn me?"

"You paraphrased him."

This was a waste of time. The conversation was going nowhere and The Pan was bitterly disappointed. He'd expected more than this. They clearly thought he was a weak, lily-livered idiot and, while they might be right, it didn't stop him feeling angry.

"I've had enough of this," he snapped. "It's alright for you lot, you're dead. I'm not. You may be Architraves, and I may be a mere Candidate, but I'm the guy on the ground, and I'm calling the shots here. Not you. You can help me if you like, or you can sit there pointing out the blindingly obvious truth, which serves nothing: that I'm an idiot."

"If you—"

"Shut it, 43, I'm talking," said The Pan, Big Merv style. It felt good. "If you want me to save K'Barth try helping me. Here are some things I need to know. One, the Grongles have some portals and judging by the way they got me here, they've reverse engineered them already. If they haven't they're close. That's an arms race I need to equalise, although how the hell I go about it when the Resistance are likely to kill me on sight, I don't know; any ideas gratefully received. Two, my successor will need some kind of guide – the basic information – in case he, or she, is like me. You can stick your heads in the sand and believe they'll be better but I can't, I have to cover the options. They'll also need a bunch of venerable elders like Sir Robin, Gladys and Ada to act as custodians, until they arrive, and as guides when they do. I need to find those people and, if you like, you can help me pick them. Three, I have some pirate portals in my cellar and I want to make some more. Yeh, I know it's a lost art but surely some of you will remember how it's done or know something that will help me to work it out. Four, if you can think of some way I can achieve any of these things in the next few days, without getting killed, that would be helpful.

"That's what I require from you. I have a pub to run now, without you lot coddling my brains, so I'll put the ring back on and give you some time to think. You decide if you're going to be of some actual use. I'll look forward to hearing your answer, later, when I take the ring off again, at which point, you will not be giving me any crap. At all. Unless you want me to put it back on for the rest of time."

"How dare you! You can't speak to us like—" began 43.

"Yes I can," said The Pan and with a small smile he put on the ring.

The voice of 39, loaded with sarcasm, saying, "Well done gentlemen, great job!" faded into nothing and they were gone. He listened to the sound of distant traffic, music playing in one of the rooms below and voices drifting up from the street. Then he was distracted by a new sound. He'd never heard a chicken laugh before.

"It's not funny, hen! Arnold, you never told me they were such a bunch of pompous arseholes!"

"Cluck."

"It didn't go very well did it?"

The chicken said nothing.

"No. How can I be related, even astrally, to these gets?"

He had a mental picture of a chicken spreading its wings in a very human search-me shrug.

"Arnold's snot, after I've snuffed it, eternity with that lot is going to last a very long time."

He got the impression the eighth architrave was raising his eyebrows, even though, as a chicken, he couldn't possibly have had any.

"They're not all smeckers, then? No, of course they aren't, you're not. Still, I wonder why they had to pick the gits to talk to me."

The chicken, or should he call it Eight, didn't say anything. He got the impression it wanted to, but perhaps, it didn't know where to begin. The Pan checked his watch.

"Come on. We'll sort this out later. It's time to open the pub."

Chapter 41

Deirdre sat on her bed. She hoped Snoofle was OK. He had been back to visit after work, along with Mrs Pargeter and a contingent of the 'girls' from the drying room, Sid the Head Launderer and the Grongle medic, Dr Dot. She wondered what he was doing now.

However, she worried about Snoofle's safety long term. She no longer trusted Denarghi and Plumby. She no longer trusted anyone, other than Snoofle and herself... and perhaps the Grongle Doctor. She trusted General Moteurs too, in that she felt he could be consistently relied upon to act like a total smecker. Not exactly the same kind of trust, that. Dr Dot had brought her a selection of books and she had spread them out of the bed while she tried to occupy her thoughts with the business of choosing which one to read first. She was still wondering when, with the standard jangling of keys, the door was unlocked. Corporal Jones appeared with one of her troops. He carried a long canvas garment bag, with a zip up the front and he was holding it by the hanger poking out of the top.

"Lieutenant, ma'am," said Corporal Jones saluting smartly.

Deirdre returned the salute.

"At ease, Corporal." The Corporal might be Grongolian but she was a truly professional soldier; the kind of soldier Deirdre would be happy to command. "In future, there is no need to stand on ceremony. You do not answer to me."

"Please accept my thanks," said Corporal Jones, "yet, I would dishonour you if I did not accord your rank the respect it deserves."

"Understood," said Deirdre. "Corporal, what is this?"

"General Moteurs requests the pleasure of your company for dinner, ma'am."

"What if I would rather be alone?"

This clearly wasn't the answer Corporal Jones was expecting.

"The General is aware you might consider his invitation impertinent but he asked me, whatever your response, to leave this with you and allow you some time to consider before I return for your answer."

"It won't change."

"As you wish, ma'am but I regret I must obey my orders. I will leave this here and return for it shortly."

While she knew her answer, right now, Deirdre bit back a scathing retort in deference to Corporal Jones. All she said was.

"Understood. Thank you."

"That's alright," said Corporal Jones and to the guard, "Leave it there."

Both females watched the guard as he laid the bag out flat on the bed originally designated for Snoofle. At the door, Corporal Jones turned back to Deirdre. "Lieutenant..." She was hesitant, shy even. "The clothes are not what you think."

"Thank you. I appreciate your reassurance," said Deirdre.

The Corporal and her guard saluted and left. When they had locked the door, Deirdre sat down on her bed and looked at the garment bag with something approaching loathing. Part of her didn't want to give General Moteurs the gratification of opening it but, unfortunately, the rest of her was consumed with curiosity. It wasn't what she thought, Corporal Jones had said. Deirdre thought it was a dress, probably low cut, flattering and extremely revealing, General Moteurs was a male, after all. Then again, he was a supremely uninterested one, crushingly uninterested. So if it wasn't a dress what was it?

Eventually, she could bear the suspense no longer. She went over to the bag and unzipped it. She could not suppress a gasp of surprise at what she found. She unhooked the canvas and lifted it up. It was a dress uniform: Lieutenant, Resistance, First Class. She didn't have to guess whether it fitted, she knew. It had been carefully made to measure, like the other clothes the Grongles had given her. It was cut from finer, softer cloth and made with greater skill but otherwise it was a stitch-perfect replica of her own.

"Arnold above." She sat down, light headed. Smecking General Moteurs! He knew what he was doing, pulling off a stunt like that. It had hit home, too. In the uniform, he'd anticipated the needs and desires of her innermost self with scary accuracy. It was the perfect gift, something she'd been missing but hadn't known she wanted. Now what? He would be expecting her to acquiesce to his request but she would not be a pushover.

"You will not play me, General," she said firmly. He might think he was pressing her psychological buttons – and Deirdre conceded, with resignation, that he might be succeeding – but she knew what was happening and she wasn't going to cooperate. Yeh. He'd be laughing on the other side of his snot-coloured face when she'd torn him off a strip. Which she was going to. Because nobody manipulated, Deirdre Arbuthnot. No-one. Ever.

"Arnold, by The Prophet!" She put the uniform to one side and tried to think. No, wait a moment. She picked it up, went over to the mantelpiece and hung it up. No point in letting it get creased. She examined it again. It was fabulous. Deirdre could afford a pretty good tailor but this was in a class of its own. It was clear that someone had been let loose on the buttons and belt to polish them to a way-beyond-factory-fresh, military shine. All the same, she reckoned she could add a little more sparkle, an extra dash of lustre. Although, clearly, she would only do so as a way to pass the time because she wouldn't be wearing it. No. Of course not, because she would NOT be dining with General Moteurs.

"No," she said aloud except that this particular 'gift' had piqued her interest and even now she was weakening, wondering, wanting to know. It was so un-male. He had asked her to dinner and then he had presented her with the one thing to wear that was not about her femininity. Something which made her feel utterly, unequivocally equal to all comers and confident in herself. He would know that, too. He'd ditched flattering her figure in favour of the altogether more sophisticated type of flattery. She had wished, for so long, to meet a male who would see beyond her looks, so why was she so annoyed when General Moteurs did just that? 'Dinner' was a loaded word. He would appreciate Deirdre's sensitivity to such an invitation. So, as she understood it, the message he was sending with the uniform was that he saw beyond her beauty; that his intentions were honourable; that he had no ulterior motives. Surely, that painted him as rather more sensitive and thoughtful than average. So why did she suddenly want him to be like every other male and run around after her as if he was on heat? Perhaps her fear of him was getting in the way, because Deirdre did fear General Moteurs. He left her feeling defenceless and vulnerable, because he was cleverer than her, and clearly attuned to her thoughts, possibly to the point of omnipotence.

Flipping Arnold, she was seriously losing the plot. If only Snoofle had been there to talk her down. She tried to imagine the kinds of things he would have said. She stood up and paced the room. Moving about seemed to help her think. Finally she took a paper and pencil, sat at the table and started to write. When Corporal Jones came back, Deirdre had her answer.

"Please thank your commander for his invitation but I regret that I cannot dine with him tonight. Although, if you are able to provide me with the items on this list, I believe I would be able to meet him tomorrow evening."

Corporal Jones took the piece of paper from Deirdre's outstretched hand and read it. Deirdre had written a list; soft cloths, metal polish, leather polish, chamois leather and boot brushes. The corporal glanced up from the list and smiled.

"This is your answer ma'am?"

"Yes."

"The General will not be expecting it." A suggestion, in her tone, that it was not necessarily a bad thing.

"No?"

"No. He was adamant that you would be joining him."

"Then I will be glad to teach him some humility."

This was clearly another unexpected answer. Deirdre waited while Corporal Jones took a second to regroup.

"Ma'am."

"Please tell General Moteurs that if he is prepared to give me such a generous gift, it behoves me to do it justice. As he will understand, that takes time."

"He will be pleased to hear that," said Corporal Jones, dead pan.

Yeh, Deirdre bet he would.

"Good," she said.

Chapter 42

The Pan turned to pick his way along the roofs the way he had come and stopped. Something was wrong. He waited, listening and watching. He had turned his thoughts inwards while he was talking to the Architraves, closing his eyes and trying to fit the fleeting visual impressions he had with the sound of each voice. It had absorbed him and that was dangerous. He'd left himself vulnerable. Extra eyes make no difference if you don't use them. He could see no-one behind him but all his instincts told him things were amiss.

"Mmm..." he said to himself. He took a step forward and three robbers leapt into his path, barring the way. At the same time, two more jumped out behind him. They weren't human, either, they were Blurpons.

"Smecking Arnold," said The Pan before he could stop himself.

"That's no way to greet a fellow traveller," said the Blurpon at the front. They were all wearing utility belts, bandolier style, bristling with weaponry. Not that they needed any. The average Blurpon is a pretty lethal weapon on its own.

"Sorry, don't mind me, I was distracted." The Pan stood to one side to let them pass but they didn't move. One of the three got out a mobile phone and took The Pan's photo.

This was not good. The spot he had chosen to talk to the Architraves was out of the way. It was a good place to spend half an hour ranting at a bunch of imaginary people no-one else could see, but a bad place to be ambushed. The thieves had him cornered and they knew it.

The irony was not lost on The Pan that he'd spent half the day planning how to get murdered and now, having changed his mind, he was close to achieving his original aim. Were he not nursing an injury he could have made off over the roofs to his right. But that route required him to swing on the pawnbroker's sign and make a big leap to the awning half way up the building opposite. With only one functioning arm, he didn't trust himself to make it – they probably knew that, too. Unless... there was another way but if he timed it wrong, he'd end up dead. Then again, if he stayed where he was he'd end up dead anyway, he suspected.

Here went nothing then.

He leapt into action, sprinting halfway up the roof next to him and springing over the heads of the three Blurpons in front of him, to the roof on his left. He was up the tiles, over the ridge the other side before they could react. Slithering and sliding down the slates, desperately trying to keep a purchase, he jumped Turnadot Street at a point where it narrowed and the buildings the other side were lower. He cursed at the pain from his shoulder, as he instinctively swung his arms. He accelerated up the gap between two roofs. A knife bounced off the stonework beside him and then he was out of range, sprinting back down the roofs the other side of Turnadot Street, towards the square where Upper Left Central Market took place. He would have to do a circuit of the square, street jumping as he went, and double back down the side of Turnadot Street he'd originally been on, once he'd lost them.

Through his extra eyes, he saw that the Blurpons had also crossed Turnadot Street. They split; two going left and two right. They were going to garden hop and cut him off at the entrance to Dumpty Street, a long wide boulevard leading up to one of the City's land mark parks. There was a washing line across Dumpty Street, which Mrs Ormaloo's Blurpon Laundry and Darning Service, on the corner, used to dry some of the larger items that couldn't be hung out in the roof top drying area. With only three working limbs he was unsure about crossing it. Needs must. He couldn't see it but he knew it was there, up ahead and if he kept going, and got across it before them, he could probably lose them while they crossed.

Checking to the sides and below in the gardens, he kept pushing on, scrabbling up and down roofs, leaping alleys and all the while exclaiming colourfully as every high speed landing jarred his broken collarbone. He thought he saw a flash of red fur as one of the Blurpons leapt over a garden wall below him. He was gaining on them. Good. He should get to the wire ahead of them if he was quick. The buildings were commercial now. He ran across the flat roof of an office block, leapt from table to table of a roof garden for the employees who, luckily, had gone home. He slowed and stepped onto the painted metal railing at the edge, walking carefully along it, like a tightrope walker and along a pipe that ran across the alley between the building and its neighbour.

Still no sign of the Blurpons. Nearly there now. He jumped onto the top of a lift shaft, walked the few feet across it and there it was, the wire.

He checked around him but he was alone.

Gritting his teeth, he wrapped his elbow of his good arm round the wire, crossed his ankles over it and began to shin over Dumpty Street. He gritted his teeth and swore under his breath with each painful movement but he must keep going, must stay ahead. His arm ached, from carrying all his weight and his shoulder from being jarred about as he ran. Normally he did this hand over hand, pushing himself with his arms, his legs hooked loosely over the wire. Today he hadn't the reserves of pain resistance to go hand over hand. Slowly, slowly he caterpillared his way across.

"Arnold they're going to catch me any minute," he muttered.

"Cluck," said the chicken, by way of encouragement.

After what seemed like half a lifetime but was probably only about twenty seconds, he reached the end and dropped down, thankfully, onto the roof of Taffy's Joke Emporium and Costumier to the Stars. He stood up. Still no Blurpons behind him. That wasn't right.

"Where in the name of The Prophet are they?" he muttered as he started cautiously across the roof.

"Right here, old friend."

The five Blurpons surrounded him, closer this time.

Arnold's nostril hair.

"That was interesting. You're good, very good but we're better," said their leader.

The Pan put his hands out in front of him, calm down style, wincing at the pain in his shoulder.

"I don't want to fall out with you."

"No you don't."

He realised he'd put the ring on his free hand, again. Idiot, he thought, as he shoved it deep in his jacket pocket.

"'S a nice ring you got there, mate," said one of the Blurpons, presumably, their leader.

"What ring?"

"The one on your finger," The Pan just managed to stop himself from saying, 'What finger?'

"In your pocket," the robber said evenly, "show me."

"I don't think that's a good idea—"

"I said show me." Slowly, all the more for The Pan to appreciate the gravity of what he was doing, he unsheathed a throwing knife.

"Alright, keep calm," said The Pan half to the Blurpon, half to himself.

He took his hand out of his pocket and held it up in the air. The head thief blew the air out of his cheeks.

"Whoa, that's some rock. A bit good for a bloke who's been standing shouting at himself, I'd say."

"Not really. I've had it for years." If only they knew how true that was. On second thoughts, no, best they didn't.

"I wonder. You see, there's only a certain type of fellow uses these paths, unless there's a fire. That building you were standing on wasn't on fire, was it?"

"No."

"Then, I believe that makes you a certain type of fellow."

"It doesn't have to. I'm only a publican, taking a walk."

"Of course you are. If that's 'taking a walk', I'd like to see you do something strenuous."

He noticed the two Blurpon's behind him creep a little closer. They seemed well organised for random foot pads. The Pan wondered if they were members of the Resistance, from its very active revenue acquisition section.

"It's the truth, unlikely as it may seem. I am a publican."

"I don't think so. Nobody honest roof jumps like that, especially not when they're nursing a broken arm."

"It's not my arm it's my collarbone."

"Yeh, whatever. I tell you what, here's how this is going to roll. You're going to give me that ring and you're going to empty your pockets and you're going to put all the stuff in a nice pile just here," he pointed to the space between them, "then you're going to tell me where you nicked it from. You see, there's only so much a fellow like you can carry but going on the quality of that stone, I'd think that, wherever you got it, there's more. So my friends and I, we're going help ourselves to the rest."

"It came from a bank."

"Oh yeh?"

"Yes."

"Which one?"

"You don't want to know. Listen, can we try to work something out? I don't want to argue but it simply isn't possible to give you this ring."

"It is if you want to live."

"I can't, it's mine and I need it for... a business meeting on Saturday. You're welcome to it after then."

"Who is this joker?" the Blurpon asked his colleagues.

"I mean it, I give you my word, Saturday and you can have it but I can't afford to die now."

"Then you'll do as I say."

"Please, if you'll let me explain—"

The Blurpon made to throw the knife and, as The Pan ducked, he really did throw it. It grazed past The Pan's face; a warning shot. There was a leathery 'thock' as one of the ones behind him caught it. Arnold he was fast. He was Resistance. With reflexes like that he must be. The Pan watched, in dismay, as he drew a second and third knife from a row along one of his belts. Arnold's pants. How many did he have?

"I don't think you heard me. I said, you'll do as I say. I'm giving you the chance to walk out of this alive but if I have to throw either of these," the Blurpon moved the knives for emphasis, "I won't miss. Are we clear?"

For a small, cute, furry guy, he packed a lot of menace.

"Very." The Pan put his hand into his pocket, taking care to ensure the first item he removed was Gladys and Ada's pirate portal, rather than the 2,000 year old snuff box that only the Candidates and Architraves of K'Barth could open. "This is becoming a habit," he muttered as he thought about the alleyway outside the Parrot and Screwdriver and put his thumb in. He landed hard and at speed, rolled a couple of times and ended up standing.

That had been lucky, he was sore but there was no harm done. He threw the jar against the wall but it bounced off and rolled back into the road.

"Arnold's bogies!" He jumped up and down on it.

Nothing.

Beginning to panic, he cast around him. There, by the dustbins, he noticed a half brick. Knowing the folks round Turnadot Street it had probably fallen out of somebody's sock. He brought it down on the jar with all his strength, finally managing to smash it.

"Definitely a bad plan to make a habit of this," he muttered. It had been close and he was annoyed with himself, there was no need to give the Architraves the gratification of being as stupid as they thought he was. He took his keys from his pocket and with shaking hands, he unlocked the pub and went inside.

Chapter 43

The Pan went through the bar and unlocked the main doors of The Parrot and Screwdriver. He turned on the lights and then retreated into the Holy of Holies for a quick wash and brush up. He had a light graze on one cheek from the knife the Blurpon robber had thrown at him, and it was bleeding slightly. Blue.

"Arnold's toe jam." He dabbed it with a handkerchief until it stopped. It was at about this point that he heard the sound of someone clearing their throat. It seemed to be coming from the bar. Ah yes. He had opened the pub; customers.

When The Pan walked back out of the Holy of Holies he was alarmed to find just about every one of the regulars waiting in silence. There were a lot of them and, as they gathered round him, he couldn't help noticing that nearly all the hardest male regulars were at the front – along with Pub Quiz Alan. As the defending trivia quiz champion for Upper Left Central Ning Dang Po, Pub Quiz Alan was the nearest to 'the brains' for their enterprise that The Parrot's regulars would have access to. Another thing The Pan couldn't help noticing was that everyone was armed; conspicuously and mostly bluntly. Lord Vernon's plan was working but at the same time, if they were here to beat him to a pulp, at least it looked as if they were going to speak to him first. He prayed to The Prophet that he could persuade them to enter into an actual dialogue rather than a statement like, 'You're going to die, scum bag,' Followed by swift execution – The Pan eyed some of the weapons – or probably not so swift. Yikes.

"Good evening ladies and gentlemen," he said in a squeaky voice. He cleared his throat and attempted to sound more manly when he added. "What'll it be?"

"We'll buy nothing from you, traitor," said Psycho Dave who was rumoured to be a professional henchman and was one of the largest and most violent-looking of the Parrot's regulars. Unfortunately, at the same time somebody else ruined the effect by saying.

"I'll have a packet of beef rubbings."

Oh.

There was an awkward silence. The other speaker, seeking bar snacks, was Giant Hairy Ron, so called because he was built similarly to Psycho Dave, that is, almost Grongle height but with a wild, unkempt and decidedly, un-Grongolian beard. Grongles don't go for facial hair.

"Sorry Ron, I don't have any beef rubbings but you can have these on the house. Then no-one has to buy anything – which'll make you happy, Dave."

Slowly because he realised they might be jumpy, The Pan retreated behind the bar and reached for one of the bags of nuts covering the female Swamp Thing.

"Nah. Not them. If it's gotta be nuts, I'll have the dry roasted."

Ah maybe that explained Arnold The Prophet's popularity over the promise of uncovered girly bits. The Swamp Thing lady's nuts were plain.

The Pan took the last bag off the famous portrait of Arnold, The Prophet, finally revealing the painted hand and notably, the ring on its finger. At the same time, the ruby on The Pan's ring, the real one, flashed in the light.

Balls. He'd forgotten about that. He realised he'd missed yet another opportunity to put the ring on his other hand where it would have been hidden by the sling. Too late now. He'd just have to brazen it out.

The Pan put the packet of nuts on the bar and the eyes of the Parrot's regulars, and Pub Quiz Alan, moved from the ring on his hand to the ring on the poster and back. The Pan pretended not to notice. He leaned his good hand on the beer pump and tried to project the persona of a calm, professional publican in complete control of his beery domain. The eyes of the punters continued to follow every movement of The Pan's hand, as if mesmerised.

Arse.

"Anyone else?" his voice sounded much calmer than he felt.

Silence.

"What can I get you?"

"First up you can come out from behind that bar and face us like a man," said Pub Quiz Alan, his gaze slid to The Pan's hand resting on the beer pump, up to the poster behind him and then back to his face.

"Alright." The Pan put up his hands, or at least, the one he could, and moved slowly out from the safety of the bar. The punters, and there were a lot of them, watched him. He had been in enough of these kinds of situations to know that calmness was essential and tried to project that perfect combination of authority without cockiness. It was difficult. He walked up to Pub Quiz Alan and stopped in front of him. Immediately, he wished he'd chosen to stand a couple of feet further away, with the reassuring woodiness of the bar against his back, "I'm guessing things look pretty bad for me right now," he said.

"That's right," said Pub Quiz Alan.

"Yer," said another regular, a man called Norris, with broken front teeth and a peculiar smell about him that nobody could quite place.

"You betrayed two sweet, helpless old ladies and we don't like that."

The Pan laughed before he could stop himself.

"Gladys and Ada are far from helpless and aren't you forgetting Trev?"

"You still betrayed them," said Pub Quiz Alan.

"You think so do you?" said The Pan. "I'd like to hear your reasoning."

"That little ceremony out there," Pub Quiz Alan jerked his thumb over one shoulder, towards the door onto the street.

"Yeh, that's right, Lord Vernon's faithful servant," said Norris. They were closing in around him, blocking his escape. A couple of heavy types The Pan didn't recognise were moving behind him. Had the punters hired in? Maybe, but more likely these'd be Big Psycho Dave's mates. Here went nothing then.

"Alright Alan, tell me something. If Lord Vernon likes me so much, why would he have that little ceremony in front of you lot? He's not stupid, he'd have known I was going to get lynched."

"We'll decide if you're going to get lynched, sunshine," said Giant Hairy Ron.

"Fair enough, Ron, the decision is yours but my question still stands."

"I dunno, but how come you're standing here, when Gladys and Ada are in the slammer?" asked Pub Quiz Alan quietly. Not good quietly, either, more, I'm-about-to-rip-your-head-off, or at least, I'm-about-to-let-my-mates-here-do-it quietly. He had a crow bar and he was thumping it meaningfully into the palm of his hand. "They took you in, they trusted you."

"They still do."

"Oh yeh?" said Psycho Dave. The Pan looked straight into his eyes.
"Oh yeh."

"Well, see here," said Pub Quiz Alan, "last night, we took a proper beating on your account, for not being friendly." He glared at The Pan as he spoke and The Pan looked right back at him, as he had with Psycho Dave, as calmly as he could. If he was showing one hundredth of the buttock clenching fear he was feeling, he doubted it would be convincing.

"Yer, the Grongles wanted us to play nicely. They like you," said Norris.

"An' that means we don't," said Pub Quiz Alan.

"I tried to stop them from attacking you and they controlled me. If Lord Vernon and his ilk are so fond of me, how come they did that?" asked The Pan. "How come they did this?" The Pan gestured to the sling he was wearing. The ring on his finger caught the light as his hand moved and, again, all eyes followed it.

"How do we know they did that?"

"I have the laser burns to prove it. Any of you ever tried to get hold of a laser pistol?"

Giant Hairy Ron shrugged.

"We'll hand you that, it ain't easy."

"Unless you're all buddies," said Pub Quiz Alan, "are you and the Grongles buddies, Hamgeean?"

"Yeh, sure we are, that's why they've set me up for a lynching."

Pub Quiz Alan scratched his head.

"OK, you got a point there. How come Lord Vernon didn't kill you himself, then?"

Good question. Again The Pan looked him in the eye.

"The honest answer is, I don't know. Lord Vernon signed my death warrant. He showed it to me." He couldn't suppress a shudder at the thought that it was still out there, somewhere, probably in Lord Vernon's safe. "I'm wondering if I got off on a technicality," he continued. "Something I'm unaware of. I'm sure they intended to execute me. It's as if they had to let me go but wanted to make sure I died anyway."

"Yeh? It sounds complicated to me. Is Lord Vernon that complicated?"

"In this case, it would seem so." The Pan shrugged, which hurt and made him wince, ruining the effect of the eye contact. Arse this wasn't going well but at the same time, Pub Quiz Alan was looking thoughtful.

"I don't get it," he said.

"Nope, me neither," said The Pan. He wondered if he should say anything about being the Candidate, or at least, that he knew where the Candidate was. No. It would just look like a pathetic attempt to ingratiate himself. "Look, all I can say is—"

"Shroud my futtocks!" shouted a hoarse avian voice. Arnold's pants. Humbert. "Bombs away! Bombs away!" shouted Humbert circling the room at just the right height to be irritating without being reachable.

"Humbert!" said The Pan as the Parrot's regulars forgot about him for a moment in their desire not to be pooed on.

"Rope 'em tight. Rope my futtocks! Bombs away!"

"In the name of The Prophet, Humbert, give it a rest. And for the love of Arnold don't pooh on anyone, or I'm toast!" shouted The Pan. Damn, there went the Mr Unruffled-Calm stunt he'd been trying to pull. On a positive note at least Humbert did what he was told, heading back towards The Pan and landing clumsily on his good shoulder.

"Will you look at that!" shouted a female voice. It was Betsy Coed, from the bordello two doors down. She pushed her way to the front of the pack and grabbed Pub Quiz Alan's arm. "Alan! Look! Humbert won't even do what Ada says but he did what The Pan told him."

"And that's a first for me too, Betsy," said The Pan.

"Wipe my conkers," said Humbert.

"You're right, Betsy," said Pub Quiz Alan thoughtfully and The Pan relaxed a bit. The arrival of Humbert had reduced the tension.

"Blimey," said Giant Hairy Ron as Humbert shuffled closer to The Pan's head. "What's got into that bird?"

"Ada always set great store by what that parrot does," said Betsy and there were a few muffled giggles from the back of the room. "Grow up boys. Not what he does; what he *does* – how he acts. She always set Humbert on new customers and tradesmen and many's the time she sent someone packing because Humbert didn't trust them. It's a good judge of character that parrot."

"I wouldn't say that. He probably just wants to eat my gizzards when you've finished with me," said The Pan.

As if in answer, Humbert made a keening noise and nibbled at The Pan's ear. The Pan glared at him, sideways and the nibbling stopped.

"The Parrot has spoken," said Norris who was prone to making mystical-sounding pronouncements. It was a sentiment The Pan didn't entirely understand since, for the moment, most unusually, Humbert wasn't saying anything.

"Yer," said Big Psycho Dave.

There was another pregnant pause and then Pub Quiz Alan stepped forward and slammed his crowbar down on the bar. The Pan flinched but managed not to actually jump in the air.

"Look after that can you mate? Oh, and unless you want another riot on your hands, you'd better get round there quick smart and start serving."

"Right," said The Pan.

"Mine's a pint," Alan added and he put the correct change on the beer mat in front of him.

"Any particular beer?" asked The Pan, as with a shaking hand, he fumbled the coins into the till.

"That one," said Pub Quiz Alan pointing to the lever purporting to dispense Gumpert's Sprockett, which was really the watered down pump for non-regulars.

"That's—"

"Yeh. I know but I'm working tomorrow."

"Fair enough," The Pan smiled. "Thank you."

"What for?"

"Not killing me. It's funny, a couple of hours ago, I was rather hoping you'd succeed."

"Not exactly fighting words, my Hamgeean friend," said Pub Quiz Alan.

"Yeh well. As you know, I'm not that kind of bloke."

Pub Quiz Alan put his hand on the crowbar.

"I'm not this kind of bloke either. I saw them control you and it got me thinking. But we had to make sure and to do that we had to get you scared."

"Yeh," said The Pan. Clearly Alan and co. didn't realise how easy it was to scare him, or perhaps they'd just wanted to push the boat out. "No harm done."

"Good. Y'know, it's strange and no mistake."

"Yeh, and they've pardoned me for all misdemeanours and given me total amnesty, for a year, while I adjust. There must be a good reason but for the life of me, I can't work it out."

"Total amnesty you say?"

"Yeh."

Alan sucked the air in through his teeth.

"So it was true."

"What was?"

"You being a GBI."

"Yes."

"We all wondered, but you hung about so long we began to reckon we was wrong. Norris and some of the boys was running a sweep," Pub Quiz Alan looked thoughtful. "You've made it look nice. Betsy and I saw the Grongles in here at the weekend. Not the usual bunch either, these had different uniforms, grey.

That sounded like General Moteurs' troops. Had they left the stuff behind, or had Gladys and Ada? Alan was still talking.

"What're you going to do now?"

The Pan smiled.

"I don't know yet but I have a few ideas."

"I tell you what, if they was serious about amnesty, there's a lot you can get up to in a year."

The Pan grinned.

"Mmm," he said. "Isn't there just? Unfortunately, I won't be around that long."

"Why not?"

"I have to go away. It's a..." how to put it subtly? "family thing."

"Where?"

The Pan thought of the voices in his head. When he was dead, would he be joining them? Who knew?

"I can't say for sure," he said.

"Oi, get a move on!" shouted Giant Hairy Ron.

"Yer," agreed Psycho Dave, "We're gasping here."

"Alright!" said The Pan and he grinned at Pub Quiz Alan. "Don't worry, I'll be here all this week, and since I am, I'd better get serving." So he started pulling pints and taking money.

Chapter 44

Half an hour after Corporal Jones had collected the list from Deirdre, she returned with some of the items and an apology for her failure to procure the rest. Deirdre thanked her and told her it could wait until morning. She had what she needed to polish her boots and belt. That would be enough to pass the evening.

While she'd been waiting for Corporal Jones, Deirdre had already removed the buttons from her uniform. Now she put them on a pair of button sticks and placed them neatly on the table, side by side. She sat down, positioned the brushes, cloths and polish around her, just so, and set about giving her boots a mirror shine. These things take a while and soon she was completely absorbed in her purpose. She started on her belt, without noticing the time passing until she was disturbed by the sound of the door being unlocked. She looked up, expecting to see Corporal Jones but it was General Moteurs who walked in. He was carrying a small bag.

As usual, Deirdre was determined to stay sitting down and, as usual her manners got the better of her before she could stop them and she stood up, politely, to greet him.

"Good evening," he said. He turned and handed his laser pistol to unseen hands in the corridor, Corporal Jones, presumably, and waited while the door was locked behind him.

"I see you are no more capable of understanding the word 'no' than any other male," she said acidly.

He chuckled. Not the reaction she expected.

"Savour the novelty. I'd wager most males do as you tell them. I'll wager that's your problem. You are very beautiful, Lieutenant, but a little too aware of it for my taste. If you wish to manipulate me to do your bidding, batting your eyelids at me will cut no ice. You will have to find some other way."

Arnold! He strolled over to the table and put the bag down beside the open tin of boot polish. He was off duty. His jacket hung loosely open and underneath he wore a white shirt, with the top buttons undone, like the one he'd been wearing the night she'd blundered into his apartment. What she hadn't noticed, then, was that he wore his uniform almost as well dishevelled as he did immaculate. She had never met a male so comfortable in his own skin. He sat down opposite her with that lithe grace of movement that she could not help but admire.

"I have brought you the rest of the items on your list," he said.

"You are too kind."

Her gaze was unaccountably drawn to the v shape of the unbuttoned shirt at his chest. He noticed. She looked away to cover her confusion. He leaned back in the chair and she felt him watching her, oozing alpha male assurance.

"I think you do not trust me."

"That surprises you?"

"No," a beat, "but I wish to change your view, for, as you can see," he gestured to the empty holster at his belt, "I trust you. I assure you, you have nothing to fear from me."

"Nothing but being returned to Lord Vernon and Captain Snow."

He raised his eyebrows.

"We are beyond that now, I think."

"But not beyond betrayal. I seek to depose Lord Vernon by any means possible, and you? I don't know what you want."

"The same as you," he said.

She looked up at him and their eyes met, briefly before she turned her attention back to polishing the belt.

"If you don't mind, I have to make these presentable for tomorrow."

"Understood, Lieutenant. But if events overtake us, I may not be available tomorrow and neither may you. If we are to fight alongside one another trust is an issue. We should get to know one another, yes?"

He leaned forward, reached into the bag and picked out a tube of metal polish.

"I have a batman who will see to these, if you wish." He picked up the first row of buttons and a soft cloth.

"He won't see to them as well as I can."

He inclined his head and the smile reached his mouth this time.

"Then we are of one accord," he said and he started to work on the button. "I believe you have not eaten."

"No."

"Good. I took the liberty of having our supper delivered here."

"I might not want it. I might have turned down your offer for a reason. I might have wanted to be alone."

"But you don't."

She let her hands – and the belt – drop to her lap for a moment. "You have some nerve, General Moteurs."

"I merely speak the truth."

"Maybe. But you are arrogant, rude and supercilious. I would hope I have shown you the respect your rank would accord, but you? You laugh at me, treat me as if I'm a child and make assumptions without asking. I am also a senior officer, yet you belittle me and treat me as if I am incapable of thinking for myself."

His reaction surprised her. He seemed genuinely taken aback.

"That- That was not my intent."

"Then you should pay more attention to your behaviour."

"I see that I must. I am sorry," he said quietly. "I do not mean to belittle you."

"Well, you do."

"And I do not intend to laugh at you. We have much in common. In another place and time, we might have been friends, I think."

Deirdre shot him a look. She was wrong-footed again. Unless she was mistaken, that had been a completely genuine apology, and as far as friendship went, there was plenty of common ground between them. Who knew, he might even be right. There was a scary thought. Now what? She watched him polishing the button. There were several techniques to polishing military kit and she noticed his matched hers. She also, grudgingly, had to admit that he was doing a good job.

"Do you always do that yourself?" she asked him.

"Yes. If I have time."

They lapsed into an uneasy silence.

"You said you wanted to talk to me. What about?"

"Whatever pleases you." He waved one hand in a go-on gesture, still holding the button stick. The polished brass sparkled as the buttons caught the light. "Pick a subject."

Right now, Deirdre was feeling a little bullish. Whatever pleased her most would be a topic that the General was not pleased by. Easy then.

"Why did you murder your daughter?"

He said nothing and continued with his work. She waited.

"Well?"

"Perhaps you should pick another subject."

"You said 'anything'."

"I did but—"

"If you want me to trust you, I have to know this."

He put the buttons and the cloth down and looked at her, levelly.

"I executed her."

"Same difference."

"Perhaps," his hand went to the wedding ring on his finger, as if for reassurance.

"Why though? Why would you do such a thing?"

"Because I could do nothing else."

"But it's barbaric."

"Yes. It is."

"Then how could you agree to it?"

"Deirdre, you know little of our ways. This will be difficult for you to understand—"

"Try me."

"I-" His eyes dropped for a moment, his mouth compressed and he took a deep breath in through his nose and let it out slowly. Deirdre waited. "My daughter was found guilty of treason. I could not save her." He spoke calmly but his voice was strained. "In Grongolia, a criminal's parents are considered to bear some responsibility for their crimes. The court sentenced her to death and offered her a choice: execution by torture or – my punishment – execution by me. She chose torture. I overruled her. I had it in my power to give her a quick and painless death: nothing more. So I did this monstrous thing. We said our goodbyes and my wife left the room. Then I put my laser pistol to the head of my only child – my daughter, who I loved more than I ever thought possible – and I pulled the trigger."

Well, she had asked but she had expected him to spout propaganda about Grongolian honour, and this sounded suspiciously like the painful truth. There was a long, long silence. Deirdre tried to meet the General's eyes but she could do so no longer and in her confusion her gaze was drawn to his wedding ring.

"And your wife agreed to this?" she whispered.

He inclined his head; a half nod. He had assumed a set look, hiding his emotions, but Deirdre could detect his disquiet.

"She did not take it well. Initially she understood but then I was lauded as a hero for my commitment to the State. It sickened us. In public, for both our safety, I had to pretend I was flattered. It seems I pretended too well. She could not bear it; neither of us could, and she committed suicide."

"Smeck," said Deirdre before she could stop herself.

"Life is harsh," said the General. "And, through my own cruelty and foolishness, I have made mine unbearable. I have placed my own advancement and honour above everything of true worth, and brought about the deaths of the two beings I loved above all others. If I'd had the courage to exert more authority on my wayward daughter, perhaps she would have been- no," he smiled sadly, "she would never have been less wilful but perhaps I could have persuaded her to be more careful. As for my wife, I was an uncommon bastard. Through my own callous stupidity and lack of understanding, I killed her as surely as if I had held the knife. My name is shamed, my ancestors dishonoured and, as the sole surviving member of my family, I must make amends or they will burn with me for eternity."

His voice was raw now. Deirdre held his gaze, watching, weighing his words.

"I am sorry," was all she said, and it felt wholly inadequate.

She thought of her own career, she'd been pretty single-minded about achieving what she wanted. She had never been in love, never married. She had placed her advancement in the ranks of the Resistance before those things, and willingly. It helped that she'd never met a male who had turned her head, but she knew that if she had, then, unless he was a fellow officer, there would have been a conflict between her traditional role as wife and her vocation.

"I know nothing of love, or you, and we are sworn enemies, but I am a soldier. I know a capable commander when I see one. Your troops love you and your dedication is understandable." What was she doing? She was aware that she was well out of her depth here and probably shouldn't have spoken.

"Understandable, perhaps, but not forgivable," he said. He might be in espionage, and he might be good at it, but she was certain the pain she saw was real. As if to confirm it, one hand went to his face. "I have come to believe that my rank, my success, are worth nothing and you— you remind me..." He picked up the button stick and started to polish again.

"I remind you?"

"Of myself."

"What?" She grimaced.

"I know what Denarghi did to you," he said, "and I know what it means to question everything you believe in."

"If I do that, it's not because of Denarghi."

"No?"

"No." She looked down, the tears pricking at the corners of her eyes. "Everything about me is a sham," she said quietly.

He raised his eyebrows quizzically.

"You did not expect that, did you?" she said.

"I confess not."

"I am nothing like you. I did not earn my rank. I bought it. That is why I am here. If I had earned my place, if I was a true leader, if Denarghi had thought anything of me, I would not be."

"I find that hard to believe," his voice was surprisingly gentle. "I have read your file, and what about your troops? Snoofle's devotion is there for all to see and, according to my sources in the laundry, the ladies in the drying room have started practising knife throwing; to some effect. Your generosity to the cause is irrelevant. You affect those around you," he smiled, "and not just the males. You are a natural leader – even if you have yet to appreciate the subtleties of espionage. You could learn much from me if you will swallow your pride and choose to."

"There is your Grongolian arrogance, General. I have nothing to be proud of and I doubt you will succeed where Snoofle despairs of me. I am an assassin. In matters of espionage, I am untrainable, and I assure you, any leadership skills I possess have had no bearing on my career. Denarghi advanced me because I financed my own section. There was no other reason. I repeat, if he had any regard for my abilities he would not have sent me here."

"Do not believe that. The truth is likely to be different."

"No."

"Yes, I'll wager he saw you as a threat—"

Deirdre laughed bitterly. "You are very clumsy with the flattery,

General! If you want to bend me to your will, you will have to do better than that."

"Ford. My name is Ford." He wrong-footed her again with another, totally genuine, smile. "Denarghi's foolishness is my gain. I think you are... quite something, Lieutenant, which is why, when you walked into my rooms I could not let my Master have you back."

Smeck. She felt her pulse quicken. Arnold's pants, how did he do it? She looked over at him, so, so, self assured, but with this intriguing skill of making flattery sound like honesty. Why did a few well-chosen words from General Moteurs affect her? He was only doing it to manipulate her and she should not let him.

"We are the same," he said, in the face of her continued silence.

"I am even less familiar with the world of psychology than with the world of espionage, but I believe this is called projection," she told him.

"Call it what you wish. Deirdre, if we cannot be friends then can we not declare a truce? We want the same thing and to achieve it we must work together. We must trust one another."

She took a long hard look at him.

"What choice do I have?"

"Is that the problem, you wish to decide your own fate?"

"No. I can't. No-one does."

"But still, you would, I think, if it were possible."

"No."

"Then, why?"

The red eyes were concerned and tender. She shook her head.

"I cannot say – I do not know."

He gave her a long, penetrating look.

"Shall we try to forget sides and causes and choices for a short time? We could just talk, over our meal."

"Are you suggesting a bonding exercise General?"

He laughed. He actually laughed.

"It would help us, I think."

This was unexpected.

"Maybe," she flicked her hair over her shoulders but he did not take his eyes off her face. "The idea feels strange."

"I apologise." He straightened the button stick on the table. "Deirdre... if you wish it, I will leave."

Deirdre didn't wish it.

"You can eat with me if you like. When I've finished this, I will send word through Corporal Jones."

"Why disturb her? I shall stay and help you."

"That will not be necessary."

"On the contrary, two hands are faster than one and I have not eaten yet today. I am far too hungry to wait."

Deirdre laughed and shook her head.

"You are a puzzle, General Moteurs. Stay then. You can do the rest of the buttons."

Chapter 45

Professor N'Aversion opened his eyes.

"Oh not again," he groaned. He hated it when he fell asleep at his desk. Stiffly, he sat up, removed the papers that had stuck to his face during the night and put them back on the blotter. He took out the mirror he habitually used to unknot his antennae and checked his face, no ink imprints. Good. Then he remembered the humiliation of the previous day.

He hurriedly smoothed down his clothes and sat up straight in his chair.

Where to begin? There was a gentle knock at the door. Ah yes, that was probably what had woken him up. He hoped it was Blimpet, his assistant. The Professor doubted there were many beings in K'Barth who could make coffee as well as Blimpet. Then again, the Resistance had little truck with such luxuries. The stuff Mrs Burgess and her people served up was made from dried acorns crushed into a powder. It had a scent and flavour which demonstrated more eloquently than any previous argument the Professor had encountered why only animals eat acorns. Then again, it was unfair to be hard on Mrs Burgess. Coffee was expensive and Blimpet was the only being in the Resistance who could get his hands on the decent stuff. Something to do with his freelance IT work, the Professor was given to understand. He had never enquired too closely. Several of his agents moonlighted in return for equipment and small luxury items, both of which did wonders for Tech Ops' morale. Naturally, such activities would not be appreciated by the powers that be, so the Professor tried not to 'know' too much, officially. Unofficially, he kept a beady eye on all that went on, putting a stop to anything he thought was getting out of hand

"Come!" he shouted.

"Hi Professor."

"Oh! Nar. Good morning to you."

Nar, placed a cup of coffee on the desk in front of Professor N'Aversion.

"Blimpet thought you might need this," she said.

Marvellous!

"Blimpet is a saint – and so are you. Thank you."

240

"A pleasure, Professor."

Nar hesitated.

"What is it?"

She put one finger against the end of her snout, pointed to her ears and then pointed to the ceiling. Ah yes, surveillance.

"Lieutenant Wright is here to see you," she said as she placed a micro memory unit on the blotter in front of him. "Also, I had a word with Colonel Smeen and he sent that. It's all your personal stuff, address books, photos and everything. He had it swept by IR so it's all above board."

"How very kind of him."

"Isn't it? I'll show the Lieutenant in, shall I?"

"Yes please, and I don't suppose—"

"Blimpet's already made her a coffee."

"Thank you, Nar."

The Professor looked down at the micro disk on his blotter, thinking. He had failed spectacularly to convince Denarghi that he should be allowed to build the Grongolian portal. But could it be that he had persuaded Smeen. He would have to be careful how he looked at the disk: use the wrong equipment and Denarghi – or at least, Colonel Melior – would be able to review his activity; the files he opened, what they contained, everything. As Nar had pointed out. Tech Ops would undoubtedly be wired for surveillance as would all his newly issued equipment, and the computer in the store room, to boot. If the disk did contain anything untoward it could cause serious trouble. He slipped it into the top pocket of his lab coat and stood up to greet his visitor.

Lieutenant Wright was human; born and bred in the sprawling Northern port of Glardy, on the Bay of Dark Interior. A lot of bad things came out of Glardy and in theory Lieutenant Wright was one of them, but the Professor liked her a great deal. She was petite and businesslike, but at the same time, bubbly and lively. How she managed to switch it all off and burgle houses he wasn't sure, but he had been told by those who'd seen her in action that she was the most silent and stealthy thief. Rumour was that Denarghi had pushed her to join strike ops but she'd declared that even if she had the stealth she lacked the detachment for killing. Professor N'Aversion felt an affinity with her, partly because of this and partly because they shared similar topographical origins, albeit at different ends of K'Barth. Glardy was hot and humid, and before they'd drained it to grow crops, the land around it had been swamp, very similar to the

Professor's home in the Marshes of Tith. Because she was the officer in command of what was, essentially, any thieving for funds that wasn't a bank job, Lieutenant Wright habitually projected the aura of a cheeky wrong'un, but it concealed a keen intelligence and, despite the Professor's somewhat patrician air, it had never stopped the two of them from getting on well.

However, today she was subdued, or possibly tired. From her clothing, he guessed Lieutenant Wright had been working. She was wearing a black all-in-one suit and a utility belt which, at a casual glance, looked as if it contained everything a cat burglar might need in the pursuit of booty. She was carrying the cup of coffee Blimpet had made. The Professor wondered if she'd been out burgling all night.

He addressed her formally.

"Lieutenant, do sit down," he gestured to the small sofa, at one side of his office, which he used for a change of scene when reading.

"Thanks."

She sat, cradling the cup it as if it were precious.

"Another coffee?"

"I'm good thanks. I need to sleep in a while," she took a sip. "I shouldn't have this one but it smelled too tasty to pass up."

"Tough night?"

"Long night," she said as she relaxed into the sofa cushions. "Did alright though."

"Ah, well, if you'd like one, there are some marvellous gingernuts in that box on the table next to you."

"Nah, I'm set. Have to watch what I eat."

"Ah yes, right o. Don't want to get stuck down someone's chimney."

"Nah," she laughed, "ah what the smeck? One won't hurt."

He handed her the tin and then helped himself to a biscuit, too. He waited.

"What can I do for you? Apart from providing Gingernuts and coffee."

"I just thought I'd drop in. See how you're recovering from yesterday."

The Professor touched his ear with his finger and pointed at the ceiling in the universal sign language for, 'We are under surveillance'.

"Oh it's nothing. Denarghi made the right choice and I expect I needed taking down a peg or two. Worse things happen at sea."

"Yeh, I guess." She unzipped a pocket in the leg of her suit. "I got something to show you." She held it out. It was a small screen tablet PC much like his own but the latest generation.

"Interesting is it... standard?" He glanced upwards.

"Nope. It's a beaut. Should help you with that laser gun you're building."

"Do you know I think it will. Thank you."

"No probs," she nodded at the tablet on the desk. "I'm guessing you'll be wanting to get those sorted so I'll be going. Thanks for the coffee. And the biscuit."

"Thank you, again, for the components," he said. With a smile and a wink she put a piece of paper on the desk and pushed it towards him.

'*Room 103, 14:00.*' The Professor read. He looked up at her and nodded.

"Catch you later," she said and was gone.

The secret note passing reminded the Professor of his rabelaisian youth, except this wasn't a come on. Indeed, he suspected he would find Colonel Ischzue as well as the Lieutenant when he got to room 103 and possibly even Colonel Smeen. He stood up, went and opened the door of his office and leaned out.

"Nar, I'm so sorry to keep disturbing you like this but can I borrow you a moment?"

"Yes, Professor." She joined him.

"Nar," he said as he shut the door. "I have some issues with this thing." He led her to the desk and picked up the tablet. "I can't seem to get it working."

'*Contraband*' he wrote on the blotter.

"Would you like me to see if I can fix it up for you?" '*Off network, on internet?*' she wrote.

"Yes please," he said, scribbling vigorously to obliterate their written exchange. The Professor thanked The Prophet the Resistance was so strapped for cash: at least he would only have concealed microphones in his office ceiling – cameras would have really made things difficult.

When Nar had gone he took out the map he kept of the HQ. It was annoying that his tablet, along with the interactive Find It! At HQ app that Blimpet had built was still with IR being screened. He guessed the rough area where Room 103 would be located and ran his finger across the map searching.

'*Room 103: stationery cupboard,*' it was labelled. He chuckled.

243

Chapter 46

Deirdre woke up. The first thing she saw was an impossibly pristine officer's uniform, Resistance, Lieutenant, first class. She smiled. She had to hand it to him, General Moteurs had done a fine job on those buttons. She wondered what he was doing now. It had been a very odd evening, the comforting normality of scrubbing up her kit had calmed her.

General Moteurs had turned out to be surprisingly good company. He was simple but complicated, conventional but mischievous. Eating together, sharing stories had felt ordinary and if not easy then certainly agreeable. She felt they had achieved, if not the truce he'd requested then, a wary respect for one another. And when he'd gone, departing with a graceful, low bow, the quiet of the room seemed amplified by his absence.

She rolled over and noticed the empty bed next to hers.

"Snoofle!" she said guiltily.

What was happening to her loyalties? How could she be so preoccupied with General Moteurs that she hadn't even thought about Snoofle's first full day back in the Laundry? She checked her watch. Six a.m. He would be having breakfast. She wondered how he was. She was still bruised and sore but on the upside, she was beginning to feel human again and even better, she had that twitchy fizzy feeling she got when she needed to exercise. That had to be a sign of recovery. She wondered if they'd let her and Snoofle have a sparring session. Just a gentle one. When the General came to see her, perhaps she'd ask.

She felt a lot better today. She stretched, stood up and headed to the bathroom.

Washed and dressed she was starting on a few of the stretches Dr Dot had suggested when the good Doctor herself arrived with one of the guards from outside, a male one. He busied himself laying the table for breakfast. Though pleased to see Dr Dot, Deirdre was also slightly disappointed that she had not brought General Moteurs with her.

"Good morning, Lieutenant, Snoofle sends his best," said the Doctor.

"Thanks, how is he?"

"A great deal better. He's asked if he can come and see you later."

"Of course."

"Good," the Doctor smiled.

"Ma'am." The guard, having finished, stepped back from the table and saluted.

"Thanks," said Dr Dot, and he left.

They waited a moment until the jangling of keys in the lock had finished.

"I've brought you breakfast; Muesli, yogurt, honey and coffee," said Dr Dot.

"I am grateful." Deirdre sat at the table. She was embarrassed, just as she had been on her first morning with Snoofle. "Please join me. There is more than enough for two."

Dr Dot hesitated, but not for long.

"Do you know, I'd love to; I never have time for breakfast on Tuesdays. I have an early surgery and they've always stopped serving it by the time I've finished. However, I would like to examine you first."

She knocked on the door, had a brief word with the guard outside and returned to the table.

"How are you feeling?" she asked.

"Better."

"Good."

Dr Dot went on to give Deirdre the same kind of examination as she had the previous day.

"Can I go back to my duties?"

"Tomorrow; but you can take some exercise today. Don't go gung-ho, but if you want to stretch yourself a little to see how you cope that's fine. You're healing nicely."

"Thanks." Deirdre looked down at her nails for a moment, "Um... Snoofle believes I would benefit from some of your cocktail."

Dr Dot smiled with obvious delight.

"And what do you think?"

"I would like to try it."

"You won't regret it. It will do you the power of good."

As Dr Dot filled the syringe, the guard returned with a second place-setting which he laid at the other side of the table.

"Thank you," said Dr Dot and Deirdre at the same time. They looked at each other and to her surprise, Dr Dot winked. Deirdre smiled.

"Ma'am," he said, saluted and left.

Deirdre gathered up her courage.

"I am ready," she said.

"OK," said Dr Dot, "can you roll up your sleeve?"

Deirdre did as she asked and the Doctor injected the liquid into her arm, cleaned the spot where it had gone in with an antiseptic wipe and put a plaster on it. Then the two of them sat down to breakfast.

Chapter 47

Ruth sat staring at another bowl of porridge with added 'seasoning' from Captain Snow. She hadn't eaten anything since breakfast at the RAC club, what seemed like aeons ago. It was only four days but she was beginning to feel distinctly light headed. Maybe? She looked at the porridge.

"Ugh," she shuddered and hugged her arms to her chest. Normally, despite feeling too miserable for food, she would have tried to eat something, if only to not feel dizzy or have this stonking headache. She wished she'd thought to ask for headache pills, not that they'd have given her any, she supposed.

She went into the bathroom where she helped herself to several glasses of water to try and feel more full. While she drank she had a stroke of inspiration – the plants on the balcony might be edible. she had paid them scant attention before, but there might be herbs.

Returning to the main room of her prison she walked across to the glass doors and let herself out onto the long terrace outside. Nothing doing. They were box bushes and olive trees but either there hadn't been any olives or someone had picked them all. Ruth sighed as she looked out over the square to the city beyond. It all looked so normal. Like home. And in K'Barth, the same as at home, it was autumn. It suited her mood. In one week, she was going to marry Lord Vernon, whom she hated and feared, to save the life of the man she truly loved, a man she had hurt and humiliated beyond forgiveness. As for her own future, she guessed living hell was an apt description but, most likely, only for the best bits. She wondered what her family and friends at home were doing. Had she been reported missing yet? Her parents would be worried sick. How would they deal with being the parents of yet another disappeared woman? There would be no body to bury, no closure, just an endless list of unanswered questions. It was horrible doing this to them. Part of her wished she could turn back time to three weeks before and return to her mundane, humdrum life in the Capital, but of course then she would never have met The Pan of Hamgee.

"For heaven's sake, I have to stop thinking like this," she muttered.

Ruth knew that other people had been through tougher times than this, pretty much any noblewoman in medieval times had to marry for political reasons rather than love – although they didn't always end up with a monster like Lord Vernon – and, in a way, they felt too removed to identify with. Someone closer to, perhaps. The women in Pinochet's regime, they weren't allowed to protest about their missing loved ones so they met up in public spaces and danced with photographs of them, instead. Closer to home, the Suffragettes. Again, she recalled Lucy's admiration for their cause and her particular heroine, Emily Wilding Davison. The Suffragettes hadn't been asking that much: a group of women, demanding equal treatment. They'd kept their dignity when they were treated like criminals, stayed strong in the face of insults and abuse, and it hadn't been *that* long ago. They were hungry too, for different reasons, they went on hunger strike but they must have felt these same physical symptoms, and in their times of hunger, they would have been in prison, too, surrounded by people who were hostile to them and their cause, or bemused at best. They must have felt the same loneliness that Ruth did.

"Yeh," she said to herself. "I can do this because they did. I will be strong." She hung onto the quote Lucy had told her about 'rebelling against tyrants is obedience to God.'

"I don't know about it being obedience to God, but I won't give Lord Vernon an easy time," she said.

She smiled wanly to herself. Lucy would approve and somehow that made Ruth feel less alone. Wherever her friend was now, they were together in this, sisters, fighting the tyrant.

Her thoughts were interrupted by the sound of the door being unlocked. Her heart sank. Reluctantly she turned and went back inside. Lord Vernon had already reached the bottom of the stairs. He cast a brief glance around the room and then looked her up and down.

"Did you sleep well, my dear?" he asked. Even the most innocuous statement from Lord Vernon seemed to be a threat.

"Oh marvellously well thanks. There's nothing like betraying the man you love to promote a good night's rest."

He walked over to her side.

"Tsk, we will have to do something about that temper of yours."

"Perhaps if you stopped provoking me at every turn, you could fix that yourself." She turned away from him but he took her arm and pulled her round to face him.

"Now, now Ruth, my love, it is time for our press call and we must choose some suitable clothing." He let go of her and strode over to the wardrobe.

Press call? Was he joking?

He beckoned impatiently.

"Come."

It would appear not. Shakily, she followed him.

She was wearing one of the few pairs of canvas jeans they had provided her with, a cotton shirt and her own boots.

"You will be making your first public appearance today," he told her as he opened the doors and ran his hands along the rail of clothes. "General Moteurs has excelled himself with these."

"I thought you chose them."

"Hardly. I have better things to do with my time." He selected some clothes and draped them on the bed, a white silk blouse, a to-die-for pair of coral trousers and a dark blue jacket. All were understated classic rather than high fashion, not that Ruth knew what was, or was not, high fashion in K'Barth. But still, knowing that they'd been chosen by General Moteurs, as opposed to Lord Vernon, made her new clothes slightly easier to wear. "Wait here." He went and banged on the door. Two of the troops outside came into the room. She looked from one to the other of them nervously as they made their way towards her.

"What are you doing?" she asked as they bore down on her. "You don't have to dress me, I'm not a doll. And I said I'd wear the bloody clothes."

Lord Vernon didn't deign to reply, speaking to the guards instead.

"Hold her still."

"No!" She dodged past them, making a run for the bathroom but she was no match for the lightning reactions of Lord Vernon. She screamed as he caught her by the waist and swung her round with such force that he practically threw her at them.

"Try to hold onto her." She let out a gasp of pain as one of them wrenched her arm behind her back. "I said 'hold her' not maim her you imbecile. I want her pristine."

"What are you doing?" She couldn't keep the panic out of her voice. He continued to ignore her and removed a small case from one of the pouches on his belt. He glanced up momentarily, checking the guards were restraining her the way he wanted them to. Then slowly, he opened the case, removing a hypodermic syringe and a vial of liquid. He placed the case on the table.

"Don't worry, it's quite painless."

Yeh right, Ruth really believed that. And what the hell was it, anyway?

He prepared the syringe with deliberate concentration, pushing the needle though the foil lid of the vial and filling it with liquid. He held it up to the light, flicked it with his finger and depressed the plunger a fraction so that some of the liquid squirted out.

"No..." she said but even to her own ears it came out embarrassingly close to a whimper.

"Don't bother, you can't escape." He jabbed the needle into her neck and injected her with the contents.

"There you are, my darling. Get dressed. I will wait for you on the balcony."

He walked over to the glass doors, pulled them open and went outside. The guards saluted and stood by the steps to the door, one either side. Ruth went to the bathroom, where none of them could see her and dressed, as ordered. Her light-headedness, and the headache, had not abated. When she was finished, she walked uncertainly onto the balcony to join her fiancé.

"Excellent, you are looking ravishing," he said.

"What did you inject me with?" Her voice was hardly more than a whisper.

"Nothing that will harm you, but I'm afraid I don't trust you. Yet."

"Yeh well, the feeling's mutual. *Darling.*"

"Temper, my precious. Trust has to be earned, one small step at a time. I have administered you with a simple behavioural inhibitor to ensure you are suitably..." he waved one hand while he pinned down the word, "compliant."

"You've drugged me?"

"Yes."

Her head span and she could feel her palms sweating. Ugh. Was that the drug though, or panic?

"Is it safe?"

"Of course, why would I hurt my betrothed?"

"You haven't been too bothered so far."

"Tsk, that temper again. This is why you have forced me to take precautions. You may find it difficult to speak in a few minutes. Short of the basic requirements – yes, no, thank you – I advise you not to. Now, I hope you are clear on..." he waved one suede clad hand, "the party line."

"If I'm limited to monosyllables, I don't need to be, do I?"

His eyes narrowed dangerously.

"Answer the question."

"Clear."

"Repeat it."

"I am the Chosen One and I love the Candidate, utterly, wholeheartedly, like no-other."

"Oh very good. Your delivery was a little wooden, but we can work on that."

The Interceptor drew up alongside the balcony and both gull wing doors hissed open. Lord Vernon took her by the arm, just above the elbow. When he guided her towards the parapet she began to shake as her vertigo kicked in. He left her there, stepped casually over it onto the Interceptor's sill and slid into the driving seat, then he drove a few yards out, turned it round and reversed up to the parapet with her side closest.

"Get in."

The moat below was a long way down. She could hardly control her shaking. As she wobbled her way over to the edge he drummed his fingers on the steering wheel impatiently with one hand and raised his eyes to heaven. Nervously, she inched forward and he drifted the Interceptor closer to the building. Still she baulked.

"Hurry up."

"I'm being as quick as I can."

"Come on."

"A gentleman would help me, not just jump in himself and sit there complaining."

"I am not a man. I am the most powerful being on this planet in all but name and you will do as you are told." He leaned over, across the passenger seat and extended his hand. "Get in. Now."

The rings flashed as he beckoned to her. She reached out and took it. The softness of the suede belied the iron grip of the hand inside. The Interceptor seemed to jink outwards as she put her foot on the sill. She slipped but he yanked her towards him, hauling her unceremoniously into her seat.

"Thank you, *darling*," she said as the doors hissed closed. Had that sounded slightly slurred? She couldn't tell. Holy smoke she felt ill.

"A pleasure, my own one," he flashed her a sadistic smile and put on a pair of sunglasses. The seatbelt fastened itself automatically around her, restricting her movement. He accelerated the Interceptor away from the parapet. The G force made her feel even more light headed. She swallowed and wished she had some water. He took something out of the glove compartment, a second pair of sunglasses. "You may put these on."

She did as she was told, grateful enough that he would not see her cry.

****

The short journey passed in silence as, with bullet-proof arrogance, Lord Vernon demonstrated his mastery over the machine. Except that he seemed to be trying a little too hard to establish his skill. Perhaps he was. Ruth sat and looked out of the window, pointedly ignoring her husband-to-be, in case he was trying to impress her.

They landed in the courtyard of a building which reminded her of the Georgian bits of London; places like Somerset House. It had the same colonnaded classical splendour and big windows. There were other Grongles gathered waiting for them, including a camera crew filming their arrival. Lord Vernon got out of the Interceptor first and then walked round to her side. He didn't open the door for her, someone else did. As she put one foot unsteadily onto the tarmac she noticed Captain Snow, much to her dismay. And standing a little behind him, all pristine uniform, sparkly buttons and lofty hauteur, was General Moteurs. He blanked her look of helpless appeal. No help there then. She remembered the Suffragettes; brave women who stood up for their beliefs and stayed strong. She could do this. She squared her shoulders, took a deep breath and stood up. Once again, Lord Vernon took her by the arm, and she tried to turn her wince of pain into some sort of rictus smile as he pulled her closer. She was shaking and dizzy. He pretended to hug her, pulling her tighter against him, as if concerned that she might fall. Well yeh, that would look bad wouldn't it?

Almost immediately the two of them were accosted by one of the smarmiest individuals she'd ever met. He was Grongolian, they all were, no species-ally impure humans allowed here, well... apart from her. He slid up to them and dropped to one knee at Lord Vernon's feet, bowing his head. As he did this, so did everyone else, about twenty of them, including General Moteurs all the same; one knee, heads bowed.

Blimey.

"Formal obeisance is not necessary. Get up," said Lord Vernon, adding, very definitely as an afterthought, "please."

"Your Gracious—"

"Sir."

"Sir. We are honoured by your visit."

"Yes, you are. I believe I have briefed you about the Chosen One, my fiancée. She will be taking part in your programme with me."

There was a moment of complete silence as everyone took in that Lord Vernon's fiancée was not a Grongle and not overly green, either. Ruth wondered if they'd even known she was coming.

"She's- she's human," said Mr Unctuous with a clear note of revulsion.

Lordy. He must have a death wish.

"You question the wisdom of my choice?" asked Lord Vernon. His tone was hostile, dangerous and everyone around him, except Ruth, drew back a little.

"Of course not," Mr Unctuous smiled at Ruth. It didn't reach his eyes, "My dearest, what a pleasure to meet you, Scrope, Carlton Scrope and this is Leighton Bromswold, our anchor." The only other Grongle in civilian clothes who wasn't part of the film crew bowed to her. "I will be interviewing you and Mr Bromswold will be providing the commentary."

"Hello. I'm Ruth," said Ruth. Did Grongles say how do you do? Tentatively, she held her hand out. Carlton Scrope took it, bowed low and planted an unpleasantly wet and rubbery-lipped kiss on the back of it. Yuk. She managed not to snatch it away but was very pleased indeed when, with an extremely nervous look at her fiancé, Leighton Bromswold contented himself with shaking it. Everyone's attention reverted to Lord Vernon, and while it had, Ruth hurriedly wiped her hand on her trousers.

They were shepherded indoors to a set where they sat on a sofa. It was hot under the lights and Ruth's head began to throb. Maybe she should have eaten the gobbed-in porridge, she might have coped with the drugs better on a full stomach. And what was a 'behavioural inhibitor' anyway? It wasn't as if she needed it. The presence of Lord Vernon, sitting next to her with his arm along the top of the sofa behind her head, was inhibiting enough. She stole a glance at him. He looked even more menacing with his sunglasses on. She had underestimated the amount of stamina required to act normally in such close proximity to him, especially for such a lengthy period. It was difficult to put the physical symptoms aside to focus on Carlton Scrope's questions. He spoke fast with a strange clipped accent and she had to keep asking him to repeat himself. Beside her, Lord Vernon became more and more angry as she spoilt the slick media event. She allowed herself to feel pleased that she was able to do something to ruin his day.

However, for all Lord Vernon's furious demeanour, it was Carlton Scrope's patience that ran out first.

"Do you have a hearing problem?" he demanded as she asked him to repeat yet another question.

"No," said Lord Vernon, except it was more of a snarl. He threw Ruth a glance and stood up. "My fiancée needs some fresh air. Come with me, darling."

Grateful for a get out, even one that would involve some time alone with Lord Vernon, she stood up. Too fast. Oh no, the world began to spin. Ooops. Calm. Breathe. She was NOT going to pass out. She took a step forward. Yes, it was OK she was going to be alright. Lord Vernon took her arm.

"Thank you," she said, except it didn't sound right and she suddenly felt as if she was sinking into cotton wool. She tried to move her legs but they seemed to be having a go slow. Her knees gave way, darkness closed in and her vision narrowed. She felt herself stumble against Lord Vernon, then the voices round her echoed and faded.

Chapter 48

"I notice your statutory target practice session is due. So is mine, want to come to the range?"

Nar handed Professor N'Aversion the Grongolian tablet.

As the two of them walked through the corridors she gave him a brief tour of the tablet's functions.

"It's completely cloaked," she told him. "If Information Retrieval see anything it will show up as networked printer activity." As the Professor suspected she already knew, they couldn't get onto the range because they hadn't booked a slot, so they started back to Tech Ops the way they had come. He got the tablet out again.

"How much internet access before I'm noticed?"

"As much as you like. That's why it's disguised as printer activity. There are enough networked printers here, they're pretty busy and the actual data will be stored on a cloud drive elsewhere."

"Off site?"

"Yes."

He remembered the gift from Colonel Smeen in Henching.

"What about flash memory? It doesn't seem to have a socket."

"Micro drive, Professor." Nar showed him a tiny slot in the side.

"Marvellous. Now, if you don't mind, I have some thinking to do. I'm going to the park."

The Professor hurried to a less busy part of the HQ, turned down a corridor and came to a locked door. He entered the code on the number pad and it clicked open. Behind it were stairs leading to 'the park' – an old sentry post. The HQ had grown over the years and many of the original sentry posts, concealed platforms built into the woodland canopy, had been rendered obsolete. These had been fitted with safety rails and were now used by agents who wanted a bit of space or fresh air, or both. They were collectively known as 'the park'. The Professor climbed the stairs, which took him some time, and came out onto the platform. Nobody was about and the air was fresh and clear. He pulled a chair across the platform with a juddery plastic scraping noise, set it in a tiny patch of sunlight and sat down. He took a moment or two to enjoy the relaxing scent of pine rising from the foliage concealing the platform and to marvel at the view. Then he powered up the tablet.

Nar had installed his favourite apps, including Blimpet's Find it! In HQ, and when he checked he discovered she had also adjusted the settings to suit his preferences. He took the tiny micro drive Lieutenant Wright had given him and inserted it into the slot Nar had indicated. It contained an executable file called, *Professor's Settings*, which he opened. It only took a moment to upload his address book and diary, then a new dialogue box appeared.

'Your mailbox is empty. Restore saved data? Yes/No.'

He thought for a moment. Saved data?

"Hmm..."

Was that what he thought it was? No. It couldn't possibly be. IR had screened it.

He jabbed *'yes'* with his finger.

A box appeared on the screen.

'Restoring original mail data'

It took approximately seven centuries to load, or at least, that's how it felt to Professor N'Aversion, but finally the line creeping slowly from one side of the screen to the other reached the end. It disappeared and was replaced with a new dialogue box.

'Mail restore complete, open mail client? Yes/No.'

The Professor touched the *'yes'*, his pulse racing. The programme opened and the most recent mail loaded. It was a round robin warning all Agents in Sector 7 that the lavatories had malfunctioned again and they would need to make the long trek to Sectors 6 or 8 if they were caught short. He deleted it. Next up was information about a social event for Agents in Henching. He deleted that.

"Arnold's toenails!" He put his hand between his antennae just in time. Where was the anti-knotting hat when he needed it? On his desk, that's where. He stared at the anonymous e-mail from General Moteurs. All the attachments were there plus another one labelled *'video message'*. He reckoned he could guess what that was.

His finger hovered over the backlit screen. Dare he do this? If it was some warped test of his loyalty set by Denarghi, he would be shot. He pressed the icon on the screen.

'Save attachments to cloud? Yes/no.'

He put a trembling finger on the *'yes'*.

'Attachments saved to cloud.'

He realised he'd been holding his breath and let it out, slowly. Then he checked his cloud drive. The schematics were all there. And the message. He'd successfully committed treason. He went back into the mail screen and deleted the e-mail. Then he opened the settings interface and reformatted the micro drive.

There would be no going back now.

He pressed the sleep button on the tablet and slipped it back into his lab coat pocket. He was going to build the portal. By their actions, Colonels Ischzue and Smeen, as well as Lieutenant Wright, were practically begging him to.

"Might as well be hanged for a sheep as a lamb," he murmured. The line was drawn, his mind was made up. And it felt good. Surprisingly good.

Chapter 49

Ruth woke up. A blinding white light hung in front of her, growing in intensity, pulsing as it moved this way and that. Slowly it focussed into a pen torch, the kind doctors used. It disappeared suddenly. He had been holding her eye open it seemed. She kept her eyes closed. She didn't want to wake up yet, she needed some time to regroup.

"She is coming round now but it will take a little time for her to fully regain her senses."

Yes, that sounded like a doctor, but it also seemed to be coming from a long way away. No obvious sign of her betrothed or Captain Snow. Good.

"What is wrong with her?" Or not. There was Lord Vernon.

"I'd say she's hungry. The behavioural inhibitor doesn't mix with low glucose. Is she eating?"

"Well, Captain, is she?" Oh and Captain Snow too, all her favourite people at once. No need to wake up just yet then. She kept her eyes closed and listened. With any luck if she lay still long enough they'd all give up waiting and leave her alone.

There was a pause.

"No, sir, she is refusing all food."

"And you did not think to mention this because...?"

"It wasn't relevant."

"Why?"

"Because they always eat in the end."

"Yes, Captain," Lord Vernon's voice was like ice, "in the end. When they are half starved and you have beaten them to within an inch of their lives. But I require the Chosen One to be alive and fully functioning."

Ruth could almost hear Captain Snow sweating.

"Sir," he said.

"This is not your usual brief Captain, I hope you understand that. I want a healthy, pristine wife and that is how you will deliver her."

"Sir."

"Let me make it simple for you. If she fails to eat, she will die and if she dies, you will too. So, if she refuses again, you will make her. Now get out. You, too, Doctor."

Ruth heard the rustling of clothing as they bowed and the footsteps as they left the room. The door closed.

"You can stop pretending now, Ruth."

She lay still, trying to keep her breathing even, trying to project an aura of unconsciousness.

"Don't make me force you," he told her ominously. "Sit up."

"What do you want?" she asked reluctantly, muzzily.

"A talk. I am concerned for your well being. The regimental doctor tells me you are suffering from malnutrition. I am afraid if you persist with this foolishness I will be forced to take... action."

"If you want me to eat any of my food then tell Captain Snow to stop spitting in it."

He laughed. That wasn't the right reaction at all. She'd expected him to be angry with Captain Snow.

"It will not harm you."

"It's still revolting."

"You are very ungrateful, Ruth. I will order him to do worse if you continue to refuse it. You will eat what is put before you and be thankful, do I make myself clear?"

"Painfully."

"Excellent, then I will leave you to rest. I do not expect to find you unwell again."

Chapter 50

The Parrot and Screwdriver had been much busier than The Pan remembered. Almost suspiciously busy. And definitely far too packed for a Tuesday lunch time. Indeed, the pub was so busy that Pub Quiz Alan had to help him at the bar, and when he suggested that Psycho Dave stepped in to clear the glasses, The Pan was only too happy for the help.

Finally, the punters were gone and the clearing up was done. The Pan opened the back door onto the alley to put the rubbish out, only for Humbert to fly past him at high speed. He ran and left the bag on the corner, ready for the dustmen, before turning and rushing back to rescue Alan and Dave from the attentions of Ada's pet.

When he returned to the bar, Alan and Dave were where he had left them. Humbert was circling them dizzily and screeching.

"Wind my handle!" at full volume.

"Arnold's toe nails, does that bird have an off button?" asked Alan.

"Sorry lads," said The Pan, "he came in when I went to put the bins out. I expect he's hungry, I'll give him some crisps."

"I reckons he wants proper parrot food," said Dave.

"Yes, he does, but crisps are all I have down here." The Pan opened a packet and put them on one of the tables nearby, making a mental note that he must remember to wipe it down again when Humbert was done. Then he sat down with Dave and Alan and turned his attention to the cashing up, which they had started while The Pan was putting out the bins. Humbert flew low over the table and dropped something heavy and rusty among the neatly stacked coins, sending them flying all over the room.

"Humbert!" groaned The Pan, "Now look what you've done! And what is this?"

"Stick it in the putty!" shouted the Parrot, attacking his crisps.

The Pan picked up the object Humbert had dropped on the table; a heavy metal key.

"Humbert? Where did this come from?"

"Put it in the putty," said Humbert.

"I wish I knew what he was on about," muttered the Pan. He left the key on the table and went to help Alan and Psycho pick up the fallen money.

"Stick it in the putty!" shouted Humbert following him.

Psycho Dave stood up, looking thoughtful.

"I reckon I knows what he is talkin' about."

"Really?"

"Yer, he is asking you to make a copy of the key."

The Pan scratched his head and looked from Alan to Dave and back again.

"You think so?"

"Course," said Alan, "stick it in the putty, make a copy, that's how it's done."

"Yer," said Dave. "I s'pect he is wanting you to do it quickly like, so as he can put it back again, before anyone notices he has nicked it from—"

"Wherever he's nicked it. Yeh, see, that's why he's all agitato," Alan agreed.

"Right, where would I get—"

Alan took a tobacco tin out of his pocket and opened it and called the parrot over.

"Humbert. Here, Humbert? This what you were talking about?"

"Polish my melons!"

Alan looked at The Pan enquiringly.

"I'm pretty sure that's a 'yes'," he said. He picked up the key and handed it to Alan. "Maybe you should do this. You seem to know what you're doing."

"Alright. You got any plastic film?"

"Right, yes, I have."

"Go get it then."

The Pan vaulted over the wooden bar and went into the Holy of Holies where there was a roll of plastic food wrap in a dispenser on the wall. He took a sheet, and then because it had all stuck together and ended up as a silver ball of crumpled cellophane, he took another one and carried it carefully by two of its corners, back to Alan and Dave.

Alan opened the tin and laid the top next to it. Both were filled with putty separated by a sheet of greaseproof paper. He removed the paper and tore the cellophane in half, without it sticking to itself, a feat of dexterity which truly amazed The Pan. Next, he laid one half over the top of the putty in the bottom of the box and put one piece aside. Finally, with a wink and a smile at The Pan, he pressed the key into the putty. There was a short hiatus.

"Mate, could you...?" he indicated to The Pan's elbow. The Pan lifted his hand and discovered the other piece of cellophane had stuck to him.

"Must be my magnetic personality," he said weakly.

"Or because you is a numb nuts," said Dave helpfully.

"Oi," he said, but he couldn't really argue.

He tried to get the cellophane off himself but it was difficult one-handed, so Dave lifted the second piece carefully off The Pan's sleeve and handed it over to Alan.

Alan put the second sheet of film over the top of the key and put the lid on the tin. He held it for a moment, pressing the two parts together and then opened it, slowly. He removed the key, took off the cellophane and examined the putty.

"I dunno about you Dave, but I reckon that's OK."

Dave picked up the box and the key and examined them for a moment or two.

"Yer, I reckons it is."

"Okey dokey. I'll have it made up for you tomorrow," said Alan. "I'll drop it by first thing."

"That's- that's- Thank you, Alan."

"All in a day's work."

"So it would seem."

"Did you know that the first primitive locks weren't used to keep people out of stuff at all?"

"Really?"

"Yep, and they were in use four thousand years before the birth of Arnold The Prophet."

"Oh."

"Yeh, the first locks were invented up in Smirn. They used them to make sure ropes didn't fall off belays. It was only later they got the idea of using them to stop stuff walking out of their houses."

"That's very interesting, Alan. Thanks. You learn something new every day."

The rustle of a crisp packet being pecked at indicated that Humbert had finished his snack.

"All done?" The Pan asked as he got up.

"Norks! Buff my nuts!" shouted Humbert, which probably meant, 'yes.'

"Well, so are we," The Pan took the empty crisp packet from the table. "Here you are." He put the key down in front of the parrot.

"Wipe my conkers!" squawked Humbert, and he picked up the key in his claws and took off.

"Now what?" said The Pan as the parrot circled the room.

"Let him out, I reckons he has ter put it back," said Dave.

Chapter 51

It was the afternoon now and Deirdre's mind was running on one track. She'd flicked through the books Dr Dot had brought her, done all the stretches she had suggested, several times, and practised her knife throwing. Nothing was able to divert her thoughts from the hours she'd spent with General Moteurs. The story of his daughter haunted her. She could not imagine how terrible it would have been to face that choice or what kind of resolve it had taken to go through with it. And she could not reconcile such a troubled past with the down-to-earth strength of the individual she'd spent the evening with. She wished she could talk about it with Snoofle but he would not be coming to see her for hours. She had run out of distractions. She would not spend the entire day psychoanalysing her gaoler. Except that unless she did something about it quickly, she would.

As she had told him herself, General Moteurs was a puzzle, and spending the evening with him had merely turned him into an enigma. He had made her feel comfortable and at ease, to such an extent that for most of the time she'd forgotten that he was a Grongle. In a perverse way the sudden relaxation of the tension between them had made her even more nervous; about dropping her guard, making herself vulnerable; about getting close to a being whose motives she was unsure of and who was, in theory, her enemy.

She kept running over the evening's events, analysing, questioning and tying herself in mental knots. She could almost hear Snoofle saying 'this is not good' and it wasn't. There was little to provide a diversion until she hit on the idea of playing the old childhood – and officers' mess – game of making one complete circuit of the room without touching the ground. To make it harder she decided that she would not allow herself to use the furniture and would stick solely, and probably literally, to the ceiling and walls. It wasn't technically difficult, there was a picture rail, a dado rail, beams across the ceiling and plenty of lumps and bumps in the plaster, even the odd stone sticking out.

Even so, Deirdre knew it would keep her absorbed. Climbing was not her metier. Although she insisted that anyone in Strike Ops attain a certain level of ability, she had found it harder to attain than many of those under her command. After planning a route she turned her efforts to trying it out. She was martial arts fit but for this she needed a different sort of strength; she found it harder.

Totally engrossed, she made her way slowly around the room and after a brief rest, started again, counting all the while to see how quickly she could do it. Just under 60 seconds, she reckoned, mid-50s perhaps. It was fast but she was sure she could go faster.

"Come on soldier," she muttered and tried again.

This time, as she was moving along the wall towards the door, braced between the beams of the ceiling, the sound of footsteps and voices in the hall outside alerted her to the fact she was about to receive a visitor.

"Good afternoon, Deirdre," said General Moteurs as she dropped down beside him. If she had surprised him, he made no sign. "So bored you are crawling up the walls?"

"I needed some exercise."

"Noted." He gave her a look and walked into the centre of the room. "I see the games in an officers' mess remain the same, regardless of the army in which it is situated."

"Perhaps everyone is similar, underneath," she felt shaky. Maybe she had overdone it, although she wasn't going to admit that to him.

"How fast?"

"Just under a minute by my count."

"You have been counting quickly, I think," there was a gleam in his eye as he said this.

"Are you teasing me?"

He smiled and looked down briefly.

"Perhaps," he took off the wristwatch he was wearing and held it up. "Shall we try it in real time? I'll wager there'll be a discrepancy."

"If there is I'll bet I'm faster than my count," she lied, all bravado. What was she doing? Where had that come from?

"Shall we find out?"

"Yeh, let's."

"On my mark, then. You are ready?"

"Of course."

She waited, the nerves fluttering in her stomach, while he primed the watch. She wanted to prove herself; pity it had to be climbing.

"Go," he said and Deirdre climbed as if her life depended on it. As she negotiated a difficult move to get round the last corner she slipped. Her fingertips burned as she clung to a ceiling beam by them, the rest of her body swinging free; but then she was able to kick her legs up and continue. Heart hammering, she finished as fast as she could and jumped down where she had started.

"Forty eight seconds," he said. "Very impressive, for a human."

"Meaning?"

"A Grongle would do it faster."

So speciesist. She met his eyes, defiant.

"Not necessarily."

He seemed amused.

"Grongles are bigger and stronger than humans. On average, we would be faster."

"Bigger is heavier," she said.

"Longer reach."

"Less agile. On the mountain, small is fast," she told him.

"Then we would both lose out to a Spiffle."

"No. Neither of K'Barth's mountain dwelling species is small."

"Exactly," he said, "I rest my case."

"But Galorshes and Blaggysomps have evolved to be the most appropriate size for their surroundings; human sized."

"This is not a mountain."

"If Grongles are so much better than the rest of us, you should be able to beat my time."

He laughed.

"I am forty two years old, a middle-aged pen-pusher. You have eight years on me and you are fitter than I ever was."

She sized him up, the way she would a new recruit. Not that she needed to. She knew he was in peak condition, whatever he pretended, and if he'd achieved the levels in Ka-Pa-Te that Snoofle thought, he would have strength and fitness levels to match.

"I think you are not. But if you are it does not matter. From what you say, even a specimen as unfit for purpose as yourself should be able to beat my time."

He laughed at that.

"Naturally," he said, "but I do not intend to try. I am above parlour games."

"Of course," she shrugged dismissively.

His eyes narrowed a little.

"I have nothing to prove to you."

"Or perhaps you cannot back up your prejudice?"

"You know I am not prejudiced. I merely state a truth; physically we are stronger, bigger and faster than other beings. There is no implication that one is 'better' than the other, merely that, given that simple fact, a Grongle is likely to exceed a human in this particular endeavour."

"Yet he seems unwilling to try. I think the General is afraid of losing."

He put his hands on his hips and took a deep breath in. His eyes met hers.

"I think the Lieutenant is issuing a challenge."

"If you can handle the pace."

He gave the ceiling a dismissive glance and handed her his watch.

"I believe I can," he said.

"So I would assume, since you are trained in Ka-Pa-Te," she said as he sat down on Snoofle's bed and slipped off his boots and socks, "black belt, level three," she added as he went and put them neatly by one of the easy chairs.

He glanced over at her.

"Correct."

"Snoofle is very well informed," she explained. She didn't mention that she was level five, herself, although she imagined he knew.

"Snoofle is an exceptional agent," he took off his utility belt and laid it carefully over the arm of the chair.

"You still spar regularly?"

"Yes," he said as he unbuttoned his tunic. He laid it over the back of the chair with equal care. She watched the muscles of his forearms flexing as he rolled up his sleeves, a sudden rush of girlish embarrassment coloured her cheeks when he glanced up and caught her.

"How regularly?" she asked, aware that, in her confusion, she sounded more abrupt than she intended.

His eyes met hers, his expression unreadable.

"Regularly enough."

He undid the top two buttons of his shirt and as always her eyes were drawn to the triangle of bare flesh it revealed. As he bent to adjust the bottoms of his britches, the shirt fell forward and she found herself leaning in a little, trying to catch a glimpse of the body inside. Arnold. Grow up trooper.

He straightened up, all finished, standing before her in his shirt and britches, a little closer than was necessary. At ease, he seemed totally unaware of her confusion.

"Shall we begin?" he asked.

She glanced down at the watch.

"Go," she said as she pressed the timer and he started climbing.

He moved fast and with the assurance of someone well within his limits. Half way round he was ahead of her. Maybe he realised, perhaps he was a little too relaxed. Whatever it was, as he made to effect a tricky transfer across the far corner of the room, his hand slipped and he fell. He bounced awkwardly across the back of the sofa, his stomach taking the full force, flipped over onto the floor and lay still.

"Smeck! He's broken his back." She had run to his side before she even realised what she was doing. "Ford."

He looked up at her. His mouth was open, gasping for air and he tried to sit.

"No," she put her hand against his chest pushing him gently. He flopped backwards, "you are winded at the least. Breathe."

He half-grimaced, half-smiled and did as she told him.

"It hurts?"

He nodded. He was very pale but he had now reached the point of wheezing like an asthmatic sea lion. So long as nothing was damaged internally he'd be alright in a minute. But what if he'd ruptured his spleen or something? Like everyone in strike ops, Deirdre had some first aid training.

"Lie still. Let me check for damage." She undid his shirt and carefully felt across his torso, up to his ribs, across his diaphragm and down the other side. His skin was warm and smooth against her fingers and again, she relived the moments he'd carried her in his arms. She wished these flashbacks would stop. She shook her head to clear it and concentrated on what she'd learned in her field first aid training. There were none of the danger signs outlined but perhaps she should double check. As she started again his hand locked around her forearm.

"In the name of the Creator stop," he gasped.

"Does it hurt?"

"No," he put his other hand up to her shoulder but high, near her neck. "I thank you." Her beats per minute tripled as she felt his thumb move absently across the skin behind her ear. She tensed, afraid to show any other reaction. He closed his eyes briefly and withdrew his hand. "When you lean forward, your hair tickles me," he explained.

"Like this?" She leaned further forward and shook her head.

"Stop that!" he sat up. Yes, he was fine, definitely. "I have received a sofa to the solar plexus!"

"And it has clearly done you no harm." She got to her feet and looked down at him with a stern expression.

"Where is the tender nurse of a moment ago?"

"Saving herself for a more grateful patient."

"Deirdre," he winced as he tried to get up.

"Here," she held out her hand. He took it and she helped him to his feet.

"It's just a light knock but it hurts when I laugh." He rubbed his stomach thoughtfully. "And I'll wager it will for some time. That will teach me to attempt to keep up with younger, fitter beings."

"You are fitter and you were faster," said Deirdre.

"You finished."

She arched her eyebrows.

"Draw."

"Draw." He heaved a sigh. "Enough frivolity." With a grunt he turned and started towards the chair where he'd left his clothes. "We must discuss our mission. You must come to the High Temple."

"Now?"

"Once I have put my boots on."

She went and knocked on the door. When the guards opened it she asked for a cold compress and two of the analgesics Dr Dot had given them. To spare the General's blushes she made a point of explaining that they were for her. She took these and went to the bathroom, where she filled the plastic cup provided with water and took all of it back to the General. He was putting on his boots. Slowly.

"Here."

He took the compress and slipped it into his shirt.

"What are they?"

"Pain killers," she told him and held them out, with the cup.

"Thank you," he said. He took them, drained the cup and handed it to her. She put it on the table and watched while he straightened his shirt, removed the compress and put on his tunic.

"Better?" she asked as he buttoned it up.

"It is only a bump." He strapped on his belt. "Put your boots on, we must go."

"Where?"

"I told you, the High Temple," he said, striding across the room. He waited by door. She hurriedly slipped on her socks and boots. "You have a coat," he nodded to the uniform hanging from the mantelpiece, "other than that?"

"No."

"Then we will find you one."

He knocked on the door.

After being locked in the same room for three days, Deirdre almost ran to join him. He turned to face her.

"I trust you, Deirdre, but I must remind you that you would be unwise to try and escape."

She thought of Denarghi.

"I have nowhere to go," she said as the door swung open.

He nodded.

"Then, Lieutenant, after you," he gestured to the open door and hardly believing what was happening to her, Deirdre stepped out into the corridor.

Chapter 52

In her palatial penthouse prison, Ruth was awoken suddenly. She looked at her watch. Lunchtime and still Tuesday. She resigned herself to the idea that her day would not improve. She sat up. No, definitely not, neither the headache, nor the light headedness had abated and now she had a stomach ache to boot. As if that wasn't enough, the door was flung open and Captain Snow filled the entrance.

"Hello, sweetheart," he said, "you look pretty as a picture."

"How very kind of you Captain. What do you want?"

"That's no way to speak to your caring gaoler. It's lunch time," he said, standing to one side to let the usual maid into the room but today, two guards followed and stationed themselves at the bottom of the stairs, one either side. As always, Captain Snow slapped the girl on the bottom as she walked past him. Ruth winced and in the fleeting moment that Captain Snow couldn't see her expression the girl raised her eyes to heaven.

More food. Did these Grongles ever stop eating?

"I'm not hungry."

"Yes you are, if you know what's good for you." The maid turned to go. "Stay there precious," he ordered her. She stood still. "I want you to wait while I check this. The Chosen One, here, is a finicky eater. She likes it with a bit more seasoning."

Just watching him putting his finger in, tasting, spitting and stirring it in made Ruth feel ill.

"That's better," he said and stood by the table, leering at her. "On you go precious."

"No."

He nodded to the guards who stepped up swiftly. One of them grabbed the servant girl. Then Captain Snow swaggered over to where she stood, and she screamed when, he drew his laser pistol and, laughing, put the gun to her head.

"Eat it."

"Which one of us? Her or me?"

"You."

270

"No. Not after what you've done to it."

"Eat it or I'm going to pull the trigger."

"Please..." whimpered the servant girl.

"OK, Captain Snow, you win. If you let her go I'll eat something."

He jerked the gun at the girl and the whimper turned into a keening noise.

"No, you eat first, non-being."

"No, I said I'll eat, and I will, now let her go, please, Captain."

The room was silent except for the maid's crying. With a grunt Captain Snow stepped away. The guards let go of her and Captain Snow pushed her away from him, towards the stairs.

"It's your lucky day, get out," he ordered her.

She ran.

"Thank you," said Ruth. She went out onto the balcony and picked a leaf off one of the olive trees. "Here we are," she said holding it up to show him as she walked back in. Then she put it in her mouth and began to chew. She hoped it really was an olive leaf and not something exactly similar but poisonous.

"You told me you'd eat it, bitch."

"No. I said I'd eat something."

The Captain's bloodshot, piggy eyes narrowed dangerously.

"You don't get to mess me around. My orders, *from Lord Vernon*, are that if you don't eat you die."

"Yes, that is usually how it works but it takes a little longer than four days."

"It won't with him. He means business. What's the problem sweetheart? All you've got to do is show your appreciation, it's just a kiss."

"And as I just told you, I'm not kissing you or eating anything you've spat in. Anyway, I am eating aren't I?" The leaf was bitter and had a mouth feel not unlike sisal string. She swallowed it with a grimace. "There, just like you asked me to."

Captain Snow put his hands on his hips and fixed her with a dangerous look.

"Lord Vernon isn't going to like this."

"That's true, he doesn't like people playing with his toys."

"Don't try that one again, precious. You think he gives a smeck for you? You think I don't know how far I can push it? One little kiss. I won't tell and if you do, it'll be my word against yours. We know who he's going to believe, don't we? I'm going to give you one more chance."

Ruth went over to the bowl. It was macaroni cheese and it smelled good. Unadulterated, she knew she would probably eat it. She took a big spoonful, turned to face Captain Snow and flicked it at him. He ducked, unfortunately, but she'd made her position pretty clear.

He didn't seem to be angry, which was worrying, instead he laughed.

"I'm glad you did that. You've just blown your chance."

"No. You did."

He shook his head.

"Nah, now I get to have some fun. I don't like doing this to a pretty girl like you," he said with leaden irony. "Boys, get in here!"

Two more Grongle guards clattered into the room to join the pair who were already there. Uh-oh. No. She wasn't going to let them catch her. She ran for the bathroom, dodging all of them, slammed the door and locked it.

There was a pause of about two seconds before Captain Snow broke the bolt off with one well placed kick. She tried to duck past him but he grabbed her by the scruff of the neck. She struggled and lashed out as he dragged her into the room. He remained impervious to the blows which she rained on him, as the others closed in.

They overpowered her effortlessly, forcing her into the desk chair. One of the guards wrenched her arms round behind her and held her tightly, another pinned her ankles to the chair legs with gaffer tape while a third pulled her head back and tilted the chair backwards. The fourth rammed some sort of metal thing into her mouth that he pushed against her teeth and then extended, forcing her jaw as wide open as it would go. The pain was intense and to her humiliation she had to bite back the tears. And then Captain Snow leaned over her.

"There, there sweetheart. It's alright. I'm here to help. You see, my Master told me that if you don't eat, I've got to make you."

One of the guards handed him a coiled length of Perspex tubing. He unrolled it and pulled it taut so it cracked. Her eyes widened as she looked at the tube and guessed what they were going to do, and when Captain Snow attached a funnel to one end, she knew for certain. She was going to be force fed. The same way they'd force fed the Suffragettes who'd gone on hunger strike. Her jaw muscles burned against the clamp but she realised, from the firsthand accounts of the process she'd read in her history books, that it would hurt a great deal less if she could try to relax her throat, keep a lid on her panic and just swallow the tube. She was in awe of those women as she lay panting, held totally immobile, waiting for it to start. She remembered, as she tried to focus on individuals, that Emily Wilding Davison was one of them. Ruth concentrated on breathing, on Emily who had been derided and misunderstood and subjected to this before her. She concentrated on anything but the details of what was about to happen.

Captain Snow handed the funnel to one of his colleagues, took the other end of the hose and leaned over her.

"I think you know what I'm going to do now," he said as one of the guards handed him a jug of what looked like soup. "You see, I told you, didn't I, that one way or another, you'd eat my delicious, nutritious food, and if you won't swallow it, I'm going to have to get it into you some other way."

He held the end of the tube in front of her face and she looked up at him, concentrating on her anger and disdain.

"Relax, pretty lady, I've done this before, it won't hurt. Much."

She closed her eyes, tried to blot out Captain Snow and the guards. They could force her, but they would not break her. She knew she wasn't alone and she held on to that thought; so many others had been through this before her, and they'd won.

****

At last, it was finished. Captain Snow took the metal thing from Ruth's mouth and his guards released their grip and tilted the chair upright. She felt them cutting the gaffer tape round her ankles but she was too exhausted to move. The pain began to subside. Her stomach heaved several times throughout the process. She was determined not to vomit. She concentrated on staying calm, taking deep breaths, in, out, in, out. She wriggled a handkerchief from her pocket and wiped the drying tears off her face. Her throat and jaw hurt.

The Captain and his heavies stood around watching.

"Alright, pretty one. You've kept that down for long enough so we'll be going, right boys?"

At last.

"But the next meal you don't eat..."

Ruth looked up at him, trying to channel the loathing and repulsion she felt into her expression. 'I dare you,' she hoped that look said, 'I double dare you.' As if it would stop him or make any difference, but it made her feel better.

"You're going to take a lot of breaking. I can see that." He leaned towards her and Ruth braced herself for the vileness of his breath. And as it hit her nostrils, her body intervened. Without warning, her efforts to keep the horrible soup where it was, ended in spectacular failure. It surfaced, at speed, and landed all over him.

There was a moment of silence, while he stared at her in complete disgust, and she wondered how such a natural process as throwing up had achieved such impressive levels of coverage. Especially on his boots. It would probably be quite difficult to get that diced carrot, which seemed to have miraculously appeared in the regurgitated soup from somewhere, off suede.

That felt *so* much better.

"Well... there's a bit... of my tasty goodness for you... Captain," she panted.

The guards struggled not to laugh and Captain Snow rounded on them.

"Smecking shut up!" he shouted, and then, as the others stopped laughing, Ruth started; a worryingly manic, unhealthy laugh but what the heck, if it ticked him off. "And as for you, you piece of human dreck!" He kicked out at the chair so hard that she, and it, fell sideways onto the floor. "You asked for this—"

One of the guards ran swiftly over and put himself between them.

"Sir, No!"

Captain Snow pulled his fist back as if to smash it into the guard's face and then finally regained control of himself. He looked down at Ruth, breathing heavily.

"You'll get yours, you filthy, crawling, dung encrusted piece of crap, I'm going to make sure of that, you—" He stopped abruptly as a new voice – a soft-yet-carrying voice – silenced all of them.

"Captain. I ordered you to keep her pristine."

For heaven's sake. Didn't he have a country to run?

Chapter 53

General Moteurs had a staff snurd, with a driver. It was dark green, sleek and high end, without being flashy. Deirdre's father had owned one at one point. Sitting in the back, waiting for them, was Snoofle. Despite it being difficult in the constrains of the snurd, when she climbed in, she hugged him. She took the corner seat, Snoofle sat in the middle and General Moteurs the other side. He gave some brief instructions to the driver and closed the glass partition between the front and back seats.

"Before we reach the High Temple, while we have some privacy, you know what we are about?"

"Yes," said Snoofle, "we assassinate the High Leader so your contacts in Grongolia can take power."

"Yes."

"And Lord Vernon?" asked Deirdre.

"Yes."

"You hesitate."

"Lord Vernon must fall, but the Candidate will be attending the ceremony and for Lord Vernon and his allies in Grongolia to be totally defeated, it is essential that the boy is allowed to prove his credentials. He will need your help."

"Even with you in charge of security?"

"Yes. If the Imperial Guard is allowed to carry out its duties I see no difficulty. However, while Lord Vernon may trust me, that is not necessarily enough. He is cautious and he may have other contingency plans in place. He may even decide that it will be his army forces who carry out my orders. If that is so, the Grongles around you will not be so benign."

"You mean they'll kill us," asked Snoofle.

General Moteurs' face was a mask.

"Unless you kill them. Lord Vernon's plan is to conceal his hand in this, by using you, and to use the fact you are K'Barthan as an excuse for reprisals."

As she listened, and the High Temple drew nearer, Deirdre felt a hint of pre-mission butterflies in her stomach.

"What kind of reprisals?" she asked.

"In truth, I do not know, but they will be brutal. K'Barthans will be little more than slaves, he may even cleanse some species entirely. If that is what he intends, it is what he will do, the exact reason he chooses to give will be immaterial."

"Smeck," said Deirdre.

"Yes. He must die, and soon, but it cannot be before the installation. The Candidate has to face him to ensure the succession and that encounter must take place on Saturday."

"Arnold," whispered Snoofle, "this is not good."

"No. You were both brought up as Nimmists. You will have seen the High Temple enough times, but you must look at it afresh today. We will cover every inch. I will give you all the information I can, I will furnish you with plans and weapons and anything else you think you need. But first, you must look, and think, and rethink, and consider every possible option. Tomorrow we will compare ideas and devise a plan."

The snurd landed and drew to a halt in the Precinct in front of the High Temple. The driver stopped the vehicle, got out and opened the door.

"We are here, sir," he said, somewhat redundantly.

Chapter 54

Slowly, muzzily, Ruth stood up. Lord Vernon was taking in the scene, the vomit on the rug, Captain Snow, pebble-dashed from head to toe and her, remarkably un-spattered.

"Captain, I see I cannot trust you to handle a simple procedure." Lord Vernon's voice was like molten lava. "Your appearance is a disgrace. I want you back here, clean and properly attired, in five minutes."

"Sir."

"Oh and Captain."

"Sir."

"I mean clean. Take a shower and brush your teeth."

Captain Snow flushed a deep dark green.

"Sir," he said and left.

Lord Vernon turned his attention back to the guards in the room.

"You!" He pointed at one of them. "Get this cleaned up."

"Sir." The guard he'd singled out saluted and marched briskly towards the door.

"At the double," snarled Lord Vernon. The guard ran. "Now... you and you," he waved a dismissive hand at two of the guards, "put her back in the chair and hold her down."

She started to move away.

"No. Not again."

"Yes, Ruth, again."

"No. Let go of me!"

Her blind panic at the thought of repeating the past few minutes gave her strength, but not enough. Yet she fought them anyway. She heard a grunt as she gouged one in the eye and the other cursed as she landed a kick in his groin. Lord Vernon watched them dispassionately as they overpowered her and dragged her back to the chair.

"I really don't know why you bother to fight. You can't escape." He waited while they put her into position. Ostensibly unnoticing, he examined the ends of his fingers, as if there might be some mote of dust on the immaculate suede.

"Any time this week, gentlemen."

"She is ready, sir," said one of them as they held her still.

"Good." He took off his sunglasses and put them in the pouch on his belt, crossed the room, carefully avoiding the rug, and looked down at her, "I have been very patient with you, Ruth, but I explained what would happen if you refused to take care of yourself. And if you will not, you leave me no option but to... intervene." He held out one hand. "Give me the tube." One of the guards proffered the plastic hose. "No, fool. The other." The guard handed him a thinner one.

Captain Snow returned. He crossed the room, to his Master's side, also avoiding the rug.

"Reporting for duty, sir," he said snapping smartly to attention.

"About time, Captain." Lord Vernon thrust the tube into his hands. "Proceed." Captain Snow made to put the end of the tube into her mouth.

"Not like that. I want her fed, not killed. Put the tube into her nose or she will aspirate."

"Sir." Captain Snow started to do as ordered but Lord Vernon stopped him.

"No, imbecile." He snatched the tube from the Captain and he leaned over her, his eyes met hers, "Calm yourself, Ruth," he spoke softly, his tone would have been gentle, reassuring, were his eyes not alive with sadistic pleasure. "The more you fight this, the more it will hurt."

It was two minutes, if that, but the pain was excruciating. Tube inserted, he took a syringe, drew off some liquid and tested it with litmus paper. He waited until it turned red and then poured in a second jug of soup. Ruth closed her eyes and endured until it was done.

"Tape," ordered Lord Vernon.

Captain snow took the roll of gaffer tape one of the guards proffered. There was a tearing sound as he unrolled a large strip.

No. Her nose was blocked. She would suffocate. Too frightened to speak, she shook her head.

"Oh but I'm afraid so," said Lord Vernon. "Give it to me," he ordered Captain Snow. "I'm sorry to do this, Ruth," he said glibly as he put it over her mouth, "but we don't want any..." he waved one hand as he sought the right word, "mishaps, or the Captain and I will be compelled to repeat this process, again." He leaned down towards her. "And again, and again until you can keep the soup where it is put. Do you understand?"

The merciless grey eyes were inches from her own. She made no response.

"I said, 'Do. You. Understand?'"

She nodded.

"Excellent." He turned to Captain Snow. "And as for you, Captain, you have carried out this procedure enough times." He cast a sweeping glance over the Captain and his guards and the air temperature seemed to drop a few degrees as he made the depth of his rage apparent. "If I have to show you again," he addressed the whole room, "I will be more than angry, I will have you executed. Do I make myself clear?"

"Sir," said Captain Snow.

"Good. You!" he waved a hand at the nearest of the four guards, "Get me a chair." He pointed, indicating where he wanted it put. The guard went outside and brought one of the balcony chairs in for him. "Now get out. All of you."

Shakily Ruth made to try and stand, intending to go and lie on the bed with her back to him.

"Did I say you could go anywhere, darling? Sit down and stay where you are. You will not move until I say."

Too exhausted to resist, she did as he had ordered.

Lord Vernon strolled over to the table, once again, taking care to avoid the rug, and took the rings off his fingers. She watched as he lined them up in a neat row and then removed his suede gloves, took a clean pair from one of the pouches on his belt, put them on and replaced the rings on top. He took the old pair between his finger and thumb and holding them away from him, little finger extended, he went to the door.

"Send those to the Laundry," he said as he handed them to the guard outside.

He returned and sat down. Sprawled casually in the wooden patio chair, he waited, never taking his eyes off her. She faced him, her own personal demon. She wanted to appear aloof and dignified, untouched by the atrocity to which he had subjected her, but she could not. The fight for each breath took all her energy.

There was no sound in the room but the laboured whistling in Ruth's nostrils as she forced each breath in and out.

A team of cleaners arrived. They washed the mess off the floor with disconcerting expertise – this was not an unusual situation, she surmised – taking the rug away and replacing it with a new one. All the while Lord

Vernon sat and glared at her. The smell of the disinfectant eased Ruth's sickness, but as they left they squirted air freshener over it. The sickly chemical smell was almost her undoing. When she hiccupped the intensity of Lord Vernon's glare increased. She lifted her chin and tried to maintain a veneer of defiance but it was difficult; she could feel the shock taking over, her shaking was almost uncontrollable.

At last, he stretched languidly, unhooked his phone from his belt and glanced briefly at the time on the screen saver.

"That is long enough."

He got to his feet and stalked slowly over to where she sat. He moved like a panther. She wanted to stand and face up to him but her fear and exhaustion held her where she was. Towering above her like some malevolent god he reached one hand towards her face and gripped it hard. Oh no. Couldn't he leave her to do this bit herself? Of course not. He took the gaffer tape with his other hand and ripped it off with a flourish. Once again, she saw his pleasure in causing pain.

"This is how it will be, Ruth. You will adhere to the terms of our agreement or I will destroy you."

"You forget, I can destroy you, too." Her voice was all over the place and why wouldn't this ridiculous shaking stop? It made speaking so difficult.

"I see you are still unbowed but it will make no difference. Do not choose this path. Do not force me. Because I assure you, if I have to, I will break you."

She ditched the undignified wobbly voice in favour of a shake of her head.

"Oh it won't be so hard. You forget, I am an expert in these matters and you are not."

'Expert'. Certain things about Ruth's husband-to-be were beginning to hit home.

"So, you are going to do my bidding, as you agreed, or there will be... consequences. It makes no difference to me, but perhaps, now, you are beginning to understand that one way, for you, will be so very painful."

Again she shook her head.

"Accept your defeat, Ruth. This is a battle you cannot win."

"I know that," she said through chattering teeth, "I will keep my promise. But I'll not give you my dignity," she wiped her hand across her eyes, "not when you have taken everything else."

"Oh you haven't begun to see what I can take from you." He took a long breath in. "If that is your choice, so be it."

Ruth didn't know how long she sat on the chair after he had gone. She was too drained to move. Eventually, slowly, she dragged herself to the bed.

Chapter 55

Professor N'Aversion wasn't certain what to expect in Room 103 but when he opened the door and slipped inside he found himself in a space rather larger than his office, lined with shelves. Like the rest of the HQ it was clean but tatty, the paintwork chipped, the shelves constructed from the scavenged bits of broken others. They were laden with pens, pencils, staplers, printer cartridges and all of the other office-related detritus he'd expect. He also found Lieutenant Wright, sitting on a box of photocopier paper. On a stack of two boxes of photocopier paper, sat Colonel Ischzue. No Colonel Smeen, he noticed.

"Hi there Prof, make yourself at home," said Lieutenant Wright with a grin. Colonel Ischzue inclined his head and waved a hand at a wooden crate which had been set aside for his guest.

"Oh, the luxury seat," said Professor N'Aversion, to break the ice.

"Of course," said Colonel Ischzue smoothly.

Each time the Professor and Colonel Ischzue met, his first, and enduring, impression was of a thoroughly shifty and untrustworthy being. Since the Colonel was a professional thief, the Professor suspected that his first impressions were largely correct. Except that he did trust the Colonel. And Lieutenant Wright was loyal to him, and she was not the kind of person to be loyal to just anyone. He took the tablet computer she had given him from the wide pocket of his lab coat.

"Thank you for this," he said.

The Colonel adjusted his whiskers and raised an eyebrow at Lieutenant Wright who nodded.

"My pleasure," he said, "have you loaded Smeen's donation?"

"I have."

"All of it?"

"Yes, very interesting." He suspected he was being asked about the video message and the schematics but didn't dare mention them out loud. "So, what can I do for you?"

"I'd have thought that was clear," said Ischzue.

"It sounds as if you're asking me to put my neck on the line," said the Professor.

Lieutenant Wright put her hand to her collar.

"It's not just your neck, Prof."

"No, quite."

"I believe we are all here because we fear the Resistance is in great danger," said Ischzue. "Unfortunately, our Leader removed the papers you gave us before I had time to read them all. However, as I understand it, you believe the Grongles can use this portal for surveillance as well as travel. Is that correct?"

"I'm afraid it is, Colonel, the K'Barthan version at any rate. The Grongle one is slightly different, it uses input map coordinates; I believe the K'Barthan one is driven by the imagination of the user."

Lieutenant Wright whistled.

"Smeck," she whispered.

"Indeed," said the Professor. "There were five original portals and they are mainly being used for surveillance. As I understand it, and I hope I'm wrong, we are completely compromised."

"You mean they could be listening to us now?" asked Lieutenant Wright.

"I sincerely hope they are not, but if what the General told me is true, yes, it is a possibility."

There was silence as the other two took that in.

"Is there any way of telling?" asked Colonel Ischzue.

"Not yet. If I can build a working portal that is something I am hoping to discover."

"How big is the Grongolian portal?"

The Colonel's question was not one the Professor was expecting.

"It's difficult to tell. The schematics we have are for something about oh... yea big," the Professor outlined a shape with his hands.

"I see." Colonel Ischzue and Lieutenant Wright exchanged glances.

"The thing is, Prof, either this General Moteurs is lying and the Grongles have made a really diddy version, or there's another K'Barthan one around. But I'm guessing it's K'Barthan and one they don't know about," said Lieutenant Wright.

The Professor leaned forward eagerly in his seat and felt his antennae mirroring the manoeuvre.

"Arnold's socks! Can you tell me more?"

"Yeh, I'll say."

"Come on then! Don't string it out."

Lieutenant Wright turned to Colonel Ischzue, who nodded and smiled.

"One of my gangs met The Pan of Hamgee on a roof last night."

"But surely they can't have done. He's in Grongle custody."

"Not any more."

"But...? Are you sure?"

She undid a zip on her cat suit and pulled something out of a concealed pocket; a photograph. "One of the lads took this. I can put the original on a micro disk for you," she said as she handed it to the Professor.

"I already have," said Ischzue, pulling a small black rectangle from one of the pouches on his belt and handing it over.

"Thank you. Are you sure it's—?"

"You bet we are. I ran it through the database – you know, discreetly. It's a 95% match."

The Professor took it from her. He looked at it. The frightened young man in the picture seemed unnervingly animated, as if he was actually there, trapped in the photograph, looking back at him. For all the obvious fear, there was something in his eyes; a confidence, a strength of character, that was missing in the photograph on the Resistance's files.

"He seems... different."

"Yeh, that's why we ran a check. We wondered if it was a relation, you know, twin brother or something, but it's the same bloke, no question. And my team say he took something out of his pocket and then disappeared into thin air."

"Arnold's socks! He still has a portal."

The Professor tried to conceal his excitement but he could feel his hands shaking. Blow the Grongle's box – maybe, if he could find The Pan of Hamgee, he could produce a K'Barthan portal. Surely Denarghi would overlook his flagrant disregard of orders for that.

"We can give you a rough location," said Lieutenant Wright. "The roof of number fifty three, Turnadot Street, Upper Left Central District, Ning Dang Po."

"Turnadot Street?"

"Yeh, and believe me, that is rough. You know it?" asked Lieutenant Wright.

"No."

"It's low class. Pass through for us."

"Pass through?"

"Yeh, as in we pass right through because there's nothing there worth nicking."

"So, a deprived area?"

Lieutenant Wright smiled.

"Depraved more like. Well, it's not so bad but you wouldn't hang around there unless you were local. Wherever he's hiding, I reckon it can't be far from where my lads found him."

"Did he say anything else?"

"According to the team leader, he said he was just a publican, going for a walk. But nobody straight goes over the roofs and he'd blatantly been thieving."

"How can you tell?"

"He nearly outran them for one, and he was wearing the loot. My boys reckoned it was the biggest rock they'd ever seen. They tried to take it off him. That's when he split."

"I see," Professor N'Aversion would have liked to have seen that ring. Unfortunately The Pan of Hamgee's hands were not in the picture. "Can I keep this?" he asked.

"Sure."

"Thank you. Have you forwarded the report to Denarghi?"

"Unfortunately it has been lost in our files. So very inefficient of us," said Colonel Ischzue. "I will have to rediscover it when the team return from duty, but they are in Ning Dang Po until Sunday. I have sent them a personal message stressing that the information is sensitive and they should mention it to no-one. That's why I've lost it myself, these damned sensitive files. I put it aside to keep it safe and mislaid it."

"Are they going to believe that of you?" asked Professor N'Aversion.

"No, but if you haven't built the portal by then I fear we will all be dead anyway; if not shot for treason by our esteemed Leader then at the hand of the Grongles."

The Professor swallowed. Certain aspects pertaining to the gravity of what he was about to do, were beginning to hit home.

"Is that going to buy you enough time?" asked the Lieutenant.

The Professor forced a reassuring smile.

"It'll have to."

He thought back to Lord Vernon's announcement of his Candidature. The first news report had contained that bit of clap trap they'd dropped in subsequent ones. It was merely a line to set the scene. It stated that Lord Vernon's announcement was made just after he'd bestowed a pub on a close personal friend. Now, here was The Pan of Hamgee, at large, apparently unmolested, wearing a valuable ring and calling himself a publican.

Could he possibly be a close personal friend of Lord Vernon? It seemed unlikely. Even so, it was clear to the Professor that he must be approached with extreme caution. There would be more information, somewhere. Perhaps Nar could help him find it.

"D'you need anything else from us? I could order my team to try and find the Hamgeean. You know, tactfully," said Lieutenant Wright.

"No. I believe I can track him down. If I need any help with that or on the Ning Dang Po side of things, rest assured I'll ask."

"If you need more time, there is... another way," said Colonel Ischzue, "I could persuade Denarghi that we must evacuate."

"He'll never do that, and where would we go? We'd need to dig another base first."

"It would keep him focussed on something that is not us."

"Hold it in reserve. But I think you would be wise to drill your emergency evacuation procedures, as well; Smeen, too, and anyone else you can persuade."

"Good point," said Lieutenant Wright.

The three of them agreed to meet the following day, in one of the trees comprising the Park.

Chapter 56

At the Parrot and Screwdriver, Tuesday lunchtime opening was over. Alan and Dave had gone, as had Humbert, and The Pan stood, alone, at the window in Gladys and Ada's sitting room. He gazed out on the street as if from behind bars. He wanted to go out, but he dare not in case he met that Resistance gang again.

He turned round, facing into the room and leaned his back against the cool glass.

He was the Candidate. And he was alone.

"What can one man do?" he asked the empty room.

"Cluck."

"OK, one man and a head full of Architraves."

He rolled his eyes, 76 out of 77 Architraves and the only one he needed wasn't there; the first one, Arnold The Prophet. He would have known what to do, whereas all his successors seemed to know was how wrongly The Pan was doing it. He felt numb, black.

"Snap out of it."

He crossed the room and flopped into an arm chair.

"Ouch."

No flopping until his shoulder was better.

He sat forward and rubbed one temple with his good hand.

"I'm a failure, hen."

Silence.

"I as good as killed my real folks and now the adopted ones are going to go the same way. And Ruth..." He made a face. "OK, let's not talk about her. But how can I make this right? One clueless man against Lord Vernon and the Grongles."

"Cluck?"

"Alright, I have half a clue. I can take the box to Lord Vernon's installation, prove he's a fake and get myself killed but someone has to get me in there."

There was a long pause and in his mind's eye, The Pan could see General Moteurs, shaking his hand and telling him 'trust me'. But what now? Should he try to contact the General or should he wait until the General contacted him?

"I wish there was someone I could talk to... If only Merv was here, I know we'd work something out." How had Big Merv put it, yeh, he quoted his friend.

'There's three rules of doin' a job. First you gotta case the joint; second you gotta lay out the moves; third you gotta trust your blokes and know 'em real well. And you know something else, mate? You can get by without one and two if you got three. Coz if them moves don't work, see, an' you got a bunch of likely lads at your back, it's still gonna go down the way you want it.'

"That's where I'm stumped. Thing Three."

"Cluck," suggested Eight.

"You think I should rescue them? Yeh right. How? It's a big ask to spring all of them at once. I can't leave any of them behind to be tortured by a vengeful Lord Vernon."

Eight didn't answer but The Pan got the impression he was sympathetic.

"And I don't know how I can do this without them, hen."

"Cluck?"

"You think I can? Sorry to disappoint you."

The Pan held his hand out and watched the ring catching the light as he turned it this way and that. He doubted any of his predecessors had been less qualified to wear it. His only hope was a Grongle, an enemy. Should he trust General Moteurs? Could he?

"Cluck."

"I know, I'm thinking myself in circles and it isn't going to help."

A picture of Gladys' recipe file popped into his head from somewhere.

The Pan had an idea. It wasn't a good one, but he knew Gladys and Ada would approve, and it would keep his mind occupied. Who knew, maybe that would give his subconscious enough time and space to work on an answer.

"Yeh. Nice going, Eight. Let's go make some chutney."

Chapter 57

In his palatial rooms, Lord Vernon drained the last dregs of his smoothie and stretched languidly. His victory was almost complete. This would be a difficult interview but Captain Snow would be anxious to please him after their last encounter and would follow his instructions carefully. Lord Vernon knew the outcome would be favourable. Success in any situation was simple enough to achieve, if one chose the right incentives. He stood up and clicked his knuckles. His sense of anticipation building, he made his way to the secure dungeons buried deep under the building.

Lord Vernon had decided that the initial interrogation would require a direct approach and sure enough, Captain Snow was waiting for him with six guards. They clicked their heels together with a snap, in perfect synchronisation, as he drew near. He rubbed his gloved hands together.

"Captain."

"Sir."

Lord Vernon ran his eye over the guards. For this part of the interrogations he had ordered Captain Snow to prepare for an interview of a somewhat physical nature. Two of the Captain's troops carried clubs, two, truncheons, and two, crowd control sticks.

"I see you understand my requirements."

"Sir."

"Excellent. Then we shall begin," said Lord Vernon.

He strode past the Captain, to the cell he had selected at the far end of the corridor. A guard rushed forward and opened the door. Inside were two more troops and one prisoner, Sir Robin Get. Captain Snow's guards went in first and stood to attention, flanking the doorway. Lord Vernon stepped in after them and looked about him. The cell was furnished for interrogation purposes. There was a heavy table with leg and arm restraints. It had been pushed against the wall, as he had instructed. He would not be using it in this interrogation.

However, on its surface was a metal tray upon which various instruments of torture were laid out in rows. He doubted he would be using these, either. He had instructed Captain Snow to put it there for effect. At the far side of the room, flanked by two guards, wearing shackles on his arms and legs stood the prisoner.

"Sir Robin," said Lord Vernon quietly.

"Lord Vernon." The old man bowed. "I expected you sooner."

"Then you overestimate your importance." Lord Vernon moved towards the table and selected a pair of pliers from the tray.

"Do I? Or are Ruth and The Pan of Hamgee taking too long to crack?"

"The Chosen One is already mine and the Hamgeean will be dead by nightfall."

"I doubt that."

"Then you are misguided." Lord Vernon pretended to concentrate on the pliers, opening and closing them a couple of times. "I saw to the matter, personally."

"You enjoyed beating that boy to a pulp did you?"

"I did what had to be done." Lord Vernon held the pliers over their place on the tray beside him and dropped them from the height of a couple of inches. They hit the metal surface with a clatter, making the old man jump. "Administering justice, where required, is always a pleasure, Sir Robin."

"And now it's my turn is it?"

"Oh no, that would be too easy." Calmly, casually, Lord Vernon turned his attention to the tray again and, after a few moment's deliberation, chose an electric drill. He rubbed it in his hair to boost the charge and held it up to the light as if examining it. "You are trained in the Nimmist arts; all of them I'll wager." He turned the drill this way and that and then aimed it, randomly, as if it were a laser pistol.

"Indeed. And you would be wise to remember that; they give me great power." He really was an old fool.

"Naturally," Lord Vernon cast a sarcastic look about him, "and that is why I require your services."

"I may not wish to serve you."

Lord Vernon switched on the drill for a second and the bit whirred with a satisfying electronic scream. He walked back to the tray and he could feel the old man's eyes on him as he placed it carefully back in its place.

"Perhaps not. Yet you will give me your full compliance in... How long will it take, Captain?"

"Ten minutes, sir."

Lord Vernon narrowed his eyes. He had instructed Captain Snow to be more thorough than that. With a nasty smile he turned back to Sir Robin.

"Ten minutes."

Sir Robin's reaction was unexpected. He laughed.

"I wouldn't do that if I were you—" began Captain Snow but Lord Vernon silenced him with a look.

"For all your boasting, Lord Vernon, you've obviously questioned far fewer true Nimmists than you believe," said Sir Robin.

"Oh I have had the privilege of interrogating many of your colleagues." As he spoke Lord Vernon waved a hand at Captain Snow who took two guards and went out into the corridor. "I can only admire their ability to endure pain; unto death in most cases." He paused, giving Sir Robin time to understand the gravity of what he had said. "Their discipline and training is enviable and I must commend you in that regard. It is devilishly hard to get anything out of you holy people without killing you first but..." he continued as he walked slowly over to the doorway. One of the guards opened the door and Captain Snow dragged Trev Parker into the room. Lord Vernon could almost smell the old man's apprehension as Captain Snow threw his only son to the ground. He was bruised and beaten and his leg was broken, spectacularly, but that didn't stop him struggling. Lord Vernon turned and faced Sir Robin, unleashing a slow sinister smile. "I wonder if the same can be said for your son." Again, he paused, giving his words time to hit home. "Oh, I know who he is, Sir Robin."

"Dad—" began Trev but his words were lost in a yell of pain as Captain Snow punched him.

"True to form I see," said Sir Robin. His voice was calm but he had lost all trace of colour.

"It's a simple choice; you can do what I require or you can watch him die."

"He won't die. You can be sure of that."

Such quiet confidence but Lord Vernon knew it was all bluff.

"Really?" Lord Vernon raised his eyebrows. "Captain Snow believes it will take ten minutes to beat him to death. I would wager that estimate is somewhat... conservative." He cast a meaningful glance at the tray with the drill, the pliers and the rest of its cargo. "Even I could not make it last more than an hour."

"Tell me, Lord Vernon, what do you hope to achieve by doing this to my son?" Sir Robin was clearly in shock but for all that, his gaze was steady.

"Your full cooperation. You will preside over my installation as Architrave."

"I will preside over the Candidate's installation."

Lord Vernon tutted.

"Are you trying to provoke me?" Without taking his eyes off the Sir Robin, he snatched a club from the guard nearest him and smashed it downwards and sideways, hard, onto the broken part of Trev Parker's leg. It made contact with a satisfying crack. The old man flinched at his son's scream but when he spoke, his voice was steady and authoritative.

"Let him go."

Lord Vernon smiled.

"I think not," he said.

"Don't worry, Dad I'm—" Trev began, and with a casual flick of his wrist Lord Vernon hit him again. A partial success he reflected wearily; it had stopped him speaking but he was still making a lot of irritating noise.

"Hold your tongue," said Captain Snow putting the boot in, and, unsurprisingly the wretch only screamed the more. A little of General Moteurs' subtlety would have carried Captain Snow a long way, reflected Lord Vernon – further than the rank of Captain. Alas, his brain was as blunt as his fists, as his behaviour with the Chosen One had shown. Some direction was required, clearly.

"Gag him, you cretin."

"Sir." Chastened, Captain Snow did as he was ordered. Despite being beaten almost senseless, Sir Robin's son fought and it took a few moments. But Lord Vernon had time, and a little more degradation would underline the seriousness of his intent to the old man.

"Let Trev go and we will talk," said Sir Robin.

"No," said Lord Vernon.

"I will not be installing anyone unless you do," said Sir Robin but Lord Vernon just smiled.

"You will do exactly as I command you," he said. He walked slowly, menacingly over to where Sir Robin stood, swinging the club as he went. The old man did not struggle but the guards who held him knew their master well enough to tighten their grip. "You cannot refuse me," this was pure poetry – Lord Vernon couldn't believe his luck – "your beliefs will not allow it. You will do my bidding for the sake of a forlorn hope," he laughed, "and because you are a spent, deluded dreamer."

"Very possibly, Lord Vernon. Better that than an arrogant one."

Lord Vernon was filled with an almost overriding desire to smash the club into Sir Robin's pompous Nimmist skull, but he demurred. Instead he looked into the old man's eyes and what he saw confirmed his suspicions.

"You think the Candidate will attend my installation?"

"I know he will."

Lord Vernon watched Sir Robin closely, exulting at what he saw; hope, defiance, a hint of fear, but confidence? No.

"Shall we see if he dares?"

"Oh, he will be there. You can count on it."

"Then I will kill him."

"No. He will vanquish you. And when he has, someone of suitable authority must install him as Architrave. I am the only one remaining."

Lord Vernon's fingers itched to swing the club but he managed to contain himself. If he wished to successfully establish a new order and access the true power of being Architrave, he must do so with, at least, the token blessing of the old one. To his chagrin, this insufferable old man was, indeed, all that was left of it.

"I thank you for your cooperation. It is I whom you shall install."

"Lord Vernon. As the instrument of The Prophet in this mortal realm I must install the most suitable Candidate. If it is you then, whatever my own personal view, I really have no choice. However, I think it highly unlikely that it will be you."

"Who else? Who can defeat me? Do tell."

"So confident? I warn you, drop this while you may. Whatever comes to pass you will never be Architrave."

"Oh but I shall," said Lord Vernon coolly, "and as you well know, I will have great power, and since you are being so..." he waved his hand while he searched for the word, "cooperative it seems I can dispense with your son. That will save us the cost of his keep. He will be publically executed tomorrow morning."

"On what charge?"

"As the progeny of the blacklisted, his existence is as treasonable as that of his parents."

Sir Robin was so pale now that he was almost blue, but still his voice did not waver.

"Do your worst, Lord Vernon. He will not die. I assure you of that," but, like the rest of Sir Robin's words, this was nothing but big talk from a small, defeated man.

"We shall see, Sir Robin."

"Indeed we shall." The old man sounded hoarse and every bit his age. Lord Vernon glanced dismissively at him and then at his broken son. "Put them back in their cells."

"Sir," said Captain Snow.

Lord Vernon was exultant. The interview had gone better than he ever could have hoped. The Nimmist fool had played into his hands. As he stepped into the corridor he smoothed his gloves over his hands. The ring, the ring worn by 40 generations of Architraves flashed deep red against the black suede. He would be indomitable. He would crush everyone and everything in his path. And he would begin with that tedious old man in there – he chuckled to himself – oh yes, once he had served his purpose.

Chapter 58

General Moteurs was as good as his word, Deirdre and Snoofle spent several hours with him at the High Temple. He was different now that Snoofle was with them: formal, his demeanour closed. As the day wore on he seemed to withdraw further and further away from her, behind a mask of brusque military efficiency. The more distant he became the more she yearned for the other General, the one who had bared his soul about his daughter, scared her by falling off the ceiling and made her laugh afterwards. But she didn't know how to get him back and she was bemused that his rebuttal, if that's what it was, even bothered her. The three of them returned to the Palace and he escorted her and Snoofle to her room.

"Snoofle, I have arranged for you to have dinner with the Lieutenant tonight, since I cannot," he told them, "and Lieutenant, you must remain here but you may return to the Laundry tomorrow, for light duties. I have arranged with Sid that the two of you will work together."

"Thank you," said Deirdre. "Will we see you tomorrow?"

She kept her voice calm and level, speaking soldier to soldier. She didn't want to sound hopeful. It would be unprofessional.

"I fear I cannot. If my diplomatic team is correct, the High Leader will arrive here tomorrow and I will be attending on him." His voice was as even as hers, with no hint of regret. It made her feel unaccountably flat.

"Understood," she said, keeping her voice formal and businesslike.

"Corporal Jones will escort Snoofle back to the dormitory, in one hour."

"Thank you," said Snoofle.

"My pleasure." With the usual bow, he was gone.

Snoofle and Deirdre sat at the table, waiting while the guards outside closed the door behind the General and locked it. Snoofle watched the closed door thoughtfully.

"You two have made your peace, then."

Deirdre was about to say yes but she didn't know any more. She shrugged. "I think so."

"Hmm," he said.

"What does 'hmm' mean?"

"Do you like him?"

She recalled their comfortable evening polishing her kit, the morning's game. Then an afternoon's lofty indifference and his absence, now, when he had originally accepted her invitation to dine. She was surprised how much it hurt. She thought about that single soft caress of his thumb, on her neck, an unconscious gesture of tenderness. He had overstepped the boundaries, there, perhaps. Had that made him shy? She couldn't lie to Snoofle but was unsure how much she should say.

"He is good company, when he is inclined," she said. "It is hard to tell but I think he is playing me."

Snoofle picked up the rolled plans.

"Maybe," he said. There was an elastic band round the middle, to keep them rolled up. He began to work it towards one end of the roll. "I don't know."

"I do, and the thing that angers me, is he is winning."

"And that's driving you up the wall, right?"

She laughed, but even to her own ears it sounded a bit forced.

"Yeh."

The elastic band pinged off the end of the rolled plans and landed, a few feet away, on the couch.

"Arnold's sandals! Hang on," said Snoofle. Deirdre waited as he hopped off the chair and retrieved it. "You know what I think?" he continued as he settled himself back at the table. "I think you're the one who's winning."

Chapter 59

The Pan stood at the stove in Gladys and Ada's kitchen at the Parrot and Screwdriver. His second day's tidying and his second evening's trade complete; he was making some cocoa as the old ladies had always done. He looked, with pride, at the five sticky jars of pickle he'd made. He would label it and put it in the cellar to prove. Gladys kept it for at least six months before serving.

"Shame I'll never get to taste it then."

He lit the gas under the saucepan of milk. He was tired. All he wanted to do was sleep.

"Jiggle my tumpkin!"

"Tell me, Humbert, how did you get here? We left you at the Underground HQ."

"Gits in a bag."

"Well yes, I suppose it wasn't very kind, but we didn't have much option, we were all a bit tied up at the time. There you go, anyway." He threw the last of the biscuits up into the air. Humbert swooped from one side of the kitchen to the other, catching the biscuit as he went in a manner more becoming an eagle or a gannet than a nearly bald parrot.

"Wipe my conkers," he shouted as he settled himself on top of the units the other side of the room.

"A pleasure," said The Pan. "That reminds me, Dave told me he'd bring you some proper parrot food tomorrow. I'm surprised Ada didn't leave any."

"Shroud my futtocks."

"Mmm. AND I've got your key here. Alan brought it round."

"Melons in a hammock!"

Humbert sounded excited.

"Good. I aim to please," said The Pan as he put the shiny metal key on the table.

Did he actually know what to do with it, though, wondered The Pan. For all he knew, the parrot might just drop it in the Dang, except that he knew Humbert was way too intelligent for that, and after 'meeting' the Eighth Architrave The Pan's own views about avian intelligence had altered somewhat. He started stirring the contents of the saucepan. He turned the radio on. It felt a bit sticky. Then again, everything did. Despite extensive cleaning up after his pickle making, the whole kitchen seemed to be faintly tacky to the touch.

It was time for the news. Gladys and Ada had always held the view that a wise publican should be able to arbitrate in any political discussions which got out of hand. True, their usual form of arbitration was to issue a warning and then, if it wasn't heeded, to get Trev to escort the offending parties out of the pub. However, they always kept up to date with the news. All types; local, national and gossip.

The Pan, whose interest in current affairs, thus far, had run little further than an ardent desire not to feature in them, was tempted to turn the radio off again. Instead, remembering that he was their stand-in, he listened with mild curiosity which turned to dismay as the bulletin progressed.

"Tonight's top story. Three rebels are to be executed for treason. Big Merv, Lucy Hargraves and Trev Parker will be publically beheaded in the City Square at first light, six a.m. tomorrow morning. Three other suspected rebels, who have not been named, remain in prison, awaiting trial. Our commentator, Leighton Bromswold, is outside the Security HQ now..."

The reporter made brief mention of The Pan's friends, calling them 'dangerous'.

"Yeh right," said The Pan, rolling his eyes.

"Cluck?"

"Oh alright, but Big Merv is only dangerous if you get on the wrong side of him."

The broadcast continued with an in-depth explanation of exactly who Big Merv was; all about the Mervinettes and what they'd done. It was the Grongles' version, of course, so as far as The Pan was concerned, it was more or less fictional. He turned the radio off in disgust and looked up at Humbert who was still slobbering over his biscuit.

"This isn't good, Humbert."

"Futtocks!" said the parrot and he swooped down, took up the key and returned to where he was perched on the corner of the cupboard.

"How will I ever find anyone to look after you when I'm gone?"

"Cluck," said the chicken.

"Well, I'm not going to be around long am I, hen?" said The Pan.

"Bombs away!" said Humbert.

"Cluck?" asked the chicken.

"Mmm," said The Pan. "It looks like I'm in for a long night." He would not leave Big Merv, Trev and Lucy to their fate. Especially not Lucy. She had nothing to do with any of this, but how was he going to save them? More to the point, should he?

Yes. Of course he should. It was the right thing to do on every moral level, but there was more to it than that. He was just one man, and his part in this was to die for his people. Someone else had to carry on the Underground after he had gone. The obvious choice was Big Merv, who knew how to fight, and more importantly, how to win and certainly had presence. OK so he wasn't much of a Nimmist but Trev could help. It was up to Lucy what she did but at least he could give her the choice.

"Now here's the million dollar question," he said aloud. "How am I going to do this?"

"Cluck," agreed the chicken.

"Knackers," shouted Humbert from the top of the cupboard.

The Pan rolled his eyes and carried on stirring.

He knew he couldn't get his friends out of gaol, he couldn't fight his way onto the platform and whisk them away from their executioners either – not alone and definitely not against the numbers of Grongle guards likely to be there with them. And anyway, he couldn't show his face. If he did, his friends were just as dead as if he'd let the Grongles execute them. Sure, he could hide them but Lord Vernon would simply take him into custody and ask him nicely – and then not so nicely – where they were until he blabbed. Then there was the bigger picture. He was the Candidate and while defeating Lord Vernon was impossible, The Pan could stop him becoming Architrave as long as he could keep himself alive and out of trouble until Saturday. So whatever he did he had to make sure that, from the outside at least, the rescue plan could not be connected to him.

If only he'd listened to the news sooner, he might have tried to borrow a snurd from one of the Parrot's customers. He might even have succeeded. But they had gone home now and the execution was at dawn. The Pan would have to find a set of wheels tonight. Which meant tramping the streets until he found a suitable target and then nicking it.

He poured the cocoa, put the saucepan in the sink and filled it with cold water. Then he picked up the cocoa tin from the side and put it back in the cupboard, but as he was about to close the door he hesitated. It was one of K'Barth's well known brands, Nectar of The Prophet, still limping along by sheer quality, alone, despite cheaper, subsidised competition imported from Grongolia. He looked at the iconic logo on the tin; a purple lorry on a yellow background.

"The delivery snurd!"

He scrabbled through any number of nameless keys in the bowl of junk Gladys, Ada and Trev kept by the phone until he found a set that looked likely and ran downstairs. The Pan skidded out into the alley behind the pub and half way across to the garage before another thought struck him and he stopped. Perhaps he should find some gloves. At this stage he didn't have a clear plan but when he finally thought of one he might not want his fingerprints all over the delivery snurd and the garage.

In all his time living at the pub, The Pan didn't recall going into Gladys and Ada's garage. He'd been too busy chauffeuring Big Merv about. Beer sales through other outlets had never been a priority to Gladys and Ada – either that or the Parrot's regulars had proved too thirsty to make them tenable – and the delivery snurd had always been driven by Their Trev. He was very cagey about letting anyone else near and The Pan was beginning to think that Trev had used the delivery van for other things, the secret transporting of blacklisted K'Barthans for example, rather than beer. Certainly The Pan didn't recall even touching it. Now he realised this was a factor which might work in his favour.

He ran back into the pub almost getting himself knocked down in the process by Humbert, who flew out of the door at high speed as he opened it and disappeared, complete with his new key, into the distance over the buildings.

"Strange..." said The Pan, watching him go. "Where was I?"

"Cluck." A picture of some yellow rubber gloves, or Marigolds as they were called in K'Barth, after the chapped-handed lady who'd invented them, popped into his head. He had a distinct impression it was put there by the chicken.

"Right, yes."

He remembered that he'd left a pair on the draining board in the Holy of Holies. He ducked in, grabbed them and returned to the ally. The garage had double doors made of wood, with a smaller postern door set in one of them so that people who didn't need to get the delivery vehicle out could come and go easily. He unlocked it and slipped inside.

The delivery snurd was large enough to accommodate at least ten barrels of beer, 30 if they were stacked. It was bigger than required, that was for sure. The Pan didn't know how long it had stood idle but appearances suggested Trev had maintained it meticulously. He unlocked the door and climbed up into the cab. Everything seemed as it should be. He tried to put the key in the ignition. It wouldn't fit. Arnold's snot. Now what?

No wait. It was an old fashioned model, the key was just for the door, there would be a second key, somewhere, for the ignition. He ran his hand along the top of the sun visor on the driver's side. Sure enough there was another key. He tried it in the ignition. Praise The Prophet, it fitted. A bank of worry-lights came on, flashed for a moment and then all bar the ignition light went off. That was normal. Good.

Probably a smart idea to see if it turned over then. Risky, in many respects – if the battery was a bit flat then, unless there was a charger, he might flatten it completely – but still essential because if it didn't go when required, it would be too late to find anything else.

He pressed the starter and the engine coughed into life, immediately filling the garage with a cloud of steam.

"Cluck?"

"Yeh, I think there are better ways to have a sauna."

Not the most fuel efficient engine, then. The Pan made a note that, if there was that much water pouring out of the back, he must make sure he put plenty in the tank. He cut the engine and pressed the button on the dash which would reveal the extra functions. If there were any.

"Wow," he said. He hadn't expected that.

It wasn't as deluxe as the SE2 but the Parrot and Screwdriver's delivery snurd was definitely top end. He read the labels under the buttons. "Aviator, submariner... sideways park. Sideways park? I haven't seen that one before." He pressed it. There was a whirring sound, a thunk and the vehicle shuddered. He leaned out and saw that all four wheels were now pointing sideways instead of forward. "Ooo very snazzy." He deactivated sideways park and looked at some of the other buttons. There was one labelled 'shields'. Until he'd taken delivery of his own enhanced wheels he'd never seen that option. Clearly Gladys and Ada's delivery van was not all it seemed. There was the ubiquitous 'machine guns', underneath which Trev had written 'fires blanks' in china graph pencil. Legally, it was supposed to fire blanks so the very fact Trev had made a note suggested the ordnance in this vehicle was usually live. That wasn't so out of the ordinary in certain circles – most of Ning Dang Po's underworld drove fully armed snurds. The MK II's ordnance had been real. Even the SE2's was – not that The Pan ever used the ordnance in either – but from Trev and Gladys and Ada who were very un-underworld, somehow it came as a surprise. The Pan shrugged, he'd check the magazine. There was another button, "Rubber bullets?" said The Pan. No way. Was there a Water Cannon option he'd missed? No. Judging by the way this thing appeared to guzzle fuel, he doubted there'd be enough water in reserve. He popped the catch to open the engine compartment and hopped out of the cab, tipping it forward. He examined the magazines, sure enough, there were several minutes' worth of blank machine gun rounds and a string of orange plastic cylinders, each one about the size of his fist if a little thinner, attached to another firing mechanism.

"Arnold's pants," said The Pan. He swung the cab back into its proper position and climbed in. Should he? Yes. It was only sensible to test the equipment. He switched on the ignition, pressed the button labelled 'rubber bullets' and squeezed the trigger on the steering wheel to fire. There was a hiss and a pop as the firing mechanism activated and one of the plastic cylinders hit the door with an almighty thunk and ricocheted straight back at the truck. The Pan ducked but luckily it glanced off the windscreen without breaking it and disappeared upwards through an open trapdoor. It hit something up in the rafters of the hayloft above with a metallic bong.

"Cluck?"

"Yeh. Oops."

The Pan switched off the ignition and put the key back under the sun visor. He was glad he wouldn't have to hotwire it after all. He locked the delivery snurd and went back into the pub. That was alright then. He had a vehicle and for all its humble appearance, it was deluxe in the ways that mattered.

"Mmm... Well, my chicken-shaped friend. We have some wheels. Now all we need is a plan."

Chapter 60

Professor N'Aversion returned to his office. There was a surprising number of staff still in the workshop. He found Nar and offered to take her to the canteen for a break because she was working too hard. He managed a short conversation in the corridors, where there was no surveillance, on the way.

"Nar, I need you to have another go at the prison records and see if there's anything else about The Pan of Hamgee."

"What sort of thing?"

"Whether he escaped."

"If he did escape I won't need the prison records. There'll be a manhunt and it'll be all over GNN."

"Which it isn't. Good point and yet one of Lieutenant Wright's teams saw him, at large, yesterday. They even took a happy snap," he took the photo out and showed her. "Apparently he told them he was a publican going for a walk. She reckoned they first saw him on the roof of number fifty three Turnadot Street, Upper Left Central Ning Dang Po."

"I'll contact Simon, Professor."

"Be careful. Melior's monitoring our calls."

"I will, Professor."

"Also," he stopped walking for a moment. "Nar, I know it isn't your job, but can you have a quick look, at least online, for any mention of The Pan of Hamgee in the press between Saturday and now or, of Lord Vernon gifting someone a pub. It was mentioned in the first round of announcements about his Candidature and then dropped. Now, I'm wondering if this person receiving the pub was our friend, The Pan of Hamgee. Even if the Grongles are sitting on it, The Free K'Barthan Broadcasting Corporation might have posted something somewhere."

"Yes, Professor," she hesitated. "We're building the portal, aren't we?"

Utterly direct, that was Nar. He smiled.

"In a roundabout way. This is the marvellous thing, if I can get enough information from The Pan of Hamgee, it won't be General Moteurs' device that I make. Denarghi's problem is with General Moteurs. I won't be disobeying orders if I build the K'Barthan version. So, yes Nar, I am going to build a portal. I have to. Although you don't. If you want to step back from this—"

"No, Professor. We're in this together. We cannot lose this opportunity. Although..." she stopped.

"Yes Nar?"

"What if it's true and the Hamgeean really is a friend of Lord Vernon."

"Then we build from General Moteurs' plans. If he's laying a trap, we're doomed but if he's genuine, and we don't build it, the outlook is even worse."

She nodded, "Is there anything else you need me to do?"

"Just the inventory, if you can remember it. Handwritten. No computers I'm afraid."

"Alright, Professor. I'll make a start."

Chapter 61

It was 5.30 a.m. and The Professor was touched to see Nar in front of him, but at the same time, he felt very guilty.

"Nar, you should get some sleep. You need to be fresh."

"I will, Professor, but first I think you should see this. It's about The Pan of Hamgee. Blimpet found it. I think he's onto something."

"I hope so. It's all our necks on the line here and our Leader is like a bear with a sore head."

"Don't worry, professor, he's been threatening to have you shot for years. I'm sure he won't," said Nar, frantically pointing at the ceiling and her ears.

"I'm beginning to think he might, this time, unless I give him a sop. That's why I want to find this lad. Come on, let's go and check the moth trap. You can tell me on the way."

There was no moth trap, it was just another ruse to visit an area free of surveillance, so Professor N'Aversion and Nar went to the Park. They made sure the tree they chose was one of the furthest away from Tech Ops because they believed it was less likely to be bugged, or at least, less likely to be bugged by anyone looking for *them*. The Professor was horribly aware that the Grongles might also be listening, but there was little he could do about that. He hoped the mention of the moth trap, and the prospect of a detailed entomological conversation, would have put them off.

He and Nar found a pair of plastic chairs and sat down.

"Alright, dear girl, let's see what you have."

Nar took her tablet pc out of her lab coat pocket and put it in front of the Professor.

"Here," she cued up a video. "You were right. When Lord Vernon announced his Candidature, GNN didn't show all the footage on the News."

"I see."

"Yes and he did present a pub to someone, too. The ceremony was clearly designed to show Lord Vernon as generous to those who are loyal to him."

The Professor sighed.

"I expect we're on the brink of another round of purges then."

"Yes, but he put it with too big a story if he wanted the population to take note. The announcement of his Candidature eclipsed everything else and the presentation part was only on GNN Local. Nobody looks at Local, it's a bad design and hard to navigate. I searched for Turnadot Street and nothing came up so I tried The Pan of Hamgee, and... Look what we have."

She swiped a furry mauve finger over the play icon and the Professor watched Lord Vernon thanking The Pan of Hamgee for his loyalty and pardoning him for all misdemeanours.

"This isn't like the Lord Protector though. A public disembowelment would be more his line." Probably with a blunt spoon, knowing him.

"I give you... The Pan of Hamgee," said the tinny voice of Lord Vernon as the camera angle widened to include the young man from Lieutenant Wright's picture. He was wearing a hat and cloak but the sling was visible underneath.

"It looks as if the Grongles treated him. That sling is too white to be anything but brand new."

"Yes," said Nar, "I agree. It's very strange."

"Hmm and you can see that he's unhappy about it isn't he?"

"Yes. He is angry, his body language is closed but aggressive," said the Professor.

Despite Lord Vernon's warm words, the lad's face was sullen, his eyes glittered and as his lips moved in reply, his expression was one of disgust rather than gratitude. There was clearly no love lost between them. The Professor felt a little out of his depth. Science was his metier, not detection.

"It looks, to me, as if they beat him first, to get him to cooperate and then patched him up."

"Yes," said Nar.

"Oh dear, oh dear. What else do we know about him?"

Nar put a finger on the pause button.

"His whole family was blacklisted five years ago, he's the sole survivor and he was on the blacklist from then on."

"Can that be right?" the Professor quizzed her. "Five years is a very long time to survive on the blacklist and he can't have been more than a boy when he was added."

"Sixteen, professor."

"Poor lad. He's not the obvious choice if Lord Vernon wants a helper, is he?"

"No."

"Do we have any idea what he said, back there off mic?"

"Not really, I ran it through the lip reading software but he's Hamgeean. It doesn't understand his accent. The only bits we can be sure of are, 'No,' and then he says 'Thank you, for nothing and I will not...'"

"Will not what?"

"I don't know, professor."

"Is that all?"

"It's in beta, Professor," said Nar defensively.

"Of course, of course. I quite understand."

"We need a newer faster computer, Professor. I've built our best from the pieces of four broken terminals but it is as we say in the mountains, 'shonky'."

The Professor knew what 'shonky' meant.

"Yes, they've installed all that expensive listening equipment in tech ops to find out what we do. You'd think they could run to some slightly more modern equipment to do it with."

"There's something else. The Grongle behind The Pan of Hamgee. We never see his face but, from the uniform, he's a Captain. Look, the evidence points to a shoulder injury." She froze the picture and pointed to the area in question. "See the Captain's hand, how the fingers are curled. He's squeezing and the Hamgeean is in pain at this point. I am positive he is being coerced."

"Yes, a logical conclusion I'd say. But why?"

"I don't know."

"This sort of thing isn't really our department. Can you find The Pan of Hamgee?"

"I think so, Professor."

"How soon?"

"A couple of hours once I can speak to Simon. He did his MSc at the University of Ning Dang Po. He might know Upper Left Central, it's the kind of area students would live in."

"I hope so but from what I've read and heard, it sounds as if even the students wouldn't want to live there."

"Oh, students will live anywhere, Professor. So long as the beer's good and nobody minds if they make a noise. Even so, I've made Simon a list of all the pubs within a three square mile radius of Turnadot Street."

"Splendid job, how many are there?"

"40."

"Oh."

"Yes, but we have the news video. If I send him the link, he may recognise it. If he doesn't he can walk the area until he finds that pub. It shouldn't take long."

"Nar... you and Simon, you are both wonderful and I would be lost without you. Thank you."

She smiled shyly.

"It's a pleasure, Professor."

Chapter 62

The Pan stood at the night desk in his local police station complaining, vociferously, to a weary desk sergeant about the theft of The Parrot and Screwdriver's delivery snurd. The desk sergeant was army, rather than police, but these days the two were interchangeable. The Grongle waited, with a bored expression, while The Pan told him thieves had broken into the garage, driven the snurd through the locked doors and made off into the night. The fact that there had been no thieves and that it was The Pan who had 'stolen' the delivery snurd was neither here nor there. To all intents and purposes it looked nicked. Arnold knew he had made sure of that.

"Where is it? That's what I want to know. I can't see how you expect me to run a business without it."

"Give it a rest, non-being. We're busy this morning. I wouldn't expect an ignorant native like you to keep up with current affairs but there's an execution at first light; six a.m. That's in..." he looked up at the clock and The Pan looked up with him, making sure his face was clearly visible to the security CCTV camera mounted beside it. "Ten minutes. So looking for some K'Barthan non-entity's lost vehicle is not a priority to us at this time."

Since The Pan didn't know how to make beer, relocating the delivery snurd was hardly a priority to him either. The delivery snurd wasn't lost, anyway. It was parked on a patch of waste ground to the north of the city and he'd left it there himself. But if The Pan's plan to rescue his friends was going to work he had to make it look as if he wasn't involved.

"Please, sir. I understand you are busy but I'm begging you... this is my livelihood, I really, really need to find that delivery snurd."

"Then I suggest you go start looking. No wonder you K'Barthans are such a waste of space. You don't need governing, you need an effing nanny."

"But it's been stolen. You're the police—"

"Yeh and we're busy."

The Pan waited which took all his self-control because he was running out of time.

"Why are you still here?" demanded the desk Sergeant. "I suggest you get lost. Unless you want to get yourself mislaid."

"But—" began The Pan.

The Sergeant reached under the desk, pulled out a crowd control stick and primed it. There was a high pitched electronic squeak as it powered up and a beep when the charge was loaded.

The Pan put both hands up in front of him and backed away.

"Right-o then, I'll be going. Don't mind me," he said and he turned and ran out of the door. Seven minutes. The delivery snurd was a good hour's walk away. Not that it would be a problem. The Pan was going by portal. The average K'Barthan knew nothing of portal travel. The Pan was banking on his supposition that many of the regular Grongle police and army were ignorant of its existence, too. In the absence of a better plan, it was all he could do. His idea was simple. To make it look as if he couldn't possibly rescue his friends without being in two places at once. If he was reporting his delivery snurd stolen at ten to six then, in theory, he couldn't possibly be at the patch of waste ground where it was parked – and where he hoped it had been seen and reported – for an hour. More importantly he couldn't be driving it when it disrupted the execution of his friends.

He realised there were holes in this plan. For a start it was likely that if he used a single use portal it would be picked up by those Grongles who *did* know about them. However, he was hoping most of those were under the command of General Moteurs and that the General could be trusted. He also knew that if he smashed it fast enough when he arrived at his destination there would be no way of telling exactly who had used the portal or where. It might be enough. The Grongles might assume that someone else was driving and if they didn't, at least it would be harder for them to prove that he was. He ran round the corner and ducked into a side alley, no-one was around. Good.

Nestling at the back of his sling, hidden behind his arm was a blonde wig. He put it on and a pair of sunglasses, too. Gritting his teeth he tried to ignore the pain from his shoulder as he removed the virulently patterned shirt he wore, leaving the white t-shirt he had on underneath. Now that he had made an impression and established his whereabouts, anonymity was key. He rolled the shirt up and stuffed it into the sling – he'd need to wear

310

it later. He'd have to take the sling off for the rescue but not until the last minute. He would give his shoulder as much support before the event as he could. Next, he fumbled a pair of Marigold gloves from his pockets and put them on. There must be no fingerprints. He couldn't afford to be connected with what he was about to do. Not if his friends stood any chance of surviving, long term. He sighed. Yes, well, none of them had much chance of that. Medium term then. Yes, survival in the medium term was the best he could do.

Clumsily, he pulled one of Gladys and Ada's tiny, individual-portion-sized jam jar portals out of his other pocket. He pictured the delivery snurd in his mind's eye and put his finger in the open top. There was a loud sucking sound, a pop and The Pan landed awkwardly next to the driver's cab. Quickly, he grabbed the hammer he'd left on top of the front wheel and smashed the jar. He shuffled the sleeve of the yellow rubber glove towards his hand so he could check his watch. Five minutes. He was going to be cutting this fine.

He climbed in, put the keys in the ignition and pressed the starter. After a prolonged bout of coughing and spluttering the snurd kicked into life, sending a plume of steam up into the dawn sky.

"Please Arnold let this work."

He pressed the button marked 'wings', gunned the engine and took off. Once airborne he realised he'd substantially underestimated the amount of flying time he would require. The delivery snurd was nowhere near as fast as his own SE2. Worse, he needed two hands to drive it and he only had one and a half. Every time he changed gear or pressed one of the buttons on the dash, the pain in his injured shoulder told him that this was not the sort of 'gentle exercise' Dr Dot had prescribed. The sky was flecked with silver. Dawn wasn't waiting on anybody and neither was the clock. He took the fastest route he could; he had to time his arrival just right. Too early and there'd be no-one to save; too late and... well... ditto.

He flew in over the Avenue, one of the larger roads into the square, but not the biggest. His target was in sight now but for all his fears about the delivery snurd's speed he was a minute early. There was a cordon. A roadblock stretched across the street below and a couple of unmarked snurds were waiting on the roofs either side. He gained height, for a panoramic view, continuing towards the square and the roadblock for as long as he dared – it was unlikely they'd let him fly over the square, even at this height. As he flew he appraised the scene, formulating a route. A crowd had gathered. No big surprise, not when Big Merv, leader of the Mervinettes was one of the prisoners. There was a heavy police and army presence around and among the crowd of K'Barthans. Protesting verbally was illegal and would result in their being controlled so they stood in silence. The Pan could almost feel their sullen anger. In the midst of the sea of silent onlookers was an island of wood and metal; a raised platform bristling with Grongle military and police. A prison snurd was arriving at the opposite end, moving slowly through the press of silent K'Barthans. The Pan had come as close to the cordon as he could without looking noticeably suspicious so he banked the delivery snurd in a gentle turn, steering it round and away. As if he'd been sightseeing, rather than scoping.

He realised that if he hit the cordon full on and at the right height, he should be able to get into the square. He must fly in the no-man's land between the police in the street and the snurds on the roof. That would make him difficult to spot from above but at the same time, difficult to stop from below. He pressed the button marked 'shields'. He hoped they'd last; they were in for a hammering.

He turned down a side street which crossed the Avenue about a hundred yards down from the roadblock. He thought it unwise to approach from too far away. He wanted to present the roadblock with a target for the shortest possible time. He would build up some speed in the side road and then turn onto the Avenue and accelerate, hard, for the last few hundred yards. His plan was not remotely subtle but it would preserve the snurd's shields a little bit longer. He slowed so he could lean over and take a pair of Gladys and Ada's single use jam jar portals from the glove compartment. As he drifted along, just above the street, he took his bad arm out of the sling and put the jars on his lap, gripping them between his knees so they didn't fall into the foot well.

"Cluck?"

"I'm sorry?"

"Cluck."

The chicken seemed to be talking about a thin panel on the dash. Wait a minute. Was that a cup holder? The Pan pushed at it and it slid out. It was a special tiny drawer for change. He put the jam jars in it. The jars were too tall to allow him to close it but the sides were just the right height to keep them in position without making them difficult to remove.

"Nice," he gave the chicken a mental high five.

"Cluck."

He switched on the radio and found a station broadcasting the executions live. Right. Now he was ready. From the speakers in the snurd and inside the square he heard the sound of a fanfare. The commentator announced the arrival of the prisoners. The Pan took a deep breath. It was time.

Chapter 63

Ruth slept little and was highly unamused to be woken by Captain Snow a few minutes after she'd finally drifted off to sleep. However, he seemed surprisingly subdued. He did nothing more than pick out some clothes from the drawers, tell her to get up and leave her. She washed and dressed in the bathroom, with the door locked, just in case he came back. Pyjamas in hand, she emerged to find her fiancé standing in the middle of the room, radiating smugness.

"At last. I have been waiting for you, my darling," said Lord Vernon. "I see you are looking ravishing, as always."

She said nothing.

"I have a surprise for you. Put your shoes on."

She went to the cupboard and selected a pair with heels that were slightly less unfeasibly high than the rest. General Moteurs may have chosen the clothes and shoes, but clearly he'd been working to a brief from Lord Vernon; one which stipulated adornment over practicality. Or maybe it was just a pathetic attempt to make her seem taller. She slipped them on.

"Excellent, come here."

Slowly she approached him.

"It's..." she double checked her watch, "five to six, Lord Vernon, if you want me to be a good wife to you, I suggest you wake me at a reasonable hour."

"Then I will instruct Captain Snow to wake you at four tomorrow."

"I meant civilised reasonable, like eight."

"I have arranged a little surprise for you, a... how shall we describe it? A demonstration of my intent. Put your spectacles on, I want you to see this."

Sullenly, Ruth went to the bedside table, snatched up her glasses and did as she was told.

"Come with me." He turned and headed towards the balcony.

"Why?" she said, staying firmly where she was.

He strode back across to her and grabbed her by the arm.

"Let go of me."

"No," he pulled her against him.

"Stop it. You're hurting me."

"Good, then perhaps you will cease your attempts to thwart me at every turn."

Touché.

"Come with me onto the balcony. I will not ask you politely again."

He guided her through the glass doors. Outside the sky was turning grey. The windows of some of the buildings opposite glowed pink, reflecting the rising sun. As she and Lord Vernon emerged a fanfare sounded. Ruth saw that there was a crowd in the open space between the Palace and the Police Headquarters opposite. They were gathered round a long wooden platform upon which were several rows of Grongle soldiers and a lone Grongle dressed head to toe in black, with a balaclava and hobnail boots. He carried a sword – not like Lord Vernon's, though – this was a broadsword, the kind of thing she imagined being used by the Knights Templar during the Crusades to lop heads off, probably several at a time.

"No—" she began but her voice was drowned out as a fanfare of trumpets sounded. The assembled crowd of K'Barthans, turned round but still they didn't make a sound.

"Wave, darling. When we are married they will be your subjects as well as mine." Woodenly, she did as she was told, holding up her free arm – Lord Vernon still gripped the other one – and a half-hearted cheer rose up from the assembled K'Barthans below. She could see the Grongle soldiers among them. She wondered if they had gathered spontaneously or whether they'd been rounded up from the nearby streets.

"You know what this is?" Lord Vernon asked her.

"It looks like an execution."

"Correct. I would usually see to such matters personally but I am sure you would prefer to have me here, by your side." Another fanfare sounded and a police snurd arrived, moving slowly through the press of people. As it reached the platform, troops stepped up and flanked the stairs. The doors opened and three prisoners were brought out; Big Merv, Trev and Lucy. They were herded onto the stage. Trev, one leg useless, was dragged to his position by two gaolers.

"Wait. Those are my friends. You can't do this!"

"On the contrary, I can. You only bought one. What did you expect me to do with the others?"

"No," she shook her head, "no."

"Oh but yes, I'm afraid. You see, Ruth, I want you to focus. You are all alone here and I can protect you or..." he gestured to the stage in the square, "I can destroy you. The choice is yours but at the moment I sense you are experiencing a little difficulty..." he paused to choose the right word, "committing yourself to the terms of our contract. I hope this will help you to understand your situation."

"I said I would marry you. That's enough isn't it?"

"Oh no..." she felt his grip tighten on her arm as he half turned and looked down at her, "I want more, so much more than that."

"Well it's a pity you didn't negotiate what you wanted when we made our agreement. I agreed to pretend I love you and marry you. Nothing more. You seem to be forgetting that I can destroy you, too. At some point in this sham you're relying on me to say the word 'yes'."

"And you will. It's up to you of course..." He nodded at the scene below them. "I can stop this."

She hesitated.

"You mean that?"

"Naturally, I own this nation. They do what I tell them."

"Then I'll do what you want."

Lord Vernon smiled.

His phone beeped. He flipped it open and held it to his ear, listening while somebody spoke.

"Excellent. Proceed," he said and flipped it closed.

"No! You said you'd stop it."

"I said I could stop it. I never said I would."

"No!" screamed Ruth but her voice was lost in another deafening fanfare of trumpets and beating drums. She tried to free her arm from his grip but he yanked her against him and wrenched it round behind her back. He turned her so that she was facing outwards, onto the square, forcing her against the balustrade and then he stood close behind her, still holding her in an arm lock, but also leaning against her to hold her there. Pinned in position, unable to move, she watched in horror as the prisoners were lined up on the platform; her new friends Big Merv and Trev, together with Lucy, her oldest and dearest. They were forced to kneel, their hands tied behind their backs trailing two long lengths of rope. Ruth couldn't see Lord Vernon's face but she knew that he was smiling. A pair of Grongle troops took the ends of each prisoner's ropes and held them taut to keep each one of the victims still from a safe distance. The executioner swung the sword in a few practise loops. Ruth couldn't bear to look and turned her head away.

"They think you requested this, so you will watch or I will be compelled to have those dear, sweet little old ladies executed tomorrow," said Lord Vernon. He pushed against her harder and forced her arm a little higher.

She was crying now.

"I will arrange an execution every day until you decide with whom your loyalties lie."

"Never with you." He laughed, put his face against her cheek and breathed in.

"Oh Ruth. So, so fiery. I can't wait until our wedding night." Pinned against the parapet she shuddered as, growling, he leaned his head down and kissed her neck.

Neither of them heard the sound of an engine. He still had her in an arm lock, pressed against the balustrade; and then the lorry arrived.

****

The Pan revved the delivery snurd and took it to the maximum speed at which it could safely turn the corner at the end of the road. Then he swung onto the Avenue and accelerated towards the roadblock, flying a few feet above head height. The Grongles started firing almost straight away. The bolts from their lasers whined past and machine gun bullets bounced crazily off the shields a few inches in front of the windscreen, but the snurds above were napping and he only saw them behind him as he flew out into the square. Now most of the fire power on the ground was coming from the Grongles on the platform and around the crowd. The snurds behind were gaining, too. They would have All Purpose Torpedoes and he was hoping that they'd refrain from using them with so many of their own colleagues in the way but he couldn't be too sure. They might at least have to seek clearance, though, which would give him a few extra seconds, and they might also be in danger from the barrage of fire coming up from the ground. He flew slower, skimming so low over the heads of the crowd that they could almost have reached up and touched the delivery snurd's undercarriage. Trev, Big Merv and Lucy were kneeling, held in position by Grongle troops.

As the executioner stepped towards Big Merv, swinging his sword, The Pan fired a rubber bullet which caught him full in the stomach. He fell back, winded.

"Yes!" shouted The Pan as the executioner crawled to the side of the platform and rolled off. Two more rubber bullets hit a couple of the guards holding the prisoners. The Pan topped it off by strafing them with a few seconds of pretend machine gun fire. While he might have known he was firing blanks in the mayhem below, it went unnoticed. The ordnance – whatever it was, cotton wool, plastic? – pinged off the wooden platform with a reassuringly realistic clatter and many of the Grongles leapt off to take cover while a core of brave souls moved into formation and began to fire at the delivery snurd. The Pan swooped in to land on the platform, waiting until the last minute to disengage aviator mode. The Pan retracted the wings and the snurd landed with a crash, Grongle guards scattering in all directions as it thundered towards them.

He was going too fast.

"Stop you smecker! Stop!" he shouted as it careened along the platform.

Presented with several tonnes of a heavy commercial snurd charging towards them at speed, any remaining Grongles stopped firing and fled. The Pan handbrake turned it, remembering to yank the wheel in the right direction so the back slewed round, away from the friends he had come to rescue. He was facing the way he had come now but the momentum was still carrying the snurd backwards at speed. The locked wheels squealed for purchase on the planks. The Pan gave up on the brakes and engaged first gear. With the snurd's gearbox screeching and grinding under the strain, he accelerated. Stinking black smoke billowed from the tyres as they spun. He hung onto the wheel and prayed to Arnold, that the snurd would stop before it fell off the end of the platform. It finally came to a halt, still facing in the direction it had come. Now for the really dangerous bit. The Pan switched off the shields. One bolt of laser fire in the right place, that's all it would take and the delivery snurd was toast. To The Pan's relief, Big Merv quickly realised what he must do. As The Pan flung open the door, both his friends ran towards Trev.

A couple of Grongles aimed their lasers but The Pan fired, compelling them to get down. The delivery snurd was surrounded though. It had no back windows and The Pan's view behind him was limited to what was visible in the mirrors. A squad of Grongles was trying to creep up, but the crowd was closing in, getting in the way, silently tripping and shoving them. The Pan turned his attention back to his friends. Trev threw himself over Big Merv's back and with Lucy helping, the three of them hobbled towards the delivery snurd. The Pan covered them with a hail of fake machine gun fire but the Grongles had realised the ruse and were standing up. Some were shielding their faces with their arms, others were wearing riot goggles but all were beginning to advance, taking no notice of the pretend ordnance pinging off them. The Pan unleashed another salvo of rubber bullets.

"Come on," The Pan yelled to his friends – as if they needed telling. Big Merv reached the open passenger door and hefted Trev inside, Lucy was half pushed in by Big Merv and then the Swamp Thing climbed in himself. The Pan wrinkled his nose. One, or all of them, smelled pretty fruity.

Everyone was inside – which was progress – but they were all in a pile, pretty much on top of one another and their hands were tied so they couldn't shut the door. Neither could The Pan. He started the snurd moving with as big a jolt as he could and the door slammed. Bonus. He switched on the shields. Now to get airborne.

****

Ruth's sprits soared as she watched the chaos unfolding in the square below. Lord Vernon thrust her from him and drew his laser pistol for a moment before thinking better of it and replacing it in its holster. Almost immediately, the Interceptor appeared and parked itself alongside the balcony. The driver's door hissed open and Lord Vernon stepped casually over the balustrade as, below him, the prisoners struggled to the lorry and got in.

The driver had long blonde hair but Ruth knew, from the way her heart skipped a beat, that it was The Pan of Hamgee. She watched in breathless excitement as he gunned the engine. The tyres span, black smoke billowing up into the sky and Lord Vernon, one foot on the sill of the Interceptor and one on the balcony turned to look back at her, his slate grey eyes burning with malevolent fire.

"Don't think they will escape," he snarled and he slid into the seat. "Won't it be a pity if the Hamgeean is driving that truck?" he said as the door closed.

"If he is you won't catch it!" she shot back with more conviction than she felt. She watched hopelessly as the Interceptor accelerated away at speed. The Pan would never escape from him. Not in that lumbering lorry.

Chapter 64

Most of the Grongles were on their feet again but wisely avoiding the platform as the delivery snurd trundled down it, gathering momentum, if little speed. It needed to be going much faster than this if it was going to take off but The Pan selected aviator mode anyway. There was no other option. It had to fly. The wings opened with a whine and locked in position. Ahead of him, Grongles and K'Barthans alike fled in all directions. As the heavy snurd reached the end of the platform it dropped onto the ground with a crash and bounced, allowing a few vital seconds of much faster in-air acceleration. It hit the ground again and bounced higher before coming back to earth one more time. On the third bounce The Pan was able to keep it airborne. He put it into a climb and removed one of the jars from the cup holder.

"Merv, take this. It's a—"

"Portal. Yer." Oh good. He knew. "You got a pair of scissors?"

"Arnold's socks!" said The Pan. He knew he'd forgotten something. He managed to crane his arm over and put the portal into one of Big Merv's hands. Now what? He noticed the long lengths of rope hanging off the three of them. "I'll have to tie you together." But he'd have to be quick. The lack of bi-directional vision made him feel blind and vulnerable. He wasn't in the habit of actually using his mirrors and he didn't trust them. As if to reinforce his misgivings, something hit the snurd with a bang. The shields beeped and reset. A warning light came on. They were down to 10%.

"What was that?" asked Lucy in Alarm.

"An APT," said The Pan.

"Hurry it up then," said Trev. His voice sounded strained. As the first one in he was also at the bottom. The Pan hoped he wasn't in too much pain.

"Yer. Another of them and we're dead," shouted Big Merv. There was no auto-pilot so, trying to keep control with his knees, The Pan fumbled to gather three of the long lengths of rope and tie them in a knot.

"Done," he shouted, "now go. Parrot and Screwdriver. And break the jar," he shouted as Big Merv put his thumb into the portal. There was a loud sucking sound, the bath watery noises and a pop. The Pan checked his mirrors again while his friends were disappearing. He was being followed but it wasn't the two army snurds from the roofs. His pursuer was canny, keeping out of sight in the delivery snurd's blind spot, but The Pan could see enough glimpses of black to know it was the Interceptor. He would have to put up a fight or it would look suspicious, but not so much of a fight that he was recognised by his driving.

"You tied the wrong ropes, numb nuts."

Of course! They'd had two each.

"Lucy. Smeck! I'm sorry..." He yanked the delivery snurd sharply round and Lucy rolled off the seat into the foot well.

"Ouch!"

"Arnold. I'm sorry for that too. Look, I only have one more portal and..." he heaved on the wheel and the heavy snurd rolled, as if in slow motion, a volley of fire from the Interceptor speeding harmlessly past it. "I have to make this realistic, can you wedge yourself in there somehow, so you stay put?"

"I'll try."

Chapter 65

Ruth stood watching from the balcony, willing the impossible, begging for the lorry to outrun the Interceptor but as she watched, with inexorable inevitability, the lethal form gained ground, shooting all the while. Then as the lorry rolled to avoid a volley of fire, the Interceptor overtook, doubling back. She watched the headlights retracting, revealing blank holes with the nose of an All Purpose Torpedo visible in each one.

****

The Parrot and Screwdriver's commercial snurd lumbered through the sky, with the Interceptor in hot pursuit.

"Arnold, Lucy, I'm so sorry—" The Pan began.

"Stop apologising and concentrate."

"Alright. And I promise we'll be fine," he said as he wove the delivery snurd frantically from side to side for a moment. "Arnold's snot! This thing handles like a waterbed on castors." He wrestled with the wheel and yelled at the pain in his shoulder. He could hear Lucy's feet scrabbling against the seats for purchase.

"You alright down there? You only have to hang on for thirty seconds, two minutes at the very outside." He reached down beside her with his good arm, grabbed one of the lengths of rope attached to her, wrapped it round his hand a couple of times and went back to his driving.

The Interceptor was too close for the Grongles below to risk a ground to snurd missile. Clearly Lord Vernon had decided to finish them off on his own. Despite the abysmal handling of his vehicle The Pan managed to dodge an APT only to receive a comprehensive strafing from Lord Vernon's lasers. The shields gave out.

"Alright, Lucy, this is it. Close your eyes!" he said and then realised she'd done that already. He held the wheel steady with his knees while he took the second disposable portal from the spare change holder on the dash. Suddenly the Interceptor was in front of the snurd, flying towards them at speed. At point blank range Lord Vernon fired an All Purpose

Torpedo. The Pan took his hands off the wheel, gripping the rope attached to his friend tightly with one hand watching the approaching torpedo, tensed, waiting for the split second he must act.

****

It had all been over in minutes. Ruth felt that something inside her had died when she saw the big lorry-snurd explode in a shower of debris and sparks. She didn't know how long she stood there, clinging onto the balustrade, watching the silent crowd leaving and the Grongles swarming all over the burning wreckage.

****

As the torpedo exploded, The Pan jammed his thumb into the jar holding tightly onto the rope attached to Lucy with the other. A huge force lifted the cab of the snurd and The Pan felt a few nanoseconds' worth of searing heat, caught a brief glimpse of the polished black underside of the Interceptor as it banked sharply upwards and then, with a loud pop, he and Lucy were tumbling over one another across the stone-flagged floor of the Parrot and Screwdriver's main bar.

****

Eventually, the balcony doors behind Ruth opened, but instead of Lord Vernon it was General Moteurs who came and stood by her side.

"Forgive my intrusion," he said. She couldn't speak and she couldn't let go of the balustrade. A fresh bout of tears ran down her cheeks and dripped onto her clothes. "Ruth, my career in the Imperial Guard spans 17 years and I have seen many things. I know better than to believe my eyes alone. Nothing is ever as it appears." She took some deep breaths and managed to talk.

"He killed them!"

"No, I'll wager your Hamgeean paramour is more resourceful than that." Paramour? Ruth knew he was only trying to help but blimey, he needed to have a word with himself. "You have seen a snurd crash and burn. You do not know what happened to the occupants."

"I can guess what happened."

324

"No. That is what he intends my colleagues to do. He would be hoping for greater insight from us."

"Do you realise how patronising you sound. Can you be a little more arrogant?"

"I am commander of the Imperial Guard in K'Barth. A certain haughtiness of demeanour is expected of me."

"Please can you try dropping it for a moment."

"Ruth," he said quietly, "there has been portal use in the city this morning. I cannot prove where but I know when: ten minutes ago, five minutes before the commercial snurd appeared here. I am expecting to hear word of a second instance. If there is, the implication would be..." he tailed off.

"Thank you," she said except it sounded more like a hiccup.

"I will uncover the truth, you have my word and I do not give it lightly."

"Thank you," she managed again.

"Come inside now... please."

"I would but... I don't think I can let go," she said in a small voice.

"You are in shock." Carefully, he uncurled her fingers and took her hands. "I will stay with you, I think, until you feel more yourself," he said, except the intonation made it into a question.

"Do you have that many days to spare?" she asked. It surprised a smile out of him. She wiped her eyes on her sleeve.

"Allow me." He took a cotton handkerchief from his pocket and handed it to her.

"Thank you."

The handkerchief was immaculately pressed and folded into a perfect square. It was far too good to be wasted blowing a nose. He noticed her embarrassment.

"Please..." he said moving one hand in a 'go-on' gesture.

She used it, copiously. Now what? She'd turned it into a soggy rag, should she give it back?

"Keep it," he said. "I have many more."

"Thank you."

They stood in silence for a moment and he picked a blanket off a nearby chair and wrapped it round her shoulders.

"I think that you know the identity of the Candidate, perhaps?"

No. She mustn't admit this. Not to anyone, least of all Lord Vernon's right hand man, or at least, Grongle. Sir Robin might trust General Moteurs but as yet, Ruth wasn't sure she should. She shook her head.

"Why would you think that?"

"Your presence here. There is no guile in you. Given a choice you would have refused Lord Vernon and faced death. You would only agree to such a complex deception if you had an ulterior reason."

"For somebody who has spent all that time in the military you certainly have a vivid imagination. I'm here because I'm in love with someone, plain and simple."

"That is understood. I merely ask if you fully appreciate who he is."

"It doesn't matter does it? He's dead," she said bitterly.

"Always assuming he was here. You have no proof either way."

"I recognised him. I know it was him. Except that now I'm clinging to your ridiculous idea that he's somehow survived being vaporised in front of my eyes."

"You are the Chosen One and I would consider such hope proof of his escape if I were K'Barthan."

"You're not though, are you? And neither am I."

"That does not invalidate the K'Barthan viewpoint. And if their tradition interprets the nature of your relationship correctly, the question is addressed easily enough. Search your heart. If he died you will know as surely as you knew it was him."

She thought a moment and he watched her intently.

"All I can feel is hopelessness." Oh great.

"That is entirely reasonable. But I beg of you, take heart and do not believe this," he gestured to the smoking wreckage in the square, "is as you have seen." She understood the logic in his words but just thinking about what she had seen made her start shaking. Not only because she feared for her friends but because she feared the monster who had brought them down: Lord Vernon, her husband to be. She felt sick and dizzy and on the brink of collapse.

"Ruth. If you cannot trust me, I understand but, please, let me look after you, " he gestured to the doorway. She stumbled and he caught her and put his arm around her waist, holding her upright as they made their way indoors.

Chapter 66

As The Pan rolled to a stop on the floor of the Parrot and Screwdriver's bar, he put the jar down on the stone flags and a foot wearing a leather zip-up boot promptly trod on it, smashing it to pieces.

"Thanks," he said to Big Merv and turned to Lucy. "I'm sorry. That wasn't my best work," he added as he helped her up. "Give me a moment everyone."

Throwing the wig onto a nearby table as he went, he ran into the kitchen behind the bar, grabbed a sharp knife from the drawer and returned. He cut the rope round Big Merv's wrists and handed over the knife. Big Merv cut the rope off Lucy's wrists. They were raw and she was shaking.

"S'alright sweets, we're safe now," he said. He wrapped one arm round her and pulled her into a brief hug before the two of them moved swiftly over to join The Pan next to Trev.

"You cut that fine mate," said Trev, smiling weakly at The Pan. "We were starting to think you wasn't going to show."

"Yeh, well, you know me, late for everything," said The Pan. Trev was very pale and his leg... It smelled terrible and it was bent at a right angle mid-shin. The Pan suppressed an urge to retch. "Arnold Trev, that must smart," he said.

"Yeh," said Trev with a weak laugh. "They put it over a step and jumped on it."

"Smeck." The Pan ran his good hand through his hair.

"Yer. Then they showed me to me dad and roughed me up some more. The pain knocked me spark out. I reckon they gave it a rinse with the slop bucket an' all when they dumped me back in my cell. Lord Vernon's an evil smecker but that Captain Snow's a piece of work an' all. One of these days, I'll 'ave him."

"Not if I get to 'im first," growled Big Merv.

"Can you straighten it up son? It's making me queasy," said Trev.

"You're not the only one," said The Pan.

Big Merv and Lucy knelt down beside them. The Pan and Lucy gently moved Trev forward so Big Merv could free his tied wrists. Then Big Merv took his hand.

"I reckon this is gonna hurt. So squeeze as hard as you like mate," he said.

"Hang on. I can help with that," said The Pan, he ran behind the bar and soon found what he was looking for, a bottle of Gladys' home made Calvados.

"Here," he said as he settled himself back at Trev's side. "Have a slug of this."

He pulled the stopper out and handed it to Trev.

"Thanks lad," said Trev putting the bottle to his lips. The level dropped steadily as he drank.

"Blimey," said Big Merv.

With more than half of it gone Trev passed the bottle back to The Pan.

"You done?"

"Yer."

"Sure? There's plenty more in the cellar."

"Ner. I'm good, son."

The Pan put the stopper back in and placed the bottle on the ground behind him.

"Ready Trev?"

"Yer."

"Lucy?"

"Yes."

"Here we go." Carefully, trying to support it, he and Lucy lifted Trev's leg a little, straightened it and put it down. Trev's eyes rolled up into the back of his head and he groaned. The Pan waited for his friend to recover, he was sweating and breathing heavily. Was that just the pain or was there something more? The Pan reached out to feel Trev's forehead and realised he was still wearing his marigolds.

"What's with the gloves?" asked Lucy as The Pan hurriedly took them off.

"No fingerprints."

"Sweet," said Big Merv.

The Pan, minus gloves, put his hand on Trev's forehead. It felt hot. Too hot. He had a fever. The bone would need setting, too, by someone who knew what they were doing.

"Trev, I don't want to move you more than we have to, and I think you need to see a doctor."

"I can't go down the Doctor's. How am I going to get treated without I.D.?"

"I was thinking more of getting the Doctor to come here. Someone has to fix that," The Pan turned to Big Merv. "I'm hoping you can help me there. You must have a few contacts."

"Yer. Last week maybe but after what happened with the robbery my doc's gonna be compromised, if he ain't already dead."

"Fair point."

Big Merv stood up.

"'S OK. Trev mate, we're gonna fix you up," he said and to The Pan. "I'll ask around."

Trev gave The Pan a doubtful look.

"Merv, you can't ask around. In case you've forgotten, you're dead, too – until I can get you some fake I.D." Except that he was a Swamp Thing and he was orange and there was only one person he could ever be. "If anyone does any asking it'll have to be me."

"Yer? We'll see, that might be a problem, mate. These people ain't gonna do business with someone they ain't been introduced to, you get me?"

"Yeh. I get you. But as a dead Thing, the closest you can get to them is if I say you recommended them."

Trev looked up at Big Merv.

"The lad's right," he said.

Lucy jumped in.

"Whatever we do about doctors, we should put Trev's leg in a splint. We need to wash the wound too, and sterilise it if we can."

The Pan picked up the bottle of Calvados.

"I'm pretty sure there's some antiseptic upstairs, but if the worst comes to the worst I guess we could tip this over it. I should think it'll kill most things. Do you know how to make a splint, because I don't?"

"I'm a first aider, I should be able to do a reasonable job," said Lucy "Normally you wouldn't move someone with a fracture like that but since we have... Trev, do you mind if I cut up your trousers?" she asked. "If you have some proper actual scissors, Defreville," she added to The Pan.

"I'll go and see. We probably have bandages, too, as well as antiseptic."

"That would be great and wood or metal to bind into the splint, thin but strong if you can find it."

She looked up at him. They all knew it wasn't going to work.

"I'll be right back." The Pan ran upstairs to the kitchen. He was sure he'd put a pair of scissors in the pot of pens by the phone. Sure enough. He grabbed it, ran into the bathroom and seized the bandages and some antiseptic from the shelf where he'd tidied them. Maybe the Grongles had done him a favour trashing the place, after all. At least after clearing up, he knew where everything was. Now he needed to find some wood or metal for the splint. He could probably saw a broom handle in two but he was thinking that the upstairs and downstairs brooms, cut to the right length, and with a cushion over the bristles, would make a fine pair of crutches. Then he remembered that Gladys and Ada had some wicked Tithian kebab swords. They looked the part but the only sharp bit was the point. Yeh, they might do. He ran back to the kitchen, grabbed the kebab swords and took everything back down to the bar where he laid it out on the floor next to Lucy.

"Thanks." She held the scissors aloft. "Are you ready, Trev?"

"Yer." Trev was looking much worse now, flushed but at the same time, pale underneath and he was sweating. He was definitely suffering from more than the pain. He turned to The Pan and nodded at the sling. "What happened?"

"Lord Vernon."

"Bastard," said Trev.

"Yeh, but then he pardoned me and let me go. I think he was hoping the punters would lynch me. Luckily they saw Captain Snow control me and chuck me in here before he and his bunch set on them."

"You a free man then?" asked Trev. His voice was quiet and Lucy stopped her cutting for a moment to give The Pan a warning look. Trev was fading. The Pan didn't want to weaken him further by chatting to him but at the same time, it was obvious that the purpose of this conversation, for Trev, was to take his mind off the pain. He was calm, brave calm. The Pan remembered what Sir Robin had said about escorting blacklisted citizens to the safety of Lucy's reality.

"Until Lord Vernon changes his mind. Hence the wig," said The Pan.

"I have to stay clean until Saturday. After that it doesn't matter."

Lucy cut Trev's trousers open up to and around the knee and laid the material out either side of his leg. The three of them looked at Trev's wound and for a moment no-one spoke.

"Trev... we're going to get you to a Doctor," said The Pan. The others looked at him.

"Thanks," whispered Trev and he passed out.

"I'd say that's infected – not that I know anything," said The Pan. He risked another look at the wound. There was something lighter poking through the skin. He tried not to look at that. Arnold let it not be bone. The area round the wound was bruised and swollen; the wrong type of swollen, red and puffy and it was what The Pan's mother would have called 'gunky'.

"It looks like a surprisingly clean break but I think it IS infected," said Lucy, she cut further up the trousers and examined his knee and thigh, "see those red lines, those are signs that the infection may be spreading."

"Then he needs treatment and he needs proper drugs," said The Pan.

"'S right. We'd better get on the case, son," said Big Merv.

"I have an idea. Look, while he's unconscious, let's take him upstairs to his room out of the way. Do what you can to clean that up and put the splint on. It'll help ease the pain and reassure him." The Pan went into the hall and Big Merv followed.

"Defreville, mate. If we don't get a doc, he's history."

"I realise that."

"Him an' all. He knows the score."

"Then your job, Big Man, is to make sure he doesn't give up. There's been enough killing."

"There's gotta be *someone*. While we sort him out, I'm gonna have a think."

"Thanks, Come on. We've got a few hours before I have to open the pub for lunch. Let's get Trev comfortable. And we should listen to the news."

The Pan helped Lucy and Merv carry Trev upstairs and lay him on his bed. Then, when the three of them had got their friend reasonably well settled, he ran into his room to change. He put the shirt he'd worn to the police station back on. Trev disparagingly referred to this one as '*maelstrom on planet Zorg*' but The Pan wanted to stand out and look as different as possible to the 'anonymous, long-haired blond' disguise he'd worn to rescue his friends.

He convened with Lucy and Big Merv in the upstairs kitchen. The Pan turned the radio on and made a pot of coffee for everyone while they waited for the news. The bangy self-important music that heralded the start of a newscast reverberated through the speaker and the three of them sat mutely as the bulletin began.

"Today our benevolent Lord Protector, Candidate and soon to be Architrave once again showed his selfless devotion to the people, by foiling an attempt by rebels to rescue three of their leaders. The bank robber known as Mister (Big) Merv, Lucy Hargraves and Trev Parker were due to be executed for treason at first light. However, a stolen heavy commercial snurd interrupted the scene. Firing indiscriminately on Grongles and K'Barthans alike, it landed on the execution platform, spraying the scene with machine gun fire."

"Blanks," said The Pan.

"The three rebels escaped in the snurd but were brought down moments later by our Auspicious Leader."

"Only 'cause I let him," muttered The Pan.

"The three felons had avowed to overthrow the State," The Newscaster continued.

Big Merv growled.

"Shh," said Lucy.

"...The vehicle was partly vaporised and the rest of it exploded. Security forces have just confirmed that they are searching the wreckage but it is believed that all three felons, and the driver – whose identity is unknown – were killed. Security forces deem it unlikely that any bodies will be found. And now over to our correspondent on the spot, Leighton Bromswold who is with Lord Vernon now. Leighton..."

"Hello, I'm here outside the Security Headquarters, the Old Palace, with his Gracious Exaltedness, Lord Protector Vernon himself. Your Gracious Exaltedness—"

"Sir is..."

The Pan stood up and clicked off the radio.

"That sounds as if we're in the clear," said Lucy. "Is it so simple?"

"Unfortunately not," said The Pan.

"Yer. We used portals, girl. We smashed 'em so the Grongles ain't gonna know where we went but they're gonna know we used 'em."

"Yep. And that means they may not believe you lot are dead. They're going to be searching for you."

"Will they come here?" asked Lucy.

"Possibly, but with any luck they won't look too hard. I went to a lot of trouble to report the delivery snurd stolen this morning, just before you were due to be executed. On paper, I couldn't have been reporting the theft and then rescuing you. It won't stick. The ones in the know will suspect I used a portal, of course – they may even know for certain – but it'll make my involvement harder to prove; anyway, I'm hoping they all work for General Moteurs."

"If we can trust him," said Lucy.

"Yeh, if, but we don't have much choice. I drove like a total plank, too. And there are no fingerprints anywhere. I saw to that."

"Nice going son."

"I aim to please. The thing is, though, it complicates our quest to find a doctor."

"Then what do we do?"

"We gotta find a bent doctor."

"Big Merv had a guy on his books who was prepared to treat unusual injuries—"

"Like laser burns and gunshot wounds?"

"Exactly like that but we had a slight hiccup during one of our robberies a few days ago and as of Thursday, Big Merv is blacklisted."

"Yer."

Lucy was downcast.

"Does that mean the same for him as you told me it did for you?"

"Yes. His existence is treason, he's classed as vermin and he can be shot on sight. Anything he owned before officially belongs to the State and his organisation will be undergoing some heavy police scrutiny. If his tame Doctor isn't dead, he'll be under investigation and therefore unable to help us. That leaves the Resistance but since they want me and Big Merv dead it might be tricky to persuade them Trev is worth saving."

"So what do we do?"

"I'm afraid our only hope is to ask a Doctor they won't be watching, someone they'd never suspect."

"Like who?"

"I think I might be able to get hold of a Grongle doctor."

"Where you gonna find one of them?"

"Well, I think Doctor Dot, the Grongle who gave me this, might oblige." The Pan raised the arm in the sling, "I did say I was the enemy and she told me she'd sworn an oath to heal and asked me to humour her."

"You barmy? You can't just go down the Old Palace and ask for her."

"Why not? I'm fully assimilated, I've done nothing wrong and I have some questions about my wounds. Who better to ask than the Doctor who treated me? Especially when she actually told me that I could. Logical I'd say, no?"

"What if they take you in for questioning?" asked Lucy.

"I'd better hope they don't. Look, I'm not going to be getting myself into trouble and I'll be back by midday to open for lunch." He glanced at his watch. "It shouldn't take more than a couple of hours."

"You ain't serious?" said Big Merv.

"Deadly. We all know the score, it's 'hello Doctor Dot' or 'goodbye Trev'. No-one dies on my watch."

"So you keep saying," said Lucy and Big Merv just shrugged.

"Ain't no use arguing with this little twonk, girl. Not if 'e's made up his mind."

The Pan got up and went down the corridor for a last check on Trev but he was still unconscious. He went to the coat-stand in the hall and put on his hat and cloak. Big Merv and Lucy followed him to the door.

While they had been busy upstairs with Trev the post had arrived. A white padded envelope addressed to The Pan and embossed with the Snurd company logo lay on the mat. He picked it up, force of habit, he supposed, and stuffed it in his pocket.

"Look after Trev, you two – and each other – and don't let anyone in. If I'm not back by 12:00, I'm dead."

"Very reassuring, numb nuts," said Lucy as he stepped out into the street.

"I try. See you around."

****

Other Books by M T McGuire

One Man: No Plan, K'Barthan Trilogy: Part 3

Confused ex-outlaw, pardoned for all misdemeanours, seeks answers...

The Pan of Hamgee has a chance to go straight, but it's been so long that he's almost forgotten how. Bewilderingly, despite a death warrant over his head he is released, given a state-sponsored business, and a year's amnesty from all offences while he adjusts.

He doesn't have a year, though. In only five days Lord Vernon will gain total power and destroy K'Barth. Much to his frustration, the only person who can avert it is The Pan: a man without a plan.

Looking For Trouble, K'Barthan Trilogy: Part 4

Cornered Hamgeean, with nowhere left to run, seeks miracle...

The time has finally come when The Pan must stand up and be counted. He must face his demons and rectify the chaos he has caused. There's a chance he can stop Lord Vernon, but to succeed he has to stay alive. He has to keep his head down and maintain a low profile. He has to be brave and clever and stay in control. And he hasn't a clue how to do any of it.

Author News

A good way to stay up to date with future book releases is to join the M T McGuire mailing list. Just e-mail list@hamgee.co.uk with 'add' in the subject field. You can also check for news of progress on future projects by M T McGuire in the following places:

Website: http://www.hamgee.co.uk
Blog: http://www.mtmcguire.co.uk
Facebook: http://www.facebook.com/HamgeeUniversityPress
Twitter: @mtmcguireauthor.
Goodreads: http://www.goodreads.com/author/show/3492555

Website	*Blog*	*Facebook*	*Twitter*

Lightning Source UK Ltd.
Milton Keynes UK
UKOW03f2327170614

233637UK00001B/134/P